Boy in

Boy in the Well

DOUGLAS LINDSAY

DI Westphall Book 2

MULHOLLAND
BOOKS
HODDER

First published in Great Britain in 2019 by Mulholland Books
An imprint of Hodder & Stoughton
An Hachette UK company

1

A CIP catalogue record for this title is available from the British Library

Paperback ISBN 978 1 473 69694 5
eBook ISBN 978 1 473 69696 9

Typeset in Plantin Light by Hewer Text UK Ltd, Edinburgh
Printed and bound in Great Britain by Clays Ltd, Elcograf S.p.A.

Hodder & Stoughton policy is to use papers that are natural, renewable
and recyclable products and made from wood grown in sustainable
forests. The logging and manufacturing processes are expected to
conform to the environmental regulations of the country of origin.

Hodder & Stoughton Ltd
Carmelite House
50 Victoria Embankment
London EC4Y 0DZ

www.hodder.co.uk

For Kathryn

I

Alarm. Eyes open. First look at the morning. Reach out and silence the noise.

Ten-minute snooze set, but I won't need it. Lie in the grey light of dawn, staring at the ceiling, and right away it's there. Depression.

No particular reason. Just one of those things that comes with the day. Any given day. Like one of those old blues songs. *Woke up this morning . . .* In my case, however, I don't tick any of the old blues men's boxes. No woman putting me down, no trouble with the law, no drink, no drugs, no long, lonely journeys on the railroad.

There was a time there, for a few years even, when I never felt like this. However, it seems to be coming more often these days, and every now and again has become once or twice a week.

Last week Mary, on the front desk, told me I needed a wife.

Sit up, legs over the side of the bed. Late enough in the year to be sleeping with the curtains open. Early November, looking out at the tops of houses, trees behind, the ridge of the hills beyond obscured by low cloud. The feeling of apprehension still sits in the middle of my head, drip-feeding lethargy through the rest of me.

Finally stand up, stretch, and into the morning routine, which as ever ends with me sitting at the small table in the kitchen, listening to *Good Morning Scotland*, eating fried eggs on toast and drinking coffee. Some days feeling enthusiastic, some days feeling indifferent, some days like today, a weight on my shoulders, wondering what's about to happen.

Into the station at just after 08:30. Nod at Mary as I walk past, but know that I'm not going to escape so easily. She either has a radar for this kind of thing, or else the signs of my melancholia are obvious to everyone, and she's the only person comfortable enough to talk to me about it.

'Inspector,' she says.

'Mary.'

I smile, slow down, try to look more enthusiastic for the day.

'Anything happen in our one-horse town overnight?'

She narrows her eyes slightly, seeing through my attempt at casual conversation.

'Assault outside the Horseman,' she says, 'but it was two hours after closing, so there's no need to speak to Robbie.'

I lift my eyebrow in question, and she says, 'Tom Arnold. He was kept in the Memorial overnight for observation. Head smashed against the wall, but he'll likely get out this morning. Broken finger, a few cuts and bruises.'

'Right. So I presume we have Debbie in custody?'

Mary smiles ruefully and nods.

We used to spend our time waiting for the inevitable break-up between those two, and the joke at the station was that when it finally happened, crime in the town would be cut in half and several of us would lose our jobs.

Time passes, however, and we've come to realise that they're going nowhere. They fight and make up in a repetitive ritual, and sometimes the police are called, and sometimes it ends with one of them in hospital.

Tom and Debbie Arnold live in a large, old house on the edge of town on the Strathpeffer Road – convenient for the police station, it has been noted – and they never bother anyone else. At least there's that. It is, however, just unutterably depressing as we watch the decline and fall, the worsening of the rift, hoping one of them will finally have the strength and sense to walk out, but knowing that when it ends it will end in the fight that goes too far, leaving one of them dead.

There was a moment, about a year after I'd been on the job. It was early morning, and I'd gone for a walk out of town on a spring day, the smell of the Highlands still fresh, new and welcoming. (Not that the sense of that ever leaves you.) I'd stopped to get a bacon roll at a van on the corner of Gladstone – a business that sadly didn't last, despite the custom we sent its way – and was finishing off the roll as I was walking in the direction of Strathpeffer, beyond the last of the houses out on that road.

Unexpected movement to my left made me turn and look towards Knockfarrel, the hump that rises between the two towns. There were two people running towards me in what appeared, at first sight, to be a scene of Pythonesque comedy. At the front there was a man, bare-chested, unshaven, hair wild, running full pelt down the hill. Tom Arnold. Debbie was about ten yards further behind, brandishing a frying pan.

I stopped to watch, torn between walking off and leaving them to it, intervening, or being a casual spectator to this seemingly comic act. Seemingly comic, because while the scene had been taken straight from the world of seventies TV comedy, this being the real world, were she to have caught him and actually hit him over the head with the frying pan, no one would have been laughing.

With one hand on the top wire of the fence, Tom jumped over, and then he was running down the street towards me. Debbie took a little longer to negotiate the hurdle, and so fell a few yards further back.

As he passed me, the worry on Tom's face eased for a second. He looked at me, nodded, said, 'Inspector,' and then continued on his way. Another couple of seconds, and then Debbie was upon me. She did the same, slowing slightly, as though slowing down might mean the police not noticing that she was actively chasing someone with a frying pan with intent to commit assault, said, 'Nice morning,' and kept on running.

It was perfect, and amusing in its way, and I would have loved to let them get on with it. But I was the police officer amongst the three of us. I was the adult.

I watched her for a moment and then said, just loudly enough for her to hear, 'Debbie . . .'

She didn't turn immediately but I could see the break in her stride. She kept running for a second, another two, three, four strides, and then finally she slowed and stopped, turning back to face me, as Tom ran on, past his own front door, not noticing that his wife was no longer in pursuit.

We looked at each other, Mrs Arnold and I, and then she said, 'I wasn't really going to hit him.'

The moment passed. No one was assaulted that day.

Soon enough it came though, and for years now we've all watched the grotesque implosion, and one day it will be over, one of them dead, one of them in prison.

'Nothing else of interest?' I ask, and Mary shakes her head.

For a few seconds, I wait to see if she's going to give me any words of advice, or admonition for living alone and not sharing myself with anyone else. When it thankfully doesn't come, I nod and walk on through to the office.

Most people already in, except Chief Inspector Quinn, who's in Inverness for the day. Nod at a few of my colleagues in the open-plan, over to the other side, and there's Detective Sergeant Sutherland, in the seat that used to be DI Natterson's, a doughnut in one hand, a cup of coffee in the other, as ever at this time in the morning.

We were due to get another DI to replace Nat, but it never happened, and the replacement inspector became a sergeant. However, another sergeant post was cut so, ultimately, when it had all panned out, and the dominos had fallen, we lost an inspector and gained an administrative assistant, Police Scotland saving £34,500 a year in the process.

Sutherland smiles and nods, I return the nod and then look around the office, and on out the window, wondering what to do first.

'All right?' says Sutherland, through the last of the doughnut, before taking a tissue to his lips.

'Yeah,' I say, hands in pockets, looking out at the clouds above the rooftops across the street, and then turning to the coffee machine. Take a moment, decide to get the second cup of the day, ease myself into things and see if I can shake the feeling of gloom that still sits like a black ball in the middle of my head.

'You all right for coffee?' I say to him, and he lifts the mug in response, indicating it's still half full.

'We heading out to the Meachers' today?' I ask.

Fraud case, small-time, involving old European Union money. The call came from Glasgow, asking us to make some enquiries. So far it's going slowly, but no one seems to mind.

'Yep,' he says, 'should be free after eleven, if that's good.'

'Yep,' I say, and turn away, walking over to the coffee machine. Constable Fisher passes by and we say hello.

And so the day begins, and just this once it turns out that my waking feeling of dread and despondency at the day is not misplaced. Soon the herald of bad news arrives, and we won't be going to the Meachers' place, and Glasgow and Brussels, and whoever else is asking, will just have to wait.

2

Yesterday this would just have been any old field on the Black Isle. One field's width back from the road, the ruin of an old croft away to the right, another couple on the low hill rising beyond. To the far left, a small copse of trees, the farmhouse behind. Woods beyond that, farmland all around. In the distance before us, the roofs of Culbokie, and beyond that the Cromarty Firth. Behind, at the top of the hill, a lone tree, before the gentle roll down to the other side of the Black Isle, to Avoch and the Moray Firth.

The last of the sheep have just been moved into the adjacent field, although they had all fled to the furthest parts of this one at the arrival of so many people.

The day is grey and bleak, a cold wind whipping up from the firth, rain in the air. There are already seventeen of us in attendance, only a few dressed for the weather. Fourteen various officials and law enforcement officers, the farmers – Catriona Napier and Belle McIntosh – and an acquaintance of theirs, Lachlan Green.

I don't know the farmers. Napier looks upset; McIntosh, who found the body, is far more composed, like she's the one already thinking over the ramifications of all this on their business.

Lachlan Green has been known to the police all his adult life, and is a regular feature of the small police notices in the local papers. Nevertheless, he has neither a prison sentence nor a story with its own headline to his name.

A couple of our team are setting up a broad perimeter around the area, and just in time, as a BBC van has parked on the road at the bottom of the next field down. Doesn't take long to get here from Inverness, presuming that's where they came from. Maybe they were in the area anyway, and were diverted. Ahead of them a lone individual strides forward, phone held out, journalist written all over him.

I nod at Sutherland, and he accepts the challenge and walks off to counter the reporter before he can casually duck under the perimeter tape, pretending to be from the procurator's office or some such.

At the far corner of this field there is an old well, the top of which has long been sealed. The well was listed in the schedule of sale when Catriona Napier and her husband bought the property; the previous owner stated that he never knew the well to have been opened.

For reasons that have yet to be explained to us, the farmers recently decided to see if the well was still functioning, and if there was a chance it could be reactivated. This morning, at just after nine o'clock, McIntosh and Green took to the task of dismantling the stone cover. She said their intention was to do it carefully, leaving the stones intact, in case the decision was taken to reseal the cover.

Once they had completely cleared the stones and the old pieces of wood which had originally been fitted as support, they lowered a light, attached to a piece of rope, down towards the bottom. There, as far as they could tell from their position on 'the surface of the earth', was a body.

And now they stand, contemplating what this is going to do for business over the coming weeks and months, Green beside them, looking as if he has other places he'd rather be.

'Ready to go, sir,' says Constable Cole, as she walks up beside me, dressed for the descent, wearing a helmet with a torch and camera attached, a harness, carabineers dangling from her belt.

Constable Ross is kneeling, looking down into the well. He is also dressed to make the descent, but only as back-up, in case Cole runs into any trouble.

I nod, and we walk over to the well, where the rest of the team are getting ready to lower Cole down.

'Sir,' says one of them, putting an iPad in my hands. It's already showing the images from the camera mounted on Cole's helmet.

'Thanks. We set?' I ask generally to the small crowd.

'Ready to roll,' another says, and I get the thumbs-up from Cole.

As she attaches the line to her belt, sits on the edge of the well and gets ready to descend, Sutherland comes back up alongside me.

'All well?'

'The guy's from the *Courier*,' he says. 'He's cool.'

I wonder about making some trite remark to Cole about being careful, but there's no need. We're not playing to an audience.

She lowers herself over the side of the well, gives another thumbs-up. The winch starts slowly unwinding and Cole lets herself go, allowing it to take her weight, and beginning her descent.

We watch her for a moment, and then shift our attention back to the iPad. The bright light of the torch moves slowly down across the stone, walls untouched and unseen in who-knows-how-many years.

'If this was a movie, you'd be doing that,' says Sutherland to me, drily.

The image on the screen is moving steadily back and forth as Cole looks around at the wall of the well, making an initial check to see if there is any evidence of the process of the body being dumped, or taken down, to the bottom.

'And you'd be scared of the dark, spiders, rats, bats, heights and confined spaces.'

'That'll do, Sergeant, that'll do.'

'Yes, sir.'

'Everything all right, Alice?' Ross shouts down the shaft after Cole.

'We're good,' she answers, not needing to shout back up as there's a microphone in the camera on her helmet. Her words are in strange stereo, from down in the well and from the iPad.

I take a moment to look away, over a scene that is suddenly very tense, as we wait for the first close-up from the bottom of the well.

A picture painted in dull grey. The crowd has grown a little, the perimeter is established. The farmers are on this side of it, although detached, while seven people stand at the tape, one with a camera on his shoulder, an officer beside them.

We either need to make sure the guy is not filming when we bring the body up, or we need to set up a tent around the well. Of course, these days there's hardly a discussion to be had. There are cameras everywhere, on every device. We'll need to set up the tent.

I look back to the two crime scene vehicles that came through from Inverness. They'll have everything we need.

'Feet on the ground,' says Cole, with a little more urgency, and the winch is instantly stopped. A moment, then she says, 'A little more slack, please,' and the winch briefly rolls again.

There are three people leaning over the well, looking down. Someone else comes and stands next to Sutherland and me, looking at the iPad.

The picture scans quickly round the well, checking for any other entrances or doorways. It feels like we're almost waiting for the moment of panic, the fear in her voice, and the desperate plea to be yanked to the surface. I probably need to stop listening to Sutherland.

This, fortunately, isn't that kind of drama. It is still drama, just one of a much sadder kind.

Finally, Cole lowers her head and we get the first look at the face of the person whose body has been deposited at the bottom of the well. A boy, dark hair, maybe nine years old. The face is dirty and marked, but it's hard to tell by torchlight if there is any blood or bruising.

The camera closes in on him, as Cole bends down to check for signs of life, although clearly there are not going to be any. Then she runs the light over the rest of his naked body, which is lying sprawled at a curious angle. There's a line running down the centre of his chest, difficult to make out in this light.

'Nothing,' says Cole quietly. The tone of her voice has changed. You don't see something like this and remain unaffected. 'Doesn't look as though he's been dead for long, though. Maybe a day or two.'

So much for the well not having been opened for several generations. I glance over my shoulder at the farmers, who are watching us guardedly.

'Looks like his chest has been cut open, then stitched back up,' says Cole, 'but that's all I can make out at the moment.' Then the picture lifts again, and she looks around the well once more, the camera a couple of feet lower this time.

We wait for the revelation, we wait for the thing that might make sense of this, or which might give us a decent head start in working out who this boy is and why someone placed him down here.

Yet, of course there's nothing, and there's hardly likely to be either. No clues, no instructions, no confession, no note, no piece of evidence accidentally dropped into the well alongside him.

Just a body, that's all. That's all we have. A boy in a well, and the sadness of it. Somewhere, someone is missing their son, waiting anxiously for news, not sleeping, not eating, waiting for the phone to ring. And later this morning their doorbell will sound, they will go to answer it, and there will be two police officers. The mother or father will open the door, full of fear and dread and hope and desperation, and they will see the faces of the officers and they will know, and their torment will multiply a thousand-fold.

3

For a while we did not know what had happened to Dr Sanderson, the police pathologist in Inverness. He left, that was all. Handed in his notice, didn't actually tell anyone with whom he worked, only had to give a month, and he was gone. Called in sick on his last day, just in case word had got around.

One of his colleagues went to see him that weekend, and he wasn't in. Tried calling, he never answered the phone. Called a few more times to no avail, eventually stopped.

The rumours started. Never married, there was talk that Sanderson had met someone online, and grabbed a chance later in life for some romance. Some suggested that maybe he was gay, and that he'd run off with another man, unable to come out to his friends and colleagues. Another obvious one – and what, I have to admit, I presumed myself – was that he was ill. A cancer diagnosis, a poor prognosis, and he had gone off to try to salvage something from what time he had left, unable to face the torment of the goodbyes, the looks of concern and the awful expressions of pity from his colleagues.

This past Saturday I walked to the top of Wyvis. A beautiful day, white clouds dotting a clear, cold, blue sky, the view out to Wester Ross unbroken; one of those days when it felt as if you could almost see Canada.

Packed a small lunch, rode my bike out along the Ullapool road to a spot beyond Garve, and on up the hill.

I was sitting near the top eating a ham and tomato sandwich when Sanderson approached, over the brow of a small rise. He was heading for what passes for the summit up on that flat plateau, when he saw me, smiled, waved and approached.

'Ben,' he said, sitting comfortably on what had looked like an uncomfortable rock.

'Peter.'

He removed his backpack, and settled into position, taking a moment to enjoy the view, for all the world as though we'd arranged to meet here, rather than it being complete chance.

'Odd approach you just made,' I said.

'Didn't use the paths. Came up from over by Loch Glass.'

'Right. Ground OK?'

'Bit marshy lower down, but ...' and he finished the sentence by tapping his boots, which were solid, expensive, high over the ankle.

'Like Sauchiehall Street up here,' he added, as a family of four walked past, in classic formation, younger kid up beside the parents, older child trailing slightly behind, tripping over her bottom lip. I'd only seen two other people for the previous twenty minutes.

He laughed lightly, and the kid at the back glanced round at him, quickly looking away when she caught my eye. 'I always think, get off my mountain,' he said. 'I mean, it's classic, isn't it? Nice day like this, and you have people dragging kids like that up here. Fair-weather walkers, the bane of the Munros. I think, where were you when the snow fell? Where were you when the wind blew?'

He shook his head, as though even he didn't have any conviction in what he was saying.

'Where were you when the Westfold fell?' and he laughed again, and finished with a bit of a grumble.

I smiled, and had a moment of lamenting the *Lord of the Rings* conversations we never had over dead bodies at the morgue.

He opened his bag and pulled out a sandwich and a bag of sea salt and cider vinegar crisps, opened it, offered it to me. I shook my head and he started to eat.

'What have you got there?' he asked.

'Ham and tomato,' I said, still feeling that there was something slightly surreal about this. I had genuinely only ever talked to Sanderson while standing over a corpse, and I'd also expected that I'd never see him again. I'd presumed he had died, somewhere in the world, while attempting to chalk off some item from his bucket list.

Maybe this was on his bucket list. Climb Wyvis.

For someone who had lived in Beauly, that would have been a pretty unimaginative bucket list.

'What about you?'

'Pan-seared Japanese beef, with horseradish, blue cheese and rocket,' he said. 'On homemade granary.'

And he made a small gesture with this artisanal sandwich, then took his first bite. He laid the sandwich on his knee, then reached once more into his bag, producing a flask.

'Would you like some?'

'Thanks,' I said, feeling unprepared in my last-minute dash up the mountain. I thought I'd done well making a sandwich and throwing in a bottle of water.

'Good choice,' he said.

He removed the cup-lid, the white cup beneath, and unscrewed the top, poured out the liquid and handed the bigger cup to me.

'That's not tea,' I said, for some reason finding it funny.

'Of course not. It's a nice day. Why would we want tea? It's sauvignon blanc.'

'I'll take the smaller one, thank you,' I said, smiling.

He passed over the white cup, we tapped the plastic together, and then took our first drink.

Have to say that sitting at the top of a mountain, looking out west across the hills, the wine tasted damned good.

'Nice,' I said, mundanely.

'There's no such thing as bad wine,' he said. 'You're just drinking it with the wrong food.'

'Did you get that from a fridge magnet?' I asked, and he laughed.

The laugh died away, the moment passed, we drifted into silence. Far in the distance we could see a low-flying plane, a fighter jet, presumably a Typhoon, although I couldn't make it out from there. Just the one, flying beneath the level of the mountain, too far away for the sound to have reached us yet.

'What happened to you, Peter?' I said eventually.

He grunted, as though disappointed by the question, but eventually, after another bite of his sandwich, another swallow of wine, another reach into the packet of crisps, he shrugged and said, 'I suppose I did just fall off the map. What were they all saying?'

'I think if you were to amalgamate all the theories into one, it'd be that you had a secret gay lover and had gone off to Costa Rica to die of AIDS.'

He laughed, loudly enough that I ended up laughing with him. It had all been kind of stupid, especially now, considering that here he was, no more than a few miles away, living much the same life as he had been before, minus having to go to a mortuary every working day.

We settled into a comfortable silence, the subject having been broached, while we ate and drank, looked at the view, and waited for him to finally decide to talk.

'The world is a shit-basket, Ben,' he said eventually. 'I wasn't fed up with work, or anything. I wasn't tired and drained by all that sadness, all the death. We're in Inverness, not downtown Baltimore; it was never exceptional, it never really weighed me down. But the news. My God, every day, the news. The world out there, this God-awful sewer that humanity has created ... I couldn't stop reading about it, couldn't stop thinking about it. And I just got to thinking ... I really believe, this world, or at least, our civilisation, is ruined. Absolutely, unequivocally, unavoidably ruined. I don't know how the end will come. Plague maybe. Climate change and colossal ecological disaster. Some terrorist gets hold of a nuclear weapon, perhaps, or not even a terrorist. One of the people that already has them just chooses to do something indescribably stupid. Russia or Turkey, the damned Yanks or just that rotund little fuck-muppet in North Korea.'

'Turkey doesn't have nuclear weapons,' I found myself saying, the only thing he'd said so far that I thought needed correcting.

'Well, there goes my theory,' he said, drily. 'We're fine.'

I laughed, Sanderson took another drink, indicating the mountains beyond.

'However it comes, it's coming. Society will fall. We will fall. Scotland, Britain, Europe, the West, all of humanity ... This year, next year, five, ten years, who knows, but it's coming. And I just thought, why am I doing this? Why am I spending my days doing *this*? The last days of human civilisation? Why not just get out on the mountains? Why do it once or twice a month, when you can do it every day? So, I moved to Ullapool. Some days I go fishing, some days I walk up hills.'

'Wow,' I said. 'That's impressive. What d'you do when it's chucking it down with rain?'

'You know how good a shower feels after you've been up a mountain all day in the freezing rain? You know how good a Château La Garde, Pessac-Léognan 2009 tastes? You see, it's not just the hills, or the fishing. Time is short, it really is. Why waste it, why waste any of it? Every meal is good, every drink should taste like this,' and he indicated his cup, taking another sip as he did so.

'You sound like you're dying of cancer,' I said, though I did not mean it in any maudlin way.

'It's civilisation that's dying,' he said. 'Greed, stupidity and hubris. But it's not like you don't know that already, Inspector. You're surrounded by it in your job, and you'll have seen far worse in your SIS days than you will've since you've been up here.'

He finished his cup of wine, then opened the flask and offered me a little more. I had hardly started mine, so he poured himself another cup.

'I have a cheesecake and a small dessert wine for after,' he said.

I laughed, but couldn't help myself saying, 'I hope you're not driving back to Ullapool. I might have to arrest you.'

'Spending a couple of nights at the Highland,' he said.

'Lovely.'

'Simple pleasures, Inspector, simple pleasures.'

'You never said you were leaving,' I said. The words sounded jarring. I regretted speaking as soon they were out my mouth. I hadn't intended saying anything about that, then suddenly there they were. Words spoken.

He continued to eat and drink for a while, looking steadfastly out over the view, then finally he cleared his throat, coughing gently into the back of his hand.

'You know how it is, son,' he said. 'Goodbyes and all that. Questions. Where are you going, what are you going to do? We'll miss you. Don't forget us. You lucky so-and-so. The going-away card passed around the building, the hastily bought present, arranged by people who didn't really know me.' He shook his head, looking mournfully at the ground. 'See?' he said, picking up slightly, 'it's depressing me just thinking about it now.'

He laughed, and I laughed lightly with him. We didn't talk much after that, sitting in companionable silence, looking out over the mountains. Somehow, though, the feeling of sadness that had suddenly appeared with the change in the tone of his voice never went away. Eventually, after a little more food, a little more conversation, we said goodbye and went our separate ways.

I didn't mention when I got into the station this morning that I'd seen him. It didn't seem right. It didn't seem to me what Sanderson would have wanted.

The crowd at the perimeter of the scene has grown, reporters and television, passers-by, and those few, attracted far from home, by the lure of a crime scene. Sutherland has taken the farmers back into their house to ask further questions. They can protest innocence all they like, but every investigation starts with where the body was found, and it was found on their property.

A white tent has now been erected around the scene, enclosing the well. The boy has been brought to the surface, and lies inside the tent, on a pop-up table. Body covered in a sheet, his head emerging from beneath, his face the forlorn, pale masque of death.

The tent has been cleared, and now it's just Dr Wade and me. The investigating officer, the police pathologist, and the victim.

'And you don't have any missing persons of this age in the area?' asks Wade.

I shake my head, which she picks up on, even though she's not looking at me.

'We've spoken to Inverness, and they've got nothing. They did a quick check for us, and there are a few possibilities from around the country, but nothing close by. I'll check them out when we get back to the station.'

Look at my watch, although the time hardly matters.

'I should be getting on. Too soon for you to have any ideas?' I ask.

Wade has been here for about ten minutes, much of which she spent standing outside the tent, looking at the view down across the fields and the crowd and the trees to the Cromarty Firth, as she slowly got attired for the job.

'On the contrary,' she says, looking up.

She's in her late forties, a tangle of sandy-coloured hair tied back, a particular harshness about her, but with a peculiar sense of humour beneath. Perhaps not so different from Sanderson.

The unexpected suddenness of Sanderson's departure meant that Wade came to the police service at short notice, having worked in Aberdeen for the previous fifteen years. There's a rumour that her departure from the Royal Infirmary came at an opportune time for her, amid talk of a scandal of some sort, but I've never gone looking for the details. None of my business. We're just here to talk about a dead body.

'The boy died approximately Saturday afternoon. Then, judging from the marks on the body, I'd say he'd been dead a good twelve hours before being dumped down there.'

'So, dropped, rather than taken down and placed there?'

'Unceremoniously dropped. Which makes sense, because it's going to be a lot of effort to get down there just to leave the body of someone you've killed. It would be curious to treat someone with that much respect, having murdered them.'

'Any idea on cause of death? Constable Cole said it looked like there'd been an incision made in the boy's chest.'

Wade replies with a nod, then she slowly lifts the cloth that's covering the body, revealing the wound that stretches from his throat down to his waist.

A recent incision, very roughly sewn back up.

'This is what we have so far,' she says. 'A brutal cut, crudely repaired, as you can see. The boy was dead when the stitches were applied, too early to say if he was dead before the incision was made in the first place. I could do it now, but if it's all right with you, I'll leave it until I get back to the lab to open him up again.'

'Sure,' I say.

'He was not necessarily awake when he was cut open,' she says. 'People normally wouldn't be, albeit, I grant you, this is hardly a normal course of events.'

'OK, doctor, thank you. If you can put a call through to the station when you've got something else . . .'

'Will do.'

There's a movement behind me, the entrance to the small tent parts, and Belle McIntosh enters. There's no artifice about her, or nervousness, or even curiosity. She just walks into the tent as if she's supposed to be here.

She glances at the doctor, then she gets a quick look at the body, but even in the act of her entering, Wade has the sheet drawn back up, and this time all the way over the boy's head.

'Who are you?' says Wade sharply, and as she says it, I step in between McIntosh and the now-covered cadaver.

'You're not allowed in here,' I say, glancing through the small opening, looking for the officer who was supposed to be standing outside.

'It's my land,' says McIntosh. 'Are you telling me some of it is now off-limits?'

'Yes, I am. Can you go back into the house, and I'll come to speak to you shortly?'

'What if I want to go out? Go to the shops? Am I under arrest?'

'No,' I say, and the antagonism starts to leave my voice. It strikes me that she's just come in here for the argument, wanting to be annoyed at the sudden influx of visitors and interest in her property. Feeling entitled in her resentment and wanting someone to blame. Arguing with her will only feed her aggravation. 'At the moment we're just doing what we have to do. No one's under arrest, no one's suspected of anything. We've just found a body, we'll deal with it and gather the evidence as quickly as possible.'

She holds my gaze for a second, gives Wade the briefest of looks, and then stares down at the covered body. This second look is not so brief.

'Mrs McIntosh,' I say eventually, and this time I take a step forward, which, given the limited space of the tent, puts us more or less face to face. 'You need to go back to the house.'

'*Ms* McIntosh,' she says. 'Who is it?' she adds, moving quickly on from admonishing me for misrepresenting her marital status, which at least makes me realise that I have no idea about her marital status.

I reply with a nod towards the flap in the tent.

A few years ago I would already have placed my hand on her arm to move her on. Now, any touch by the police is considered an offensive move, one that invariably leads to escalation or accusation.

Her eyes remain on the sheet for a short while longer, and then she turns quickly back out of the tent, the flap falling into place behind her.

'What d'you suppose was going on there?' says Wade, lifting her eyebrows at me.

'Not sure,' I say, 'but it's hard to imagine it was anything more than her trying to impose herself on the situation. She wants us to know that we're on her land, and she wants us off as soon as possible.'

'Hmm,' says Wade, 'I'll leave you to it. I'll concentrate on finding out how our sorrowful young friend here died,' and she pats the corpse on the shoulder.

Once again she pulls the cloth back from the head, and then slowly from the rest of the body, and we stand and look down at him again for a few moments.

'Right, doctor, thank you,' I finally manage to say. 'I should be going. I'll see you later.'

She nods, and I'm back out into the fresh air, looking at a scene which is exactly the same as it was when I went in there. The same crowd, the same work being done to secure the area, the same checks being made of the surroundings. Up above, the same grey sky flecked with darker grey; in front, the same fields stretching away, down to the same lifeless water.

4

Standing at the kitchen window, looking out on the same view. The farmers sitting at the table, Sutherland across from them. The three of them are drinking tea, poured by McIntosh from an oversized pot.

Lachlan Green is waiting elsewhere for us to interview him. The farmers and Green have been taken separately into the white tent to see the dead child. In the case of McIntosh, this was obviously a more formal, second viewing. None of them claim to be able to identify him.

McIntosh and Napier are married, and have been for a little over a year. We've yet to get to their background story, and with people getting married in their fifties, same-sex or not, there's usually one to tell, but there's plenty of time for that.

'It's clear that the well has not remained sealed since the nineteenth century or whenever,' says Sutherland, 'so we need to start from there.'

'We hadn't touched it until this morning,' says Napier, and I turn to watch them. Napier looks nervous, troubled, as she might reasonably be expected to be; McIntosh looks angry, ready to lash out.

'Can you explain to us how the dead body of a young boy got in there, then?'

Napier drops her eyes, head shaking.

'For goodness' sake,' says McIntosh, 'he must've been put there a while ago, and the well was resealed in a way we didn't

25

notice. That's a reasonable explanation. Don't tell me the child just died this weekend.'

Sutherland holds her gaze, and although she does not wilt, the understanding is evident on her face.

'I don't believe it,' she says, although the stress and anger in her voice reduce a notch or two.

'You saw him, Ms McIntosh. First estimate is that the boy died on Saturday afternoon,' says Sutherland, causing Napier to look up – a helpless, desperate look – and McIntosh's face to harden. 'Someone killed him,' continued Sutherland, 'and then they dropped his body down into the well. How did that happen?'

They stare back across the kitchen table. A moment, and then Napier turns and looks at her wife. McIntosh holds her gaze for less than a second, and there's nothing there. Her face, her look, is expressionless.

'Well, that's for you to work out,' she says, turning back to the sergeant. 'What d'you think we did? Kill someone, hide the body in the well, then the following day call the police and report what we found? Seriously?'

Her tone is unnecessarily harsh and accusatory. At least her words have a point.

'And yet,' says Sutherland, 'it seems a very particular coincidence that you open the well the day after someone just happens to have disposed of a corpse in it.'

McIntosh does not wilt from his gaze, but has no answer.

'Why did you choose this moment, today, the start of this week, to open the well? Did you hear something? Suspect something?'

'Nothing like that,' McIntosh answers, her voice low.

'Why today?'

McIntosh glances at me, aware that I'm the unknown quantity in the room. Watching, waiting, saying nothing.

First impressions, that's what she's wondering. What are my first impressions?

'Right, here we go,' says McIntosh. 'Although I don't know why it's any of your business . . .'

'Don't,' says Napier, shaking her head.

Sutherland almost smiles as he looks at her, then turns back to McIntosh.

'Oh, that sounds interesting,' he says.

'Oh, I don't think I'll bother now,' she says.

'Why did you open the well, Ms McIntosh?' I throw in from the sidelines. 'Until we get answers to who this boy is, where he came from and how he came to be at the bottom of a well on your land, and until we know who else it is we ought to be speaking to, you're all we've got. You're in the spotlight. Answer honestly and truthfully, get it over with, and that spotlight will shift away from you all the more quickly.'

McIntosh looks round at me, and I can see the stiffening of her resolve. We come to the first answer, at least. Another look of uncertainty from her wife, just before she speaks.

'The water, of course,' she says. 'We were wanting the water—'

'Don't bring me into it,' says Napier. 'You and your conspiracy theories.'

'Ooh, conspiracy theories?' says Sutherland. 'Excellent. The Illuminati? Paul is dead? Stanley Kubrik faked the moon landing?'

'Amateur hour,' says McIntosh with a grimace. 'Look, I had no idea why the well was closed. There's no one around to talk of it.'

'There must be land records somewhere,' I say, and she shakes her head.

'I've got no time for officialdom. You see a bit of paper, supposedly dating from a hundred and fifty years ago or whatever. How do you even know? How do you know someone didn't just mock it up the previous week? Even if it is a hundred and fifty years old, how can you trust what was written back then? Who do *you* trust, Inspector?'

'I can't believe you didn't at least look into it.'

'Why? Why bother when you're not going to be able to believe anything you read?'

'What's the matter with the water you get through the mains?' asks Sutherland. 'Not enough of it for you? We're on the Black Isle, average rainfall seventeen inches a day.'

'For God's sake,' interjects Napier, 'you've got a dead body on your hands, and you're sitting here talking about this drivel. Go and find out who the boy was. You think this is going to be good for us? Good for our business? For goodness' sake, why on earth, seriously, why on earth would we dispose of a body on our own land? You think we turned round and did a study on the effect of a dead body on profit margins, and decided on balance that it'd be positive?'

'Effect of a dead body on profit margins?' I say, smiling. Can't help myself, and she scowls.

'Ms McIntosh?' says Sutherland, ignoring Napier.

'It's poisoned,' says McIntosh. 'Don't you read the . . .?' and she finishes the question with a shake of her head.

'Don't I read the what?' asks Sutherland.

'The Internet,' she says, to the accompanying shake of the head from her right. 'Don't you ever, ever look at the Internet? The things that are going on out there? The way the world's run? Seriously? You people that live with your heads in the clouds,' and she glances with annoyance at Napier as she says it.

'If the water's poisoned, why are we not all dead?' asks Sutherland, and McIntosh barks a laugh, sitting back, looking scornfully between us two police officers.

'What would you care?' she says. 'The two of you. Senior officers in the bloody police. You're part of it.'

'If the water's poisoned—'

'Not that way!' says McIntosh loudly, cutting off the sergeant. 'They don't try to kill us. It's mind control. It's to make us compliant. Think about it. Politicians lie. We know they lie. They know that we know, and yet they still do it, and we still vote for them. Total compliance, thanks to the water.'

Sutherland holds her gaze for a moment, and then looks round at me. Hard to tell whether Belle McIntosh has just decided to pretend to be crazy to throw us off the scent, or whether this is the real thing. Either way, it's usually best not to humour that kind of talk for too long.

'Aye, scoff if you like,' she says. 'I can see the look between the two of you. Just ask yourself how, when we have a democracy of consenting adults, you end up with the complete bunch of retards in power that we do? When the whole system is rigged, and no one ever does anything about it.'

'It's the water,' says Sutherland, nodding.

'Exactly. I'll give you the website addresses, you should check this stuff out.'

'Thank you,' says Sutherland, 'we'll take a look.'

'Not that you'll learn anything that the likes of you don't already know,' she adds bitterly.

'So you decided to see if you could draw your own water, so that you wouldn't be using the system?' I ask.

She turns and looks at me.

'Yes,' she says.

'Why now?' asks Sutherland, and McIntosh turns back to him.

'It's time,' she says. 'Time to fight back.'

'She watched a documentary a few months ago, and she's been banging on about it ever since,' says Napier, although her tone is not quite as dismissive as her words. She gets up and heads towards the door. 'You three have a nice chat now, I've got work to do.'

'We're not finished,' says Sutherland.

'I'll let you know if I decide to run away to Australia,' she throws over her shoulder, and then she's gone.

Sutherland looks at me, poised to go after her, I shake my head, and he turns back to McIntosh.

'What was the documentary?' he asks, and McIntosh scowls.

'Aye, mock me all you like, you two, but consider this. I was thinking, starting today, I might be able to free myself from government mind control. Instead I find a dead body at the bottom of my water source, and suddenly the police are here.'

'What's your point?' asks Sutherland.

'My point, officer,' she says, 'is fairly obvious, don't you think? I've been thwarted. I was going to do something bold and brave against the government, and instead, here you stand. Do you suppose that's a coincidence?'

'Do you really believe that?' asks Sutherland.

She shakes her head, but not in answer to the question, embraces us both with a scowl, and then the mug of tea is raised to her lips and she disappears behind her drink.

Lachlan Green is leaning against a wall at the edge of a field, close to the farmhouse, looking down towards the firth. He's visible from the crowd of onlookers and media, and someone will have taken a photograph of him. Somewhere along the way he'll be identified, and two will be added to two to make fifteen, and the petty criminal will become a suspect in the case of the dead, unidentified child.

I nod at Constable Andrews who's been watching him as I approach, and she steps away a few yards, but does not leave the scene.

'You'll be spotted, Lachlan,' I say.

'I've got no part in this. People can think what they like.'

'You often do work for McIntosh and Napier?'

He doesn't immediately answer, and I turn and join him in looking down over the view, although without settling back against the wall. Slightly clearer for the moment, but the rain will be back.

'Known Catriona for a while,' he says. 'Help out every now and again. Belle asks me to do stuff sometimes, like today.'

'And they pay you?'

'If you'd call it that.'

'Off the books?'

He doesn't answer, then when I turn to look at him he says, 'You investigating me for tax fraud?'

'It'd make a change from public disorder, possession, and driving without a licence.'

He laughs, shakes his head.

'Aye, well, good luck, Sergeant.'

I've spoken to Lachlan at least ten times in the past. Always calls me sergeant. We're never done laughing about it.

'When did McIntosh first speak to you about removing the well cover?'

''Bout two months ago.'

'Did she say why she wanted to do it?'

He smirks.

'Some crazy-assed garbage about the water turning us all into lizards or something. She's full of all this crackpot shite she reads on the Internet. I tried telling her to watch porn like everyone else.'

Can't beat it. Interviewing a two-bit thug who has the smug self-assurance of a smart-assed eighteen-year-old. Could do it all day.

'So if she'd been talking about it for two months, why'd she just get around to it this morning?'

Another pause, finally brought to an end by a careless shrug.

'That's what happens, isn't it, Sergeant? We all make plans, we all say we're going to do this or that. Do the garden, kick drugs, stop drinking, run a marathon, save a whale, invest in stocks, build a new house, get a job, stop being a prick. We've all got plans. Mostly they never happen, and then sometimes we get around to them. Like taking the top off a well, which Belle got around to a couple of months after she started talking about it.'

Smug self-assurance he may have, but he's not wrong. Of all the plans in all the world, what meagre percentage ever see the light?

'And it just happened to be the weekend someone dumped a body down there.'

'How d'you know?' he asks. 'How d'you know the body hasn't been down there for years? Decades? Centuries?'

'He's been dead for two days.'

'That's what it looks like,' says Lachlan. 'Maybe there was something down there preserved his body.'

'Right enough, we did find a large refrigeration unit,' I say, drily.

'Look, there's weirder shit than that in the world, that's for sure. Maybe, sealed in that well, his body's been preserved for two hundred years. Like it was mummified. Or maybe someone did something to it. I mean, you ever seen the body of that bastard Lenin on the TV?'

'I've seen the real thing,' I say.

'Been to Moscow, eh? Check you. Well, if you found that guy's body lying around, you might not think he'd been dead for long.'

'You obviously haven't seen Lenin's body.'

'Maybe when they send it out on tour.'

'I think the pathologist might have noted the presence of embalming fluid.'

'Does she know what she's doing, though?'

Casual sexism to add to the casual arrogance. I choose to ignore it. He picks up my disdain, and folds his arms, slouching back a little further against the wall.

'We'll stick with the facts for the moment,' I say. 'Can you describe how the cover of the well looked when you arrived this morning?'

He smiles, looks over towards it, although it is now, of course, out of sight.

'Same as it did two weeks ago when we started talking about it.'

'Thought you started talking about it two months ago?'

'Oh, Sergeant, nice. That eye for detail that made you cock o' the north. Belle mentioned it two months ago. Something like that. Might have been longer. One night in the pub, part of some rambling shite about the additives in the water. Then I was here two weeks ago doing some work. Nothing major . . .' and he pauses, looks round, points away up the hill, 'helping with that fence up there, the whole lot needed redoing, then when we're done, she starts talking to me about the well, and we come down here and look at it. That's what we did then, and it looked the same this morning. There'd been three or four planks of wood placed across the top of the well, then stones joined, fastened together over the top and around the wellhead. But the pieces of wood were still sticking out. Rotted to fuck, now, of course, been there so long, but you could still see the edges of them in a couple of places. Obviously the wood hadn't been preserved as well as the kid,' he adds at the end with a smirk.

The comedy keeps coming. Finally the smirk dies, beneath the tired, unremitting, unamused stare of the investigating officer.

'And it looked untouched when you started work this morning?'

'Just like I already said,' he mutters.

'What about the stonework around the wall of the well? Some of that looks pretty shaky.'

He looks at me for a moment, but decides to take advantage of the fact that I didn't really ask much of a question, by answering with a shrug.

'You know any other way someone could have got into the well?'

He holds my gaze seriously and then, shaking off those few seconds of doldrums, breaks into a broad smile.

'Aye. There's a secret portal from space. Belle's not wrong, you know. There really is something out there, and it's coming this way. So, you know, you'd better check the kid for alien shit. Maybe his blood's green.'

'I can rely on you not to go anywhere,' I say, and he laughs.

I meet Sutherland a few minutes later, as we walk together through the field, the white tent up ahead, the growing scrum of media and onlookers down to our left.

'Anything else from McIntosh?' I ask, having relayed the details of Lachlan's testimony.

'Nothing there,' he says. 'Seems worried about the business. Says her wife isn't really up to it. Does a decent job, but no head for money. McIntosh has taken ownership of the family common sense. One of those people you come across who you know were mature and sensible by the time they were twelve. Early onset adulthood. She knows all the answers, thinks everyone else needs to grow up. Including her wife.'

'How does that square with her thinking that we're all controlled by giant space pumpkins?'

'She seems pretty definite about that as well.'

I take a look back towards the media.

'I need to go and have a quick word with this lot. Won't be long, won't give them much. There aren't any particular missing persons cases in the news at the moment, are there?' I ask, head shaking as I speak. I already know there aren't.

'There'll be the usual collective, but nothing the press have their teeth into,' he says. 'Not sure about down south, though. England, I mean.'

'No,' I say. 'Better watch what I'm saying. Don't want people from all over the UK calling up, asking if it's Uncle Harry who went missing in 1989.'

I start to walk off in the direction of the press, indicating the white tent as I go.

'Just go up and have a quick word with Dr Wade. She can fill you in. We'll head back to the station in about five minutes, and we can get into the process of trying to identify the boy.'

'Right, boss,' he says, and then I turn away and start heading down to the small press pack that has assembled in the middle of what is, really, a very small crowd.

5

'Nothing?'

2:17 p.m.

Room Two, windowless and forever bleak, set up as the situation room for the case of the unidentified boy. Sutherland and me, Constables Fisher, Cole, Kinghorn. Quinn's been notified, but is still in Inverness. He'll be here when he can. We won't wait for him.

On the wall we have pictures of the boy, the well, the field, the farmhouse. That's all we have for now. Very early stages, and it's going to be tough to progress this at all until we make an identification.

Cole shakes her head.

'There's no missing child like him in our system. The photograph and description have been sent to every force in the country, and we've had nothing back.'

'And by the country . . .?'

'UK-wide, sir.'

'Nil returns?'

'Several,' she says, 'a few yet to reply.'

She's about to make the point that no police force is going to get this in, process the photograph, and then not make the call if they have a match, but stops herself. Instead, she says, 'I'll get on it, sir.'

'Thanks, Alice. Elvis, you too, the pair of you split them up.'

Kinghorn nods.

A moment, and then I indicate the door.

'We've got nothing until we establish the boy's identity . . .'

'Yes, sir,' they say in tandem, and then they're up and out, door closed behind them.

I turn back to the board, looking at the photograph of the victim, taken as he lay on the table inside the white tent. Pale face, eyes closed. Thick, straight, dark hair, damp and pushed back off his forehead. Long eyelashes. Cheekbones pronounced, the cold purple lips thin and slightly parted.

'Dental records,' I say. 'It's hard to believe it'll come to that. That someone's going to find out their child is missing via their dentist.'

'It could be they thought he'd never be found,' says Sutherland. 'Maybe the kid had been taken out of school. Home-schooled, not a member of any clubs, the parents kill him, get rid of the body, no one knows for a long time.'

'Meanwhile they're fleeing the country,' says Fisher.

'That doesn't sound so far-fetched,' I say, nodding. 'Would explain why nothing's been reported.'

'What about Interpol, sir?' says Sutherland.

I've been looking at the face of the boy the whole time; now I finally turn away, look across the table at Sutherland.

'Yep, let's do it. We'll stay within the system for the moment, then if we don't get anywhere, we'll need to go public and see what we can get. However, let's do what we can to avoid someone finding out their child has died by seeing his picture on Instagram.'

Sutherland and Fisher nod, and there's an air of needing to get on with things. Regardless, despite the feeling of urgency and the desire to get stuck in to this and try to get it wrapped up quickly, before it becomes a story that grips the attention of the press and the country, for the moment there don't seem to be too many places to go.

'There's unlikely to be any CCTV of use in the area,' I say. 'I was looking on the way back, didn't see anything obvious.'

'I'll check it out,' says Fisher. 'There'll be one somewhere along the line.'

'Please.'

Stare at the picture again, then turn to them once more.

'Any thoughts on how he got down there?' I ask.

That, for the moment, seems a more immediate question. Yes, it's odd that we can't identify the child, but he's a child, he was alive, he existed, and somewhere out there will be someone who'll be devastated, or who will be in hiding. We should find out soon enough, but it's a waiting game.

How he got there, though, is a mystery that can be tackled now.

'If we take the farmers at their word,' says Sutherland, 'and I presume we're not letting that go just yet, the only explanation can be that someone created a gap at the top of the well, dumped the body, then fixed it back into position.'

'I didn't study the wall of the well closely enough, though it looked pretty worn. Did you get a look?'

'Hmm,' says Sutherland. 'Impossible to tell from a cursory glance whether it had been tampered with, but it did look old. Ropey.'

'Still sounds a bit of a stretch,' I say.

'No,' says Fisher. 'The killer would've had a lot in their favour. Plenty of darkness, and the boy was slender, so they might have been able to insert the body by removing a few stones, and possibly even just a single plank. There's no reason why Belle McIntosh would've had a photographic memory of what the well cover looked like. Aside from the coincidence of the well then being opened, it could've been a perfect place to dispose of a corpse.'

Her last sentence gives her pause, and we're all thinking the same thing. Pretty damn big coincidence.

'Do we know where we are with testing the materials used in the well cover?' I ask.

'Checked ten minutes ago,' says Sutherland. 'Some of the stuff's back in Inverness already, but our people are still out at the farm. Preliminary findings in an hour or two.'

'All right. I'm going to go and see Dr Wade shortly, I'll stick my nose in to see Lyle while I'm at it.' Pause, contemplate leaving the discussion there, as it's another one that can't really be progressed until we've got more information. Nevertheless, there's something about it all that's making me uneasy.

'So, what if forensics prove that the well was untouched until this morning? How else did they get the body in there?'

A moment, and then Fisher, practical as ever, shakes her head.

'There's nothing. If the cover hadn't been removed and then repaired in a way that McIntosh didn't notice, then the only other explanation is that she removed it over the weekend, dumped the body, then created this narrative about why she opened the well in the first place.'

'Which would make Green an accomplice,' I say.

'Unless McIntosh started setting him up to be an unwitting accomplice a couple of months ago. Either way, it has to be one or the other of these options,' she says, and Sutherland is nodding.

'I mean, someone could have dug through the ground into the side of the well,' he says, 'but that's a decent-sized job, and there's going to be a lot of collateral damage there. Earth dug out, the mark on the land, the side wall of the well put back in place. That's a lot of work. And it didn't look as though the wall had been disturbed.'

He glances at Fisher, then back to me. It's another theory, but he's right, it would require so much work, in such a short period of time, that it becomes more or less impractical.

'And not only would you have to break into the well from the side, through a tunnel,' he continues, 'they wouldn't just have been able to make as small a gap as possible, insert the kid, then try to close it back up. They'd have to make the repair from inside the well, so that it wasn't obvious. But if they made the repair from the inside, how do they get back out again?'

'Maybe we missed a repair on first inspection, but forensics should've been down there by now . . . I'll check it out. It would be careless, though. Why go to all that trouble, then leave some obvious sign of what you did? Surely you'd flood the chamber, something along those lines.'

'I don't think it's this,' says Fisher, 'but we can make a geological check of the surrounding ground, tell if it's been disturbed. If we're going down this route, it's far more likely to have been that they used an older, existing passageway.'

'I'll speak to Lyle,' I say. 'So, the well was opened up then repaired, or Green or McIntosh dumped the body then claimed to have discovered it when they dismantled the well cover. Or, there's some mysterious tunnel dug into the side of the well, with a mysterious opening that we somehow managed to miss so far . . . Any other options?'

Fisher and Sutherland stare blankly back, then shake their heads in unison. A synchronised negative.

The image of the boy lying at the bottom of the well comes into my head, and I think of Lachlan and his suggestion – his theory, if that's what it was. The boy, down there for decades, hundreds of years perhaps, his body held in some sort of weird stasis by the sealed chamber.

I need to fight that part of me, the part that is too like Belle McIntosh, the part that gives credence to the fantastical. Of course, I've worked for SIS, so I know there's a lot that is indeed fantastical out there; I know a lot of the conspiracy theories are true. A belief in political conspiracy, however, is some way short of a belief in the supernatural. And even if there are spirits, trapped in some netherworld, it's still a long way from there to a physical body, immune to decay.

'Sir?'

I look at Sutherland and shake my head.

'Sorry, formulating. We'll leave it for now,' I say, waving off the moment. 'Right, we need more of a background check on Napier and McIntosh. Can you do that, Iain, and also look at Lachlan Green. There'll be plenty on record for him, but try to get further into it. The main things we're after are links between Green and the farmers, and any dealings they've had or have with children. Maybe, ultimately, we establish the boy's identity by getting into the weeds, from this direction, rather than someone coming forward.'

'Yep,' says Sutherland.

'And, Fish, we need to find out about the well. The history of it, if that's possible. Are there records anywhere, indicating when it was closed down? Did it dry up, did the water become toxic and it was closed off? If it was dry, why wasn't it just filled in?'

Fisher nods.

'Good. Right, I'll go and speak to Dr Wade again. She's had a couple of hours. Give me a call if anything turns up. We'll regroup when I get back.'

Another couple of nods from across the table, and we're up and out.

'There's nothing about his person, no fabrics or fibres.'

Dr Wade and I are in our usual position. The only one we ever stand in. Wade and I and a cadaver, the three of us bound in death.

This is only the third time that I've worked with her, neither of the first two occasions ultimately requiring the detective branch. She seems a little different today. A peculiar mix of tension and sadness. But then, neither of the previous two cadavers were that of a nine-year-old boy. She probably has children herself. Perhaps, in fact, she once lost a child. I really don't know anything about her.

I heard she lives on the Black Isle, and previously must have been commuting to Aberdeen. If that's the case, no wonder she got a transfer to Inverness. The commute to Aberdeen every day would drive anyone nuts.

Sanderson didn't ask about her, and I didn't mention her. Some people, in Sanderson's place, might have thought to enquire about the person who'd taken over, the one who was now occupying the place that they themselves had occupied for years. Sanderson, though, clearly wasn't interested. He has the mountains, and his food and his wine. Why should he care? If he did, he'd still be in the job.

'How about building materials?'

'Building materials?'

'Something to suggest he'd been pushed through a narrow gap. Any hundred-year-old mortar in his hair?'

'No,' she says drily, 'nothing like that. Prior to his death the boy had been bound by the wrists and ankles. Not too tightly. You can see, it's not just his pallor. He was a weak child. Not a lot of strength in these muscles.'

As she says the words, she squeezes his right bicep.

The cadaver is naked on the table. The wound up the middle has been reopened, but Wade has put the skin back in place after making her internal examination, so that the ribcage and viscera are not currently exposed.

'He was bound and drugged. Good dose of Methohexital, but given his age and size, it didn't have to be too heavy. It'll have knocked him out, for all the world like he was going into the operating theatre. Which, given what was done to him, is more or less what happened.'

She looks up and I ask the question with my eyebrows.

'Well, it's up to you to find out whether what we have here is a ritualistic thing, or if the boy was an unwilling donor, but his heart has been removed. And that's all. Just the heart. My initial thought was organ donor, which reminded me of course of that case you had here a while back. But then, if you're killing a child to illegally harvest his organs, why not take the others?'

'They could just have wanted the heart for a specific person, though I guess they'd have to know it'd be compatible with the transplant patient.'

'Yes,' she says, 'but I really don't think that's what we have. If you're going to this trouble, if you're killing someone to save someone else's life, you're going to take care with the heart.'

She gestures to the wound, shaking her head.

'There was no care taken. A very rough cut through the ribcage, and then again, with the removal of the heart. This last one is particularly telling. If you're going to remove the heart for transplant purposes, you wouldn't make the mess that has been made here of the pulmonary aorta. Sure, the heart was cut out, rather than ripped, but nevertheless, it was a brutal job. Whatever was done with this heart afterwards, it was not transplanted into the body of another human being. Nor, I suspect, would it have been used for any scientific or research purposes.'

'And nothing else was touched?'

'Clean,' she says.

'Aside from the fact we all know roughly where the human heart is, can you tell if the surgeon here, such as he or she was, knew exactly what they were doing, or whether they had to root around?'

'It was blunt and brutal, but it'd be a stretch to extrapolate anything further than that.'

We're both looking at the body, then lift our eyes at the same time.

'There's no sign of abuse prior to the murder,' she says. 'No historical bruising, no indication of anal penetration.'

'Any better idea on the time of death?'

'I'm going to stretch it out a little. I think he'd been dead a full twenty-four hours before the body was disposed of. So, time of death is going to be late Friday to early hours of Saturday morning.'

'So plenty of time for the corpse to have been transported here from elsewhere?'

'Oh, yes.'

'Anything else? You said he was weak. Was there an underlying condition?'

'No. Just a low-level, runt-of-the-litter kind of weakness.' As brutal as the heart removal. 'There's just not much to him,' she adds, squeezing his arm again.

'And what about the teeth?'

'Sure,' she says, 'he had teeth,' and she pulls his lips back as far as she can. A couple of gaps, a couple of adult teeth not fully grown in yet. Some evident plaque, not especially clean. 'Reasonably healthy teeth, despite their appearance. Little evidence of eating sugar at least, which is unusual.'

I look up again, away from the pale, expressionless child, as she allows the lips to close.

'We're sure he's nine?' I ask.

'Yes. If not, then he's not been ten for long.'

'OK,' I say. 'Anything else?'

'That's all for the moment.' She makes a small back-and-forth movement with her head. 'I'll get the final report to you as soon as possible, but I doubt there'll be anything else. If there is, I'll give you a call.'

'Thank you, doctor,' I say, somewhat formally, in response.

For a second I get lost looking at the boy's cold, dead face, the words *cold dead face* in my head, as though I have an internal narrator describing the scene in front of me.

'We done?' asks Wade, to snap the moment.

'Sanderson used to listen to music all the time,' I say, the words just appearing on my lips, my head still down, still staring at the boy. 'Laments. Seemed appropriate.'

'I know,' she says. 'He left his CDs behind. I put them in the cupboard. Feel free to take them away; you can make yourselves miserable listening to them at the station.'

I look up at her, and she raises her eyebrows in a way that asks if really, at last, are we done, so that she can get on with her job.

'Thanks,' I say, and with her reserved nod of goodbye, I turn and walk slowly from the mortuary, somehow taking the weight of sadness of the dead child with me.

6

Another building, another office, another expert. We trust in these people, same as they trust in us. The first time I met Inspector Tomes, who's in charge of SOCO division in Inverness, he introduced himself with the words, 'They call me Lyle.' This, it transpired, wasn't because Lyle was any part of his name, but because he'd played a masterful long bunker shot on the eighteenth, once, when he was about fifteen. The name had stuck, although if you introduce yourself to everyone with your nickname, that's going to happen.

I called him out on it, nevertheless. I liked him straight off, which helped.

'Literally no one introduces themselves like that in real life,' I said.

He laughed and shook my hand.

'I also impart information by starting sentences with *know this*,' he said, and I laughed too. Given that at the time we were standing over the blood-spattered site of a vicious stabbing, it might have been considered a little insensitive. In view of who'd been stabbed, however, I doubt anyone would have cared.

'Lyle,' I say, walking into the small office, which opens out onto the main lab. He's leaning over the desk, tapping at a keyboard, and straightens up to acknowledge me as I enter. There are three other people at work in the lab, none of whom pays any attention to my arrival.

There's something about him today, the usual ebullience missing. He's only a couple of years younger than I am, but normally he has the good humour and roguish joviality of a twenty-year-old snowboarder.

'Inspector,' he says, 'doing the rounds?'

'Been to pathology. Now you. Then on to make-up and special effects.'

One of our regular jokes, he greets it with a nod, then he sits down, gestures for me to sit in the regulation blue plastic chair opposite, and I join him at the desk.

'Where d'you want me to start?' he asks.

'You all right, Lyle?' I ask, ignoring his question.

He's obviously not all right, and for a moment I can see him contemplating talking about it, the conversation playing out in his head. His eyes drop and he seems to come to a conclusion with a small shake of the head. I take that, though, as a decision to not have the discussion, rather than him answering the question. His conversation was with himself, not me.

'Let's talk about this,' I say, moving on, and immediately I see him relax. 'Tell me about the stones and mortar used to seal the well.'

He nods, the moment having passed, accepting that there's work to be discussed.

'The question was, when were those stones last sealed together?'

'Yes.'

'Looks like it's around two hundred years ago,' he says.

And there it goes, the simplest explanation of how a body came to be dumped in a closed-off well, driving off down the road into the distance.

'That wasn't what I was wanting to hear,' I say. 'Not even a hint that it might have been done at the weekend?'

'That's all we've got. If the well cover was removed and

then put back in place, it wasn't resealed. We're not completely done, of course, but so far we've got no positive indicators for recent activity around the well, beyond what those people did this morning. That lid hadn't been lifted in a long, long time. Maybe we'll be able to pin down a more precise date for you, but it's not going to change substantially.'

'And the stones on the side wall of the well? Above ground, I mean.'

'We're checking them out. If one of them had been taken out and the body pushed through, presumably the body would've shown some signs of … it would've picked up residual elements of the binding agent between the stones. Unless they'd pulled out half the wall on one side.'

'There's nothing on the body,' I say.

'Fine. We're looking at that anyway, and we'll let you know. Might be harder to tell, as that wall is pretty worn. There might have been stones that have fallen out and have just been rammed back into place over time. The cover itself we know hasn't been moved.'

'And prints?'

'Two sets,' he says, 'already confirmed as your two principals out at the farm, McIntosh and Green. Nothing yet to suggest anyone else was there.'

'Footprints, or is that too much to ask, given the melee that ensued?'

He nods a rueful affirmative.

'OK,' I say, parking the disappointment, and feeding the information into the mix, such as it is. No prints of any use. Confirmation, rather than information.

'So, how did the boy get in the well?' I ask, the question rhetorical, staring blankly at the monitor from side-on.

'It's got to be through a gap in the wall. We'll find something.'

49

'And if not?'

'Teleportation out of the question?' he says.

'Far as I know. I met a guy a while ago who thought it existed, but he didn't provide any actual evidence. Have you put someone down into the well yet?'

'Toby and Mick're there at the moment. They'll be straight back here, and we'll look at what we've got. We've already reviewed the footage from Constable Cole, and I didn't see anything especially interesting. Ran it through K-500, and there was nothing exceptional.'

More confirmation. I watched that footage live, and have looked it over three times since. I know that nothing stands out.

'A sealed pit, no way in or out,' says Lyle. 'Awesome,' he adds, but without his usual good-humoured enthusiasm, as though the word is just automatically there, a learned response, what everyone is expecting him to say.

'Thanks,' I say. 'Every officer likes a mystery with absolutely no possible explanation.'

'Well, there's one,' he says dully.

'That McIntosh and Green opened the well, dumped the body, and then claimed to have found him shortly afterwards,' I say, nodding. 'Given that they're all claiming complete ignorance of the boy's identity, if we find out any connection whatsoever between them, that'll puncture their cries of innocence pretty quickly.'

'If you've nothing else, and if we don't find anything amiss with the stones at the side of the well, it has to be them,' he says. 'Just has to be. What's your alternative?'

'You might find us a secret entrance into the side, underground,' I say. 'You'd earn your money if you did that.'

'One of the well-known elaborate series of tunnels that runs beneath the Black Isle, from Muir of Ord to Cromarty, branching off to Avoch and Rosemarkie,' he says, his voice deadpan. 'You want us to ultrasound the surrounding area anyway, just in case?'

'Please.'

'OK, we're on it. We've got a drone for that. I'll e-mail the preliminary report within the hour, then get back to you as quickly as possible with whatever findings the guys make from inside the well itself.'

'Wait, you've got a drone?'

'You don't ask, you don't get. I think they got it from Argos.'

Another joke, humourlessly told. We hold a gaze across the desk, the general tone of the conversation and the atmosphere in this small corner of the lab weighing heavily upon us, then he places his hands on the desk and lifts his eyebrows, as he looks to bring the conversation to an end.

I've got no reason to feel insecure about my working relationship with Lyle, so I'm not presuming for a moment that he's off with me. But there's something there, something big enough to change his personality. There's always a fine line between gently enquiring to give the person an opportunity to talk, and just seeming to stick your nose in, quickly getting to the point where they feel pressured.

I elect to keep my distance. Get to my feet, business-like nod.

'Thanks, Lyle,' I say, 'speak to you later.'

'Ben,' he says, and then I'm up and out, closing the door behind me, and walking along a long white corridor, windows to an internal courtyard on one side, information posters on the wall, dotted between closed doors, on the other.

I stop by one that reads, *Vigilance Is Security*, illustrated with a picture of a young woman wearing a backpack, looking over her shoulder on a busy street. The tagline reads like something from the Cold War, and I walk on, thinking that that is more or less where we are at the moment.

7

The afternoon grows dim on the drive back from Inverness, the headlights of the cars getting brighter by the minute, picking out the rain. I contemplate stopping off at the farmhouse, just to look at the scene again. A new perspective, a fresh take. However, apart from believing it's unlikely there are any answers out there, with fresh eyes or otherwise, I really need to get back to the station.

We have the body, we have where it was disposed of, and we know how he was killed. We don't have how the killer gained access to the well, so for the moment our focus needs to be on discovering the victim's identity. Until we have that, there's little progress to be made.

Back into the station, acknowledge Mary as I pass by.

'Quinn in?' I ask, without slowing.

'On his way,' she says, and I'm off along the corridor and into the open-plan.

Get to my desk, and Sutherland is there, in place, tucking into a doughnut, a cup of coffee at his right hand. There's also a doughnut and a steaming cup of coffee on my desk.

'Boss,' he says.

'Knew I was coming?'

'Jedi powers,' he says, tapping the side of his head.

'Thanks,' I say. 'I wouldn't normally, what with my body being a temple, but I'm hungry.'

He smiles through a mouthful of doughnut, puts the mug to his face, starts talking all at the same time.

'You get anything further from Wade?'

'Oh, yes,' I say. 'Haven't quite got a handle on her yet, though.'

'Know what you mean,' says Sutherland.

'There was a story about her leaving Aberdeen. Have you heard that?'

'Just that there was a story,' he says. 'I don't know the detail.'

'No,' I say, 'me neither. Everyone's got a story.'

'You want me to ask around?'

'Oh no,' I say, shaking my head. 'Shouldn't even be talking about her. She'll be fine. We'll manage to train her in our ways soon enough.'

Sutherland laughs.

'Anyway, you first,' I say. 'We have an ID on the boy yet?'

I ask the question, presuming the answer's no. That piece of information was going to be worthy of a phone call.

'Nothing. I mean, whoever the kid was, he hasn't been reported missing in the UK. We've gone to Interpol, but we're already getting nil returns from around Europe.'

'We're going to have to put the photo out,' I say. 'I really don't want to have to do that.'

'The parents must already know he's gone. They're not going to be sitting watching the TV in the evening, then up comes the picture of dead little Timmy, or whoever, and they're like, ah, that's where he went. Malcolm, quick, come and watch the TV, Timmy's not been at the shops for the last week like we thought. He's dead.'

Allowing him to talk – or witter on, as my father would have described it – has at least given me the chance to take a couple of bites of doughnut. The late afternoon doughnut can be a little too far gone, but this tastes fresh. It's not from a morning batch.

'Are you finished?' I say.

He nods, shrugs, says, 'Just saying.'

'It could be the parents are separated, one of them thinks their son is staying with the partner, or on holiday with their partner, while the partner is currently running away. There are all sorts of scenarios. I don't like it, but if we have to post the picture, then we do it.'

'Any chance it was an accident, the adult in charge panicked and dumped the body?' suggests Sutherland.

'You saw that the abdomen had been cut open and stitched back up?'

'Of course.'

'The heart had been removed.'

'Jesus.'

'Just the heart. Nothing else.'

'Jesus.'

'Yes. And very roughly, so Wade's pretty confident it wasn't removed for transplant purposes. Too early to say what it means, but we potentially have some sort of ritualistic element.'

'So it could be that whoever killed the boy, just did it to get a human heart,' says Sutherland. 'They needn't necessarily have known him at all.'

'Yep, not out of the question. But then, surely the boy would've been reported missing by now. The only reason I can think why his disappearance hasn't been called in, is that the person responsible for his death was also responsible for his life.'

Another bite of doughnut, finally take a seat.

'Where are we on the farmers?' I ask, bringing the monitor to life.

'Just writing it up now,' he says. 'Interesting. Napier used to be married to Belle McIntosh's brother. No children. The farm was failing, they struggled on for years, seems like it was really tough for them. The husband suffered from depression, and three years ago . . .' and he completes the sentence, the part of the story that involves suicide, with a slight shrug, a regretful look. 'Seems that not long afterwards, Belle moved in, and they got married about a year and a half ago.'

'Were they having an affair beforehand? That why the husband killed himself?'

'Not according to my reliable local source,' he says. 'Although, she did suggest that there was an inevitability about the sister ending up at the farm. There had been rumours about Catriona Napier, apparently. And, on top of that, it sounds like the new wife knows how to run a business, unlike her wife, or her dead brother. She's turned things around, and Catriona is little more than a farmhand. That's the local word.'

'What about children? Any sign of them in either of their lives? McIntosh didn't have an old husband? I mean, where did the name McIntosh come from?'

'Their family name is McIntosh. Napier is Catriona's maiden name, which apparently she reverted to when she remarried.'

'She un-took her wife's family name?'

'Yep.'

'Novel.'

'So, McIntosh, Belle McIntosh, has no family, no other partners. We're still raking through her life. There are a couple of gaps, but nothing so far. Further to that, we can find no involvement with any children's groups for either of them. No football clubs or Scouts, no Guides, no school visits, no youth group involvement. Nothing to suggest that they have contact with children in any capacity.'

'So, for the moment, all we've got is that the body was found on their property?'

'That's it.'

'Spoke to Lyle. In short, nothing of significance, and nothing to suggest any tampering with the well prior to it being opened by McIntosh and Lachlan. Not yet, at any rate.'

'That doesn't make sense,' he says.

'Unless the two of them killed the boy, tossed his body into the well, then came up with their story. Hard to think of any other explanation, in fact.'

He lowers his eyes, thinks about it for a moment, automatically lifting his mug of tea.

'Or we need to find another way into the well,' he says.

'That's not looking good either, but he's going to get back to me on that too. Did Fish find out if the existence of the well is generally known about? Anything else about it?'

'Yeah, she asked around. Some people know of it, but not many. Course, there's obviously no way to work out who all those people are. We need to look into the land registry side, and see what kind of records there are.' He looks at her empty desk, then says, 'There was a domestic in Strathpeffer she was asked to go out to.'

'OK, we can get on it,' I say. 'It'd be just too perfect if the records of the well are not online, they're held in an office somewhere in town and we can find out who's been asking.'

'That would certainly be leaving a pretty big footprint.'

'And CCTV?' I ask.

'Useless,' he says. 'We really need something to look for and, even then, we're looking some way away from where the body was found. I also sent Kinghorn and Cole back out, to go round the nearest neighbours. But as we saw, of course, none of those neighbours are very close.'

'OK, thanks.'

Last of the doughnut, take a sip of coffee. Not too hot, take a longer drink. Notice Sutherland looking over my shoulder and turn to see Quinn walking towards us. He doesn't break stride as he passes, but nods towards his office.

'Is it possible someone brought a child from overseas, just to drop his body down a well in the far north of Scotland?' says Quinn. 'Seems remarkable. And a lot of trouble.'

'The body could easily have been hidden in the boot of a car,' says Sutherland. 'Driven over from the Continent, they dispose of the corpse, they drive away again.'

'They would be betting then on it not being found this quickly,' says Quinn. 'If we had managed to identify the boy, we could already be looking out for his parents, and they wouldn't necessarily have been back, ready to cross the Channel, by this morning. Nor would it make sense for them to get on a longer ferry crossing, as they'd be stuck on the ferry when the word went up.'

'Maybe they dumped the car, then got on a plane.'

'Yes, possibly,' says Quinn.

'The boy weighed just under twenty-two kilos,' I say. 'He was slight in build. A kid that size could easily have been placed in a suitcase, flown in, disposed of, et cetera . . .'

Quinn looks slightly put out by this notion, but I think it's more at the idea of it, than any dismissal of its likelihood.

'Horrible to think that he might have been alive when he was put in there,' he says.

'I don't think that was the case,' I say. 'I mean, air holes could have been cut in the suitcase, the kid could have survived in the hold, although that's dependent on the temperature down there, but why transport him alive? Wade thinks he was dead twenty-four hours previously. That's plenty of time for him to have been killed, a booking made, and flown here from virtually anywhere on the planet. As time frames go, it's really only a push if you consider Australia and New Zealand, or the Pacific islands. Europe, western

Asia, India, Africa, the Americas, even South America, are all within this scope.'

'Well, thanks for narrowing it down, Ben,' says Quinn dolefully.

'Obviously I'm not,' I say, playing it straight, 'but at this stage it just means we have to keep all our options open. The more we ask, the less likely it looks like the child is British, but we need to put the picture out before we can really settle on that.'

'That's not a good look,' says Quinn.

'I share your reluctance. But we're going to have to do it soon. Tomorrow morning's news bulletins at the latest.'

Quinn nods, runs his hand down the side of his face in a peculiar, slightly affected gesture.

'Very well. You should get back to the task, gentlemen. Keep me informed, and make sure you run it by me before you go public with the photograph.'

'I will, sir,' I say, 'but at the moment, unless we get anything else definite beforehand, I'm looking at an 8 a.m. press conference. Then we go worldwide with the picture.'

'Yes, yes,' he says, and now, without looking at either of us, he indicates the door.

As we're halfway there, he coughs, in just the kind of way that makes us turn back to him.

'Sorry, one more thing. I heard some sad news, I'm afraid.'

He looks at the two of us, almost as though he's giving us a moment to prepare for it. Like we need to adjust our settings to Grief Mode. Not being entirely sure what kind of sad news Quinn could bring, I just look curiously at him. I hear Sutherland swallow beside me.

'You'll remember Dr Sanderson, of course. Peter. Left rather abruptly.'

He pauses to shake his head. I almost say that I saw him at the weekend, but somehow I know not to say the words.

'I'm afraid . . . It turns out he left abruptly because, as one might have suspected, he'd received a sudden cancer diagnosis. He didn't want to be around for the quick decline. Apparently he fancied himself going off and living a last few months of freedom, but it never happened. Fell ill too quickly.'

He looks troubled as he tells the story. I swallow, as I know what's coming. I know that this story is going to end with the death of Sanderson. The thought of it, the thought of Sanderson walking happily along the top of Wyvis, sitting on that rock, drinking a fine wine, eating a sandwich, staring away over to the hills of Wester Ross, has the hairs standing on the back of my neck, a cold shiver creeping slowly across my skin.

'He died on Saturday. Such a shame. Decent man.'

Sutherland makes a small noise, but doesn't have any words.

'Saturday?' I ask.

'Afternoon,' says Quinn.

'He was in Raigmore?'

What does it matter where he was? I talked to him on Saturday. This conversation is just words to fill the space, to allow me to process this completely implausible circumstance.

'No, no, he left Inverness altogether. He had family down near Glasgow. Managed a few days hillwalking around Loch Lomond and the Trossachs, but soon enough even that was beyond him. He died in a nursing home near Strathblane.'

He lets out a long sigh.

'I'm not sure how many of the others would have spoken to him, but maybe if you could let them know. The funeral's in Glasgow on Friday. I'm not sure . . . it would be proper if someone could go from here to say goodbye, but it's taking a day out of the office, and at the moment, what with this . . .

We'll talk about it again later in the week. Maybe we'll just send flowers. You could speak to Mary, Ben?'

The shiver finally comes to a head, and I shake it off. I nod at Quinn, but I don't really have any words either, and then I turn to the door, open it and let Sutherland walk out ahead of me.

We walk back to our desks in silence.

Maybe we'll have this case wrapped up this week – although at the moment, I wouldn't bet on it – but even then I don't think I'll be volunteering to drive to Glasgow to go to Sanderson's funeral.

I don't need to do that to say goodbye. I already have done.

8

Get home just after ten in the evening. Too late to eat a proper meal, so I decide to forgo food and just have a cup of tea and a flapjack, the last of five I bought from the Tesco's bakery a few days ago.

Almost at the end of a day that seems to have been unusually long. It's not like we get many murder enquiries around here, so when they come, the single event can seem like a thunderstorm.

Tea made, into the sitting room, flapjack on a plate. Fire up the iPod, put the Turin Brakes mix on shuffle, and sit by the table, looking down over the town and out to the Cromarty Firth.

I've got all their slow, acoustic numbers on one playlist. 'The Optimist' and 'Above the Clouds', 'Time Machine' and 'Bye Pod'. The music I use for when the melancholy and tiredness take me. And yes, inevitably, it seems to be happening more and more often.

I look out at the water, the lights of the one boat I can see, moving slowly away from Dingwall. The tide is in. A boat that size wouldn't be there if it wasn't.

I need the space, the quiet time. A bite of the flapjack, a sip of tea, a long gaze across the town and the water to the dark hills of the Black Isle beyond, where sometime in the last forty-eight hours a boy was impossibly dumped in a well.

A day of keeping the media at bay, with the plan to go public in the morning with the photograph of the dead child.

Already we've got the heads-up on the *Human Remains Mystery Leaves Police Baffled* lead in tomorrow's *P&J*. None of the other Scottish papers lead with it, parking it on a front page side column, or on page two or three, waiting to see what happens. The English papers might have looked at it for a moment or two, but on discovering that the Black Isle is a peninsula rather than an island, they likely got too confused and decided to park it.

And that's what I need to do for the night. The only trouble with doing that is that it frees up thinking space.

I spoke to Sanderson. He spoke to me. We sat there on a mountaintop. Several people walked past us. Was I talking at that point? Did they see Sanderson, or was there just a gap on the rock and some strange guy talking to himself? Regardless of whether either of us was talking, did they see Sanderson at all?

I start to wonder if there might be some way to try to find these people, walkers who were at the summit of Ben Wyvis on Saturday. An advert in the *Ross-shire*? A plea on Facebook?

But what would be the point? What if they had seen him? It was definitely Sanderson, and Sanderson is definitely dead.

Maybe he's not, that's where my thoughts go next. Maybe he faked his death by some means, and he bled away into the fringes of society. Yet he didn't look furtive when he saw me, and if he'd been intending to disappear off into the world, he wouldn't have been walking up Wyvis. Anyway, that's not it, I know it's not.

Why me? I wonder. Why did Sanderson come to talk to me when he died? Was it that in his time of passing he found himself in his happy place, at the top of his favourite mountain in the Highlands, with so much of the country spread out before him, and I just happened to be there? Or would he have found me wherever I was? Would he have knocked at my door if I'd been at home? Would he just have appeared opposite me at the table, or sat beside me as I settled down for *Match of the Day*?

Perhaps I just provided him with some comfort on his way out. That's all. Or maybe he's still out there, still wandering Wyvis or some other Munro. Maybe the next time I'm up there we'll see each other again.

Here now is 'Chim Chim Cher-ee', peculiarly magnificent, and I get up from the table and stand by the window. Tired now, lost track of how long I've been sitting here, but it's time for bed regardless.

All that thinking, to no end. Just processing the day, putting it through the filter, little emerging on the other side. I might as well be sitting here playing a mindless game on my phone, joined with the rest of humanity in the most trivial of trivial pursuits.

Acoustic guitars and quiet vocals are overtaken by waves of electric sound, and tomorrow awaits, at least with some sense of direction. A media campaign to launch, and the mystery of how the well was breached to be addressed.

Out on the water, the lights of the boat disappear into the night. There's a spit of rain against the window, the sound of a car accelerating away along the Old Evanton Road.

9

We walk away to the sound of chairs being pushed back, a final question thrown needlessly and with no intent into the room, no one listening, everyone getting on with the job. Some of the journalists will sit there for the next couple of minutes, tweeting photographs of Quinn and me, and of the unknown dead child, telling the story – such as it is, and such as they wish to describe it – in two hundred and eighty characters.

A quiet bedlam of noise, and then we close the door behind us and walk along the short corridor in silence, back towards the main office in Inverness, and a brief chat with the chief constable of the Highlands.

Not being equipped for this kind of national campaign in Dingwall, the search for the identity of the boy in the well is being run through Inverness. Greater capacity, greater visibility, greater reach. All calls, e-mails, tweets and Facebook posts will first be monitored at the ops room here in Inverness, the garbage weeded out, the serious possibilities then forwarded on to our smaller ops room in Dingwall.

As we reach the chief constable's door, she's just emerging from her office, and she smiles, in that grim way of hers, closing the door behind her.

'David, Ben, good job.'

'Thank you,' says Quinn.

'I could kill for a coffee,' she says, then laughs, shaking her head. '*Outrage As Addict Cop Slays Kids for Caffeine Fix.* Come on, we'll talk in the canteen.'

As usual, in her company, Quinn laughs because he thinks he should, and I laugh because I enjoy her peculiar sense of humour.

There's many a chief constable would drink coffee alone in their office, or in the company of people of influence, with whom they would also lunch and dine. Chief Constable Darnley prefers to sit in the canteen as much as possible. Not intrusively, however. She won't walk in there alone and happily insert herself at a table with people. But she's available if anyone needs her, and she'll regularly end up sharing coffee and lunch with junior members of staff.

Through the main open-plan at Inverness station, and she stops for a brief chat with a desk sergeant. Quinn and I turn away, looking over the office and out the window.

'I thought it went well,' says Quinn, as though reviewing a performance. Needless words, spoken presumably because he feels he has to say something. I'd prefer silence, or an arcane conversation out of nowhere on any given subject. The Dutch tulip craze or the Voynich manuscript.

'Yes,' I say, nevertheless.

Fortunately there's not really anywhere else to go with the conversation. We presented the information that we have to the media. We showed the picture of the child. We asked that they disseminate the image as quickly and as widely as possible. This being the social media age, that's not something we have to worry about. It's an interesting story that will be picked up and spread around the world in seconds.

Even now, as we stand here waiting for Darnley, possibly millions of people will be looking at the photograph, wondering how a child could come to be missing without his parents having reported it. Some will be looking at it and placing themselves in the narrative. Could it be that they know the boy? Could they be the one to make the identification? The picture might not entirely resemble that kid who used to be in their son's primary three class, but it's been a couple of years, so he's going to have changed. Maybe they should make the call.

'Sorry,' says Darnley, breaking into my thoughts, 'come on.'

'What are we thinking?' she asks, once we're settled at a table, three coffees between us. We don't get anything to eat, as though having a pastry at a time like this would be trivialising. I can imagine Sutherland's face. The horror.

'Nobody's child goes missing and they don't know about it,' says Quinn. 'So we have several options, but we can neither discount nor favour any of them, such is the information currently at our disposal. Ben,' he says, giving me the floor.

Darnley takes a sip of coffee, shifts her attention across to me, a slight raising of the eyebrows.

'The boy has now been missing for over three days,' I begin, 'and even that's on the basis he was killed as soon as he disappeared. So our most likely option is that one or both of his parents killed him, then hoped they could dispose of the body well enough that he'd never be found.'

'Even then they would have to be living on the margins,' adds Quinn.

'Yes,' I say. 'Or maybe the parents are separated, and one of them is yet to find out he's dead. I fear this is where we're going, although obviously all options are bad. But this way, some mother, or father, separated from their former spouse, thinking their child is fine, discovers he's dead when they're watching the news, or a family member sees the picture on Facebook.'

'Yes, I feel that's the most likely,' says Darnley. 'Dead in a well at the edge of a field on the Black Isle . . .'

'Despite the conversations the chief inspector and I were having yesterday, about the possibility of people coming in from overseas, I think the perpetrators are much more likely to be from around here,' I say, and she nods. 'You don't travel from miles away just to stumble upon a closed-up well.'

'Then there's the kidnap theory,' says Quinn.

'You have a kidnap theory?'

'Yes,' I say. 'It could be the boy was kidnapped, he was being held somewhere, and the parents had been told not to contact the authorities.'

'Plausible,' says Darnley. 'If that's the case, it will certainly bring the parents forward very quickly.'

'Unless more than one child has been taken,' I say.

'Oh, God,' she says quietly. 'Let's at least hope it's not that. In the meantime, we're proactively chasing this with police forces and departments around the world?'

'Yes, of course,' says Quinn. 'We disseminated the picture around the country, and then with Interpol and around Europe as soon as it became apparent that the boy wasn't recorded as missing in the UK. Simultaneous with our press briefing this morning, the picture and associated details have been sent to every police organisation around the world; we've sent it to embassies, we've . . .' and he finishes the sentence with a vague hand, indicating that he's run out of things to say.

'You've thrown shit at the wall to see what sticks,' she says, and Quinn nods, a little uncomfortably. 'You're going to get a lot of false positives.'

Quinn holds her gaze for a moment, and then indicates for me to comment, as though speculation is not his game. He needs facts. He needs to be able to say we did this, and we didn't do the other thing. He struggles with the vague or the ambiguous.

'Yes,' I say. 'We're ready for that. Each one has to be investigated and put to bed quickly if it's not appropriate. However, in most cases, it's going to be up to the local law enforcement to make that enquiry. If someone calls in from Pasadena or Christchurch and says, yep, we think we know who your boy is, the local feds will need to establish the likelihood, before anyone starts getting on a plane.'

'A missing child,' she says, 'we should get purchase in the news cycle.'

'Maybe. But the news cycle is like anything. I don't know, like a movie, or a book, or a video of an anthropomorphic animal. There are always certainties. People will always talk about the new *Star Wars*, the next Bond, people will buy the latest Harry Potter incarnation, and a video of a cat cuddling a great white shark will be seen by fifty-eight million people in under two hours. But then there's the out-of-left-field, just another movie, just another book, just another video of a cat falling out of a tree, that suddenly takes off when no one would have expected it, or really understands why. *Slumdog* or *Fifty Shades*.'

'And so it will be with the boy in the well.'

'Yep,' I say. 'It just depends what we're competing against. Is there going to be a terror attack today? A mass shooting at a school in the US? A plane crash? Will a rock star die, will a bank collapse, will Russia invade the Baltics, will Wikileaks leak? Will some British TV legend be accused of sexual assault? Will some YouTuber, who the three of us have never heard of, call someone "black" rather than "a person of colour", or release a photograph of themselves topless in a mosque, so that the Internet breaks or explodes or does whatever it is the Internet does every other day?'

'What a world,' she says. 'Seems to get worse every day.'

'It has a near infinite capacity to do so.'

'My daughter was asking me yesterday if I could

remember a time when things were this bad.' She smiles, and adds, 'You know, now that she's moved on from claiming that I was born in the 1600s.'

Quinn and I, we two childless men, smile in response.

'It's like we're living in this time of inexorable madness. And obviously things were worse during the wars, and things were worse during the black plague, and fifty other times in the history of the planet, but now, right now, given that we ought to be living in a time of relative stability, the world seems so screwed up.'

'And on the verge of something worse,' says Quinn, his voice low and soft, his head turned away, looking out the window.

An unusual interjection from him, a peculiar tone to his voice, adding weight to the apocalyptic words. Words he could have taken from the dead Sanderson.

He seems lost in his own thoughts for a moment, and then turns when he realises that he's brought the conversation to a halt.

'A reckoning,' he continues. 'A great reckoning. You don't accumulate weapons like this planet is doing, not to use them. We got away with it once before, the first nuclear arms race. God knows how. But the leaders back then, they were statesmen, they were serious men who had lived through war. They had all lost people, they had all suffered. They knew what they needed to avoid. They cut their teeth on divisive conflict, the horror that can come from failed international relations. Politicians today cut their teeth in the banking sector, or working as interns to government ministers, and in the offices of NGOs. The only thing they ever lost was their virginity on a gap year doing VSO work in Indonesia.' A short pause, and then, 'It's coming. The realignment. God knows what it'll look like on the other side. God knows if there'll even be anything to look *at*.'

He looks from one to the other of us, and then lifts his coffee, the gesture of raising the cup a metaphorical shrug of the shoulders. The *that's all* of his conclusion.

'If only I'd thought to tell Cissy that we're all going to die and there was no hope for the future,' says Darnley ruefully.

'It's impossible to compare, though,' I say, feeling the need to lift the conversation. Not that I don't agree with Quinn, but it'd be nice to leave the table without feeling that there's barely any point walking out the front door and getting on with the rest of the day. 'How can you relate today with forty years ago? If in mid-1970 there had been a terror attack in France, if you didn't have the radio on, you got to hear about it on the nine o'clock news. It was in the paper the next day, another mention, further back, on the news the following evening. Maybe you put the radio on if you wanted more immediate information. Either way, it was something that was happening over there, news that came and went. Now, you know it's happening, while it's still ongoing. You watch it unfold. You don't just get the perspective of the BBC, you get a million people telling you how terrifying it is. You hear about the lives of the dead. Every minute, every hour, every day, you look at social media and it's there. #terror #fear #endtimes. It's relentless. And it's all like turbulence on a plane. It's not that little bit of bumping around at thirty-five thousand feet that worries you. It's the *what's coming next?* It's the *how much worse is it going to get?* It's the *when is it going to end?* Social media and the twenty-four-hour news cycle drive that home, not letting you forget it, much more than at any time in the past.'

'And the beast of humanity feeds on negativity and disaster,' says Darnley.

We have a moment that finds all three of us simultaneously with coffee cups at our lips, and the peculiar synchronicity somehow seems to herald the end of this mutually driven descent into melancholic reflection on the coming apocalypse.

'Where are we on how the killer accessed the well?' asks Darnley.

I got up early this morning, showered, dressed, walked the long way to work. Good thinking time. Decent night's sleep – didn't meet Sanderson again in my dreams, which I'd half been expecting – so walked with a clear head. Funny how the depression of yesterday morning, which I felt seemed to have settled upon me and might be here to stay for a while, has been pushed to the side when confronted with something interesting to do. Something out of the norm of everyday fraud and thuggery.

Nothing came to me on my walk, though. Nothing obvious, nothing new, nothing fiendish.

'Every idea we hit upon, and there haven't been many, has been shut down so far. We really need forensics to come up with something, something about the well that indicates how they could have got access, but—'

'Lyle hasn't found you anything?'

'No. He sent his full report over last night, after I'd left the office. Must've worked late. Access to the well was definitely not made through the cover, so there's that. The above-ground side wall of the well is another matter. It was pretty shaky in places. There are one or two spots where individual stones might have been eased loose, then put back in place, but the question is whether they're big enough to allow someone to squeeze through a body, particularly given that there's nothing about the corpse to indicate such an action. Lyle's gone out for another couple of tests, but it might be a while before we hear anything. But if there's nothing there, that leaves the only possibility being that the people who discovered the body tossed it down there in the first place.'

'You haven't brought them in again?'

'We'll speak to them again this morning. As for bringing them in officially, we're not ready for that yet.'

'I'm inclined to be suspicious,' says Quinn to my left, 'but the only thing we have is based on a process of elimination. And while nothing else making sense certainly points to them, we can't arrest them, and certainly can't charge them, without something more concrete.'

She's nodding by the time he's finished, and as she takes another drink of coffee, I get the sense that the meeting is coming to an end. We've all got things to do.

'We should get back to the station, sir,' I say, setting my cup back on the table. 'The public won't wait to make contact with us, and while it's likely to be cluttered with unnecessary speculation, there's also a very good chance that we'll have our name.'

Quinn is nodding long before I finish speaking, but I get to the end of the sentence nevertheless, getting to my feet at the same time.

'Good call, Ben,' says Darnley. 'And well done for rescuing us from turning into miserablist triplets born of the bizarre union of Eeyore and Private Frazer. We'll stop by the ops room on your way out.'

We share a smile, while Quinn noisily pushes his chair back, and I realise that he's uncomfortable at the ease with which Darnley and I talk to each other. Or perhaps there's a layer of jealousy, considering himself excluded.

It doesn't matter. If I speak to Darnley twice a year it seems exceptional, and whatever slight resentment is playing itself out in Quinn's head will be gone within two minutes of returning to the car.

IO

It didn't take long.

I'm standing at Constable Fisher's shoulder, looking at the screen as she moves quickly down a Twitter feed.

#boyinthewell

Not yet two hours in, the social media feeds are jammed. Not so many phone calls, and the bulk of those that have come in have been quickly discounted. Some remain outstanding after the initial call, but gradually, one, two or three further calls down the line, the lead ends.

As yet, in fact, nothing has been put through from Inverness. Nothing concrete. Nothing with even the potential to become concrete.

'What's that?' I say, noticing an unusual line, out of tune with all the other expressions of interest, shock, amusement and horror.

'It's a song, sir. REM. "The Boy in the Well",' says Sutherland.

'I don't know it,' I say.

Fisher shakes her head, indicating her own unfamiliarity. I look at Sutherland, who's standing next to me, a cup of tea in his hand.

'Thought about that as soon as we found him, sir,' he says. 'Song was in my head. Usual kind of REM obtuse lyric, but it's not actually about a boy in a well.'

'It's a metaphor?'

'It's a metaphor,' he repeats.

'What's it a metaphor for?'

'Being stuck in a shit life, trying to get out.'

'Not our boy, then?'

'Definitely not.'

'Should I check it out?'

He shakes his head. 'I'll keep an ear out for anything coming in that's reminiscent of the song.'

'Thanks.'

Fisher jumps back to the top, looking at the latest tweets, a new batch every few seconds. On the left-hand side of the screen, the UK trends, the current list of top ten most popular items. #boyinthewell is third on the list. It was fifth when we started looking.

I don't think we've been standing here long, but it's hard to tell. How quickly one becomes wrapped up in the banality of social media.

Poor kid. Thoughts and prayers with the family. #boyinthewell

Looks like wee Ryan, Danny's boy. Saw him last night tho, so #probablynotRyan #boyinthewell

#boyinthewell Fuck's sake, people r cunts

Looks like Madeleine McCann lol #boyinthewell

#boyinthewell less people should be talking shite and should be looking at this. More to this than meets the eye. #conspiracy

Sad for the kid. Should of been a warning sign on the well. Someone at the council gettin his baws felt. #boyinthewell

'Can you reply to that lady and tell her it should be *fewer* people?'

Fisher turns, about to object, then sees that I'm joking and smiles.

'I'll correct *should of been* while I'm at it,' she says. 'People on the Internet would be delighted to find that the grammar police were literally the police.'

Share the joke, then turn away with a shake of the head.

'All right, enough, Fish, thanks. Just get rid of it for the moment, leave it to Inverness.'

'Yes, sir,' she says, and she closes the screen.

Sutherland and I walk back to our desks, Sutherland draining his mug of tea as we go. I feel restless. We need something to happen. We need the definitive lead, the phone call, the visit.

'We should get back out there,' I say, as he sits down at his desk, and I remain standing, unable to think about mundanely getting on with work.

'The well?'

'Yep. The ladder's been fitted, so we can go down and have a look. If we're going to have to wait for a positive ID, it at least gives us time to concentrate on this. And we can have another word with the happy farming couple while we're there.'

Sutherland nods, glances at his monitor, quickly gets back to his feet.

Last look over at Fisher, to see if she's about to turn and give me some new piece of news, worthy of the station's attention. She's on the phone, but her demeanour is not one of urgency.

'Think we'll fit down the well at the same time?' says Sutherland, lifting his jacket and walking beside me as we head out the office.

'With the amount of doughnuts you eat?' I say.

He laughs, then says, 'That's bullying, by the way. That'll be going in the office survey. You know what the chief's like when the BHD scores go up.'

And we're walking past Mary, smile and nod, and on out the station.

Despite the glib remarks on the way out, we quickly settle into sombre humour on the road to the farm. No words exchanged. Usually we'd be poring over the details of the case, but there are currently so few details to talk about that the discussion seems redundant.

All we currently have is a dead child, and we don't know the identity of his parents. There's very little lightness there.

We do the same as the day before, parking at the bottom of the fields, rather than driving round and up the driveway towards the farmhouse. Get out the car, doors closed, stand and survey the surroundings for a moment.

Late morning, the freshness of the new day still lingering. Very still up here, on the side of the hill. For a moment, not even the sound of a distant car, no wind to move the last of the leaves in the trees. A lone gull cries somewhere away to our right. The Cromarty Firth lies grey and still beneath us, just over a mile away, across fields and scattered homes. As ever, there is little happening out on the water. No blue sky, but the clouds are high and light, and the rain that was promised still some hours away.

I turn and look up the hill, across the fields, to the farmhouse and to the tent set up around the well. I can see Catriona Napier, sitting on the steps at the front of the house, working away at something in her hands. The only other person in sight is Constable Ross, standing outside the small white tent.

'Seems kind of quiet,' I say. 'When did we take the other officers off the watch?'

'This morning,' says Sutherland. 'Inverness recalled them. Or, more to the point, didn't replace them when they went off duty.'

Another look around. Roads still quiet.

'Isn't it odd that more people haven't come out? I mean, now that the kid's become this morning's Internet sensation?'

Sutherland follows my lead, looking around the area, becoming aware of the silence.

'Possibly,' he says. 'But then, we're on the Black Isle, sir. These people . . . well, not only are they largely hundreds of miles away, or not even in the UK in the first place, they're on the Internet. They could be in Culbokie, but it hardly matters. The drama is playing out, there, in front of them, on their phone. Why come and stand in a cold field?'

'They came yesterday,' I observe, not convinced by his argument, albeit seeing no other explanation.

I open the gate, he follows me through, closes it behind us, and we start walking up the well-trodden path through the lower field.

'The boy in the well wasn't on the Internet yesterday,' says Sutherland, continuing the discussion. 'Yesterday, if you wanted to take an interest, you had to be here. Today . . .' and he lets the sentence go.

'The media will be back, if nothing else,' I say.

'I don't know. They got their shots already. Their budgets are all just as tight as ours. Why come out to shoot an empty field with nothing going on, when they can use the shots from yesterday. Same field, lots more activity.'

We walk on. In the distance, the silence broken at last, there is the sound of an approaching car.

'Nevertheless, Sergeant,' I say, 'can you get on to Inverness? We're going to need at least two more officers back out here. If they can't give them to us, we'll have to do it.'

'Yes, boss,' he says, without any argument.

I walk on, as he takes the phone from his pocket, stopping to make the call. Up the hill, into the next field, look across at Napier but, apart from seeing each other, there's no acknowledgement from either of us, and then I'm up to the tent by the well, Constable Ross outside.

'Quiet morning?' I ask, coming up beside him, then turning to look away, back down the hill.

'Dead quiet, sir,' he says.

'No media?'

'None.'

'No onlookers or random passers-by, a car slowing as it drives past?'

'Couple of cars,' he says, 'but nothing of note. They could easily just've been people who knew nothing about it, saw the tent, saw me, slowed down as they looked over.'

As we watch the road, a white van comes into view, SKY NEWS emblazoned on the side in red. It slows as it approaches the field, and then stops. The driver looks up at us, glances over his shoulder, and then starts reversing back along the road.

'Crap, he's coming up the driveway,' I say. 'I'll stay here, you get over there and make sure Napier gets inside, right now, and don't let them bug her.'

'Yes, sir,' and he's off, heading over to the farmhouse even before the news van has turned into the driveway.

Still don't know who it was making the decision to cut back on the amount of officers at the scene, but we're back up to some sort of proper level of policing now. Those lines of tape that people are happy to step over or under or to push aside have been re-manned, allowing them to serve their purpose.

Inevitably the truth of the situation has turned out somewhere in between what I expected and what Sutherland presumed would be the case. The Internet generation aren't here, but some locals are back, and the media have reappeared, few though they are in number.

I'm in overalls, ready to go down into the well. The inside of the tent is brightly lit, there is a light at the foot of the well and another fitted into the wall, halfway up. Sutherland is here, as is Constable Ross, who has resumed guard duty outside the tent, although he is standing half in and half out of the doorway, watching me get ready.

'You want me to go down after you?' asks Sutherland.

'If you mean, when I get back up, then yes,' I say, and he nods. 'You should see it too, see if you spot anything I've missed. You should get togged up, ready to go.'

Sit on the edge of the well, feet over the side. I'm aware that Ross takes a further small step inside the tent, and turn to look at him.

'You're not going down yet, sir,' he says. 'You need a harness and a helmet.'

I glance at the table, and the equipment I've eschewed for the descent.

'Excellent health and safety points, Alex,' I say. 'But I'm good.'

'You're not allowed down without the required safety equipment, sir.'

I pause for a moment, those few seconds when I decide what kind of person I'm going to be, then glance at Sutherland, who nods in return.

'You'll do better with the torch on the helmet anyway, sir,' he says, 'even with the lights in the well. And if anything happens, the harness'll help us yank you out.'

'What d'you think's going to happen?' I say, but I've already swung my legs back over, conceding to the inevitable.

'You slip, you fall, you break your leg. Mundane,' he says, 'but hardly out of the question. And that's not to mention the fifty or so other horror-movie-type situations that descending into a dark, confined space offer up.'

'You're right,' I say, glibly, 'give me the harness.'

And five minutes later, here I am, decked out like Constable Cole yesterday, a police expert in some sort of mining or excavation speciality.

'Gentlemen,' I say, nod at them both, with an extra look of acknowledgement to Ross, and then start slowly climbing down the ladder.

I'm not going to find anything new, of course. It's not about that, particularly as the scene has now been compromised by our people, but I need to come down here. Somehow this boy was placed or dumped at the bottom of this well, and the only way to work out how it was done, is to process each possible explanation, all of which starts with Sutherland and me taking a look for ourselves.

I descend slowly, stopping briefly every couple of steps, making a three-hundred-and-sixty-degree examination of the wall. Nothing to see, as slowly the bright light of the circle at the top of the well recedes, and the lights set up within the pit take over.

Down to the halfway mark, the light on the wall at my back as I go past it.

'Everything all right?'

Sutherland, with the obligatory call.

'Yep!' I shout back up, although neither of us really needs to raise our voice.

The temperature drops markedly as I near the bottom. The area where the body was discovered. Tempting to put the cold down to some evil chill, marking the place of death, but it's logical, that's all. A hundred feet underground, away from the sun, any warmth in the air in here rising to the top and out and away.

Nevertheless a shiver courses through me from nowhere, and I take a sharp breath as I look around. Shake it off, and focus by looking at the bare walls, the last ring of stones a couple of feet from the bottom, and the well-trampled dirt at the foot of the well.

Looking around, I wonder what became of it. Did the well run dry, or did someone decide that it wasn't needed any more? The well itself is as much a part of the mystery as the boy, and we need to find out everything we can about it.

I tentatively put my foot down, as though expecting the floor to give way, sending me plummeting into a shaft of freezing water. I stand for a moment, and then start feeling the walls, my hands running over the old stonework. Nothing. No sign of life, no moss, no cobwebs, no worms. Not even the feeling of damp that one might anticipate. I do a full turn, shielding my eyes from the light on the floor as I pass it, inspecting the walls as I go. I begin to feel as though the bright light is impairing me, as though I'd see better with nothing but the light of the headlamp or, perhaps, with no light at all.

Stand still, close my eyes for a moment, but the light is still too bright. Open them again, look around. There's nothing to see in any case. Bare walls that, prior to the last couple of days, hadn't been looked upon in decades. Perhaps hundreds of years.

'Kill the lights, Sergeant,' I say, looking up to the circle of light, Sutherland's head in the middle of it.

'What?' he shouts back down, much too loudly. The well really isn't all that deep, and now we've been down here and illuminated it, the atmosphere feels completely different from yesterday morning, when Cole descended into the unknown.

I'm sure he heard me anyway. It was more a question of process, than of understanding. Why would I possibly want the lights turned off?

'Kill the lights,' I repeat.

My request this time is greeted by silence, and then a moment later he's gone, and the lights are off.

I stand for a second, adjusting to this new level of dark, but with the area in front of me still illuminated by the headlamp. The quality of the light, and the features now visible in the wall of the well are different, but still, of course, there's nothing to see. No door, no access, no way in or out.

I reach up and turn off the headlamp, then stand still for a moment in the darkness. Sutherland doesn't leave me standing there like that for very long, however.

'Everything all right, sir?' he shouts down.

I look around, still aware of some vestige of light from up above, the well not deep enough for the bottom to distance itself from the brightness at the top.

'I need darkness,' I say, prosaically, once more turning my head upwards. 'Can you put the wooden cover back over, please?'

'What?'

'Sergeant!'

I shout this time.

'You sure?'

'Sergeant, put the damn cover on!'

A moment, then the quieter, 'Yes, boss,' and his form disappears. I'm staring up at the light of the entrance to the well the whole time, then he returns, resting the roughly made wooden cover – four planks of wood nailed together, not cut into a circle – on the edge of the well.

'Thanks, Iain. I'll shout or tug when I want the lights back on.'

'Right,' he says, and then the cover is slowly lowered and pushed over, and the light quickly dims, disappearing into nothing, and the darkness is complete.

I stand for another moment, my head still staring up, as though expecting Sutherland to immediately withdraw the cover and ask if I'm sure this is what I want, and then I finally lower my head.

At last the darkness is complete, as deep and chilling as the silence that accompanies it. I stand absolutely still, eyes open, and can see nothing. The wall is no more than two feet in front of me, but it might as well not be there. For all I can see, I could be in the middle of a cavernous, underground hall.

I reach out and touch it, and then slowly circle, my hands on the wall, all the way round, until I'm back, as far as I can tell, in the same position.

The noise of the movement, the sound of my feet and the rustling of the overalls, comes to an end, and silence once again embraces the dark.

I let the silence settle into itself. Eyes still open, but they may as well not be. There is no adjustment to be made in vision down here, no trace of light to reflect off any surface. The darkness will not shift in time, the walls will not slowly creep into view.

I close my eyes, allowing the hush to slowly wrap itself around me.

What can you hear down here, beneath the ground? The workings of the world, the machine that drives the earth . . . Geological forces, grinding and pulling and fighting and squirming in eternal, monotonous rhythm . . . The gurgling of deep magma, the noise conveyed through the strata . . . The sound of a drill, carrying through rock, from hundreds of miles away . . . A vole or a mole or a mouse, squirrelling through the ground, a few yards either side . . .

Nothing. Shallow, inaudible breaths. Cannot even hear the sounds of my own body.

Yesterday morning the unnamed boy was lying down here, dead. His body was dropped into the well, from somewhere. Up there, where the opening was not opened? Or was there some strange fracture in space; he was dropped into another well, another well in another part of the world, and he ended up in here?

I allow myself this thought, something that is as absurd as Lachlan's suggestion that he could have been down here all this time, his body somehow immaculately preserved. I don't need to take the thought back up there, into the bright world, of light and sound.

But down here, where I can think, I need to consider all possibilities, if only so I can disregard them and concentrate on what's left.

I think of the moment when he dropped down. Already dead, his heart already removed, no life, just sound. Forensics found no evidence of him hitting the wall of the well on the way down. A perfect drop. The whoosh of wind, a blur of pale colour, and then the loud, ugly thud as his heartless corpse hit the ground.

I'm standing where he was lying, trying to imagine him, trying to feel him. But of course there's nothing to feel. He was never alive in this spot. What vestige of life could there be in this place?

And how long does a sound reverberate around a confined space? What is the half-life of a dull thud? Could one stand in silence and detect a noise from ten minutes previously? From an hour ago? A day?

The feel of it? The sense of it? The final, distant, minuscular vibrations. The awareness that this thing had once been here. This sound. This event. It happened not so long ago.

Yet how much noise has there been down here in the past twenty-four hours? People have come and gone, a ladder has been attached to the side of the wall, a body has been removed, pictures have been taken, boots have clumped up and down, words have been spoken, instructions have been shouted, lights shone in long-concealed corners, the equilibrium of a dead body lying at the bottom of a dried-up well has been broken.

No . . .

Silence.

I swallow, move slightly, adjusting my head, suddenly aware of the quickened beat of my heart. That sudden, horrible fear, every nerve end tensed. Listening. Trying to listen harder, in the way that one would run faster or push more vigorously. Standing in silence, ears straining.

The darkness is still complete. The silence still—

Another sound. A sigh. A sound of sorrow.

I turn quickly, the noise coming from behind. Air on my face. Not a breath of wind, not someone blowing. It's like it was just there, a patch of air, hanging a few feet off the floor of the well, waiting for me to step into it. The temperature is not different, the air is not cold, not humid. It's as though the air is clinging to my skin, sucking on it.

Another gasp of breath, another chill sweeps down my back. *There's no mystery* . . .

'What?'

The voice, the words, somehow inside the well and faraway at the same time. The voice young, and so sad.

I step back, and now my back is pressed against the wall. I should turn the light on, but somehow I know when I do that, it will be the end of it. The end of the voice.

Four days ago I talked to Sanderson. Perhaps that was how it began. Me going from being someone who can occasionally sense the dead, to someone who talks to the dead. That's why Sanderson came. He was saying, *you need the practice, my friend. You need to get used to it.*

The wall, that's all . . .

Turn the headlamp on! Tug on the harness!

'What d'you mean?'

Is he here? If I sat and spoke to Sanderson, if I shared a glass of wine with him, if I looked out over Wester Ross with him, then could I not speak to the boy? Would that not make everything so much easier?

Silence. I strain and listen, desperate to hear something else, desperate for there just to be silence. I should turn on the light, but I'm scared he'll be right there, down here, in this space. A foot away from me. Pressed against me. His face at my chest, looking up, his abdomen prised open, a bloody space where his heart should be.

There's nothing there! No sound! There is no sound! I'm standing in total darkness and my imagination is getting the better of me. Get a grip, you fool! Hand across my face, as though I can get rid of the feel of this air. The clawing grasp of it, that has stuck to me no matter where I turn.

Did I really hear that voice? *The wall, that's all* . . . That wasn't someone else. That was me. My voice. My inner voice, telling me where to look. It's obvious, isn't it? The body can't have been teleported in from space. There is no secret passageway. If the lid of the well is undamaged, there must have been something done to the side of the wall.

That was no child talking to me. The mind doesn't just play tricks. Everything about the mind is a trick. I came down here wanting there to be something, and I got it. How had I been expecting it to arrive?

A noise from above, a shaft of dim light, and I look up. Sutherland peers over the edge, although I can't see his face.

'You all right down there, boss?' he asks.

I feel enfeebled. I feel shot. I feel like I don't really understand what just happened.

'Sure,' I shout up after him. 'Nearly done. Give me another couple of minutes.'

'Really? You've been down there ten minutes. What are you doing?'

'What?'

Ten minutes.

He must be exaggerating. Rounding up.

He's not rounding up. I know he's not rounding up. I stood in the dark, and time got lost, just the same as I got lost.

Suddenly I feel the claustrophobia of the well, the walls and the darkness and the air, and this meagre ray of light which is all that stands between me and where I was thirty seconds ago, and without even seeming to have any positive thought to do so, I'm reaching for the ladder, foot on the bottom rung, and climbing quickly back up to the surface.

Up at the top I study the sides of the wall that rise about three and a half feet above the ground. The stonework is old, much of it in need of repair. Impossible to tell from this kind of cursory glance whether any of the blocks have been removed and put back in place. Hard to imagine, though, that the boy, however slender, could have been squeezed through there, and how there would not have been some noticeable effect on the body.

Perhaps we have to bring him back out, to see if he can be dropped back into the well.

We can't do that.

I study the wall while Sutherland makes his descent, and while my composure returns. Sutherland chooses not to experience the foot of the well in total darkness.

II

'What did you think about the decision to reopen the well?'

In the farmhouse, talking to Catriona Napier. First her, then her wife. Probing for the hole in their stories, the inconsistency that opens up the path to the next stage of the investigation.

Napier's sitting at the table, hands clasped before her, eyes down. Looks as unhappy as she did yesterday.

'I thought it was odd,' she says. 'She has her theories, after all, about giant lizards ruling the world. It keeps her amused.'

'How much attention did you see her paying to the well cover before yesterday morning?'

A beat. She slowly lifts her eyes from whatever spot on the kitchen table she'd been staring at.

'What does that mean?'

'Did she spend much time at the well? Did she know exactly what she was going to do to take the well cover apart?'

'Are you asking me if I think she might have removed the well cover prior to yesterday morning, then replaced it again?'

I don't answer, just hold her gaze across the short distance of the table. That is exactly what I'm asking, and of course it's not about her answering the question at all. She's never going to do that.

'Did she spend much time at the well?' I repeat.

She sighs heavily, pointedly, says, 'No', and doesn't add to it.

93

'Does Belle have any dealings with children's groups? Scouts, Boys Brigade, Sunday school, youth clubs, anything like that?'

She holds my gaze for a moment, then slowly her eyes drop back to the kitchen table. She looks as though she doesn't want to be having this conversation, but then, that needn't be because she's trying to avoid anything. The list of reasons people don't like being interviewed by the police is long.

'She wanted to go and talk to schools,' she says, without looking up. 'About a year ago, she contacted a few in the area. Didn't go any further than Inverness. She was looking to raise a new breed of cynics and conspiracy theorists. She wanted to talk to pupils about how the world is really run. About the value of the education that they were all getting, and how they were all being brainwashed. She was offended no one wanted her.'

'And has she tried to reach out to children in any other way?'

For a moment it's as though she hasn't heard me, and then finally she shakes her head, the word 'No' sounding small from her lips.

One must deal with the impossibility of reading someone in this situation. It could be she's scared, hiding something, and dealing with it by curling up into an uncommunicative ball. Or, it could just be that she's haunted by the whole thing, and all she wants is for it to go away, to be left alone.

'What about Lachlan Green? Is it possible he's been involved with children's groups, and Belle ended up doing him a favour?'

'Seriously?' she says, the word accompanied by a small, bitter laugh. She leans forward, placing her forehead in the palm of her hand. 'You people. *What's that, Lachlan, you killed someone? Gosh, that's inconvenient. Just bring the body over here, we'll get rid of it for you, we've got the perfect place. But even though it is the perfect place, we'll still need to tell the police about it . . .'*

Time for another quick change of tack.

'Were you having an affair with your sister-in-law while your husband was still alive?'

A beat, then the despondency on her face increases, as though she's talking to a child for whom there is no hope.

'Inspector, I'm not even having an affair with Belle now.'

'I know,' I say, 'you're married to her,' and she rests her forehead in her hand again.

'The police,' she says, head shaking. 'For what it's worth, here goes. There's nothing between Belle and me. Nothing. Never has been, never will be. We've even got separate bedrooms, which I'm happy to give you a tour of. She'll probably not be happy, but to be honest I've never been into her room, so I don't know what it's like.'

'You've never been in your wife's bedroom?'

'No,' she says defiantly.

'You've never so much as taken her a cup of tea in the morning.'

'She drinks coffee first thing, and she likes to make it herself,' she says. 'Look, Inspector, Robert and I had an awful marriage. The farm was failing, he was in this free-fall, and there was nothing I could do about it. He wasn't . . . he didn't have cancer or liver disease or anything like that, but he was ill, and there was nothing anyone could do to help him. You ever watch anyone die, Inspector? You ever stand there, utterly helpless, and watch someone slip from your grasp? There was nothing I could do, and then he was gone. Dead. Killed himself, and some days I tell myself that there really was nothing I could've done, and some days I think that I might as well just have handed him the rope for all that I did to stop it.'

Her voice is starting to break, she takes a deep breath, she pulls it back. I let her gather herself, too experienced to be anything but sceptical at any show of raw emotion.

'The farm was falling apart by the end, and I was this close – this close – to just letting it go. Belle helped me pull it back. She'd been to business school, she knew what she was doing. That was all. A clear head. She lived south of Drum, though, so it made sense for her to move in, save on the forty-minute drive every day. And then, at some point, we realised it was financially to our advantage to get married. Her suggestion. Tax reasons, something like that, I didn't really pay attention. It was a business deal, that was all.

'So we went through the motions, the deal was done, and now, here we are. The married, lesbian couple, who aren't lesbians. I expect people talk, which is why I'm not surprised that you've blundered in here, wearing your size fifteen clodhoppers, asking questions ... Now you know the truth. Maybe when you're next interrogating the village gossips, you can pass it on.'

'Can you tell me the root of your husband's depression?' I ask.

A slight change in the eyes, a deeper, darker shadow crosses them, an almost imperceptible drop in the shoulders, like another weight has been placed on them. Not necessarily anything to be read into it, of course.

'Just talk to me, Catriona, please,' I say. 'It's much easier to do it here than down at the station.'

'You have a reason to take me down to the station?' she says, her voice still lifeless, her gaze still vacant.

'I just need you to answer questions, that's all.'

The look in the eyes does not change; there is a small movement of the head.

'You don't suppose that this is very painful for me, do you, Inspector?'

'I understand it could be.'

'*Could* be? Well, thank you for that, sir, I bow to your compassion.'

I don't say anything to that. Her tone has shifted enough that I know she's going to answer at least; I just need to give her the time.

'Well, what does it matter now?' she says. 'We couldn't have kids. Big fat cliché, right? *He* couldn't have kids. Just that. We got married, and he was ... There was no honeymoon period for us, for me, there was no adjustment to married life, no suggestion that we could enjoy ourselves for a while, a new couple, no responsibilities. He wanted to start a family straight away.'

She smiles at a memory, an expression that looks sad and unfamiliar on her face today, and soon enough the smile fades and dies, and the vacant, haunted look returns.

'Except we couldn't. Over time, excitement faded to worry, worry became anxiety. He'd convinced himself that it wasn't going to happen even before we went to the doctor. I thought the issue would be with me, he thought it'd be him. He was right.'

'What was the problem?'

'Seriously?'

'You didn't want to adopt?'

'No, Inspector, we did not want to adopt. Robert did not want to bring up someone else's child. He wanted his own, and he couldn't have them. And as soon as he found out that was the case, that was us. We were finished, right there, right then. Might as well have split up. Never had sex again, barely spoke to each other again, but neither of us went anywhere. We clung on here, doing what we were supposed to be doing, living a God-awful, miserable life, year after bloody year. And then he took his own life. And while Belle and I might not have the best thing going on earth, at least it's not as sad and desperate as the life I was living with Robert for over twenty years. That, Inspector, was the true horror.'

'And what about children?' I ask, and in the quiet of the room the sound of her swallowing is loud.

'What about them?'

'You wanted to have children,' I say, voice cold. 'How have you lived with that? How have you accommodated that?'

She's holding my gaze now, her eyes impossible to read.

'I'm a woman, therefore I must in some way have exercised my needs? I couldn't possibly just have lived with the pain?'

'That's what I'm asking.'

We hold the gaze for a long time, before finally she looks away, eyes dropping, head turned slightly to the side.

'I've lived with the pain,' she says. 'That's all.'

That I don't entirely believe her is not because there's any particular reason I shouldn't. No change in her voice, nothing that sounds forced or contrived. It's just the years of experience. Of questioning and interrogating, of reading people and investigating what they say.

People lie. Often enough they might not mean anything by it, but they lie anyway, because that's what people do.

'We only, realistically, have two options before us, Ms McIntosh,' I say.

We're standing in the sitting room, McIntosh having refused to take a seat. As though she's decided to grant us one seated interview, and if we want another, we'll have to escalate matters. Perhaps she thinks standing will make the interview a fleeting affair.

'There are always more than two options,' she says.

'Well, perhaps you can share some of them with me.'

'What two d'you already have?' she asks.

Even chippier than yesterday. I expect she feels she's said everything that needs to be said, and now we should be getting out of their hair and letting them get on with the important work of the farm.

I still feel empty. Washed out after being down at the bottom of the well. The life was sucked from me, and is yet to return. Voice flat, questions coming out in almost an uninterested monotone, as if I'm going through the motions. Not helped by the conversation with Catriona Napier, when she talked as though she felt the same thing.

'Either you removed the well cover, or part of the side wall, tossed the boy's body in, and then claimed to have found it down there; or else it was done before you got there, and you didn't notice the repair that had been done to the cover when you opened it.'

'That didn't happen,' she says.

'Which one?'

'I meant the second one, because I would've noticed. I'm just not replying to the first one because it's so absurd.'

'And now that you've heard mine, what explanations do *you* have?' I ask, and she rolls her eyes.

'Classic,' she says. 'So ingrained in the system that you can't see the inherent corruption.'

'No, I can't,' I say, 'but I'm looking forward to you explaining it to me.'

'Oh, all right then,' she says, sarcastically, 'I'll do that, shall I? Hmm? So who is it who says there's no sign of the well cover being repaired to such a remarkable standard that I wouldn't notice? Your people I suppose. The police.

'And who says the boy's only been dead a few days? And who says the boy's even dead at all? Given how often the police have lied over the years, how can I believe anything you say? Seriously, if you found out some bigwig or some rich landowner was responsible, can you honestly tell me that you wouldn't set me and Lachlan up, while covering for the toff?'

She delivers all this in a steady tone, no bitterness, as though it's just an accepted fact of life. I give her the space to see if she'll continue, then when she doesn't, I say, 'So, basically, you have no other explanation?'

Nothing. Just the well-practised, resentful look, with which we're so familiar. And so, on to the next question on the slate.

'Did you help out at the farm before your brother died?'

'Talking about that now, are we?' she says. 'I tried to stay out of it. It was obvious what was wrong, and it was obvious there was nothing to be done about it. It was just one of those things. A bad lot, call it what you will. A ship heading for the rocks, the captain insisting on not changing course. You try to argue for a while, but at the same time, you know there's nothing you can do.'

She stops for a moment to shake her head, glances at me, then looks back out the window.

'I ended up staying away. Couldn't stand it any longer. I tried to help them and was rebuffed at every turn.'

'What was your relationship with Catriona at the time?'

She lowers her eyes in a kind of staged movement. The knowing, sideways glance, the *here we go, just what you'd expect from the police* look to the TV audience.

'You mean, were we having an affair?'

'What was your relationship with Catriona?'

Have never been a fan of the real-life sideways glance to the audience, as though we are all permanently playing to the masses. It's a more prevalent gesture from the young, whose every action is conducted alongside a running internal narrative of how it will play out on social media. There's a deal more acerbity about it from someone Belle McIntosh's age.

'I felt a degree of pity but, at the same time, she was utterly hapless in the face of Robert's depression. Didn't have a clue what to do. I mean, none of us did, and I'm not sure who would. Nevertheless, Catriona was particularly useless.'

'So why did you come here after Robert died?'

'Catriona was thinking about selling up,' she says, her voice heavy with the weariness of having to share, 'and I said I'd look over things for her. I came to advise on how to put things in order before selling, but didn't realise how shockingly badly it had been run. So much potential just being frittered away.' A deep breath, a long sigh. 'I gave myself the challenge of turning it around. Found I enjoyed it. Six months in, procedures were in place and it was obvious it could be a going concern and that she didn't have to sell.'

'And then you got married?'

'Yes,' she says, the look on her face adding that that's all she's got to say on the matter.

'That must be a particularly good tax break to put up with the innuendo.'

'Inspector, I genuinely don't give a shit about innuendo. I don't give a shit what people say or what they think. I don't give a shit about what you say or what you think. There's nothing going on here except two people running a farm, and the sooner you accept that, get out of our hair, and let us get on with it, the better.'

'Can we talk about children, then?'

A further hardening of her face. Her head twitches a little. 'Jesus,' she says.

'You've never had children?'

'Really?' she says. 'You're asking a woman in her fifties? What are you after? A sob story? Tears? The baby I lost, the baby I never had? My life as a non-mother, the incomplete woman that I am? How can I even sleep at night knowing that I fought my biological instincts and won?'

'Are you done?'

'Are you?'

'You never wanted children?'

'Jesus,' she says, turning away.

Her back turned to me now, she stands at the window, looking down over the lower fields of the farm.

'Is that so wrong of me?' she asks eventually, some of the annoyance gone, her voice tired. Tired, at least, of the discussion.

'Why did you never have children?'

She sighs heavily. 'You're not letting it go, are you, Inspector?'

'No.'

She turns back, finally, and the fight has gone out of her, the look on her face resigned. I know, however, that I can't trust it for a moment. That look, the give up and shrug and act like this is all too much to even think about, is the easiest one to fake.

'I just didn't,' she says. 'Does that make me such a bad person?'

I find Lachlan Green, a caricature of the village fool, sitting against a wall, his backside on a waterproof jacket, looking out over the Cromarty Firth, a blade of grass in the corner of his mouth, drinking Weston's cider from the bottle.

While I talk to Green, still going through the motions, Sutherland – having spent the previous hour going all over the farm property with Constable Cole, and coming up with nothing new – stays in the car, on the phone, sorting out our next port of call.

'Tracked me down, Sergeant,' Lachlan says. 'It's like trying to escape from the Mounties. Or Jason Bourne. *Jesus Christ, it's Sergeant Westphall!*'

'Did you work for the farm when it was still run by Robert McIntosh?'

The bottle is raised to his lips, but he lowers it again without taking a drink, looking at me curiously. I think it's my tone, which he likely finds unexpectedly subdued, rather than the question itself.

'No,' he says. 'I knew the guy, that was all. When he died, Catriona needed some extra hands. Came looking for the cheapest worker she could get,' and he raises his arm. 'That'd be me. Like I said yesterday.'

'You ever see any children up there? Ever hear talk of any children?'

He barks out a laugh, follows it with another headshake.

'Yeah, sure, of course. They used to get visits from school groups, which would mysteriously always leave with one kid missing. Happened all the time. Surprised no one told you about it.'

'Did you ever hear talk of any children?'

'Huh,' he says. 'You've changed, Sergeant. You're usually up for the fight. No fun today.'

'Did you ever hear talk of any children?'

'No,' he says, finally answering with a resigned tone. 'No kids, far as I know, not when Robert was there, and there's not much chance of it happening now, is there? Not a lot of ammo getting fired up there these days.'

'What about you?'

He shrugs. 'What does that mean?'

'Do you have any children?'

'You know I've got no children.'

'I know you live alone, it doesn't mean you don't have children somewhere.'

'Classic. Unemployed, uneducated, smokes, drinks . . . one plus one equals three, and therefore the guy must've fathered a bunch of illegitimate kids. Jesus. Well, turns out I'm gay. So, no, no kids.'

He's not gay. I know he's not gay. Not that it matters either way, but I'm not rising to anything today.

'Are you involved with any youth groups? You ever do work in schools?'

'Yeah, of course. I teach Latin over at Dingwall Academy. Just on a Wednesday, mind. The other days I'm too busy helping autistic children cross the road.'

'You're being a dick, Lachlan,' I say, voice still level, but exasperation beginning to emerge. The negativity is just wearing sometimes.

'Oh, I am sorry, Sergeant,' he says, affecting a slightly posher than normal voice, albeit he doesn't really have the talent for it. 'I simply must try harder, and I'll be sure to do that next time. For the moment though,' he says, the voice dropping again, 'why don't you just fuck off and leave us alone?'

The door opens, and Sutherland half stands out the car.

'We're good to go, sir,' he says. 'The afternoon's getting on, we should move.'

'Thanks, Sergeant,' I say over my shoulder.

I look down at Lachlan, we hold each other's gaze for a few moments, and then I turn and walk away.

'We good?' asks Sutherland, as I get into the car.

'No, Sergeant,' I say. 'Not at all.'

12

Just before four in the afternoon. Darkness already coming across the land. We're in Ross and Cromarty land registry, a small office in the town of Cromarty, by the harbour, with a view facing back down the firth, towards the oil rigs. The rigs are illuminated, heightening the feeling of oncoming gloom.

I still haven't recovered from the well. Feel exhausted. Spent. Absurdly, like I gave everything, physically and emotionally, down there. Yet all I did was stand still, staring into the darkness.

Interviewing the only suspects we have, such as they are, seemed to pass in an interrogational haze. I was going through the motions, putting questions that I knew would be dead-batted back at me. At this stage, there's little to be gained, other than taking in information that might later be used against them.

If they did have nothing to do with it, there's little extra to be learned from them. If they are involved, they're going to lie anyway. If it's the latter, then we need to be speaking to them as often as possible, manoeuvring to catch them out. Either that, or we need to identify something from their past. Everyone has a past, after all, and everyone's past feeds into their present.

Jesus. Must have read that in a fortune cookie.

I have no feeling, so far, which way this will go. For the moment, however, they're all we've got.

Sutherland went down into the well after me, but I knew he wouldn't have the same reaction, he wouldn't feel the same things. He certainly wasn't going to hear the same voice, because that voice was in my head. It couldn't have been anywhere else.

Not that I talked about standing in the dark, the strange sensation of air sucking at my face. Sutherland came back to the top, shrugged a little, said that he hadn't been able to see anything of significance and then made a glib comment about lunch.

The lunch itself, taken before we interviewed the farmers, was conducted in a peculiar silence that I presume Sutherland did not understand.

He turns his phone off and slips it back into his pocket, and I ask the question with a raised eyebrow.

'Still nothing,' he says. 'There was a potential call from Devon, a real likeness about the face they said, then it turned out the kid's only been missing since yesterday afternoon.'

'How's #boyinthewell coming along?'

He smiles, shakes his head.

'Still the top trend. Been a few hours now, so you know what that means.'

I look at him, until he turns away from the water.

'No?' he says.

'Not really. We're not to take it as a positive?'

'Well, it's certainly getting the story out there, so there's that. The downside is, of course, that 99.99 per cent of these tweets and posts, and whatever else, are absolute trash, many of which breed or promote conspiracy theories.'

'Belle McIntosh got involved yet?'

'Ha. Not so I know, but we can look into it. Wouldn't put it past her.'

'So what's the favourite, then?' I ask. 'You never know what truth may come. Or what truth someone wants planted as a way to inculcate the story into the national consciousness.'

He smiles.

'Nice,' he says. 'Just the kind of talk the conspiracy theorists like.'

'Given where I used to work, I know.'

'Used to plant one or two stories yourselves, did you?'

'All the time,' I say, drily. 'There was literally nothing we couldn't pin on rogue elements within the Labour Party.'

He laughs, nods, glances back out to the sea as he speaks.

'Well, there are two emerging as favourites. The first, more straightforward conspiracy is that the boy is the son of a government minister. An unnamed government minister, as obviously no one has been able to find a government minister with a nine-year-old son not currently present and accounted for.'

'Westminster or Holyrood?'

'Either will do, but the general preference seems to be for Westminster. Considered, by the Internet at least, to be more naturally salacious.'

'And the other?'

'Classic. Started on Facebook, it's a little more involved. This theory states that the boy is a plant. That they, whoever *they* are in this case, but the "they" with a capital "T", they found some kid who'd been kept away from general society, they made his family disappear,' and he smiles grimly at the euphemism, 'killed the kid, then planted his body in such a way that he was going to be found at a specific time.'

'Why?'

'To cover up something else that's happening today, or tomorrow, or whenever it is that we hit peak #boyinthewell. This same theory has it that it's the government who are driving the viral reaction to the story. So people are responding to it, for the most part, by stating that most other people responding to it are fake government accounts.'

'Nice.'

'Yeah, the perfect conspiracy theory,' says Sutherland. 'The more people talk about it, the more self-fulfilling it becomes. Nice job from whoever started it.'

'Probably GCHQ.'

He laughs, although there's still nothing in my tone. Still feel empty and discombobulated.

'Oh, and since #boyinthewell is a little clumsy, they've started calling him Boy 9, because that was how it was being written. Boy, 9 . . . Now it sounds like there were eight other boys before him. So we've also had to start keeping an eye on #Boy9.'

'Boy 9,' I say, letting the name fall sadly from my lips. 'Well, at least it's a name.'

The door opens, and two women enter, one carrying a tray with three mugs of tea and a small plate of biscuits, and the other with a large map partially rolled, which she's obviously been looking at in another room, and has gathered up to bring through to show us.

'There's your tea,' says the younger of the two women, the few words a way to cover her general embarrassment at walking into a room with two older men she's never met. First job, work placement, I decide, though I hardly think about it. We smile, Sutherland says, 'Thanks!' his face brightening, and she's gone.

Elizabeth Rhodes stands with the map held in her hand, looking at the tray in the middle of the table, then looks up at the two of us useless men, standing there waiting for something to happen.

'Sorry,' I say, getting to the point marginally before Sutherland, then lift the tray and place it on the large shelf beside the window.

'Thanks,' she says. 'Help yourself to the tea, they're all the same.'

'Smashing,' says Sutherland, and one of the mugs has disappeared almost before I've removed my hands from the tray.

'I'll get mine in a moment,' says Rhodes, absent-mindedly, speaking to herself more than us, as she starts to unroll the map. Looks distracted, a little distant, and not necessarily because she's thinking about the map in her hand.

It's a land registry map, boundaries, roads, paths, streams, rivers and holdings marked out in black and white. At first glance an impossible jumble of figures and lines, which will gradually sort itself out in time, the longer we look at it. Presumably Rhodes sees it all from the off.

The confusion of the map is added to by the numerous amendments, all done in pencil, in various different handwriting. Notes and figures and lines.

She holds it out, her arms stretched wide, as we stand on the other side of the table for a few moments, trying to make some sort of sense from it, then she catches my eye with a weak smile, and, just as slow as I was with the tray on the desk in the first place, I realise she needs help pinning down the corners.

'Sorry,' I say, rolling my eyes.

The plate of biscuits, a stapler, an empty mug and the old-fashioned red desk phone are each placed at a corner, and the stiff paper of the map is flat against the surface of the desk.

'Thanks,' she says, straightening up. I lift the two mugs of tea and pass one over to her, which she takes without lifting her eyes.

'Thanks,' she says again, and silence falls as we are absorbed in the lines and numbers of the map.

As one stares at it, it begins to organise itself, almost as though a sorting spell has been cast upon it. The rivers become clearer, the placement of the roads. Here a stream has taken a slightly different path, here a small development of four houses, here a croft has fallen into disuse, here a field has been given up and returned to wild grass. I find the road leading up from the B9169, and from there I can identify the farm and, within the grounds of the farm, the spot on the land occupied by the well.

'Got it,' I find myself saying, then glance at Sutherland, feeling slightly foolish, in case he'd spotted it straight away. He nods in such a way as to suggest that he's just spotted it himself.

'What's the reference by the well?' I ask, indicating the series of numbers scribbled beside the symbol.

'That, Inspector,' she says, 'is the system at work. It's a reference to the database, where we go now to get the history of the well.'

'How many other wells are there in this area?' asks Sutherland, scanning the map as he speaks.

She takes a moment, looking quickly over, then says, 'Four. Three of the others are also closed, and one . . . well, obviously isn't. Still used by Mr Fenders, just along the road from here.'

She continues to scan the map, then indicates another point inside the boundary of the River Conan.

'There was also one here, but it was swallowed up . . . I don't know, over a hundred years ago.'

'When does the map date from?' I ask.

She points to a line, right down at the bottom, albeit one that Sutherland and I couldn't possibly see from here.

'Printed in 1937,' she says, then looks up. 'You know, there's a replacement programme, but these things take time.'

'Is everywhere in Scotland like that?' I ask, not at all surprised.

'No,' she says, shrugging. 'Places change, new maps get done. This is more a testament to the Black Isle than anything else. Not many motorways, high-speed rail lines or massive housing developments been built here in recent times. We're on the list for an upgrade, but we keep getting pushed down.'

'You're obviously not lunching with the right people,' I say, and she smiles ruefully. Given who she's married to, I'm not sure who else the right person would be in this area.

'Maybe now that everyone's suddenly paying attention to us, we'll get bumped up.'

We all stare at the map for a few moments, then she takes a drink of tea, and sets the mug down on the edge of the table.

'Right,' she says. 'In another turn-up that will shock you to the core, I'm sure, I can't get the information we need on this computer here, and need to go into the other room. If you can just bear with me for another few minutes, sorry.'

'Of course.'

And with another weak smile she turns and is off out the room again, neither Sutherland nor I looking up as she goes.

'You'd think they'd just buy a new Ordnance Survey map and mark that up,' says Sutherland.

'Different scale,' I say. 'This is far more detailed. Or, at least, detailed in a different way.'

'Hmm,' he says with a nod, quickly followed by a slurp at his tea. He looks round, hesitates, then retreats from the table, lifting a biscuit as he goes. I hear the first crunch, am aware that Sutherland is now back looking out the window, but don't turn.

Is there really anything to find from the map, or am I clutching, standing here looking down at it because it's in front of me? It's giving me something to do while I wait, something to divert my attention from earlier today. Stare at the mass of writing, and at symbols I don't recognise, and hope that something emerges slowly from the mire.

'She's nice,' says Sutherland.

A moment, and finally I look away from the map.

'Really?'

He looks back, smiling.

'You know, she's attractive, that's all. Nice smile. Seems to like you. And she's got that, you know, air of melancholy that . . . well . . . matches yours.'

'You think I need a girlfriend?' I ask, and he makes a small movement with his head, then lifts the mug to his face. 'And you think I should start with someone who's married to Councillor Rhodes in Dingwall?'

His eyes widen as the mug gets lowered from his face.

'She's not married to Harry Rhodes?' he says, a little more incredulously than I would have thought the news warranted.

'I think you'll find that she is.'

'Harry Rhodes, who's on the local police committee?'

'There is, as the football fan likes to say, only one Harry Rhodes.'

'But how d'you know she's his wife?'

'Because I read the *Ross-shire*,' I say. 'You should too.'

'It's shit.'

'No, it's not. It's the local paper, with local news. What d'you want it to report? The melting of the Greenland ice sheet and queues for food in Caracas? Local papers are vital to a community, and you should read it. If you had, you'd at least know that Elizabeth Rhodes is married to Harry Rhodes.'

'Wow.'

'No, Sergeant, I don't really think it's a wow moment. It's just a thing. A small thing at that. Enough, nevertheless, to prevent me asking her out on a date.'

'Hmm,' he says, and finally he appears to be retreating from his moment of surprise. 'Yeah, probably best. So, when were they in the paper? I mean, do the councillors' wives and husbands usually get a mention?'

'Not usually, no. Photographs from grand Dingwall occasions. Openings, charity events, that kind of thing.'

'She was in the paper recently?'

I have to think about that one. Take a moment, step forward, lift a biscuit, and then look out over the water, the lights of the rigs seemingly brighter than they were a few minutes ago.

'Last year, maybe. Been a while.'

'And you remembered her?'

Since the answer to that is obvious, I don't reply, and we once again fall into silence, standing still, looking out over the water.

Shortly, from our right, three tugboats sail into view, in a perfect line, having entered the Cromarty Firth from the Moray Firth. In the grey light of dusk there's something old-fashioned in the scene, as though we're watching it in black and white, and these are military vessels sailing home from the war.

Nothing to say, we stand and watch the silent movie, slow and grey and strangely mesmerising. And then, lagging a few hundred yards behind the formation, comes a fourth tug, chugging along at the same pace.

Wherever they're going, they're almost there, in strange and silent beauty.

'It's like a scene from a Bergman film,' says Sutherland, some time later, breaking the captivating silence. 'What d'you suppose they herald? Four horsemen of the apocalypse?'

'In tug form?' I say, the moment having finally been broken. 'More likely they herald a couple of rigs needing to get towed out to sea.'

The pedantic answer sounds even more mundane as it crosses my lips, and I don't have time to wave it off before the door opens.

'Sorry about that,' says Rhodes, as she re-enters the room, a large book in her hand. 'Had a few things to look at.'

'That's all right,' I say.

She takes a drink, lays the book on the map, then sits down at her desk, looking around for two other chairs as she does so. There are no more chairs. We glance at each other and the entire conversation of apology is played out silently between us, and I indicate for her to continue.

'So, basically, your well was sealed in 1814. There's nothing to suggest that it's been reopened since. The land around here . . . well, you know how badly the Black Isle was affected by the Clearances. This land here was owned by a Lord Balfour, and Balfour was quite brutal in his actions; as were many, of course. The well would have serviced four or maybe five crofts in the surrounding area. They were all cleared, and turned over to the sheep.'

'The well is dry,' I say. 'Was it running dry back then, or was it just topped off?'

'It was decommissioned from an operational status, but before the well cover was put in place, the stream that fed the aquifer that fed the well was diverted onto land that the laird viewed as more favourable to his needs. So it's not recorded if the well was completely dry by the time it was covered but, if not, it possibly would have been soon afterwards.'

'So Gillian Napier's farm, when did that come into use?' I ask.

'Well, as you can see, the farm is on this map. It was just after the first war. The present house dates from the early 1930s.'

'And there's no record of the well being opened, or anyone attempting to restart the well, in all that time?'

'Nothing,' she says. 'But then, they wouldn't necessarily have had to tell us.'

'What happened to the people on the land?' asks Sutherland. 'The ones who were cleared?'

'Well . . .' she says, and here she taps the book which she placed on the map. 'You've got some reading to do. This is the ledger of the land owned by the Balfour family, 1806 to 1826. There are other editions, up until the time of the Great War, but this should cover the required period. If you want to see more, then we have them.'

'Maybe we could just take them with us,' I say, 'if that's all right.'

'You'd think it would be,' she says, sympathetically.

'It's not?'

'Sorry.'

'Can we take this one?'

'Sorry.'

'You're not allowed to give out a book that was written in 1826?'

'You can look at it, you can photocopy it, you can take notes and commit every word to memory, but I'm afraid I can't let you take it out.'

A moment. Not a tense one, or anything. She's only doing her job, and we're all the same, all of us who work for government. We have to do what it says in the job description or someone somewhere will get upset.

'Sorry,' she says again.

'That's all right,' I say, voice level. It's not all right, of course, it's bloody irritating, but there's little to be done.

'So we can photocopy the relevant pages and take them away.'

Another pause, and this time she looks even more embarrassed.

'Actually, no,' she says.

I ask the question with a look.

'Photocopier's broken. Been waiting three weeks for it to get fixed.'

'And we can't take it to a shop in town to get the photocopying done?' asks Sutherland, joining in.

'No, sorry.'

'Not even for ten minutes?'

Shake of the head.

He heaves a deep breath, one of those that says much more than any words, and threatens to alter the tone in the room, so I quickly accept the position as it is and get on with it.

'OK, you know roughly how many pages we'd need to read through in order to cover the timeframe around the well closure and clearance?'

'Hard to say,' she says, her tone not quite as soft as before. 'Details of the well closure, if there are any at all, might be in any one of about thirty pages. The land clearance . . . I don't know, maybe a couple of hundred.'

Quick look at the watch, calculating. What are the odds that the book gives us anything useful? What could it possibly be? And if there is something, does that imply that the motive for the killing goes back two hundred years?

'You could take pictures of them, if you like,' she says, then she opens the book, not especially hopefully, showing the size of the print and the way the words are crammed onto the page. 'With your phone. Might not be great, but you could give it a try.'

'How long are you open?' I ask.

'We'll be going in about an hour,' she says. 'Maybe a little later. But you can stay, lock up after yourself, put the key through the letterbox.'

'So, you'll trust us to lock up, but not to return a damned book?' says Sutherland, his annoyance beginning to spill over.

'You have rules you have to follow, Sergeant?' she says. 'Do you? Because I do. I did not write them, I just have to stick to them.'

'That's all right,' I say, touching Sutherland's arm, 'we understand, it's fine.'

She contemplates saying something but decides to back off, as does Sutherland. Quickly run it through my head, make the decision.

'Call the office,' I say to Sutherland, 'see if there's any news. If there is, we'll head back there now.'

There's not going to be. They're not sitting there with the name of the dead child, waiting for the senior investigating officer to call in for the information.

'And if there's not?' asks Sutherland, phone out of his pocket, scepticism in his voice.

'I'll stay here and look at the book, you get back to the station. It'll be good to study the book itself. If I get into anything, find any long passages of use, I can take pictures of them to bring back.'

'And how're you going to get back to Dingwall?'

I glance at Rhodes to see if she'll have any easy answers, although of course there are none. I can wait for a late bus and sit on it for over an hour, or I can get a taxi. The same answers that there usually are when you don't have a car.

'I'll work it out,' I say, when Rhodes keeps herself out of the conversation. 'Is there somewhere I can sit?'

She seems to relax again.

'There's not a huge amount of space, sorry. You can sit in the records office, there's a desk in there, but it is a rather gloomy room with no windows. I find it can be quite claustrophobic, but if you don't mind that.'

I don't immediately answer. I'm not claustrophobic at all, at least I never have been before.

'Or, of course,' she says, recognising my hesitation, 'there's the small desk there by the window, I'm happy for you to sit in here if you like. I can get you a chair.'

I look over at it. After the thought of the well, this office and the desk by the window, with its view out onto the water, the Cromarty Firth leading to the Moray Firth, leading to the North Sea and the rest of the world, brings a feeling of relief.

'Perfect, thanks,' I say, and the next hour or two of the investigation has taken care of itself.

13

There were, at the beginning of 1814, exactly one hundred and fifty people living and working on Balfour's land, thirty-seven of whom were under the age of sixteen. Two years later, there were fifteen people living on Balfour's land, including three children.

Of the one hundred and thirty-five who left, two were hanged, seven were sent to prison, and another five were sent on prison ships, three to Australia, two to Canada. Forty-three were recorded as having moved to Scottish towns, principally Inverness, Glasgow and Edinburgh. One family of seven moved to England, and were never heard of again. Forty-nine left on the same boat to New England. Two families went to Canada, one to Virginia. There is no record of what happened to thirteen of those evicted from the estate.

The well was capped off while the crofters were still on the land. Closing it appears to have been part of the process of making their lives so miserable that they wanted to leave; a simple act of malevolent expediency.

The record of the estate is detailed, the print small, the words densely packed. The period we're interested in covers a couple of hundred pages. I have found the details of the closing of the well, so what is it that I'm now looking for, my eyes trailing across words and paragraphs, scanning, searching, hoping?

I'm in *I'll know it when I've found it* territory, that's all. If it seems vague, it also feels like I can't let it go. We're struggling, a day and a half in, there's no denying it. The boy in the well may be today's go-to talking point on social media, it may have been consequently bumped up the news, footage of Quinn and I might even make the national news at ten this evening, but no one has come forward with anything useful. He's a boy that no one knows, that's all. Boy 9, conjured up out of nowhere.

So, what would I be doing if I headed back to the office? Gone eight o'clock, I might well just have gone home by now. So instead I'm sitting here, searching through 200-year-old papers, hoping that something peculiar pops out at me.

I have a vision of this being a TV show on some awful satellite channel that no one watches. *Extreme Cold Cases* or *Desperate Investigations*.

The door opens behind me and I turn away from the book and the view out to the firth, although mostly all I can see is my own reflection, and the reflection of the room.

'Hey,' says Elizabeth Rhodes, 'how are you getting on?'

'I'm getting there,' I say, 'but not ready to go just yet. You worked late,' I say, sitting up, stretching my back and my neck, taking advantage of the break. 'I thought you'd left.'

'Just been into town for dinner – my husband's at a thing in Edinburgh tonight; saw the light on, and thought I'd pop back in before I headed home. Culbokie. Thereabouts.'

'Right,' I say, as she closes the door and walks further into the room.

The room is dim, the blinds are drawn on three of the five windows, the only two still open, the ones closest to me. The only light is a desk lamp, set up next to me, shining directly onto the estate book.

'You find anything about the well?' she asks.

'Everything I need,' I say. 'I was just looking through, trying to see if there's anything else.'

'What are you looking for?'

'Literally no one knows the answer to that question,' I say, and she laughs, but the sound is kind of sad in itself, quickly dying away.

And there we are, in the dim light, looking at each other, the natural conversation having come to an end. The book is still open, the light is dim, the Cromarty Firth chops in darkness outside, the tugs long gone, no life out there but the lights of the oil rigs, and the lights of the towns along the northern coast of the firth.

'I can give you a lift back to Dingwall, if you like,' she says.

'A bit out of your way.'

'Twelve minutes,' she says.

'Twenty-four once you've gone home,' I hear myself saying, and somehow, bizarrely, there feels as if there's the implication that she might not be going home. Not straight away, at any rate.

'The offer's on the table,' she says, her voice matter of fact, then she looks at her watch. 'I'll give you five minutes.'

Hold her gaze for a moment, then turn back to the book.

What is it I'm searching for again?

'Let me photograph a few pages and we're done,' I say, and she nods, takes a step or two away, and then stands looking out the window to my right. Out onto the firth, either looking at her own reflection, or through it to the sea.

The book lies open easily, the size of each page somewhere between A4 and A5. No illustrations in this part, although there are elsewhere. I take a picture of half a page at a time, and then quickly go through it, one after another. I could have done this at the start, obviously, but I needed the break from Sutherland, time sitting on my own, concentrating on the words on the page, not letting my thoughts wander to anything else. Not letting them wander to the well and the strange air that pulled at my skin.

I use up my five minutes and a little more, aware that she's standing behind me, although not getting any sense of urgency. The five minutes was an entirely random amount of time, plucked from nowhere, and I could likely stretch it far beyond that. However, I know I'm just chasing this because there's nothing else to chase, wary of leaving the hunt for the wild goose in case the goose steps into view just after I turn my back.

I photograph around fifty pages, and then close the book. She turns at the sound.

'Done,' I say, 'although I can't guarantee that I won't be back one day to read some more.'

'You can take the book with you if you like,' she says.

I hold her gaze for a moment, then she smiles and touches my arm.

'I'm kidding,' she says, although there is not much light in her voice, then she lifts the book, opens a desk drawer, places the book inside, closes the drawer and turns the key. 'Come on.'

The road is as quiet as ever. Elizabeth Rhodes drives steadily, as though aiming to precisely hit the thirty-three minutes as predicted by Google Maps, the journey taken largely in silence.

The Black Isle is swallowed up by the evening dark and, looking out the side window into the black, silent fields, the thought of the well returns; of standing down there in total darkness, of straining to hear, and of then being desperate for the silence to return.

I went down there wanting to feel the presence of the boy, wanting to know something about him. I wanted it to be like it has in the past, uncomfortable though that's been. The sense of something lingering, something just out of reach. Air so thick with the recent past you can touch it.

And that, more or less, was what I got, and it was horrible, the feeling having crawled inside me and refused to leave.

'That's us up there,' she says, her voice juddering into my thoughts. I snap out of it, wherever it was that I'd gone, and look round at the large house, set back from the road on a slight hill. Sloping driveway, four large windows overlooking the firth and the hills of Ross-shire beyond.

I feel as if I've just been woken up, that muddled sense of turmoil that comes when an early morning phone call judders rudely into the middle of a deep sleep. Watch the house disappear around a corner, look at Rhodes for a moment, she catches my eye, and I stare straight ahead.

'You all right?'

'Yes,' I say.

Hungry, thirsty, the only food or drink I've had in the last several hours being the mug of tea left half drunk on a small desk back at that office. I need a glass of water at least. I really do feel like I've been asleep, and it's as though we've been driving a lot longer than it takes to get from Cromarty to Culbokie.

'You know my husband?' she asks, another minute or two gone by, now out onto the A9 and crossing the bridge.

'I've met him at a couple of things,' I say.

I feel as if I'm just clinging on to the idea of conventional discussion by my fingertips, regular, oft-spoken sentences plucked from the morass of conversational orthodoxy.

Another moment, the car doing no more than fifty, and I get the sense that she's got something to say. I've been awake, or aware more like, for the past couple of minutes, but only now seem to be coming out of the funk, switching on to the situation.

'I'm lying, of course,' she says. 'Harry's not really at a work thing in Edinburgh. He's in London . . .'

She lets the sentence go, and it's difficult to tell whether she's looking for me to show interest, or whether she's genu-inely unsure about sharing.

'You have a slight accent,' I say, 'but I can't quite pick it out. What is that?'

Look round at her, and she's nodding.

'Not bad,' she says. 'No one's noticed that in a long time. Well, Mr Detective, what d'you think?'

That last sentence was one step away from *You're the detec-tive, you tell me*, but I decide to let it go.

'It's pretty faint,' I say, 'so a tough call. There's a bit of American in there, maybe, but I'm going to guess Canadian. East coast. And you left when you were, I don't know, eight, thereabouts.'

'Decent try,' she says, turning off the bridge and heading along the A862 towards Dingwall. 'I left when I was twelve, and we lived in Maine. What made you so wise in the ways of the North American accent?'

I hold her gaze for a moment, then she looks back at the road and I don't answer. It doesn't need to be a secret that I was in the security services, and that I have training in all kinds of things that regular people aren't trained in, but I don't need to go telling everyone.

Into the outskirts, and I indicate with a slight movement that she needs to take a right. And so it goes, another couple of turns, and we're parking outside my house without another word having been spoken.

She doesn't look at me as she stops the car, takes a moment, and then turns off the engine. And there we sit, in silence, both of us staring forward, down the deserted, poorly lit street that's been my home for almost eight years.

I would usually have been out the car by now. I would usually, in fact, not even have taken the lift.

'Can't work you out, Inspector,' she says eventually.

I don't reply. I'm not used to people trying to work me out.

Quinn maybe; as my boss, he might have given it some thought. In fact, he said the same thing to me on one occasion. *I can't work you out, Ben.* But that was different. He wasn't trying to work me out. I'm his senior detective, and all he needs is for me to be able to do my job, and that's all I've been doing since I got here.

Elizabeth Rhodes, however, is definitely trying to work me out, trying to decide what we're doing here, two people in their forties, sitting in laboured silence.

'I take it you're not married,' she says. 'The lights are off in the house, and you wouldn't be sitting out here in the car if you had a wife sitting in there, wondering who you were talking to.'

And even in that line, in that thought, there's some explanation to the silence, albeit not the complete one. Had I been married, I would likely quite happily sit in a car talking to a woman, if there was no reason why I shouldn't. The discomfort of the situation comes from the attraction.

'What is your husband doing?' I ask.

I don't care. I'm not making any decisions in the next few minutes that are based around what Harry Rhodes, Councillor for Dingwall and Seaforth, is doing this evening. It's a holding tactic. It's saying something just to move the next few seconds along.

'My husband started a business dealing in used tyres. That was it. Used tyres. He sold it three years ago for fifteen point seven million euros. The point seven million has always been important to him. Despite selling it, he retained his position as chief executive. So he got all that money, big business took the overall financial responsibility, he was still running the company and someone else was paying him. He viewed this as a win-win-win. That's the phrase. Win-win-win. I've heard it often enough.' She pauses, doesn't look at me, stares straight ahead. I give her the space. 'He travels extensively.

There are moves to kick him off the council, but he hangs on, and he pays enough, and does enough for SNP fundraising, that no one in the party dares get rid of him. On any given night, he could be in London, Amsterdam, Berlin or Paris. That's his life. And when he's there ... well, we have an agreement, that's all. And when I say agreement, he told me how it was going to be, and I didn't say anything. If you can call that an agreement.'

'So why is it you work in a small land registry office in Cromarty?'

A pause; finally I turn and look at her. She returns the gaze, and I wonder if there's the predictably sad answer coming. *I made a series of bad life choices.* A few moments, and then she says, 'I'm clinging to the notion of financial independence. It's pretty much all I've got left.'

Then we sit in silence.

There feels like an inevitability about me asking her in, yet I'm not sure that it's what either of us wants. It's just going to happen. I'm going to ask, she's going to say yes. Like an unstoppable force is drawing us together. As though somewhere, out there in the world, a decree has been made that we must end the evening together, and there's nothing that either of us can do about it. We are compelled, even if we don't know by what.

I know she's not a suspect, or a witness, or attached to the case in any particular way, but I shouldn't be getting involved with someone I've met through the investigation. And she's married to Councillor Rhodes, which should be enough for her not to get involved with me, and lends even more weight to me not getting involved with her.

Yet here we are. And finally, when I undo my seatbelt, squeeze her hand and say, 'Come on,' she takes the keys from the ignition and follows me into the house.

14

'Don't you find that it's got to the stage where you look at the news in the morning, and there's been an earthquake somewhere in the world, which has killed a few hundred people, and some part of you is relieved in some way. At least it's not a terrorist attack, or a civilian plane shot down over a war zone, or a war in the Middle East or in a former Soviet republic. At least it's not flooding or some other God-awful thing caused by climate change. It's just an earthquake. There have always been earthquakes.'

He pauses, takes a drink of coffee, makes a gesture out across the hills, indicating the world beyond – even though he's pointing out in the direction of the North Atlantic – and then says, 'And then you realise the measure of your own humanity. And everyone else's. This is how terrible our world is.'

'I thought your plan was to get away from it all,' I say. 'Come out onto the mountains, forget everything, leave the world behind you.'

He cuts a piece of cake with his fork – coffee and walnut, a thick slice, one of two he produced immaculately from his backpack, as though removing them from a tray in an upmarket tea house – puts it into his mouth, enjoys it for a few seconds, then says, somewhat forlornly, 'You see everything from up here. Can't avoid it, that's the trouble.'

'What's to be done?' I say, after taking another bite of my own piece of cake, indicating its quality with the fork.

'Usually these things come to a head,' says Sanderson. 'Usually it takes something monstrous. A war. A great reckoning. I don't know how the reset happens without that.'

Where have I heard that before? A reckoning?

'On the plus side,' he says, and his voice has a rueful, almost comic tone, 'if there's a nuclear war, the ensuing winter will help reverse climate change. The sea ice can recover, and it'll be boon time for polar bears. If there are any polar bears left after the nuclear war, of course. There's that.'

'Always looking on the bright side,' I say, and he laughs.

I take some coffee, continue to look out west from the summit of a mountain that I'm not even sure I know the name of. Another fine day – it always seems to be fine when Sanderson and I meet at the top of a mountain – and the sea sparkles blue-grey in the sun.

'So what have you got on at the moment?' he asks.

I nod at the question. Of course, that's why we're here. I'm not entirely sure how I come to be looking out to sea from the top of a mountain sitting beside a dead pathologist, eating coffee and walnut cake and drinking Tanzanian coffee, but there has to be some reason.

'The boy in the well,' I say, and he nods.

'Toughie,' he says. 'Heart removed, abdomen crudely sewn back up.'

'Yep.'

'You don't know who he is?'

'Nope.'

'And you don't know how he got dumped at the bottom of the well.'

'I'm not obsessing on that one. Has to be something simple that'll come out in the wash soon enough.'

Another piece of cake, another drink of coffee.

'What's your gut instinct, detective?' he says.

'That, doctor, is the problem. I don't have it. I'm not saying it's the first time I don't, but on this occasion ... phht ... Nothing there. No one wants to claim him. That's the thing. No one knows him. How can that be?'

He scratches the bottom of his chin with the end of his fork, lifts his coffee cup halfway to his mouth, leaves it hovering there as he formulates his next thought. I watch him for a few seconds, waiting for him to speak, then finally look away, back across the hills and out to sea.

There is a single vessel in sight, one of the old, traditional fishing trawlers, heading north, tiny and insignificant on the expanse of blue, the sea stretching far into the distance to meet a blue sky.

'When was the well closed off?' he asks, obviously having thought of the question just as he put food in his mouth, the words muffled by cake.

'Eighteen fourteen. Forensics don't think it's been opened since.'

'They just closed the well to piss people off, eh? Help them on their way?'

'That's about the size of it.'

'Have you considered that the boy's body has been down there ever since?'

I don't immediately reply. Take some coffee. Watch an approaching crow, which lands on a small rock, several feet beneath us, and starts picking at something in the grass.

'Someone else said that,' I say.

'Maybe it's something you should think about.'

'The someone else was, as far as we have any, one of our only two suspects. Although I'm using the term *suspect* very loosely.'

'So he might just have been trying to throw some shade on the matter.'

Shake my head, tip the coffee cup into my mouth, and then hold the empty cup in both hands, elbows leaning on my knees.

'I think he was just talking. Empty words.'

'Here's the funny thing, detective,' says Sanderson and, as he says it, he's already lifting the flask to pour me some more coffee. 'The notion that a human body could have been at the bottom of a well for two hundred years and not have decomposed, that it could lie there for two centuries and then be brought to the surface for all the world like the boy had died that weekend, is utterly preposterous. It's supernatural. It might make it onto the front of the *Daily Star*, or be part of a paranormal show on some low-grade digital channel, but it's not something for serious people to think about. Yet, here we are. I just said it as an offhand remark, and you didn't scoff. You didn't move on. You didn't ignore me. I could see you thinking about it. Detective, I could *hear* you think about it.'

'We've got nothing. Absolutely nothing. Yet there has to be some explanation, and whatever it is, it's going to be out of the ordinary, that's for sure . . . If the body had been down there for two centuries, it would explain both our mysteries. How did it get there, and why does no one know him?'

'Did you ask Dr Wade if the boy could have been down there two hundred years?'

I take a drink of the new cup of warm coffee, then say, 'Not yet. What would you have said if asked the same question?'

'Perhaps there's something in the air down there, something strange that preserved the body immaculately in its sealed environment,' he says.

'So it could be explained by science, rather than by strange mystical and ghostlike forces?'

'Exactly.'

He finishes off his piece of cake, which he seems to have been eating for a long time, and then lays the small plate on the grass by his feet, the fork clinking to a rest.

'Have you Googled it?' he asks. He laughs as he says it, and I laugh lightly with him, head shaking.

'I'm serious,' he says. 'The Internet knows literally everything. Ask it.'

'Is that what you used to do?'

'Sure,' he says. 'Soon as no one was looking, I was checking my phone. Disseminated intravascular coagulation? I'd be like, really? Myelodysplastic syndrome? What even *is* that?'

'I believe you,' I say, laughing.

'That's the beauty of the Internet. Indeed, that's why humanity has made it in its own image. Five per cent incredible insight, ninety-five per cent God-awful garbage.'

We stare out to sea, coffee cups in hand, a slight breeze blowing across the top of the mountain. No other walkers in sight, mountains to our left and right, the air a perfect temperature. A few white clouds strung across a pale blue sky; the sea, at least from up here, serenely stretching beyond the limit of our vision.

'This is beautiful,' says Sanderson. 'There's much to learn up here. Nevertheless, detective, there are lessons to be learned everywhere. Stories to be told, facts to be plucked out of obscurity. Maybe you should look at your phone.'

'You think?'

He laughs lightly. For some reason I think of that awful word 'chuckle'. He chuckles.

'Look at your phone, detective,' he says, and then once again the cup of coffee is raised to his lips.

I wake up with those words in my head, and the clear recollection and awareness that I've just been talking to Dr Sanderson.

Talking to the dead. I don't really want it to become a habit.

Was that just the second time we've chatted at the top of a mountain, or has it happened repeatedly? It seems so familiar. And of course, I'm not necessarily talking to the dead. The entire conversation took place in my head, didn't it? I wasn't actually on that mountaintop. That particular mountain might not even exist. It wasn't a case of the dead pathologist forcing himself into my dreams, it was a case of my subconscious inventing someone to talk through the peculiarities of the case. Having a conversation, and expressing ideas that I don't feel comfortable discussing with Quinn or Sutherland.

Or else, Dr Sanderson has decided to insert himself into my life, now that he's dead, whether I like it or not. Perhaps for the duration of this case, or perhaps he's here for good. The rest of my days subjected to comment and analysis from the sage, dead doctor.

Look at your phone.

It wasn't Sanderson saying that, it was me. Telling myself. Waking up in the middle of the night, telling myself to get on with it.

There's a movement beside me and I turn at the jump scare. In the orange light of the street lamps, the fright dies quickly. I can't see her face the way she's lying, but there she is, Elizabeth Rhodes, wife of Harry the councillor, who came into my house and into my bed and did not leave when the lovemaking was ended.

She sleeps soundlessly, the slight restlessness is fleeting, and once again she is still. For a moment I look at her bare arm, folded over the top of the duvet cover, then sit up and place my legs over the side of the bed.

Naked. We fell asleep in each other's arms. When was the last time that happened to me? And still Sanderson came in the night, not leaving me alone, urging me to get on with the job.

I stand up and walk through to the bathroom, checking the time on the way. 02:43. Contemplate jumping in the shower, instead decide to just wash my face, brush my teeth, drink a glass of water. Boxer shorts, T-shirt, lift my phone and into the living room, the door closed softly behind me.

This isn't about trawling through the Internet, though. Maybe the answer's on there, but how would I even know where to start looking? There's something else far more likely to produce results, or at least, more specifically germane to the investigation.

I print off the pages from the estate ledger, rather than staring at the small screen and, although the quality is not great, and in my rush I missed a couple of paragraph edges, there's more than enough there to be able to process the information.

Another glass of water, and then a cup of tea, and I settle down at the table, tea in one hand and a pile of paper in the other. Not long before 3 a.m. and wide awake.

Details of business as well as general goings-on on the estate from the years 1813 to 1815. Everything from the price of a head of sheep and the grain produced, to the roads maintenance budget and the number of children born.

The latter figure is noted to have been falling year on year for the previous twenty years. It is only elsewhere in the long document that it is apparent that this is as a result of the Clearing of the civilian population.

For administration purposes, the estate was split into four sections. East, West, North, South. The numbering system for plots of land, fields, structures and waterways within each area differed, suggesting that each section had its own administrative head.

Field N17 left fallow; Field E12 potatoes, 14 tonnes; Field E7 produced 45 bushels of wheat. And so on, data broken down, through barley and carrots, turnips and cabbage.

Morrison family, Thomas Morrison, 41, wife, Agnes Morrison, 29, four children, vacated crofting, 14th March.

Sales of butter, milk, bread, eggs, ham and beef.

Next to the bald statement of facts, and the statistics, the maps and the diagrams, there is more anecdotal telling of tales. Stories of everyday life, and the evolution of the estate – many of the specifics obviously heartbreaking – told in a dry style, emotion subservient to detail.

Unlike the statistical analysis, these are all written in the same style. The ledger obviously had one writer/editor to compile and tell the estate stories.

A child dying of sepsis. A wife dying in labour, the baby removed from the father to be brought up by another family. Deaths at sea. Marriages. A fire that destroyed two outbuildings, killing three head of cattle and no humans. A flood in late March. An outbreak of paratuberculosis amongst one flock of sheep, the contagion isolated, the flock destroyed before it could spread. Birth, death, illness, marriage, employment; the bald statistics fleshed out in tales from the administrative districts.

And then, at some time after four in the morning, reading slowly and trying to ensure that I can recall everything – because one never knows which piece of information it is that's going to be the one to suddenly prod the investigation in the right direction just when it's needed – the passage I've been searching for, the terrible story that Dr Sanderson entered my head and forced me to get up for, is told in a short, stark passage, dating from the bleak and miserable autumn of 1814 on the Black Isle.

On the morning of 24 September, the housekeeper was asked to raise the nine-year-old Master Ewan Balfour who was late attending breakfast. She returned shortly afterwards, in a terrible state, as Master Balfour was not in his room, and was not to be found anywhere in the house. The grounds were searched, as was the entirety of the estate. The boy was not found, the case quickly went cold.

One morning, three months later, as winter's grip began to take its toll on the estate, a small box, addressed to Lord Balfour, was left on the doorstep of Balfour House. The box, opened by one of the servants, was found to contain the heart of a child.

Ewan Balfour was never found, living or dead.

I read on, going more quickly now, but that's all there is. The stories from the rest of that year, from in between the disappearance and the return of, what was presumably, his heart, are not so different from the previous months, except the speed of land clearance increased. Perhaps in that there is the only telltale sign of the effect of such an awful crime. They could not find the perpetrator of the kidnapping, so they expelled anyone even remotely under suspicion.

There is no further mention of the story, and this long-forgotten dark episode is confined to these few brief paragraphs.

I get to the end of the papers some time around five. I'm wary of missing something, especially when there is an obvious story leaping off the page that's liable to make me ignore everything else. I've taken my time, gone over it all, assimilated as much as possible. Nothing else crops up, leaving me with just this one, obvious storyline.

The son of the laird went missing, a heart turned up on the laird's doorstep, the boy was never found. They would have had no way to tell, in 1814, whether the heart was the child's. Presumably they took it for granted, although the stark retelling of the facts gives no indication of the reaction of the boy's family.

An hour later, I'm still sitting at the table, looking out on the dark of morning, thinking over the implications and how we can use this to progress the investigation, when I'm aware of silent footfalls behind me.

She sits down at the table, one seat away from me, and follows my gaze out the window. She's obviously had a quick look through my clothes drawers, now wearing a T-shirt and a pair of tight-fitting boxers. Maybe not so tight on her.

'Feeling guilty?' she says after a while, her voice soft and sudden in the dark.

I look curiously at her, and she turns to meet my gaze.

'What about?'

She stares at me for a moment, and then smiles and shakes her head.

'Sorry,' she says. 'There was me putting myself at the centre of your narrative. Thought you might have been sitting here thinking about me. You're working.'

'Yes,' I say, not feeling any need to pretend otherwise.

'How long have you been up?'

'A while. Couldn't sleep.'

'You got up in the middle of the night to read through those pages you photographed?'

'Yes.'

'Find anything?'

A hint of dawn, the faintest of grey lights evident in the sky above the dark shape of the land that spreads out to the east.

'There's a story about a child. In the middle of the Clearances, the child of Lord Balfour went missing. Ewan Balfour. His body was never found. You ever heard that story before?'

She doesn't answer immediately. Her right hand, resting on the table, taps silently.

'I don't think so. When was it?'

'Eighteen fourteen.'

'Were there any suspects? Was anyone arrested?'

'There's no record.'

'There must have been suspects.'

'Given what was happening, there would've been a hundred of them. Maybe they just deported everyone as a result.'

Elbow on the table, lean into the discussion, look out into the dark.

'It feels like it should be the kind of story that people know about. I mean, that is still known about, even today. A part of history.'

'Maybe they do,' she says, 'but I'm not familiar with it. And, of course ...' and she lifts her hand and indicates the darkness beyond the window. I wait for it, but she doesn't complete the sentence.

'Really,' I say after a few seconds, 'I know we slept together, 'n' all, but I don't think we're quite at the "finishing each other's sentences" stage just yet.'

She laughs, but as with her usual laughter, it has a mournful quality.

'It's a big world out there, that's all. There's a lot of history. There must be so much, so many events, so many incredible stories that have been lost.'

'This one was written down.'

'Yes,' she says, 'but it was written down in an estate ledger. Who read that, d'you suppose? It might have been put officially in print, but there's a good chance that was the only copy, or one of only a few. And how many people read those copies? And though it sounds like it was a big story at the time, maybe they tried to keep it quiet. Maybe, I don't know, maybe Lord Balfour himself killed his own kid, and then concocted the story.'

'Maybe the boy was killed and his body was dumped at the foot of a well that was then sealed over,' I say.

The gentle movement of her fingers stops. She holds my gaze, her face expressionless.

'And you just found him this weekend?'

'Well, not me personally.'

'Did the body look like it had been dead for two hundred years?'

I shake my head.

'It's not Ewan Balfour,' she says.

'Probably not, no.'

Another moment, her head is lowered, staring at the table.

'It can't possibly be, and yet . . . you have no idea who this boy is, therefore you have to give any theory a chance, no matter how far-fetched.'

'Yes.'

The real connection here is the heart in the box. That particular detail about our boy in the well has not been released, so it's not something I can bring to the table with a civilian.

'Members of the public can come and look at your records at any time?' I ask.

'Yes.'

'Would you have a note if someone had been in to look at the records of the estate?'

'Yes,' she says. 'But they haven't.'

'How d'you know?'

'I work there. When you and the sergeant turned up yesterday, it was like Macy's Parade at Thanksgiving. We'll probably celebrate next year on the same date, or declare it a Someone Actually Used Our Office holiday.'

Her tone does not fit the flippancy of the words. As though they're being written by a different personality from the one who's speaking.

'You must've taken leave at some time?'

Of course, the only way that this connection matters is if someone went there searching for something else, and happened to stumble across this story, which they then used. They wouldn't have gone to Rhodes's office thinking, *I wonder if there's an interesting story that I could recreate in order to wreak my revenge.* More likely, they knew it beforehand, in which case they wouldn't have needed to check the history.

And is that where this thought process leads? That someone is taking revenge on the descendants of a noble family, who carried out evictions more than two hundred years ago?

Maybe it does. There are hatreds in this world that date back a lot longer than that. And it's not like the Clearances haven't been invoked by some in the last few years in the increasingly politicised Scottish world.

That might sound preposterous, but certainly not as preposterous as a 200-year-old body defying the laws of science and failing to decompose. Preposterous nevertheless. Wherever we've got to in Scotland, we're not there. And anyway, it wouldn't explain why the family of the child hasn't come forward.

'I should probably leave you to it,' she says, and this time she reaches over and squeezes my hand, her fingers soft in mine. 'The wheels are turning.'

'Sorry,' I say.

'That's OK, you've got a job to do. I'll check when I'm in the office today, see how many visitors we've had recently. How far back d'you want me to go?'

'If you're not exaggerating the paucity of those visitors, you could go back to 1814,' I say.

'I'll see what we've got.'

I realise our hands are still together when she squeezes my fingers again, then she gets to her feet.

'I'll just get changed and be on my way. Call me later.'

I nod, she smiles, and then she's walking away, and my eyes don't follow her; they don't look at the hang of the T-shirt, or the boxer shorts against her skin. Already thinking about the case, the boy in the well, the heart in the box, wondering where the boy's heart is, and if it's already been left on someone's doorstep.

I check the newspapers before heading into work. The press have taken to the story, and while it's what we need, much of what they print is unhelpful dross, intent on muddying the waters. Still, it doesn't really matter. We've no reason at the moment to believe there's anyone else out there in peril, there's no reason to believe this is a life-or-death situation. The death has already occurred, now we're just waiting for the phone call, anonymous or otherwise, to set us off in the right direction.

Is Boy 9 Madeleine In Disguise? probably takes the combined prize for stupidity and tastelessness. Otherwise, we have general speculation that his parents are on the run; that the boy must have grown up in the American back-woods, a story helpfully illustrated with a photograph of a banjo; and that he's a runt member of the royal family, of whom they have attempted to quietly dispose.

None of them have the information about the heart, as we chose not to give it to them. Neither are they aware of the peculiarity in relation to access to the well. Soon enough, however, those who are digging will be rewarded, and then we'll have to suffer an even greater onslaught of frivolous and hyperbolic speculation.

Rarely, if ever, does it go well with the media.

15

Until I started meeting Sanderson at the top of mountains, I'm not sure that we ever talked when we weren't standing over a corpse; or, at least, were in the mortuary. It seems peculiar, then, to be meeting Dr Wade over coffee. New hospital canteen, a surprising view out over the city down to the Kessock Bridge.

Not as much of a surprise, obviously, as if the view had been out over the Strait of Hormuz, but I still hadn't been expecting it when she said she'd meet me in the staff canteen. I imagined some antiseptic cave somewhere out of the way; instead, it's a bright room, top floor, a clear view out over the city to the firth.

She sits at the table, lowers the tray, then places a coffee and a pecan maple Danish down in front of us both.

'I know you didn't ask, Inspector, but I was having one, and it seemed rude.'

'Thank you,' I say, as she settles down.

She immediately lifts her coffee, makes a small 'cheers' gesture, and takes a sip, her eyes on me the whole time.

'What?'

'Who was she?'

I don't immediately answer, and shortly she shakes her head, seems to internally chastise herself.

'That's all right, you don't have to answer.'

'Is it that obvious to everyone, or do you have a superpower?'

'Definitely the latter,' she says. 'Although, as superpowers go, it's pretty lame. You're all right to meet here? I've been in since six. Thirty-three-year-old male died of a heart attack in Westhill last night. Footballer, though not for the Caley Jags.'

She says Caley Jags as if she's reading a foreign language written phonetically.

'Look suspicious?'

'Yes,' she says. 'Anyway, while some of us were still lying in bed . . .'

'Been working since three,' I say.

'Very good,' she says. 'All right, Don Juan, what can I do for you?'

Funny.

I take a bite of the Danish and a sip of coffee, just to try to get back on an even keel, to shake off that uncomfortable feeling of being slightly behind the curve of the conversation. And given the conversation that we're about to have . . .

'This morning I read an old story from the time of the Clearances. The son of the lord went missing, no sign of him was ever found, but his heart was left on the doorstep of the big house.'

'When was this?'

'Eighteen fourteen.'

'How did they know it was the boy's heart?'

'I guess they presumed. It's not clear whether there was a note with it, in case they hadn't made the connection themselves.'

'Hmm,' she says. 'You think that someone is recreating that event?'

'Possibly, but that's way ahead of us here. Is it possible that the heart wasn't the boy's heart at all, I mean, wasn't even a human heart? If they'd packed a pig's heart in a box, would they—'

'Well, given the time period, it might have been easily done. A surgeon would have recognised the difference, but a layman ... Well, a layman still wouldn't, even today. You would suppose that they'd have shown the heart to the authorities.'

'The estate was the authority.'

'Of course.'

'And they may have had reasons to keep it secret,' I say, staring out at the bridge, the words barely part of the conversation.

Another bite, some more coffee, out of my right eye I'm aware of her looking at me, waiting.

'You didn't want to have coffee to discuss a pig's heart,' she says eventually, and I look back round.

'No, not just that, although it is relevant. The other question is considerably more far-fetched, which is why I'm here.'

'Couldn't ask it over the phone as you wanted to look me in the eye?'

'Exactly.'

'Well, ask away, Inspector, my eyes are poised, ready to react.'

'OK, OK,' I say. 'Is it possible, even in the most extreme imaginable case, that there was something down in that well, some sort of preservative, that slowed, or indeed, completely halted, the decomposition of the boy's body?'

'So he was down there a lot longer than a day after he was killed?'

'Yes,' I say.

'How much longer?'

Nothing for a moment, and then I make a slight *not sure* gesture, as of course, now that we're here, discussing it, it sounds laughable. She watches my face for a moment, and then the previous question comes back to her and quickly she fits it all into place.

'Really?' she says.

I nod.

'Could the boy have been down there since 1814?'

'Or thereabouts.'

'You're serious?'

'Not entirely,' I say, just to rein in the conversation before she gets too incredulous, 'but we're onto day three now. No one knows this boy. No one. And the story's out there. We're on the front page of every newspaper today, even down south. We've been on the TV. The poor kid is having his fifteen seconds of superstardom, top trend on Twitter and whatever else.'

I pause, holding her gaze, waiting to see what she's going to do with this. She, however, seems to be waiting for me to go on.

'The sensible, rational thing is that someone will recognise him. Someone somewhere. And no one has. So, whatever the actual explanation for that is, it's something unexpected, it's something out of left field.'

'It's a 200-year-old corpse that's decayed at a rate of one day for every hundred years?'

'I don't know,' I say, more defensively that I intend, 'I'm just looking for explanations. Maybe he's a thousand years old, maybe it's fifty. Maybe, and most likely, it's exactly as you suggest.'

'Maybe?'

'But there has to be something, and I just want to know if that's it.'

'Fine,' she says, 'you make a decent argument. Well, an argument of some sort. I like your capacity to consider all possibilities, even when they're impossibilities. I am not, however, writing you a report.'

'No,' I say.

'Neither of us want our names on paper as having discussed a supernatural explanation.'

'No.'

She takes a glance around at the nearest tables, lowering her voice as she continues speaking, even though there's no real need to.

'I'm not sure I even want it to be a phone call.'

'I'll pop back over,' I say. 'How long d'you think you'll need?'

She lifts her eyes as though thinking about it, then says, 'Five seconds. In fact, I can probably tell you now.'

'Go away and consider every possibility,' I say. 'Even, as you just put it, the impossible possibilities.'

'Is that what Dr Sanderson would've done?' she asks humourlessly, putting the last of the Danish in her mouth.

There's a hold-up on the Kessock Bridge. Accident. Two lanes of solid traffic. I can see the blue lights up ahead, so don't feel the need to get down there and try to help sort things out. Not, I should add, that what any accident situation needs is a detective. Paramedics, traffic police, vehicle recovery. Nevertheless, I could easily have felt bound to get involved. Instead, I sit in silence, the road blocked, traffic to the front and to the right and behind me; to my left, the pavement and the barrier and then the plummet over the side of the bridge into the water, where the dolphins roam and where the Beauly Firth becomes the Moray Firth.

If we're going to pursue the notion that this case is connected to the one from 1814, but in a more regular, 'revenge for the sins of the fathers' kind of a way, then we need to trace the Balfour's descendants, at the very least. Perhaps that will lead us straight to the heart of the darkness.

There's a pale sun now, something of autumn in the air, but no early hint of winter. I wind the windows down and enjoy the stillness. Everyone has turned their engines off. There are a few people out of their cars, one or two smoking.

Up ahead I can see someone walking along the bridge towards the accident, looking to find out how long she's going to be stuck here. There's no urgency in her stride, however.

An acceptance seems to have come over the traffic queue. No one seems angry, no horns impatiently sounding.

Lift my phone and call Sutherland.

'Boss,' he says, answering before the first ring is done.

'Anything?'

'Quieter than a church on a Sunday morning,' he says.

'Nothing from the States or Canada overnight?'

Given the possible Clearances connection, I wondered about that. That there might be something from what used to be the New World.

'Nothing. And,' he says, 'I mean, absolutely nothing. Mind you, Fish has been checking it out, and we haven't had anything like the same amount of purchase over there, which is fair enough. They've got enough shit of their own to worry about, so why would they care?'

'I found something from the files at the land registry. There's a story of a kid disappearing, the son of the lord, kidnapped and never found.'

'When was this?'

'Eighteen fourteen . . .'

'OK, so unlikely to be our boy, then.'

'Yeah,' I say. 'However, a few months after he disappeared, the heart of a child, or what was thought to be the heart of a child, was delivered to the parents' house in a box.'

'Holy crap.'

'Yeah. So, there is some sort of connection. One that leapt off the page, at least.'

'What was the boy's name?'

'Ewan Balfour. His father was laird of the estate. I'm not sure you're going to find out much more on the

146

disappearance, or the heart-in-the-box story. I'm looking to find out what happened to the family and its descendants.'

'Right. You got anything else to go on?'

'That's more or less it. I'll send you the page just now, while I wait.'

'What are you waiting for?'

'Stuck on the bridge.'

'Ah, crap. You hit that, did you? Sorry, should have called and warned you off.'

'You know how it's looking?'

'Not sure, I'll check it out if you like.'

'No, it's all right, not a lot to be done but wait.'

'We could get you a helicopter,' he says.

'That'd go down well. Go for it. One that can airlift the car, and not just me,' I say, and he laughs. 'Anything else to report?'

He sighs, takes a second or two to consider if there's anything he feels he should be telling me, then says, 'Nah. This thing is just . . . it's weird, sir. It's like the boy never existed. How can a child die and literally no one have any idea who he was? He must have been off the grid, sir, I can't think of any other explanation. And if he was off the grid, we might never find out.'

I have a sudden notion, a fleeting thought on identity. If he was off the grid, was he actually anyone in the first place? Maybe he never had a name. A pale, scrawny kid. Perhaps he was the result of a secret pregnancy; a home birth, and then he was raised, living in a basement, no one ever knowing he existed. And then, at some point, the mother, or the father, or both of them, decided they'd had enough. The boy in the basement became the boy in the well. No name, no NHS number, too young for a National Insurance number. No schooling, no friends, no relatives, no contact with the outside world. A life of nothingness. Bereft of all the things that mark our place in society from the moment we are born, he never truly existed.

It might be horrible, but it makes more sense than the idea of him having died two hundred years ago.

'Beginning to wonder about that myself,' I say. 'We'll get the team together when I get back, start going over the rest of our options. I'll be there when I can.'

I hang up, place the phone down by the handbrake. Glance in the mirror to see if the police have started clearing the queue from the rear – to divert traffic through Inverness and back down to Beauly, to Ross-shire and the Black Isle by the long way round of old – but there's no sign of movement from back there either. Finally I get out the car and take a look in either direction, but there are too many vehicles in the way to get a good look.

Instead, I do what many others are now doing, and step onto the cycle path and stand by the railing, looking down over the side of the bridge.

The surface of the water is slate grey, flat calm, the only movement from the wake of a small boat puttering beneath the bridge to the southern side of the firth. The road is so still that the sound of the boat's engine travels quite clearly, and for a moment it feels like sitting on the edge of an old harbour in the East Neuk, a still autumnal day, the only sound, bar the ululation of the gulls, a single small fishing vessel heading out to sea.

'Have you seen any yet?'

I keep looking down at the water for a few moments, then turn to my right. A woman in her thirties maybe, wearing the kind of clothes you see in the House of Bruar. She's the one who actually buys them. She's not looking at me, and for a moment I wonder if she was talking to me – indeed, if she said anything at all – then she turns with a questioning look.

'Dolphins?' I say.

'No, ichthyosaurs,' she says, waits a moment, seems to enjoy the fact that I'm just staring at her blankly, then she smiles. 'Yes, dolphins.'

'I wasn't looking,' I say.

'No,' she says, 'I can see that now. Lost in thought. Busy day?'

'Lot of thinking to be done,' I say, falling into conversation, 'nothing really happening. What about you?'

'On my way to Brora to play golf,' she says. 'No tee time, not meeting anyone, so it doesn't matter if I'm late.'

'Why Brora?'

'You play golf?'

'Occasionally and poorly.'

'Nice little course, perfectly suited to my limited abilities,' she says. 'There are sheep. I like sheep on golf courses, makes them seem less intimidating. And I like the drive up. Makes it more of a day out than if I go to Castle Stuart or Loch Ness.'

'You don't work?'

We're not looking at each other now, both with our heads turned to the water, waiting for a dolphin to break the surface, as if it's a daily occurrence in November. There's no weird feeling or anything, but it's like we're on one of those speed dates, get to know someone in five minutes before moving on to the next table. We'll have a quick chat, and then we'll shift one to the right, and talk to the next person along the bridge.

'Husband died eighteen months ago,' she says.

'I'm sorry.'

'That's all right,' she says. 'We didn't get along. And I mean, it was quite ugly by the end. We had it all right for about ten years, then he had an affair, and I had an affair, and his business got into trouble, and yeah, yeah, yeah ... that's way too much information, right?' and she laughs. 'Sorry, you didn't need to know all that.'

'No, it's fine,' I say. 'Keep talking, and later I'll tell you about the time I inadvertently tortured a guy to death in a prison outside Kabul.'

She laughs, then looks at me, and the laugh dies a little as she's unsure whether I'm joking.

'Well, you're an interesting fellow to just bump in to,' she says. 'I really can't tell if that was a joke.'

'Neither could he.'

'Nice. I like you. What's your name?'

'Ben.'

'Good to meet you, Ben. Martha,' she says.

We shake hands. The moment feels slightly bizarre, and I find myself looking past her to see if the traffic has started moving yet.

'Anything?' she asks.

'No movement,' I say, slightly embarrassed that she noticed me looking. Some ex-spy.

'Gives you time to tell me about the guy in Kabul,' she says.

'Gives you time to tell me about your husband.'

'Yes it does. Well, I guess I started it. Wait, do you always end up talking to women like this? I mean, I haven't spoken to *anyone* in, like, months.'

'Not usually, no.'

'Hmm,' she says, then she takes her turn at glancing over her shoulder in the direction of the accident, before turning back and looking down at the water.

'I don't come out of this sounding great,' she says, 'so I don't usually tell people the details. Or, in fact, the truth.'

'Which particular lie do you tell?'

'I say he died of cancer.'

'And he didn't.'

'No. He committed suicide.'

'Oh. Sorry, that must've been awful.'

'Well, you'd think.'

She smiles sadly to herself, the quick-witted chatter comes juddering to a close, and she stares down at the water. I watch her for a second or two, then turn away, giving her the space. I begin to wonder if that's it for the conversation, and soon enough we'll be heading back to our respective cars in a strangely uncomfortable silence, but then she sighs and makes a small, hopeless gesture.

'May as well tell it like it is,' she says. 'Like I said, we both fucked around. Sorry, that's a bit rude, isn't it? We slept with other people. He did it first, and . . . well, I did it more often. And better quality, I might add. Then the hardware store that'd been in his family since the 1850s went down the tube. Homebase opened less than a mile away. He was edgy as soon as he knew it was happening. The project was delayed, but that just meant it was a very slow death, a long time coming. Business hadn't been great anyway. He waited for the worst, and when it came, it was like he'd locked the doors overnight. All those people who'd said they wouldn't desert him, they flew away like dust in the wind. He had days with more or less no customers at all. No business can survive like that. It was just . . .'

A pause, a shake of the head.

'It was a horrible time, and I was no help. I was working as a PA in Aberdeen, staying late, sleeping with the boss, just letting James drift away. He drank, he never discussed the business with me, wasn't interested in what I was doing or what I thought about the shop. We were so angry at each other.'

She smiles sadly again, looks at me, looks up at the blue sky. 'Such a beautiful day. Hard to imagine, on a day such as this, that one could be consumed by so much spite. But I hated him, and he hated me. Then one day he told me he was going to kill himself. We had good life insurance, and the mortgage would be covered in the event of his death. I'll kill myself, he said, and you'll be fine. I'll be dead, and you can live your stupid life. I hope you wake up every day feeling good about that. That's what he said. Just like that, those words, that tone.'

'And he did kill himself?'

'The next day, while I was at work. Stood on a chair in the hall, piece of wire attached to the light fitting. Slashed his wrists first, waved his arms around so that the blood flew, then he kicked the chair away when he was very weak and he'd already created the mess. First thing I saw when I walked in. And it was early March, so it was dark by the time I got home, which he knew, so I walk into a dark house, put the light on, and there he was, about three feet in front of me, a bloody mess around him.'

She turns to look at me again, the look on her face growing slowly more forlorn as she speaks, her tone at odds with the distress of the story.

'That's brutal,' I say.

'Yes,' she says, 'it was. That was James. That was how much he hated me. He left me himself, bloody and dead, as a present. And he set me up for a pleasant future. I mean, think about that. He didn't sink me, or leave me a mountain of debt, which he could've done. He sorted out his finances, left everything in order, and ensured I'd be well off. Brilliant in its way. If he'd done the opposite, I'd have hated him. I wouldn't have felt guilty about any of it; he was as much to blame as I was. But this way . . . this was his way of trying to get me to feel my guilt. Rather than waking up hating him, he wanted me waking up, every morning for the rest of my life, mourning him. Feeling bad that he wasn't there any more. Regretting the things I'd done.'

'Did it work?'

Another long, exhaled breath, another shake of the head.

'My therapist thinks I'm doing all right,' she says.

'Probably a good sign that you can talk about it,' I say.

'Hmm,' is all she replies.

We stare down at the water for a while, and then we turn at the same time to look at each other. A long stare from a short distance.

'You hide the torment well,' I say. 'The bit about liking sheep on the golf course. Nice cover.'

'Thank you.'

'Was the story true, or did you really murder him?'

A blunt question, that was just out there without me thinking about it. Must be the police training. Ask questions, consider the consequences later. She doesn't look taken aback, however.

'That was harsh,' she says. 'You're not a cop, are you?'

I don't answer, which she takes as an affirmative, then she bows her head again with a slight smile.

'Should've guessed,' she says.

'Kabul,' I say, nodding.

She sighs again, and once more she turns to look towards the head of the bridge, where at last there is a sign of movement, as the first couple of cars in the outside lane are starting to edge their way past the accident.

'Bingo,' she says, turning back. 'Looks like I don't get to hear your story.'

'I wasn't telling it anyway,' I say.

'No, I guess not. There are talkers and there are listeners,' she says.

I extend my hand and we shake formally in parting as we did on finding ourselves standing together in the first place.

'I wondered if we might end up, I don't know, having lunch when we got out of this traffic,' she says, when she's halfway to her car. 'It had that kind of feel, don't you think?'

'Working,' I say, with a shrug. 'And you've got your sheep golf.'

She looks at me, and then over her shoulder towards the Black Isle, as though needing to see it to make sure it's still there.

'The boy in the well?' she asks.

I don't answer that question either, and once again she takes the silence as an affirmative.

'It's been nice talking, detective,' she says. 'I play Brora most Tuesdays, unless the weather's really bad. Come and join me sometime.'

This time she doesn't wait for my silence before she turns away, gets into her car and closes the door.

The councillor's adulteress wife. The suicide victim's adulteress widow. For a moment I watch the space where she'd been, and then I open the car door and get back inside.

16

'Nothing. Social media, sure, it's doing its thing. Given that people get excited on social media when someone wears a new bra, of course, that doesn't really count for much,' says Fisher. 'But real life . . .? I don't understand. Someone's got to know who the boy is. How can someone exist in that much of a vacuum? How can someone exist and literally no one knows who he was?'

We're back in Room Two, windowless and grey. A central table with chairs for eight people, three of which are currently unoccupied. Sutherland, Fisher, Cole, Kinghorn, and me. There's a whiteboard on one wall, and no other decoration. In the corner there is a large ficus, which has somehow not wilted and died in this airless, depressing environment.

There's an unspoken rule in the office that whenever the room is not in use, the door is left wide open, allowing in as much light as possible. Perhaps that's enough to keep the plant ticking along, that and a little care from Constable Cole, the plant expert. And for all that it's a plant, it's the only thing that gives the room any humanity.

On the table is a large plate of doughnuts, which is slowly being worked through. We're not quite in *Twin Peaks* territory, but Sutherland is certainly owning the doughnut narrative.

I should ask him about Ellen. Maybe that's where the constant eating is coming from. Pain. Denial. Avoidance.

'How often, d'you suppose,' I ask, 'does someone turn up at the doctor with a teenage kid or a ten-year-old, and say, they're not in the system, but they're ill? How often are people forced to bring invisible children into the light?'

'But it's not just about them being kept out of the system, sir,' says Fisher. 'It's completely out of society. It's one thing the parents of Boy 9 choosing to not come forward, if they're responsible, but literally no one knowing about him? No one? Or a raft of people who know, and who all choose to stay quiet . . . It really doesn't make sense.'

'What about a cult?' says Sutherland.

A couple of nods around the table.

'That would tie in with the heart removal,' says Kinghorn.

I look expectantly round the room, to see if anyone else is going to chip in on it, because it is a reasonable point. It's not somewhere that I want to go, but it's not the most outrageous suggestion. Much less outrageous, in fact, than a couple of the things I've been considering so far.

'Any potential cults currently operating in Scotland that we know about?' I throw into the silence.

A moment then Cole says, 'The SNP?'

'Don't even start,' I say. Kinghorn laughs, Fisher gives Cole a harsh look. 'Any actual, active religious or otherwise cults that we're aware of? In the area would be a good place to start, but as we know, they could've come from anywhere.'

'There's one over near Aberdeen,' says Cole. 'Something like the Church of the Divine Christ or something. There've been stories in the *P&J*, all unsubstantiated of course. Not sure if the station over there has investigated. Not, mind you, that the stories have been about child murder, or weird rituals involving human hearts.'

'OK, maybe you can look into it, but don't speak to them yet. We've got to be careful. It's one thing some bunch of religious nut-jobs wearing funny hats and chanting in circles, totally different ball game to be keeping undocumented children and ritually slaughtering them.'

She nods, and I turn to Sutherland.

'Get me a list. All cults known to be operating in Scotland, something like that. Even, I'm afraid to say, Internet rumours. Just a starting point, that's all.'

'Yes, boss.'

'What about other wells?' asks Fisher.

'Yes, we were thinking about that.'

'We could open up other disused wells in the area. Could be Boy 9's not the only one. If McIntosh genuinely stumbled across this by accident, and the timing was coincidental, maybe other wells have been used as a dumping ground.'

'Yep,' I say, 'although, of course, why not just always use the same one, if you don't think it's going to get uncovered? But it's a decent thought. Elvis, the sergeant and I had a look last night, but we didn't keep a copy of the map. There were another three disused wells in the area. Can you get the details, please, then we can think about checking them out?'

'Sir,' he says, nodding.

Look up at the whiteboard, and decide that it needs to be added to. Get up and write 'Wells' and 'Cults' on the board, space beneath for lists to be made.

There's a knock at the door, and Mary opens it and leans inside.

'Ben, two things, sorry, came in at the same time. The chief wants to see you, now, in his office. The Justice Secretary's on the phone. And Dr Wade called. Asked you to come to Inverness immediately.'

'OK, thanks, Mary.'

Look around the room, nod at Sutherland.

'Better go. Make sure everyone knows what they're doing.'

'Boss,' he says, and I'm off.

An hour later, walking back through the corridors of the hospital on my way to see Wade. The driving back and forth isn't weighing me down yet, just comes with the territory. Happens every now and again. I did call her and ask if she could impart the information over the phone, or send photographs to illustrate any new information she might have uncovered.

'Oh no,' she said – those were her words – and she refused all attempts at conversation.

Still, a more pleasant experience than speaking to the Justice minister on the phone. The Justice minister is not happy. *What the fuck is going on up there, Inspector?* he yelled. A fine introduction to any conversation.

On a list of the most important cases going on in Scotland at the moment, ours is likely not that high up. We have a body, and nothing else. We don't know where he's from, and so far no one seems upset enough by his death to come forward to speak to us about it. Today, all over the country, there will be imminent threats. People in danger. There will be abuse and rape, bullying, fear, robbery and extortion. There will be scams, there will be drunkenness, there will be suicide brought on by terror and intimidation. That's human society for you. It's everywhere, and there's nothing to be done about the bad elements, other than to try to stop them, and to protect the innocent.

It could be that our boy in the well is the tip of a cult-driven, murderous iceberg. It could be, and most likely is, a sad, one-off tale of a cruel parent, raising a child in isolation, before deciding to dispose of him. At the moment it's a mystery that needs to be solved, but there's no need for it to be on the Justice Secretary's immediate agenda. And there's certainly no need for him to be calling us up about it.

However, headlines like *Clueless Cops in Dead Child Shame* are going to pique the interest of any politician, especially when reporters start calling him up, demanding that the matter be resolved immediately, and putting the onus on him to make sure that happens.

We took the abuse, the Justice minister did not seem to calm down – although he threatened to relieve neither Quinn nor I of our duties – and I've once again made the trip to Inverness, driving past the site of the earlier accident, now in the knowledge that a sixty-nine-year-old woman, struck by a van, was killed at the scene.

I did not feel her as I passed by, just as I hadn't earlier. Whatever happened to her following the crash, she did not hang around.

Into the morgue, and there's Wade, her back turned, making notes on a clipboard. There are three bodies out around the room, all covered, and I make the assumption that our boy is the one she is standing closest to.

'Doctor,' I say. 'Nice to be back so soon.'

She turns.

'Sorry about that, but really, I wasn't talking over the phone.'

'That's OK.'

We stand in silence for a moment, and then I indicate the cadaver that lies between us.

'So, what d'you have to show me?'

'Oh, not this,' she says. 'Traffic victim, crushed by a van on the other side of the bridge this morning.'

'Right,' I say. 'I got caught up in it when I left here earlier.'

'Wondered if you might. I've got some news, by the way. We got the results back on the boy's DNA, sorry it's taken so long. Wait, what am I saying? Two days ... Nothing, I'm afraid. No match, no matches approximate enough in the system to indicate close family ties.'

'Well, that would've been too easy,' I say. 'Where's the boy?'

She indicates the body furthest away, which has been removed from cold storage, and is lying on a trolley.

'Another one,' I say, walking past the third body, heading towards the boy. 'Grim morning in Inverness.'

'You're right. Suicide,' she says. 'Woman in her thirties. Hanged herself from a light fitting, having already slashed her wrists. Husband found her when he walked into the house late yesterday evening. Blood on the walls, she was hanging in the hallway. Nice greeting.'

I stop beside the body, looking down at the pale blue sheet, the form of the unmoving corpse beneath. Mouth dry, the old familiar symptoms, feeling that strange mix of exhilaration, fear, confusion and dread.

'What?' she says.

I look down at the covered head, wanting to pull the sheet back to look at her face. At the same time, it's the last thing I want to do.

'I don't know,' I say.

My fingers go to the sheet and, as I touch the end, the tremble in them is evident.

Sanderson, the voice in the darkness at the bottom of the well, the woman on the bridge . . . the omens and the portents and the unnatural continue to build, piling one on top of the other.

I jump at her touch, and turn, Dr Wade directly behind me.

'Inspector,' she says, 'everything all right?'

I take a step back, away from both of the women, the living and the dead, deep breath, try to get my thoughts under control.

Nothing to see here, that's all you need to tell yourself. Nothing to see here. Move right along.

'What have we got?' I ask, looking over at the third and final cadaver.

'Well, I cannot explain this,' she says, 'not yet anyway, but you definitely needed to see it.'

She holds my gaze as we walk over beside the covered corpse. 'However, given your reaction to seeing a corpse covered by a sheet there, I'm not sure how you're going to be able to take this. You ready?'

'I'm fine,' I say. 'Really.'

She looks doubtful, lifts the edge of the blue sheet and slowly pulls it back so that it's revealing the entire length of the boy. She then neatly folds the sheet at the bottom end of the trolley, although of course I'm no longer watching her.

I'm looking at the boy. I'm looking at the horror.

17

I was seven when it started, as far as I know. That's how I remember it, although of course there might have been some earlier incident or accident, some strange occurrence that I didn't understand at the time, and which soon passed out of memory.

Like an astronomer inspired by watching *Star Trek*, or an RAF pilot inspired by *633 Squadron* or *The Battle of Britain*, my aspirations of joining SIS began with watching old Bond movies on TV. Connery, of course, not that hapless fop Moore, nor any of the imposters who followed. Not that I ever admitted that at the old office, but then, I was hardly likely to be alone.

So aged seven, having watched *You Only Live Twice* on a late February Sunday afternoon, I went out on my bike to the back field, a long, wide slope of late winter grass, leading down to a 1970s housing estate, the gable end of the terraces abutting directly onto the field. How this one field had clung on amidst the spread of urban sprawl wasn't something I ever thought about; and it is, in any case, now long gone.

There was a rock near the bottom of the field, and the game we all played was to ride down the hill as quickly as possible – or, more like, as quickly as we dared – hit the right-hand front of the rock which sloped at a perfect angle, take off, and then slide to a stop on the other side before hitting the six-foot wooden fence which marked the boundary of the housing estate, the end of the terrace rising directly behind.

Some of the older kids had mastered the art of sliding, staying upright, and then riding through the turn, keeping their momentum going throughout. I wasn't there yet, so concentrated on speed on approach, and jump height.

There was always a moment, coming downhill, when you applied the brakes. Always. Tough not to, as the hill was long enough and the grass, especially at that time of the year, short enough, that you could pick up fantastic speed. But the fear was always there.

That afternoon, emboldened by James Bond, I went for it. Two of my mates were there, and Gerry, this older kid, who I was trying to impress. Full pelt at the rock, I kept my nervous fingers off the brakes.

I'm not sure what I hit just before reaching the rock. A rut maybe, or a stone that I hadn't noticed. I didn't get the chance at the time to go back and check. The front of the bike twitched, my heart was in my mouth, and before I could brake or do anything to avert disaster, I'd hit the left side of the front of the large rock, which did not slope so smoothly. The lower left side, in fact, jutted out of the ground at a ninety-degree angle.

Over the top of the bike, through the air, smacked into the wooden fence full bore.

Bond would have got up and continued chasing the bad guy. I woke up in hospital.

As landings go, however, ultimately a wooden fence was a soft one. Bang on the head, with an ugly, bloody cut above the hairline, dislocated collar bone, broken tibia, three broken bones in my right hand, and a mass of bruising that grotesquely moved through the colours over the ensuing weeks, running into a couple of months.

I remember the feeling when I came round in the hospital. It was a ward with four beds, two of the others occupied. My mother and father were there, and a doctor or a nurse, I don't remember. My mother, having imagined me being in a coma for years, while she lived out a painful bedside ritual, squealed at the first movement of my eyes, and then sobbed and laughed, borderline hysterical for a couple of minutes. My dad squeezed my hand and didn't speak; all his efforts, I now realise, directed at stopping himself crying.

And I lay there, overwhelmed by a sadness that I couldn't understand. I hurt, a lot, in a variety of places, but that didn't bother me. I never minded the pain. I didn't then, and I still don't. Someone mentioned my high level of tolerance to it, but I was quite detached from the conversation.

'You've had a big shock,' mixed with, 'You'll take a long time to get over it,' and a restrained argument between my parents, to be played out at much greater length, and volume, once we were all back at home. My dad, conventionally, thought I should get back out on the bike as quickly as possible. My mum, equally conventionally, was ready to lock me up in a room full of feather pillows, and was adamant that I should never ride another bike again for the rest of my life.

When I finally thought about it myself, I was reinvigorated. I'd hit the wooden fence at full pelt and survived. Maybe I hadn't walked away unscathed, but I'd walked out of hospital the following day. I was ready to take on that rock at full bore and make the turn.

Lying in hospital, though, I couldn't think about it. All I could feel was this suffocating veil of sorrow enveloping the ward. How could my mum laugh like that, even while crying? How could my dad smile? How could the doctor nod his head in relief? How could anyone feel anything other than choking, crushing grief?

And yet, I couldn't understand why that was. There was me, a few minutes in, sitting up in bed, drinking orange juice. There was the boy directly across the ward, reading a football magazine. There was the kid to my left, talking to his friend, a conversation about *Star Wars*, some of the words of which I can still remember.

And there, diagonally opposite, was the empty bed.

I didn't have to ask anyone why it was empty. I could still feel the boy. He hadn't left the ward yet. It was the last place he was going to be on earth, and he couldn't leave. Maybe he didn't know how. Maybe he was hanging on, hoping for a miracle, although his body was long gone. Maybe he was just a normal kid, afraid of the change, afraid to take the next step, whatever that next step was.

I couldn't speak to him. I couldn't see him. His family didn't return, for why would they? There was just this space where he'd been, and the overwhelming sensation of despair, and I knew he was still there. That was all.

I slept through the night, and in the morning he was gone. The sadness was still there, but it was different. It was within me. The boy had gone, and all he had left behind in the ward was my feeling of loss, mourning a kid I had never met.

I asked around about him, I even contemplated trying to get to his funeral, but that would have required my parents' buy-in.

That was the first time it happened, but ever since, that kind of feeling has persisted around death, although it is fleeting and occasional. What happened with Sanderson, however, and what seems as if it happened with the woman on the bridge: those are new, and I really don't understand.

Maybe in years I will look back on that mountaintop glass of wine with Sanderson in the same way that I look back on the time I ended up in hospital after riding my bike, flush into a rock. The first time that something happened. The first of many.

So, where are you, Boy 9? That's what I'm wondering. If I have this ability to sense the dead, and talk to the dead, where are you? Why aren't you waiting for me at the top of a mountain?

Why aren't you standing here in the mortuary with the rest of us? Why don't you just turn up and give us the answers we need? Some of them, at least. Where are you, Boy 9?

Instead, we have nothing, and every passing development makes the case all the more confounding. The questions continue to mount. The horror increases. Boy 9 remains invisible to me, bar what is on the table before us.

'Does that make sense?' asks Quinn, his brow furrowed, an expression of concern on his face.

The expression of concern seems an inappropriately restrained reaction. What we're looking at is horrific, baffling, terrifying.

Or perhaps it's just a lie, and Quinn is absolutely right.

Wade and I are still in the mortuary, having been joined by the chief constable. Quinn is on the other end of a video call. Boy 9 – maybe Boy 9 – lies on the table. I'm holding my phone over him, having run it up and down the entire length of the body, so that Quinn can see what has become of him.

Wade is watching proceedings with a professionally raised eyebrow. Cool, perhaps with the air of someone who sees this kind of thing all the time, but nevertheless in the presence of some strange circumstance that she doesn't understand.

Darnley is staring sceptically down at the body.

'No,' I say to Quinn, 'it doesn't.'

'And you're sure it's Boy 9?' asks Quinn. 'You didn't pull out the wrong drawer by mistake?'

'No,' says Wade, her tone neutral. 'That's what I thought myself, at first, but of course, we wouldn't keep such a body in here in the first place, and from my initial tests, and from looking at the teeth, it's definitely the boy from the well.'

'Definitely?' says Darnley, and Wade nods, her eyes on the body.

'And you can tell us what happened?' asks Quinn.

'I'm afraid I don't have an explanation yet.'

'When did you discover this?'

'I came to look at the body about an hour ago,' says Wade, 'having not looked at it since Monday afternoon. I was finished with it then, and there have been other matters, other cases, needing to be dealt with.'

'Why did you return to the body today?' asks Darnley.

The woman is hard and cold and not at all fazed by what is lying before her.

Wade glances at her, then turns her eyes to me. Ball's in my court.

'I asked the doctor to re-examine him,' I say. 'There was something I wanted her to check out.'

Another moment looking down at the cadaver, the body now wasted away to nothing but decomposed skin and bone, and looking not unlike a corpse that might have been lying at the bottom of a well for two hundred years – then Darnley asks, 'What was it?'

I glance at the phone, where Quinn is still staring at us as though he's from the 1930s and has never before seen a live video feed, then back to Darnley.

'Well, Inspector,' she says, 'this looks like it might be interesting. Did you ask the doctor to check the corpse for signs of premature decomposition?'

'Not exactly.'

'Sounds like we're getting closer,' she says. 'Go on.'

'Two hundred years ago, the son of the lord of the estate on the Black Isle disappeared. The son's heart was apparently cut out and sent to the landowner, and the boy was never seen again.'

A beat. A nice little pause to the conversation, almost as though there's a metronome ticking back and forth, counting in the time to the next instalment of disbelief.

'And you wondered,' says Darnley, 'if this might be that boy?'

I don't answer.

'And he'd somehow lain un-decomposed for two hundred years?'

Still no answer.

'You asked Dr Wade to check out if there was anything that could've prevented the body's natural decomposition. She was sceptical, but pulled the body out to start having a look. And *voilà* . . . the body has suddenly decomposed, two days after being removed from its unnatural environment.'

'That's the way it is,' I say, having not taken my eyes from her throughout. 'I know the first half sounds incredible, and was certainly clutching at straws. The second half of that, the part where this happened,' and I indicate the body, 'I really don't know. I wasn't expecting that. I was . . . we were desperate. We still are. We have a boy dead, and no idea who he is. We're not even sure how his body got in the well. This story was at least something with which we could run. If nothing else, there has to be the possibility that someone who knows the story is re-enacting it in some way. Perhaps carrying out an act of vengeance.'

'For the Clearances?'

'Like no one talks about that any more,' I say, and she nods thoughtfully in acceptance, then turns back to Wade. She is clearly staying remarkably open-minded. No way we would have got this far having this kind of conversation with Quinn.

'Doctor,' asks Darnley, 'any explanation?'

'Not so far,' she says. 'I did call the inspector as soon as I discovered this. I've taken a few more samples, but it'll be a while before we see the results.'

'I meant, any explanation as to how someone could have got a completely different body in here, and what they did with the actual body of Boy 9?'

'Hmm,' says Wade. 'I alerted security, and they've looked at the CCTV footage. There was no sign of a break-in, and no sign that anyone has been down here who shouldn't have been. I understand this seems the most likely option, but I also believe we need to consider every eventuality. That's what I'm doing.'

'All right,' says Darnley, and there's an obvious tension between the women, 'what can you tell us about the decomposition? It looks pretty far gone, but internally, is this the body of someone who died two hundred years ago, or four days ago?'

'Good question,' says Wade, and she nods to herself, looking down at the corpse.

'And is there an answer?'

'Yes,' says Wade. 'Internally the decomposition is consistent with what is displayed externally.'

Darnley now has her hands on her hips. Classic pose.

'However unlikely it is,' she says, 'that someone evaded security to break in, and then switched round a body, it is still far more likely than this. This transmogrification – this instant decomposition – that lies before us here. We surely have to give the possibility of a body swap a damn sight more consideration.'

'No one broke in,' says Wade, staying very matter of fact. 'But I will have security go over the footage again . . .'

'I'll send a couple of my team down,' says Darnley.

'Of course,' says Wade. 'However, like I said, initial indications are that the body is the same, but we will need to wait for the DNA tests to come back, and as you know . . . this is not an episode of American television.'

'Thank you,' says Darnley. She shakes her head, looks back at the body, sighs heavily and gives in to considering the option that we've so far been discussing. 'All right, if we are to take it that this is the same . . . person, that this is Boy 9, what are the options? Could a body have lain un-decomposed for two hundred years? Could it have taken a couple of days, and then suddenly shrivelled up? Is there anything else that could've happened while the body was in here to cause this effect? I mean, we're spit-balling here, I'm not going to hold you to anything. At this stage, it's not a matter of tests, it's a matter of possibility. *Are* there any? Are there any possibilities?'

Wade holds her gaze for a moment, turns her eyes to me, and then looks down at Boy 9. Quinn continues to be ignored. Quinn may as well not be on the other end of the phone.

'No,' says Wade. 'I can't think of anything. But I need to check. There may be possibilities that I don't know about. I'll do some research; there might be other tests I can do.'

'Thank you,' says Darnley.

'Maybe we should speak to a forensic anthropologist, an expert in decomposition of bodies which have been dug up after centuries.'

I look at Wade as I say it, wondering if she'll take it as a slight, but she just nods and says, 'Sure, I can find someone.'

'Good,' says Darnley, 'let me know what they say.'

She takes another long look at the corpse, and then looks up, taking in both the doctor and me.

'Seems you have your work cut out for you. Keep me posted, and nil returns every couple of hours, if there's nothing definite.'

She nods at us both, glances at Quinn, having ignored him but having been aware of his remote presence throughout, says, 'David,' then turns and walks quickly from the room.

Sutherland calls as I'm on the way out the building, but I get in there first before he can speak.

'How are we doing on tracing the descendants of the Balfours?'

The short silence at the other end gives the answer.

'It's not—'

'Don't worry about it,' I say, cutting him off, 'but I need you to get on it now. It was the family of the lord of the estate; it shouldn't be too hard to trace what happened to them. Maybe get a genealogist to help. Whatever else you're doing, drop it, get to work on that.'

'Right, sir, but there's something else. Managed to fill in a gap in those early years of Belle McIntosh's life.'

'Go on.'

Standing by the car, waiting to end the conversation before heading off.

'She was married for three years. Mrs Tom Daniels. Lived over in Inverurie.'

'And?'

'They had a kid. Born with a heart defect, never got out of hospital, died at four months. She and her husband separated the following year.'

'How'd you get this?'

'Tracked it down through university. Spoke to hospital records, just had a chat with the husband. Engineer with Balmoral Offshore in Aberdeen. Remarried, three kids.'

'And?'

'Didn't know anything about her now. Said his wife hadn't been able to cope with their boy dying. Felt . . . he was aware that he hadn't been of much use. He'd reacted to it by going out drinking with his mates. He coped in his way, and didn't help her, though he doesn't think it would have made much difference. Either way, the marriage didn't last.'

'Right. Good catch, Iain.'

'You want me to bring her in?'

'No, we'll go back out. Let's be careful. She might have lied, but let's not get carried away here. We can't be bringing someone in because she doesn't want to talk about the most heartbreaking thing that ever happened to her. I'll be back first, though. Twenty minutes.'

Hang up, into the car and get going. Contemplate putting the blue light on, just because I suddenly feel pissed off and needing to get on with it. Not annoyed at anything in particular. But there's a dead child, and the start of the investigation should be straightforward. We find out who the child is, we speak to his family, his friends, his school, his teachers, we find out his last known whereabouts, and soon enough we know who killed him. But this? No identification, no family, no friends, no school, and here we are with body decomposition peculiarity, forensic anthropologists and genealogists and land registry and cults and picking ideas out of the sky hoping that something, anything, fits.

It feels like a shambles – an omnishambles – of an investigation, and I'm the one in charge of it. At the very least, we need to take some of the ideas and bin them. We need to start taking ideas off the board; we need to start narrowing the playing field. We need a working and plausible hypothesis, that doesn't include non-decomposing, 200-year-old bodies, or instantly decomposing 72-hour-old corpses; it doesn't include me standing at the bottom of a deep, dark pit, sensing God knows what in the darkness, and it doesn't include any input from the recently deceased pathologist.

Back across the Kessock Bridge, already doing seventy-five by the time I pass the point where I stood and talked to the woman who now lies dead in the morgue.

I don't look at the spot as I drive by. I don't sense her presence. The image of her leaning on the railing comes into my head, and is gone in an instant, and by the time I'm off the bridge I'm hitting ninety in the outside lane.

18

Still feeling chippy as I walk back into the station, wanting to grab the investigation by the scruff of the neck and crack on. However, such as is regularly the way of these things, I'm barely in the door when Mary indicates with a relatively polite hand gesture, with which I'm familiar, that the boss wants to see me.

I stop dead, looking at her, quickly contemplating turning on my heels and heading back out. I could speak to Sutherland on the phone, then head straight to the farm to talk to McIntosh. The former Mrs Daniels.

'You're all right,' says Mary, 'he said it'd be quick. He's got a dial-in he can't miss in,' and she looks at her watch, 'less than ten minutes, so he won't be able to keep you.'

Heavy sigh, we share the look of exasperation exchanged between employees the world over, when there are times that their boss is like one of their children, and then I head for his office, quickly knocking and entering.

'Sir?' I say, standing by the open door, letting him see that I've no intention of being dragged into a long conversation.

'Ben,' he says. 'I thought that went well.'

'What?' I say, so many different strands and thoughts running through my head that I really have no idea what he's talking about.

'The phone link.'

We stare at each other for a moment, while I adjust to the fact that he's asking for my input, and that his version of events is so far from reality.

'I don't think it did, on this occasion, sir.'

'No?'

'You were detached, and the chief constable more or less ignored you. We were looking at physical evidence, and your view of it was sufficiently compromised to render your involvement entirely nugatory.'

Perhaps that was blunter than I intended. Nevertheless, nothing breeds intent and determination like making a list and getting on with it. And nothing gets in the way of intent and determination like standing around, aimlessly talking.

'I, em, didn't see it that way,' he says, sounding unusually unsure of himself, but I'm not in the mood to try to make him feel any better.

I have nothing to add, and when it appears that he doesn't either, I decide it's time to excuse myself from what is clearly a pointless meeting.

'Sir,' I say, 'I need to get on. There are several balls up in the air, and if I'm not on it, they're going to start dropping.'

The ball-in-the-air metaphor. Was just out there before I could stop it.

'Yes, of course,' he says, and I nod and leave the room, closing the door behind me as I go. A wasted two minutes.

My phone goes almost immediately, and I answer it, annoyed, without even looking, assuming it will be Sutherland not realising that I'm back at the station.

'Inspector.'

Elizabeth Rhodes. Her voice soft and sad, and utterly jarring. I don't immediately reply, looking at the clock above the door of the open-plan. Already after three. The day seems to have passed with me sitting in the car on the A9, every new piece of evidence, lack of it, or discussion about it serving only to immerse the story further in the mire. The presence of Elizabeth Rhodes seems to date from some time ago. Not quite another life, but not from this morning, and definitely not from last night. Last night could've happened to someone else for all the effect it's had on my today.

'Elizabeth,' I say. 'Sorry, I was going to call.'

'That's all right,' she says. 'I've been following the online adventures of Boy 9, so I've got all the latest. I like the new theory about him being Princess Diana's lost son, albeit the timing doesn't really seem to add up.'

'I haven't heard that one,' I say, 'but it's not like we've got a whole lot more than that. Do you have anything for me?'

Business, business. My tone might be a little milder, but I'm no more invested in general chitchat with Elizabeth Rhodes than I am with Quinn. I need to get on with the investigation.

'Of course,' she says. 'There has been literally no one recorded as looking at the ledgers of the Balfour Estate in the last twenty-five years. They have drifted into misuse and disinterest. Extraordinary, really, that we keep the maintenance of th—'

'Does that mean there was something twenty-six years ago, or is that as far back as you went?'

'Someone checked it twenty-six years ago. Prior to that, there's nothing back to 1950, which is as far back as records go.'

'So who checked it twenty-six years ago?'

'You're serious?'

'Yes,' I say. 'If it's all you've got, we might as well have it.'

'Very well, Inspector,' she says, then there's a slight pause as she finds the spot again, then she says, 'And . . . there's no name. I thought there was, but it's just the registry clerk of the time. So, sorry, I'm not much use to you.'

'That's OK, thanks for checking.'

A beat. I'm trying to think if there's anything else I need to ask her, but even as I'm sorting my thoughts into order, I know she'll be thinking that I'm wondering how to end the conversation. Are we seeing each other again? Was it a one-night stand or the start of something more serious?

What do I know about having affairs, and what do I know about Elizabeth Rhodes? Maybe I was her fiftieth lover this year, maybe I was her first ever transgression.

'I will leave you to your investigation, Inspector,' she says, but there's nothing other than understanding in her voice.

'Do you have the information on when the Balfour estate was sold off?' I ask, as that obvious thought finally forces itself upon me.

'Yes, that'll be in there. But I do know it already, of course.'

'And?'

Standing in the doorway to the open-plan, watching Sutherland, realising that we saw each other as I came in, and that of course it hadn't been him calling.

Think straight. Less haste, more clear thinking.

'After the Great War, like so many of these estates around the country. The Balfour family suffered heavily in France, and there was nothing else for it. The story's quite well known.'

'And were there any Balfours left?'

'There were three generations of women, I believe. No male survivors. They moved to a much smaller estate north of the Cromarty Firth, although I don't know the details off the top of my head. Or the names, obviously. I can try and find them for you.'

'No, it's all right, I can look into it.'

Another pause, and now we come to it. This is the real one. This is the pause at the end of the conversation, with which neither of us is comfortable.

'Thank you,' I say. 'I need to get on, but I'll give you a call.'

'That won't be necessary,' she says, and again there's a forlorn quality to the voice, a quality that suddenly sounds very attractive. Obviously I'd found her attractive the evening before, but this particular conversation has been conducted to the minor key of business, and for a brief moment I'm reminded of why last night went the way it did.

'Well, there's little in life that's actually necessary, but plenty of it still happens,' I say.

'The language of Shakespeare,' she says, ruefully. 'How terribly romantic. Well, I shan't hold my breath, knowing how busy you are, but you know where to find me.'

She hangs up, the conversation ends, and I find myself momentarily distracted. Shake it off, brain in gear, try to recapture the energy and purpose with which I walked into the station a few minutes ago, and then into the open-plan, and across the desk from Sutherland.

'How are we doing, Sergeant?' I ask.

He puts down his mug of tea, automatically dabbing at his lips, even though there doesn't seem to be any food in the vicinity.

'It's like Christmas all of a sudden,' he says.

'What?' I say, voice harsh, not in the mood for flippant analogies.

'Just after I spoke to you about Belle McIntosh, we've got this,' he says. 'Alice found it when she wasn't looking for it.'

He tosses a photograph onto my desk. Black and white, taken from a CCTV camera. Catriona Napier walking along High Street, Dingwall, not far from the Wimpy, hand in hand with a child. A boy, but obviously not ours. Five years old maybe, no more.

I look across the office, but Cole is not around.

'We know who this boy is?'

Sutherland shakes his head.

'When was the photograph taken?'

'Friday.'

'Friday,' I repeat, nodding. 'Right. Well, I'm not sure what it does for us. It wasn't as though we asked her outright *do you, or have you ever had any contact with a child?* We haven't caught her in a lie, but this, coupled with the McIntosh story . . .'

'You're sure you don't want to bring them in?'

'No, we'll go out there now,' I say. 'Where are we with the Balfours, by the way?'

'Early stages,' he says. 'And there are a lot of them out there.'

'Yes, and any surviving family members are unlikely to have the name Balfour. The entire male line was dead by the end of the Great War. Only women survived. The estate was sold and broken up, they moved to a smaller place in Ross-shire.'

'You didn't want to mention that before?' he says, although he manages to keep any tone from his voice.

'Just found out. Spoke to Mrs Rhodes at the land registry.'

'Shall we head there after the farm?'

'Not at the moment,' I say. 'But this is your starting point. The break-up of the estate. This angle of the investigation isn't about the land, but about the people who sold it. We need to trace them.'

'Right.'

I look round the station, virtually every desk occupied, Fisher and Kinghorn in place.

'Still nothing concrete from the call centre, I take it?'

'It's completely died off,' he says. 'It blew everyone out the water for twenty-four hours, there were lots of calls – albeit none of any consequence – the boy in the well was that moment's thing, and now . . . Well, apparently someone called B-Ziz tweeted that Selena Ramone's fat, and there's a rumour doing the rounds there's going to be a new Frank Malcolm album released online at midnight.'

A beat.

'I don't know who any of those people are,' I say.

'That's all right, sir,' he says, 'you're not supposed to. And it doesn't matter anyway. If it wasn't them, it'd just be something else that means nothing to anyone and will be forgotten tomorrow. Unusual that our story lasted as long as it did. Nevertheless, we need to keep paying attention. It could be that something crops up after the furore has died away.'

'Where are we on the cults?'

He looks over at Fisher, says, 'You'll need to speak to Fish, sorry. Haven't had a chance to catch up.'

Fisher, out of earshot, but somehow in tune with what we're saying, as though she felt the vibrations of her name being used from across the office, turns to look at us.

'Just pinged you something, sir,' she says.

'K, thanks.'

I sit down, open up my computer. Realise I haven't looked at it all day. Two hundred and seventeen unread e-mails.

'We'll go in ten minutes,' I say to Sutherland, absent-mindedly, quickly scanning the title lines and list of senders, repressing the usual urge to just delete everything, then go back to the top and open the message from Fisher.

She stands beside me as I do so.

'This was in the Scottish *Daily Star*, sir,' she says. 'The only other mention of the cult I can find was in the *Ross-shire*, but that's a far more muted piece. Just about the house, and the people. Difficult, in fact, to reconcile the two articles as being about the same organisation. The fact that the *Star* story wasn't picked up by any other outlets, and that the *Star* didn't run with it the following day, is probably significant.'

'This is the only possible cult?' I ask, bringing up the *Star* article, as Sutherland comes round to stand at my shoulder.

'There's the one near Aberdeen that we mentioned yesterday.'

'The Divine Christ?' says Sutherland.

'The Free Church of the Living Christ,' says Fisher. 'And another down near Drum. Unlike the other two, that one doesn't have a big mansion attached to it or anything. There's no central figure or guiding hand. More of a loose collection of professional people. Doctors and lawyers, and police officers too, if we're to believe it. Nothing in any of the newspapers.'

'How d'you find it?' I ask, beginning to scan down the *Daily Star* story.

'Some Internet talk,' she says. 'It's pitched as being somewhere between a lame attempt at a *Da Vinci Code*-type conspiracy – you know, old men and women in cloaks molesting young virgins, almost—'

'Where'd they find *them*?' asks Sutherland. I'm looking at the screen, but I can imagine the look on Fisher's face.

'A comic book caricature of a secret cult,' she continues, 'and a genuinely sinister death cult, luring homeless young people.'

I turn away from the *Daily Star* for a moment.

'Presumably, if there was anything genuine about it, our guys in Drum, or in Inverness, would've been looking into it?'

'Unless they're involved,' chips in Sutherland.

'Can you make some calls, please?' I say. 'Same with the crowd through in Aberdeen. This shower,' I say, turning back to the newspaper report, 'well, given that they're based up near Tain, it'd have come through us, so we know there's been no police involvement.'

Another look at the clock, turn back to the screen.

'I'll send you the report from the *Ross-shire* too,' says Fisher, turning away and heading back towards her desk.

'Thanks, Fish.'

Sutherland laughs lightly beside me, reading the report, pointing vaguely as he does so.

Sicko Witch's Cult in Animal Carnage

A sick witch's cult in a remote glen in the highlands of Scotland has been accused by angry townspeople of kidnapping family pets and sacrificing them in acts of disgusting ritualistic slaughter.

The shocking midnight ceremonies are said to take place once a month at the headquarters of the cult, Cafferty House, a Gothic mansion built by slave money in the early eighteenth century, and said to be haunted by the ghosts of previous owners.

'You can hear the animals squealing,' says Iain McQueen, landlord at the Covenanter's Hat in nearby Tain. 'At first we thought a dog had got caught in an animal trap. But now, it's like every full moon. They deny it, but there are a lot of pets gone missing in the town. It can't be a coincidence.'

There are some suggestions that the cult, known as The Devil's Ring, has been running in various guises since the Middle Ages, and includes politicians, celebrity film stars and elite businesswomen in its number.

Owner of Cafferty House, Georgina Franklin, denies the allegations.

'We run a not-for-profit, agrarian project,' says Franklin. 'Volunteers come throughout the year to learn about agriculture and farming. These accusations are an outrage.'

Nevertheless, there are claims that volunteers are forced to sign a non-disclosure agreement, and that many of them are not volunteers at all. Ellen DeGeneres and actress Ellen Page were sighted in the area, as well as the likes of Cate Blanchett, failed US presidential candidate Hillary Clinton, and leader of the Conservatives in Scotland, Ruth Davidson.

'It's terrifying,' says local unemployed man, Bill Ness, 19. 'Animals? It's not just animals. These freaks are sacrificing actual people. Raping them, defiling them, cutting their hearts out, then burning the evidence. The smell around here on the

morning after the full moon is rank. It's a disgrace that the police are doing nothing about it.'

Chief Inspector Quinn of Dingwall Constabulary was unavailable for comment.

'Well,' I say, 'I'd been sceptical that this was going to be of any use to us, up until the point where Mr Ness got involved. He seems to know what he's talking about.'

'We should get him in,' says Sutherland, in a tone that naturally suggests the complete opposite.

'Yep, looks like we've stumbled across a vital clue,' I say, and he laughs and heads back round to his desk.

I read the report from the *Ross-shire Journal*, which sounds, as Fisher suggested, as though it's been written about something else, and then I park it and move on to the reports that Fisher has sent through about the other two potential cults.

Of course, we're quite possibly wasting our time. Any decent cult would surely be completely invisible, only revealed when some poor, young, brainwashed girl managed to escape to the local village, bruised and bloodied, telling tales of horror. Or, at least, that's how the *Daily Star*, and the movies, would have it.

19

Catriona Napier sits staring at the photograph for a few moments. I'm sitting opposite, Sutherland standing at my shoulder. Belle McIntosh is in another room, annoyed at our return. Unaware, as yet, that we know what we know.

'You're watching my every move?' says Napier, finally lifting her eyes.

'Can you confirm when this was taken?' I ask.

'You must know when it was taken. This is CCTV footage. Doesn't that always have the date and time on it?'

'Do you see the date and time on it?'

'You probably cut it off.'

'When was it taken?'

'Friday afternoon, I expect,' she says eventually, voice flat, resigned. 'Could have been Wednesday, but it was raining on Wednesday. No coats.' She indicates the picture. 'You probably managed to work that out for yourselves.'

'Tell us the identity of the child.'

Her head is lowered again, her words dry up. Her left hand is resting on the table, the fingers moving slightly with a nervous tremble. Perhaps she's always like this, although I didn't notice it previously.

'Is it illegal to walk down the road with a child?'

'Of course not,' I say, still with the business clip in the voice that I had earlier. It's time we were making progress. Somebody, somewhere, knows some*thing*. We need to find out who that is and get them talking. And yes, that's the same with every investigation. There's always someone who knows, someone who's keeping the secret. This one, where we haven't even found out the identity of the victim, feels much worse.

'What then?' she says, still not lifting her head. 'A child is dead, and here's the farmer with a completely different child. There must be a connection. Arrest her!'

'No one's arresting you. Tell me who this is.'

Another pause. She presses her fingers against the table, and the tremble is transferred to a tenseness in the back of her hand.

'I can't,' she says.

'Seriously, Ms Napier, you can. Who's the child?'

'All I was doing was walking along the street with the son of a friend, while the friend got her hair done. Call it forty minutes' babysitting. Is that a crime?'

'No, it's not,' I say, trying to keep my voice patient. And failing. 'Who's the friend?'

Another pause, and then, 'I'm not going to tell you.'

Tap. Tap. Tap.

My forefinger, slowly on the tabletop. Trying not to get annoyed. Getting annoyed rarely gets you anywhere. There are occasions in police work, of course, where the well-timed outburst, the air of threat, is all that's required. This isn't one of those times.

'Can you at least tell me why you're not telling me?' I ask, a question that seems dreadfully dull. Like something some poor wordsmith would find amusing.

Another moment, answers now being dragged from her, blood squeezed from the tiresome, proverbial stone.

'I need to check with his mother first,' she says. 'She probably doesn't want you lot turning up on her doorstep.'

'That's not your decision to take.'

'Maybe not, but what will you do? Arrest me for holding a child's hand in public?'

'I don't know. We could release the picture, and get the public to tell us who the child is. I'm sure the mother would be even more delighted about that.'

That, at least, gets her thinking. That's somewhere she presumably doesn't want to go, as releasing the child's picture also puts her face on the news.

'Let me check with the mother,' she says. 'It'll save you the time.'

'What's the story?'

'What d'you mean?'

'There's obviously a story, or else you'd just tell us. Sure, no one wants the police just turning up on their doorstep, but really, we'd be verifying why you were with her child, she'd agree with your story – or not – and we'd be gone. Why should she care?'

Nothing.

'Which means there's more of a story. Doesn't mean you're hiding anything from us in particular, but there must be some reason you need to check. So what is it?'

There's a slight shake of the head, little beyond a twitch, and then she looks up.

'I'll speak to her, then I'll call you. Or maybe she'll call you,' she says, glancing at the clock.

'And meanwhile you do a runner?' chips in Sutherland from the back, just to see the reaction, as we both know she won't. And she glances at him, a sad look, then her eyes drop once again.

Maybe it's the subject matter – which is obviously heart-breakingly sad – but we're not seeing the same pugnacious Belle McIntosh of previous interviews. Like her wife before her, when presented with a fact that she has so far hidden from us, McIntosh retreats into an unnatural reserve. She could be hiding, of course, but here we are, dredging up the past, and were she to react by descending into a melancholy that has been locked away in a compartment in her head for decades, we could hardly blame her or suspect her of anything untoward.

'Yes,' she says, 'you're right. I lied.'

'Tell me.'

She's sitting down, all part of the air of defeat that haunts her. Just the mention of the death of her four-month-old baby had the same effect as punching her in the stomach. The shock, the eyes closed, the slump down into the chair by the table.

'Tells itself, doesn't it?' she says. 'Tale as old as time. Like *Beauty and the Beast*. Just more painful, that's all.'

'There are plenty of marriages that survive the loss of a child. Where the couple will try again, find a way to move on. What happened with you and Tom?'

'Sure,' she says, 'generalise, that's the way to go. Maybe people try again, maybe they don't. Everyone's different, and that was us. We were much too young to face up to that kind of thing. I mean, we were only married because I was pregnant in the first place, right? That's how long ago it happened. It was still what you did back then. Then the boy died, and Tom was an asshole. I was on my own. Hey, I don't know,' she says, her voice still lacking that familiar bite, 'maybe I should've just upped and got on with it. Ditched Tom, married someone else, had a tonne of kids. But . . . I couldn't. I couldn't forget him. William, that was his name. Did you know that? William . . . He was . . . I never saw him without a tube inserted in his nose, a line attached to his arm, a monitor on his chest. I never got to give him a proper cuddle. Not even when he was born. They knew there was something wrong with him in the womb, they gave me a Caesarean, then they whisked him away soon as they had their hands on him.'

Such a small voice, such pain. Yet, as the interviewing officer, you can't give in to it. You can't allow it to colour your judgement. Can't allow yourself to be sucked in. It might be honest, it might not, but it doesn't matter either way, you have to remain above it.

'I don't even have that memory. The feel of my son in my arms. Being able to wrap him up warm and make everything better. Why couldn't I do that? Why wouldn't they just let me do that? They didn't save him, did they? All their medicine and their tubes and their expertise, all for nothing. Just . . .'

Her voice is small, but not breaking. It's been a long time since she cried over William. The memory is still painful, but the tears have dried.

'I always thought . . . I don't think he would necessarily have lived, but he would . . . would he have lived any less if I'd looked after him? And even if he hadn't lived as long as four months, the time he lived would have been so much better. He'd have been with his mum.'

'You never found anyone else?' I ask.

She looks up, her face hardening a little.

'I never found another child? What d'you mean?'

'You never found anyone else with whom you wanted to have children?' I say, ignoring her tone.

Her lips tremble slightly, she looks annoyed for a moment, and then her eyes move in an affected gesture of hopelessness. How could I possibly be expected to understand?

'No,' she says, the light in her eyes dying away again, 'I never found anyone else. My mother used to say my life ended alongside William's.'

She stares at the table, looking perfectly lost, swallowed up by the past. Finally, after I've allowed the silence to drag on into awkwardness, she lifts her head, making a small shrugging movement as she does so.

'She wasn't wrong,' she says.

*   *   *

Day has passed into late afternoon and early evening, darkness rolling in from the east. I put a call through to the operations room in Inverness to get the latest updates. They confirm what was already apparent, and what Sutherland posited earlier. The country has moved on, other fish to fry, other stories to care about.

Perhaps there's something about a dead child with no name. Something impersonal. There are no grieving relatives, no story to tell. No villains, no heroes, no open and terrible displays of sadness. Just a body, detached from all humanity. With no one apparently grieving his passing, he might as well have been a mannequin.

A sad notion, that has of course found its way into existence as a conspiracy theory.

No relatives? Is it even a body? Crash test dummy maybe. Police bigging up workload, looking for more cash. Classic. #Boy9

One of many. It may have slipped down the rankings, so that the general public has moved on, but that leaves behind the genuinely concerned, the genuinely invested (for whatever reason), and the genuine conspiracy theorist. Beware the latter.

It would help, of course, had we updates to give, another instalment to keep the media, and therefore the public, engaged. If we were PR-driven, it's what we would do. If we were managing a singer's drug detox crisis, while selling their latest CD or their new biography, we would be drip-feeding information, fuelling the frenzy.

But that's not our game, because this isn't a game at all. Real life, in all its horror. We've given the public what we have, and they've had nothing to give in return. They might want more, but until someone comes forward, until a new piece of evidence presents itself, we have nothing else to give.

The day has passed and we haven't yet made the decision to bring in Belle McIntosh or Lachlan Green, currently the only real suspects we have. I'm just not convinced by the possibility of their guilt, and am not ready to go after them, to start putting together a case to accuse them. With the exception of finding the body, and Belle omitting to tell us the sad tale of her dead child, there's literally nothing else to connect them to this, and we need to completely exhaust all other possibilities before concentrating fully on them.

The new Catriona Napier angle is peculiar, and as the day approaches its end, there's still nothing back from her. I'm aiming to leave it until morning, and then I'll head back out there. This time we'll be bringing her in, and we're just going to have to focus on it for a while. I get the feeling, however, that she's telling the truth. The likelihood is that her friend was doing something she shouldn't have been, and Napier was covering for her. That's all.

Which gets me thinking about Elizabeth Rhodes again as the end of the working day draws nearer, the desks around the office starting to slowly empty. What was it she said as we lay in bed last night? I was tired, and the conversation seemed somehow remote. Her husband was away for another night, back for a night or two, away again at the weekend.

Was that her trying to make plans? Putting feelers out to see what I'd say? I hardly thought about it at the time.

Here we are now, though, and I have to ask myself who I am. Am I the kind of man who has an affair with another man's wife?

It's not like I haven't already stepped over a line and given Councillor Rhodes reason enough to dislike me, regardless of what Elizabeth said about their marriage. There's already enough there for some newspaper, should they care, to run with a salacious copper and councillor's wife tale. The interest everyone has taken in our current investigation makes that more likely.

Nevertheless, no reason for anyone to pick up on it yet, unless Elizabeth is playing a game in which I'm the classic unwitting pawn and she goes public, for some reason I cannot imagine, to embarrass me.

Yet, here we are, and there are choices to be made. A one-night stand or something more involved and, as a consequence, more innately wrong and more likely to be revealed? Maybe the one-night stand would become nothing more than a two-night stand. Maybe there would be mission creep.

When it comes to sex, there is usually mission creep. That's where the trouble starts. I smile at the thought, at the fact that I even used that term in my head in relation to it. Sutherland glances over, catches my eye, looks curious, amused, but I shake my head, and he turns back to his monitor.

She's still there, though, the thought of her, the thought of last night. Funny how the mind works. Have barely given her consideration all day, even after speaking to her, having been very focused on the task at hand. And yet, the end of the day draws near, and the mind and the body start to wind down from the day job and think about the evening ahead.

I know I'm going to call her, so I may as well get on with it. If she's made other plans in the meantime, in the face of my earlier indifference, then it barely matters. That part of my brain will likely switch itself off again, and we can move on.

'Sir, we have the map of closed wells in the area,' says Kinghorn, walking up beside me, an A1 map of the Black Isle folded over in his hand. I nod, and he lays it out in front of me on my desk. 'Sorry it's taken so long.'

'We're good. What have we got?'

I ask the question, but the answer is immediately obvious. Three crosses have been made on the map, and I recognise their position from seeing them on the more detailed map that Elizabeth showed us the previous evening. One near Fortrose, one on the northern side of the peninsula, and one to the western border, just this side of the Black Burn.

'OK, do we know what state any of these are in, or what kind of property they're on now?'

'Haven't been around them yet. This one is on farmland, this one is on council-owned land, hard to tell from the map exactly what's there. If my memory serves me right, I think it's just border grassland. It's quite close to the road.'

'And the Fortrose?'

'Directly beneath a private dwelling-house, sir,' he says.

Sutherland and I both give him a look.

'A private dwelling-house?' I say. 'Have you swallowed an estate agent, Elvis?'

'A house, sir,' he says. 'It's beneath a house.'

'Well, that should be fun,' I say. Take a moment to think about it and then add, 'Can you two go around tomorrow, please? Take a look at them, see what state they're in, gauge how much effort it'll be to open them up and then speak to the relevant party?'

Sutherland nods, while Elvis stands, in the manner of the junior officer, awaiting further direction.

'Get back to me before you do anything.'

'Yes, boss,' says Sutherland.

'Thanks, Elvis,' I say, turning back to Kinghorn, and he nods, and starts gathering up the map.

'Bring it over,' says Sutherland, and Kinghorn moves round the desks, the map in his hands, and lays it out in front of Sutherland.

My part in the investigation of other wells over for the moment, I leave them to it. I stare at the map for a few seconds from across the desk, my thoughts already having moved on to other things, and then, almost without thinking, I lift the phone.

Elizabeth Rhodes answers after one ring, and I know that my plans for the evening are set.

20

'We used to live in Nairn, at the far end of Dunbar Golf Club. We had a dog. Our only ever dog. A springer spaniel called Noodle. Noodle and I would walk along that beach every day, twice a day, to the pier and back again. You know Nairn beach?'

Lying in bed, almost midnight. Curtains open, the room illuminated by the orange of the streetlights. We're under the covers now, on our backs, lying apart, with our fingers loosely entwined, in concession to the conventions of post-coital etiquette. Her voice is soft and melancholic, blending seamlessly with the muted light in the room.

'Yes,' I say. 'Haven't been often, but it's nice.'

'Yes, it is. I miss it. Stupid to miss something that's so close, but there you are. I haven't been round there in ten years.'

'It's different having something on your doorstep,' I say, mundanely.

'Yes,' she says.

She lapses into a natural silence, as she considers what it is she's going to tell me about Nairn beach. There's something interesting in the pause, as though she's not sure how to frame the narrative, that it's a story that demands careful telling.

In the silence, our fingers entwine a little more tightly.

'There was a man on the beach,' she says. 'We used to see him every day.' Another short pause, from which she emerges slowly. 'I say we . . . I don't know if Noodle ever saw him. He certainly never paid him any attention. But I always noticed him. The Beige Man. That's how I thought of him.

'It troubled me for a time, or intrigued me perhaps. No matter the time of day, there he'd be, my Beige Man, walking along the beach. Head always at the same angle, his stride always the same, and always dressed in the same beige clothes. Shoes, trousers and jacket in slightly different shades, with a beige backpack.'

Another break in the story. Her voice is perfect, beautiful and lilting, taking me to Nairn beach, and I'm there when I close my eyes. I can see the dunes and the long stretches of sand, I can see the ever-shifting sandbar and Noodle the dog, and I can see the man, beige in all respects, walking a silent trail across the sand.

'I began to wonder if he was trying to blend into the sand. Was that why he wore so much beige? Was that why he spent all his time on the beach? He was trying to become part of it. Trying to blend into it, disappear into it. And I genuinely began to wonder if that might be possible. That probably sounds silly.'

I reply with a tighter squeeze of the fingers. Nothing to say. It doesn't sound silly at all. That's all.

'Or, I wondered, is it possible that this man does not, in fact, exist. Perhaps this dull, directionless man is nothing more than a reflection of myself. That in some way I could not possibly understand, the beach was a mirror, and that this was me. Colourless, dry, stuck in a rut, blending dully into my surroundings, a hopeless chameleon.

'One day, seeing him coming from some way off, I decided it was time we started talking. I wasn't going to rush it. I didn't see us having a great conversation right from the beginning. Indeed, I wasn't even sure he'd ever even noticed me, despite so often passing within a few yards of each other on a deserted strand of sand.

'I said hello that first day, that was all. A smile, and hello, delivered from a respectful few yards. It was like I'd never spoken. He didn't look through me, or past me. I wouldn't even have said that he ignored me, because to ignore someone you have to at least know that they're there in the first place. But the Beige Man? There was nothing. It wasn't like I'd never spoken. It was like I wasn't even on the beach.'

She takes another moment in the narrative, her fingers press more tightly, and for the first time since we separated, I feel the touch of her leg against mine.

'But I was on the beach. This was no strange existential crisis on my part. Noodle knew I was there. Gosh, I said hello to other regulars, and they all said hello back. So, if I was on the beach, perhaps it was the Beige Man who wasn't. Perhaps he existed in some other plane. I know, it doesn't make sense talking about it lying here, and it didn't make sense even then. But I felt there was something. And you understand what I mean, don't you? It wasn't just that there was a strange silent man, always walking on the beach. There was something about him, and you could feel it.'

'A ghost?' I ask, although I know that's not it. Ghosts don't walk along beaches in solid form.

'No ghost,' she says. 'Noodle would've had something to say about that, but Noodle didn't even seem to notice that he was there. Although it did occur to me one day that Noodle never passed very close to him, like he knew there was something wrong, and was just staying away from it.

'I tried saying hello to the Beige Man a few times, but it was always the same. It was as though I was talking into a void. A space that swallowed up sound, thought . . . existence even. Just . . .' and now she lets the sentence go, and I feel the slight movement of her head on the pillow.

'Did you speak to anyone else about it? Didn't Harry ever walk along the beach with you?'

'Just once,' she says, and I realise that she's answering the first of the two questions, and I automatically understand that there's to be no discussion of Harry. For our purposes, lying here in the glow of orange light, Harry does not exist. 'It felt like my own world. It was my beach, and the Beige Man was my problem.

'Then there was a day when I was standing talking to another dog walker, a member of the golf club. We were discussing the following week's medal, when along came the Beige Man. I watched him approach from behind her, and I couldn't stop myself. I said, "Funny how he's always here." The tide was out, and he was a good sixty or seventy yards away.

'She looked out over the beach at my words, then she turned and glanced over her shoulder, then she looked back, and her face had resumed . . . her face was where it had been ten seconds previously. And she said, "Margaret thinks she'll be able to play next month, but her back's still tight after the operation . . ."'

Her hand, the one that is currently resting in mine, lifts up in a gesture of hopelessness, and then she lays it back down again.

'I don't know whether she didn't see him, or there was something so uncomfortable about him that she didn't want to talk about it. I don't know.

'So, that was Annabelle, and she was the only one I ever tried to talk to about him. There didn't seem to be any point in discussing it with anyone else. It was just me and him. Me and my Beige Man. And, I don't know how long it had been going on now, but there I was, thinking about him all the time. If I couldn't talk to him, could I even touch him? He didn't have to acknowledge me. It would be about me touching him. I didn't need a reaction from him; I just needed to know that I could lay my hands on him. That he actually existed in physical form.'

She laughs lightly, then says, 'He was in my dreams, strange things happening. I even attempted to construct some sexual fantasy out of it, but that was a non-starter. Too weird. It wasn't about that. The trouble was, the compelling, obsessive thing was, that I had absolutely no idea what it was about.

'Winter came and went. I hoped for snow. Would the Beige Man become the White Man if there was snow on the beach? But there was no snow, and the Beige Man remained beige. In fact, he seemed to blend more and more into the sand . . . Then there was a day in early spring, that feeling in the air, clear blue sky, a weak March sun. It was beautiful. That was the day Noodle ran off.'

She stops again, her fingers move softly in mine, the night so quiet and still that it's almost as though I can feel the blood flowing through her veins.

'Noodle was scared of kites. I don't know why, but they spooked him for some reason. Often enough there would be someone flying a kite on the beach, and I'd see it from a distance, and we'd make sure we'd go nowhere near. There was plenty of beach to go around. But that day, that beautiful clear day, there was a young boy up ahead, and I thought he was just playing in the sand. But suddenly he was running towards us, something in his hand, and then the kite was trailing behind him, and the wind was blowing, and it shot up in the air. And there went Noodle. Spooked, scared, running like the wind. Up over the dunes, and he was gone.'

'He ran home,' I say, not really asking the question.

'I walked the dunes for a while, calling out. Waiting for him to appear from within the long grass, tongue hanging out, bounding towards me. I didn't give it long, because yes, I thought he might have gone home. Except he hadn't, so I returned to the dunes.'

199

The story goes quiet, and again I'm left to wait for her to resume when she's ready. The questions I ask, the statements I make, never seem to have any effect on the telling and the pace of the narrative.

'I walked the beach that afternoon, into the evening. I was back on the beach first thing in the morning. I walked the beach all day, and the next day. Noodle was gone. He hadn't come home, he hadn't come back to the beach. And there was the Beige Man, walking up and down, solitary and reliable. And there was I, the Beige Man's reflection, or the echo of this man who walked up and down every day. The two of us, and the beach, intertwined in some way that I couldn't understand. And perhaps it was that simple. He too had lost a dog on Nairn beach. He too was searching for something that he would never find.'

A car drives past outside, the first sound I've noticed other than her voice in such a long time. I have no idea what the time is now, or how long we've been lying here. She hasn't said much, but there have been the silences. The silences that seem to last for ever.

My eyes are closed, and I can feel myself drifting further and further into sleep. But I can't fall asleep. I need to know what happened to the Beige Man. I need to know what happened to Elizabeth. I need to know if she ever found what she was looking for, and how she managed to free herself from the peculiar prison of the beach.

The silence that comes with the passing of the car into the night and the distance seems to grow. Our legs press more firmly against each other, our bodies slowly come closer together. The warmth of her touch lulls me more deeply towards sleep.

'The Beige Man,' I say, words tired and lost in the orange light.

I feel the movement, and then her head is on my shoulder,

her body pressed fully against mine, her hand lain softly against my stomach. There's a softness and looseness about her body that suggests she is also close to sleep.

'One day,' she says after a long time, 'he was walking towards me, and Noodle was there. The Beige Man had Noodle on a lead. I stopped. I could hardly believe it, it seemed so strange. So surreal. How could he have Noodle? And then he stopped, maybe fifty yards away. I'd never seen the Beige Man do anything other than walk before, and now, here he was, walking my dog, and stopping. And he bent down, unclipped the leash, and Noodle was free. He raced towards me, and jumped up into my arms. Noodle was so happy. I was so happy. I hugged him, and he licked my face, it was funny and ... funny and wonderful. And I finally looked up, and there was the Beige Man, far in the distance, walking away.'

Another short silence, the conclusion of the story held on the tip of her tongue, then she says, her voice heavy with sadness, 'And there we were, Noodle and I, reunited.'

Her fingers run across my stomach for a moment, and then come to rest. On my chest I feel the dampness of tears, and I lift my hand to her blonde hair, and for a moment my fingers press against her skull. I relax, and stroke her hair for a short while, before tiredness takes even that away.

'But it wasn't Noodle,' she says at last.

21

Get into work early, having awoken filled with the guilt of sleeping with another man's wife. Funny, where was that yesterday morning? Where was the guilt? I was too occupied with work, waking in the middle of the night to get on with the job; I had no time for it. This morning, however, I wore it like a suit.

'Guilt is for me, if I choose it, not you,' she said.

It didn't matter. I looked at her in the morning light – she was wearing the change of clothes she'd packed in her overnight bag – and thought she looked beautiful and sad, and the guilt weighed even more heavily upon me.

My guilt has no outlet. I'm not going to give Harry a call and confess, hoping for absolution by means of a free pass from the cuckold, or a call to arms, and a dawn duel in a Culbokie field. And so I tackle it the only way I can. By immersing myself in the job at hand.

What logic does my brain allow me in this? You may be a lesser person for your actions, but at least you're a hardworking detective. Now go and prove it.

Only Elvis is there when I arrive, and we exchange a nod and no words. I don't stop to ask if anything happened overnight, and he obviously has nothing of significance to tell me.

I get a drink from the back of the open-plan, standing in silence, staring at the wall, while the machine noisily spits out the milk and then the dark stream of coffee. I'm still consumed by thought when the sound has ended, the flow of liquid has stopped, and it's only the rich smell of the coffee that pulls me from the momentary stupor.

Back to the desk, first sip, open the inbox. Nothing from the situation room in Inverness relating to our story. Nothing in amongst the dross to help us progress the investigation, so I reduce the inbox to a small icon in the bottom right-hand corner, take a brief look at a picture of the sheer face of the Dawn Wall in Yosemite, another sip of coffee, and then pull the notepad over. Time to make a list, in the old-fashioned way. Things we need to get done, and who's going to be doing them.

Sutherland and Kinghorn to check the status of the three other closed-off wells on the Black Isle.

Progress report from Wade. Any further test results on the corpse, establish whether she's been in touch with a forensic anthropologist.

Find out from Inverness if they've discovered any sign of a break-in at the morgue.

Report from Fisher on the three cults she was looking at, and whether any of them require my further attention.

Establish the whereabouts of any descendants of the last of the Balfours.

I need to speak to Darnley and Quinn about where we go from here on identifying the boy via the public. It feels as though it's become accepted that no one knows who he is, and that can't be right. I'm not sure what else we do, having embraced (and been embraced by) the media, social and regular, but doing nothing, and changing nothing, will not get us anywhere.

There's still Catriona Napier, and the possibly innocent photograph of her walking along High Street, hand in hand with a young child. And neither should we forget Belle McIntosh, and the farmer's mate, Lachlan Green. As I've allowed my mind to wander, and as the apparent strangeness of the case has grown by the day, Lachlan, in particular, seems to have slipped beyond thought, as though his part in this is no longer of interest. And we caught Belle McIntosh out in a painful lie, but a lie that on the surface tells us little. The telling, if there is any, is in the obfuscation. If she can hide that, what else might she be choosing to hide?

But it was Belle McIntosh and Lachlan Green who started it all, and who still represent the most likely, basic and straightforward explanation as to how the boy's body was placed at the bottom of the well in the first place. The two of them need to stay on the list, and they certainly need to be spoken to again. Yet we have no tangible evidence on which to bring them in, and we certainly have no tangible evidence on which we could base an arrest warrant, and that is what we need. A plain-thinking cynic could see no other possible account for the boy's presence in the well. It must be them.

Unable to immediately think of anything else, I get to my feet and step away from the desk. Coffee in hand, I walk to the window and look out on Knockfarrel as it's touched by the first light of a thin autumn sun.

How's the guilt coming along, detective? Well, it had been fine, until it just juddered back into my head there. Not sure where it came from, but then, guilt hardly needs an invitation.

A noise behind me, and I turn at the arrival of Sutherland, walking into the office at the same time as Fisher. And out of nowhere, here comes the Beige Man, the first time the thought has come back to me. Elizabeth Rhodes and her tale of the Beige Man. How curious. I try to remember how it ended, but there's nothing there.

I remember the mood of the tale, and the beach and the sand and the dog named Noodle. And I remember Elizabeth's lonely feeling of detachment, and what almost sounded like fear when she talked about him and the hold he had over her, but I don't recall the end.

Who was the Beige Man?

Fisher nods at me as she takes a seat on the other side of the office. Sutherland approaches, holding aloft a brown paper bag.

'Doughnuts,' he says. 'Emergency over,' he adds, smiling, 'you can stop looking so worried.'

'Thanks, Sergeant,' I say, and I head back to my desk.

'Chocolate, jam-filled, sprinkles or regular?' he asks.

'You got four doughnuts?'

'Eight. I always get eight,' he says, and I feel like the parent who doesn't pay enough attention to his teenage children.

'Regular,' I say, taking another sip of coffee as I sit down, and thinking that I might need another coffee after I've eaten the doughnut.

Sutherland places a regular, sugared-frosted doughnut on a napkin on my desk, then walks round to his own desk, the first bite of a chocolate doughnut already taken.

'Thanks, Iain.'

'Boss,' he says.

'Sir,' says Fisher, coming up alongside my desk.

'What's up? You heading straight back out?'

She looks curiously at me, then realises she's still wearing her coat.

'No, sorry, sir. I left this note for myself last night, and wanted to tell you as soon as you got in. I'm usually in before you . . .' she tacks on at the end, and then shrugs. I don't think there's any need for me to explain why that wasn't the case this morning.

'What have you got?' I ask.

'Well, you remember the crackpot witches' cult from outside Tain we were talking about? The ones who made page five of the *Daily Star*?'

'Of course.'

'I think we may have to go out there after all. Alice was working last night on chasing up the descendants of the Balfours. After the estate was sold off, the family moved to a smaller property north of the Cromarty Firth. Large house, extensive grounds, but far fewer outbuildings and subsidiary dwellings. Then, inevitably, they had to downsize further, there were poor marriages, there were mistakes, and gradually the family was broken up. Ultimately we seem to be no nearer pinning down actual living descendants, but we're still working on it.'

'But from what you first said, I presume that the house the Balfours moved into is now owned and run by the crackpot witches. Who probably aren't crackpot witches at all.'

'Exactly.'

'Bang on, Constable, good work.'

'Thank you, sir, but it was Alice mostly. She won't be in until after ten.'

'It was both of you, thank you.'

Quick look at the clock, dawn still not fully emerged from the dark of night. Just over half an hour to Tain.

'Can you just have another check for anything on them, please; even the dry, official stuff, like how long they've been there, details of the woman who owns the house, that kind of thing. I'll head up there in forty-five minutes or so.'

'You want me to give them a call and set it up?' she asks.

'I'll doorstep them.'

'Forewarned is forearmed,' she says.

'Yep. Thanks, Fish, just see what you can get.'

She nods, and she's gone.

'You off to look at the wells?' I ask Sutherland, turning back to him.

'Yep,' he says.

'We need to speak to Catriona Napier too,' I say, and he nods. 'I'll go round there after I've been out to the cult house. More than likely I'll bring her in.'

Look back at the list. Coffee and doughnut to hand, guilt suddenly dispatched to the long grass, time to start chalking things off.

There's no guard on the gate. Indeed, even the gate is of little use as security, a regulation farm gate incongruously placed between two broad gateposts of pale, smooth stone standing far apart, leading to a straight driveway up to a large sand-stone house.

There is a broad expanse of grass on either side of the driveway, with seventy to a hundred sheep liberally dotted across. To the right, the lawn ends in woods, with a low hill rising behind. To the left, farmland. Hardly the remote glen as claimed by the *Daily Star*, but that's unlikely to be the report's only exaggeration.

There are several cars parked in front of the house, but also an area for parking outside the estate wall, just off the A9, and I make the decision not to drive onto the property.

Park the car, through the gate, closing it behind me, and walk up the long driveway towards the house, the sheep regarding me warily as I go, the two or three closest moving slowly away, still eating grass, not really looking in my direction, and with little enough drama to not cause a mass stampede to the far corner of the field.

I stop near the top of the driveway and look back. Although it's not far from the coast, there's little sight of the water from here, bar a stretch of the Dornoch Firth to our left. Nevertheless, the air is clear and has the quality of being by the sea, so that even if you couldn't see the water at all, you would know it was close by.

The trees have almost all shed their leaves, bar a few in a small copse on the other side of the A9, down towards the town. The air is autumn air, winter still a few weeks away.

This may have been a smaller house and much smaller estate than the one on the Black Isle, but it could hardly have been a hardship moving here for what was left of the Balfour family. One supposes that the hardships came in guises other than location, with so many of the family lost to the war.

'What do you see?'

I turn at the voice, having not heard the footsteps behind me. A woman in her early forties, dressed for farm work. Mud-spattered Wellingtons, although the mud is dry, jeans and a checked shirt, the sleeves rolled up above the elbow. Her hair is loosely tied back, strands falling over her face. There's something almost clichéd about the way she's dressed, but then, she's working on a farm, so why wouldn't she be wearing mud-spattered Wellingtons?

'Detective Inspector Westphall, Dingwall,' I say, holding out my ID card.

She's looking me in the eye, not interested in the ID.

'Avoiding the question, I see,' she says, smiling. 'Classic detective. Always asking, never answering.'

You never know what you're going to get with people, and I don't have the measure of her yet. A beat, then I turn and look back down the gentle slope of the driveway to the limited vista of the woods beyond.

'I didn't mean it literally,' she says, as I turn back.

'I wasn't going to answer literally.'

'No, I don't expect you were,' she says, then she indicates with a small nod for me to follow her, and starts to walk towards the side of the house.

'We're round here,' she says. 'You can join us for breakfast, although I don't think you're going to find anyone who can identify the boy in the well for you.'

That's one downside of being on the news. Everyone sees you coming. Everyone knows why you're there.

'Can I ask you your part in the set-up?' I ask, stopping.

Always better to speak to people on their own, and I'm about to be placed in the middle of a crowd of I don't know how many.

'Set-up?' she says, and again she's smiling, although this time there's a withering quality to it. 'Don't you mean operation? Dodgy outfit? Sacrificers of small children and drinkers of blood? Coven, perhaps?'

She gives me the look that's supposed to make me feel bad at the use of the term, accompanied by shame for whatever assumptions she supposes are being made in my head, then continues, 'We're an agrarian commune. People have been living the way we do for tens of thousands of years. It's perfectly natural, and all the cretinous morons that make up so-called society, living vicarious, detached lives in their detached houses, connected to the world around them by Wi-Fi and the phone in their hand, think that *we're* the freaks. Makes me so cross sometimes.'

She's quite animated by the end, and I let her run through her small speech, thinking it a little defensive given nothing more than the word *set-up*. It's not much to base anything on, but it does immediately point to a siege mentality, and I shall log that and see if there's anything else to support it.

On the other hand, if a national newspaper printed a story telling everyone you murdered the household pets in the area on a monthly basis, you can see how a siege mentality would set in.

'What is your part in the agrarian commune?' I ask, deadpan.

She gauges the question and my tone, to see if there was any mockery implied in its simplicity, then says, 'I'm the accountant.'

I can't stop my eyes looking down at her Wellingtons, and she can't stop herself smiling, her annoyance of a few seconds previously disappearing.

'There's not a huge amount of accounting to be done. I help out on the farm.'

'How many people are here?'

Another beat.

'You really are classic, aren't you?' she says. 'Looking to get someone on their own, hoping to make a little more of a contact, hoping to loosen the tongue. You've got your eyes and your smile . . . Come on, I'll take you round. I've got work to do. These sheep won't milk themselves,' she adds, the joke delivered in what must be a familiar tone.

You've got your eyes and your smile . . .

I haven't heard that before, although I was aware that I had eyes. That smile, that the women are all apparently talking about, comes to my lips as I walk behind her around the side of the house.

The extent of the farm, such as it is, becomes clearer as we get to the side and back, and the area opens up. There is a long, patchy field of heather, in various declining colours of autumn. There are greenhouses down to the left, and a couple of short polytunnels.

As we come around to the back of the house, there is a large fenced-off area with perhaps fifty chickens, many slowly on the move in various directions. Beyond this there is an extensive herb garden, and behind that, and running round to the other side of the house, a field of raspberry and straw-berry plants, which have settled down for the winter, and fields of root vegetables which are coming to season's end, or have already been cleared for the year.

A large extension has been added to the back of the house, with huge windows looking out over the land, up to the slight rise behind the property, and to the hills beyond. There is one long dining table in the extension, people packed around it eating breakfast.

The accountant stops, now that we're within sight.

'You want to come in for breakfast?'

'I'll wait here,' I say, and she nods.

'Fine, I'll get Franklin.'

'Thanks,' I say, and she walks away, and is quickly inside.

A few moments, and as I turn away and look down at the random movement and noise of the chickens – the smell of them their most arresting attribute – I see the turn of heads, as the workers of the agrarian commune look over in my direction. I choose not to watch them, as they watch me.

I wonder if they eat the chickens, or just have them for the eggs? Perhaps they put a couple of chickens to the sword on special occasions.

'You know what's worse?'

I turn quickly, not having heard the door open, nor the approach of footsteps.

'Franklin?'

'The worst thing is the people it attracts,' she says. Short, greying hair, something of the Katharine Hepburn about the face, and a broad Glaswegian accent. 'I don't care about the mindless, I don't know, the mindless shit. You know? I don't *care* what people think we're doing here. I don't *care* if people think we're stealing their animals or murdering their children or whatever, because ultimately, you see, when someone says, *that's a disgrace, who was it got their pet kidnapped?* they don't have any answers, because no one got their pet kidnapped. Literally no one.

'So the gawkers and the complainers, Jesus, they can all get to fuck. But the worst, the very worst thing, is the fucktards we get up here. You wouldn't believe. Ha!' she says, and she shakes her head. 'You polis, you know about fucktards. Well, we get 'em all, every last one of them. They think we're into spells and potions and live sacrifice, and they can't get up here quickly enough. Then we show them how we live, and what we do, and some of them go off, tail between their legs, disappointed, and some of them get abusive, assume we're lying and don't want them, and cause all sorts of trouble, and some of them just slyly piss off, certain in their own knowledge that we're just as bad as the newspapers want to make out.

'And yet, do any of these fuckers have one iota of proof?'

Another shake of the head; she looks around her domain, glances back inside the building where our meeting is being treated as a spectator sport – although quite a few of them look away as she turns towards them – and then she's back, looking at me with all the disdain she can muster.

'Smells like shit standing next to the chickens,' she says, 'but we're not moving. What d'you want?'

There, in fact, is a decent question, because I'm not here to accuse them of anything, and I haven't turned up, SOCOs in tow, to search the place. I'd been hoping for more discretion and a better welcome, and it's up to me now whether I choose to make the conclusion that can be drawn from their obvious displeasure at the arrival of the police.

'You know the history of the house?' I ask, nodding in its direction.

This seems to surprise her, and she turns warily to look at it, giving herself time. That instant guardedness with which we're so familiar, while the interviewee assesses just how underhand she thinks the interviewing police officer is going to be.

'What d'you mean?'

'I'm not here because of stories in the papers. I'm not interested in your commune, or in whether or not the Devil's Ring exists . . .'

'It doesn't.'

'I'm interested in the house.'

'Why?'

'Because the boy in the well, the death of whom I know you're aware I'm investigating, was found on property on the old Balfour estate. When the Balfour estate was broken up, the family moved to this house.'

I leave it at that for the moment, and she gives me what I can only admit is the appropriate look.

'So fuck?' is how she eventually expresses her complete disinterest in this connection. 'Seriously,' she continues, 'what possible shit am I supposed to give about that?'

'I'm not looking for you to care,' I say, 'or even for you to be that interested. I'm interested in the connection between the estates.'

'Why?'

'That's none of your concern.'

'Well, please feel at liberty to fuck off.'

'Yes, I certainly can do that. And I can also be at liberty to return later this afternoon, mob-handed, to run a thorough investigation of your operation, in answer to numerous complaints received by my station in the past six months. What would you prefer?'

She gives me the regulation harsh stare. She doesn't need to know that we've never received any complaints.

Yet, despite the attitude and the coarseness of her language, there is an attractiveness about her, a softness even, that goes against the grain of her demeanour. Like she's putting on the gruff tone for my benefit, and not quite pulling it off.

'Would you like me to show you around, or do you want free rein?' she asks. 'I'm sure most of us wouldn't mind you rummaging through our bedrooms. Perhaps you'd like to set up cameras in the bathrooms and showers? Wouldn't be the first time some man's asked to do that.'

'Are you done?' I ask, and there's an acknowledgement in

her look that her petulance is wasted on me. 'I'll just look around. Tell me what's off-limits, and I won't go there.'

'Seriously?' she says. 'If I tell you anywhere's off-limits, it just gives you reason to be suspicious about why I'm not letting you see it. I was being facetious. I'll walk round with you, if you can handle it. You can choose what you look at, and if it's everything, then so be it. I don't want you having to come back.'

'Thank you.'

'Don't.'

She walks quickly away, back towards the extension. When she opens the door, she doesn't march straight through, but stands waiting, her back turned to me, until I'm walking up behind her and entering the breakfast room, and the beating heart of what may be the Devil's Ring.

The members of the Devil's Ring, such as they are, are feasting on yoghurt, porridge and seasonal fruits.

22

'How will you get back up?' I ask.

In the car on the way down the road. The accountant is staring straight ahead, eyes open, lost in thought, and she takes a moment to come around.

'Oh, hitchhike, probably. It's no big deal.'

'You always find someone to pick you up?'

'Sure. I have breasts. I don't even have to put them on display.' A moment, then she adds, 'And I can take care of myself, so don't give me any police crap about being careful.'

'When did the rumours start?' I ask, moving on.

'Which rumours?'

I give her a few seconds to see if she's going to go on and answer the question, but she seems happy with the silence.

'The witches,' I say.

'Ah, those rumours. Of course, how silly of me forgetting. What was the question again?'

'When did they start?'

'Honestly, Inspector, they started even before we got here. I was here from the beginning, and I know. The locals heard that there were a bunch of women coming, and they straight away assumed lesbians, perverted sex, some sort of coven, and by extension, sacrifice. People have very limited imaginations. They've seen movies, so why think for themselves when they can think what other people tell them to?'

'Who appointed Franklin leader?'

She laughs.

'Really? We're not that kind of organisation. Franklin was in the City. London, I mean, not Inverness. The City. She was making shedloads, a woman amongst men, in that dog-eat-dog shitstorm. Raking it in, then she got out. Escaped. Came up here, decided to start the commune. It was her money that started it all. She owns the house. No one appointed her the leader, but simply, if she wasn't here, none of the rest of us would be.'

'Have you ever played to the witch rumours?'

'What d'you mean?'

'Have you ever done anything to encourage anyone to think there might be something in it? Played to your audience?'

'What? You mean, like danced naked around Clach Chairidh, and then made Sapphic love, drenched in the blood of skewered unicorns? Because we've done that, if that's what you're implying.'

I don't answer. Having decided that there was likely nothing to see at the house, I make the call to let the conversation go. I can feel her looking at me, an amusement about her, but when I don't reply, her amusement goes, and she turns away.

We sit in the car together in silence. The journey passes into routine nothingness.

The house, of course, gave up few secrets. It didn't matter that Franklin walked around with me, I was never going to find anything anyway. I wasn't up there to solve anything, or implicate anyone. I was there just to get a feel for the place, to find out if I thought it was somewhere worthy of us spending a little more time.

I asked at one point if there was any trace left of the Balfour women who came here after the war. Had they left their mark on the building, or in the grounds? I got the hesitation then, the moment when you could see that the cool customer has

been asked the slightly more awkward question than antici-
pated. And she thought about it, and then she led me out of
the house to a small pile of stones, a cairn, on the northern
side of the grounds, beyond the polytunnels. It took a few
minutes to get there. We walked in silence.

The cairn was about six feet in diameter at the base, rising
four or five feet, and thinning to around three feet in diameter at the top. The placement of the rocks seemed ramshackle,
and yet there was a solidity about it, and one could imagine
that these rocks would look exactly the same, if left without
human interference, several hundred years from now.

'It's said that they left this,' she said.

'Beyond what's obvious,' I said, 'what is it, and how do we
know they put it here?'

Franklin smiled.

'Ever the logician, detective,' she said, and I elected not to
tell her that I could be anything but. 'We don't know the
purpose of the rocks. Maybe someone, or something, is buried
beneath them, but there'd only be one way to find out. They've
only been here a hundred years, so if you want, you could get
some of your police mates to come and get the rocks to fuck,
see what's underneath. I'm sure no one'd object.'

'How d'you know it was the Balfour women?'

She stared at the cairn for a few moments, then finally
turned to me and shrugged.

'That's all I've got,' she said. 'A hunch.'

I took a moment and then stepped forward. Franklin was
behind me, and, in such a simple movement of my feet, out
of my mind. Strangely, instantly, like I'd taken a step forward
in time by a second or two, we were out of sync, and she was
no longer there.

It was just me and the cairn. I thought of that as I stood
there, a couple of feet from it, me looking at the rocks, and
somehow the rocks looking back.

The rocks weren't looking at me: that didn't make any sense. And there wasn't someone hiding inside, peeking out between the cracks.

I thought of the cairn near where Sanderson and I had been sitting last night, when we chatted near the top of the mountain I didn't recognise.

But wait, I thought. Last night? I didn't think I'd talked to Sanderson last night, and yet, when I thought of it, it felt like something that had happened only a few hours earlier. Sitting at the top of the mountain, with that cairn just to our right, etched against the familiar pale blue sky.

She said something behind me, but the words were blurred. I was concentrating on the stones, and it was as though my brain, just for that moment, couldn't process anything else.

The stones on the mountaintop, the stones around the wellhead, the stones in my head, the stones in front of me. I reached out, hesitated for a second, my fingers hovering next to the cairn, and then touched one of the stones, about two-thirds of the way up.

There was no blinding flash, no sudden insight, no shock, no vision, no wishing well of perception. But I could feel it. I could feel something in the stones. The pain of loss, perhaps. A pain of melancholy and sorrow.

I held my hand there for a moment, as that pain crept insidiously inside me, as though it was taken into my veins and shot round my body, much more quickly than my heart would have been able to carry it, and when I lifted my hand away, it was almost as though the synthesiser zapped to a sudden crescendo in my head, before a stunning silence returned, and I was standing there, Franklin just behind me, my hand, shaking slightly, still hovering beside the cairn.

'What was that?' she said.

*   *   *

'What was that?' says the accountant, and suddenly I'm back in the present, driving on the A9, on the way to Dingwall. Already beyond Kildary, and I realise I've been doing that thing, driving on autopilot, barely aware of my surroundings, the part of my brain that's been navigating the traffic and the roads, doing so without any conscious input from me.

'What was what?' I ask.

'You were a million miles away,' she says. 'I've been watching you, Inspector.'

I don't say anything. Bizarrely, even though I've been sitting in complete silence, I feel as though she's seen right through me, that she was inside my head, thinking the same thing I was, looking at the cairn, sensing its presence in the way that I've just been doing.

'Then you shivered,' she says. 'That was interesting.'

There's nothing to see here. The sense of loss. The cairn at the old Balfour house. It wasn't for a young boy, dumped at the bottom of a well, either two hundred years ago, or last weekend. It was for the men lost in France. It was for the war dead. It was for a family shot to pieces, a way of life lost for ever. It was those women marking the past they had left behind, and the pain of their loss still lingers in the stones.

And those women up there, defensive in the face of intrusion, are nothing to do with this.

So says my intuition. So says nothing.

The phone rings, the noise sudden and sharp. I wasn't aware of shivering, but maybe I did. Maybe I did when I took my hand off the stone. Another loud ring from the phone, my hands still on the steering wheel, pressing hard, my knuckles beginning to turn white. As I notice them, the accountant seems to see it too, and she smiles as she follows my eyes.

'Stressful driving along this straight section of road when there are no other cars, isn't it?' she says. 'Would you like me to get that for you? You seem occupied.'

I lift the phone.

'Iain.'

'Boss,' says Sutherland, 'where are you?'

'On the road. Should be with you in ten minutes.'

'Come back out to the farm,' he says.

'What's up?'

'There's been a death. Murder or suicide, too early to say.'

That's all. No name offered off the bat. I glance at the accountant, who is watching me, perhaps interested to see what my expression will bring, and it's hard to tell if that's because she heard what Sutherland had to say.

'Right,' I say, 'I'll be there in fifteen minutes,' and hang up.

Whoever it is, they're not going anywhere, and in fifteen minutes they're still going to be dead. I can find out when I get there.

'I'm sorry, I can't take you into Dingwall. I'll drop you at the Ardullie roundabout.'

I don't look at her as I speak, but I can sense the smile, something sly about it. The knowing look.

'Quite the switch,' she says. 'The officer in you just emerged, like a butterfly from its chrysalis. One minute, introspective and, if I'm not wrong, a little confused, and then' – she snaps her fingers – 'the detective boldly arrives, business-like and pure of heart. Makes me wonder who you really are.'

'I'll drop you at the Ardullie roundabout,' I repeat, feeling as if I need some sort of acknowledgement from her of the change in plan.

'You said,' she says, and that is all.

A few minutes later we arrive at the roundabout, and I pull into the side of the road, the act of doing so another piece of driving undertaken almost subconsciously. Already thinking about the farm. Who is going to be dead, and how is it going to help?

That's the cold detective in me right there. I almost don't care who's dead (unless of course it was one of our own, but Sutherland would have said). Everybody dies, that's what happens. But not every crime gets solved. Not every body gets identified.

'Thank you for the lift, detective,' says the accountant, as she opens the car door.

I glance at her, mind far away, and she smiles again.

'Work mode,' she says, and then she's gone, closing the door behind her.

Quick check in the mirror, and then I'm off, not even glancing at her as I'm on my way. Over the bridge across the Cromarty Firth, and heading back to the farmhouse on the Black Isle, where another body awaits.

23

I stand beside the body, then turn and look away, down across the fields, across the firth, to Wyvis on the other side, the broad, flat top of the mountain unobscured by cloud.

Catriona Napier gave herself a good view for her final seconds. Assuming, that is, that she hangs here by choice.

The rope is attached to the railing of a small balcony, stuck uncomfortably onto the side of the house facing away from the tent around the well, outside which two officers still stand. They would not have seen the death, and would have had no reason to be suspicious, despite her dying no more than a hundred yards from where they were on guard. It doesn't look good for them, but there really was nothing they could have done. They'd been tasked with watching the well, not the farmers.

'The door onto the balcony was open,' says Sutherland. 'If she did kill herself, it's likely she walked onto the balcony, tied the rope, climbed over the railing and jumped. She'd have died pretty quickly, I'd have thought.'

He joins me in looking over at the mountain, and the green hills to either side and beyond.

'She wouldn't have got to enjoy the view for very long once she fell,' he says, almost wistfully. 'If you can enjoy anything when you're dangling from a rope.'

'So, do we presume this is related to the seemingly simple matter of Constable Cole discovering a picture of Catriona Napier holding the hand of a child while walking down Main Street?'

'Definitely,' says Sutherland. 'There's been no hint of depression, no hint of anything psychological from her. We've looked into her background, and there was nothing to suggest any kind of medical history pointing in this direction. Her husband, yes, but nothing from her. So, if she killed herself it was because we'd found something out, and she didn't like the direction that was going to go in.'

'Or someone killed her, because she'd become a liability.'

'Yes.'

I turn and look around at the scene, a couple of guys on the balcony taking prints, the photographer still minutely capturing every detail from the ground, another couple of officers in place. Along the road at the bottom of the hill, I can see the steady approach of Dr Wade, her white car slowing as she reaches the lane up to the farmhouse.

'Do you suppose we're going to be able to find the identity of the boy in the picture, or d'you think we've come across another child that no one will know?'

'Oh,' he says, 'that's interesting. What are you thinking?'

I don't answer, take another look around the scene, step to the side of the house and look along the front, up to where the two officers are standing by the tent.

'You haven't spoken to McIntosh yet?'

'No, she's in the sitting room.'

'Someone's with her?'

'Elvis.'

'Did she call it in?'

'Yep. Called 999, asked for the police and an ambulance.'

'Can we get the recording of the call?'

'I'll get on it.'

'Right. I'll have a quick word with Wade, then I'll go and speak to McIntosh. Join me there if you're not ready by the time I go in.'

He nods, turns away, takes the phone from his pocket.

'Iain?' I say, and he turns back. 'Sorry, forgot. How d'you get on with the other wells? Anything?'

He shakes his head, a slight roll of the eyes at his own forgetfulness.

'Yes, sorry. Three wells. The one on the farm, almost an exact replica of what we have here. The covering of the well dates from around the same time, and was probably done for the same reason. We got the farmer to open it up, which, you know, didn't go down well, but the usual threat of sending in storm troopers with a warrant increased his enthusiasm for the project. Had a look . . . nothing. The one on the council ground is also defunct. Covered with a pretty solid manhole, very well sealed, but there's still access. Managed to get someone out to open it for us, though there was a good amount of grumbling about it. Had a look inside, similar kind of thing to what we have out here.'

'Except no body at the bottom?'

'No,' he says. 'There's already a ladder down, so I took a quick look.'

'I hope you were wearing the right clothes, a helmet, a head torch and had taken out extra insurance.'

I deliver all that without a trace of a smile, and he rolls his eyes.

'It's a little damp at the bottom, but no sign that anyone has been anywhere near it in the recent past.'

'What about the house? Fortrose?'

He nods at this one, and looks away over at the hills.

'Hmm, yes, that one caused a little more upset. The house was literally built over a well.'

'And?'

'The well had been closed up many years previously, part of the same drive of closures as we've talked about. In recent times the land was sold, building permission was sought and given.'

227

'But why over the well?'

'There are trees nearby; they didn't want to cut them down. Didn't think it that big a deal to fill in the well.'

'When was this?'

'Early nineties.'

'Did you get a look in the basement? Wait, I don't suppose there was a basement.'

'Yes, there was a basement,' he says, and he shakes his head ruefully. 'As an avid reader of the *Ross-shire*, you'll be aware of Councillor Rollins.'

I hold his gaze for a moment.

'You're fucking kidding?'

'Hmm,' says Sutherland, with mock seriousness, 'the Inspector never usually swears at home.'

'Jack Rollins?'

'Yes, it was the house of Jack Rollins.'

'He's a chippy bastard.'

'Yes, he is. And he was. Not at all impressed with the police turning up at his front door. He wasn't there when we arrived. The wife answered. She is his equal in chippiness. I don't know how she did it, because she was in our company the whole time, but we're there for about twenty minutes, chatting and whatever, and Jack Rollins turns up, demanding to know what's for.'

'Bollocks. Did he throw you out? Are we going to need to—'

'No, it's fine. He calmed down once he accepted that we weren't just there to harass his highly strung wife. He told the same story about the well that she did, then showed us down to the basement. Quite affable in the end.'

'And?'

'You know, it was a basement. Something of a games room about it, no sign of the well. There was a floor covering, I've got to admit, and we didn't go so far as to rip it up, so . . . I mean, he didn't dash down there to sort it out before we went down, and I didn't leave with a feeling that there was anything a—'

'OK, that's fine. It's hardly like we've got this definite link to the wells, is it? We'll leave it for now.'

I'm thinking, partly, that this strand of the investigation has gone as far as it's going to; but I'm also thinking that the last thing I want to do is go ramming another town councillor up the backside. Potentially upsetting one as much as I've been doing the last two days is quite enough.

No need to share that with Sutherland.

'I can make further checks if you like. Speak to the builder.'

I watch Wade as she gets out the car, taking a few moments to gather her things.

'Sure, when you get the time. I don't know where that's taking us, but have a look. Maybe find out what shape the well was in before it was filled in.'

'Yes, boss.'

'OK, thanks. You should get on, I'll see you inside.'

'Boss,' he says, and turns away again.

Wade glances over at me from beside her car, we nod at each other, and then she takes a moment, turning away to look down over the view.

Yes, there are oil rigs away to the right, and Dingwall is bigger than it once was, and there's the A9 crossing the firth down to our left, and wind farms, those bastard lovechildren of the Scottish government, atop several hills, but so much of this view would have been the same as it was two hundred years ago. The hills are the same, the colours are the same, the feel in the air that soaks through you like water is the same.

Beneath us, hovering about fifty feet above the ground, a kestrel awaits its moment, just the same as kestrels have been waiting their moments here for thousands of years.

I walk over beside Wade. She, as ever, does not seem to be in a rush. The dead, as she would point out, are not going anywhere.

'Doctor,' I say.

'Inspector. Becoming a well-worn path.'

We watch as another white car approaches, tries to turn into the driveway, is stopped by the officers on duty, then travels further along and parks at the bottom of the lower field. Two men get out, one with a small camera in his hand, and they survey the scene, looking up the hill, to see if there might be a better way to access the property.

'Murder or suicide?' she asks.

'Looks like suicide, smells like murder.'

'I'll see what I can do.'

'You get anywhere speaking to a forensic anthropologist?'

'Yeah,' she says, although there is disinterest in her voice. 'Spoke to a young woman over at Aberdeen University. Didn't tell her too much, but enough to get her interested. She wants to come over and see the evidence for herself. I said sure.'

I don't immediately say anything, and I can feel her eyes on me.

'How does that make you feel?' asks Wade.

'As long as she's discreet. Can you make sure she's discreet?'

'I will use all my powers,' she says, drily. 'She'll be here around six this evening. Come over, if you're worried.'

'She wants to see the body as well as the well?'

'Yes. I mean, fair enough, she's coming all this way.'

Six this evening. I try to think that far ahead, but a clear picture of what the day will look like by then does not come to me.

'You can let me know,' she says. 'We might know a bit more about your murder-stroke-suicide by then, so maybe you'll be coming anyway.'

'Yes,' I say.

We stare at the hypnotic scene of an unchanging Highland landscape, tied to it for a few moments.

'This what you envisaged when you came over from Aberdeen?' I ask.

'I live fifteen minutes from here.'

'That wasn't what I meant.'

'I know, Inspector.'

And that's all I get. She gives me a cursory nod, then walks past me and round the corner of the house.

'She was nervous about something,' she says.

Head down, Belle McIntosh has barely looked at me since I came in. No wariness about her, no fear that she might be under suspicion for being the one who has discovered two bodies on her property within four days.

Maybe it's not even occurred to her that her wife might not have killed herself. If she didn't, then McIntosh is currently the one and only suspect, just as she's one of the two suspects for the death of Boy 9.

Instead, she just looks a little lost.

'D'you have any idea what that was?'

'I didn't know anything about her,' she says, voice quiet and low, words forced out from a still well of sudden bereavement. 'You know that already, of course. We weren't ... our marriage was a business arrangement. I'm sitting here ...' and she pauses, shakes her head, finally looks up at me. 'I'm sitting here trying to remember her, trying to think what it was she liked, what it was she cared about. I can't begin to even think why she might have killed herself. But then, to have known that, I'd have had to have known *her*, wouldn't I?'

'When did you speak to her last?'

'Last night, if you can call it speaking.'

'When? I take it you didn't sleep together.'

'No, we've told you that already. We never slept together.'

The final word is cut short, as though some memory inter-rupted the sentence.

'I don't suppose it matters. We had sex once. Big deal that was. It just happened. It was, I don't know, you see films and read books and listen to songs, and there's supposed to be something about it, isn't there? Something romantic, at least in the broad, big sense of the word, if not in the emotional sense. And what did we have?' She laughs ruefully. 'Pathetic. What were we doing, two women in our fifties, like that? We literally bumped into each other one night in the corridor, and it was like this . . . I don't know, just the touch, it was like we had to have each other. God.'

Another look, part forlorn and part self-loathing.

'Maybe she just wanted to see what it was like and it didn't do anything for her,' she says, head dropping again. 'Didn't do anything for me. Felt like an animal, just meeting my basic urge. It was like watching sex on a David Attenborough show. They do it, they go their separate ways, it's like nothing happened.'

'So, you didn't sleep together last night?' I say. Usually happy to let people talk. But I think we've heard enough about the one-off instance of their unsatisfactory lovemaking.

'No,' she says. 'We were, I don't know, we ate dinner together. She was distracted. She'd been somewhere, seemed funny when she got back.'

'Where'd she go?'

'I don't know. But it was after you lot—'

She breaks off, looks up at me again. Turns to Kinghorn, then back to me.

'What were you speaking to her about?' she asks.

'Didn't you ask her?'

'Yes, but she wasn't saying. I wondered if it was just about me, but I didn't really care. I expected you'd be coming back and forth until you'd found out who this Boy 9 was. To be honest, I'm surprised you haven't tried to pin it on me and Lachlan, seeing as we're your only suspects.'

'How d'you know we're not pinning it on you? And how d'you know you're our only suspects?'

For a moment it looks as if we might be about to get some of her old annoyance, and then it's as though she remembers that there's something to be upset about, that life has changed, and her eyes drop again.

'How long was she away?'

'An hour maybe,' she says. 'Maybe longer. I made dinner, we sat and ate it, she went back out for another walk.'

She pauses, then turns and points roughly in the direction of the well.

'Saw her up there, speaking to your guy. Very cosy. No idea what that was about.'

'You didn't talk when she got back to the house.'

'Nope.'

'And you didn't talk to her this morning?'

'Nope.'

'Did you see her?'

'Once, sort of. She was over the far side of the farm. Saw her walking. Not sure what she was doing, I didn't think there was anything to do over there at the moment.'

'How can you be sure it was her?'

The door opens behind us, and Sutherland enters, just as she's looking at me with an air of contempt for the question. Sutherland nods and I turn back to the bereaved widow.

'When did you come across her body? Were you looking for her?'

'I was up on the top field for much of the morning. Had some fence work to do, and then I . . . I spent some time up there, just sitting, looking at the view. Quiet enough morning.'

'You couldn't see the far side of the house from where you were sitting?'

She shakes her head. 'I came back down, I made lunch. I called her, looked out the window at the front, couldn't see her. Presumed she was still out walking. I had lunch, washed up, she still hadn't come back. So, yes, then I went looking for her. And I found her. When it came to it, I didn't have far to look.'

'How long did it take for you to call us?'

'Five minutes maybe, I don't know. She was obviously dead, she'd obviously been dead a while. There was no ambulance going to be able to do anything.'

'Did you talk over dinner?'

'Sure,' she says, and her voice drops a little lower, so that when the sarcasm comes it's only the words that show it and not the tone. 'We chatted about the Syrian conflict, and how it's all being orchestrated by Brussels. She asked me about my childhood, and I asked her about her succession of lovers at university. Then we debated transgender rights in school classrooms and discussed Wittgenstein's picture theory of language.'

She pauses, looks up at me – and still the sorrow defines her – and says, 'I think that was about it. Just the usual topics.'

'Did you talk over dinner?'

'We did not talk over dinner,' she says. 'Just like we usually didn't talk over dinner.'

'Did she say *anything* over dinner? Anything at all? Pass the salt. Would you like some more broccoli? Did you have a nice day? Would you like another glass of wine? We're going to have to get the vets in.'

'Would you like a napkin?' throws in Sutherland.

'Maybe we said three words to each other,' she says, cutting us off with exasperation. 'She just died. Am I supposed to remember everything she said?'

'There was so little of it. What was the last thing she said to you? Thanks for dinner? I've got a headache? Good night?'

She smirks, a rueful look but unattractive.

'We finished dinner at the same time. Ate the entire meal with barely a word. Then, as we placed our cutlery back on our plates with perfect synchronicity, we finally looked at one another. You know what she said?'

She pauses, as though Napier's final words to her are going to be of some significance, then she says, 'Well, well,' and laughs. 'Then she washed up and went back out. I went out to check on the chickens a short while later and she was talking to your man. You can ask him what she said. Maybe she confessed everything.'

Another in her rich panoply of dismissive expressions aimed at the police. I choose not to linger on it and ask, 'Have you any idea why someone might have wanted to kill Catriona?'

'Kill her?'

'Yes.'

'She committed suicide.'

'It looks like she committed suicide. That doesn't mean she committed suicide.'

She possibly looks even more lost at that thought, and her eyes drop again.

'No, I suppose not,' she says. 'Well, if that's your way of asking if I killed her, I didn't.'

'D'you know anyone else who might have wanted to?'

'Really? I mean, she was lovely. Quiet, just got on with things. Yes, she was terrible at running a farm, but that didn't make her a bad person. That didn't give anyone a reason to want her dead.'

I lift the brown envelope that I'd placed on the table and her eyes move back to it. She noticed it when I entered, but seemed to have lost interest since I hadn't produced anything from it yet.

I take out the photograph of Napier from the previous Friday and place it across the table, in front of her. She opens her mouth, as though an automatic denial is on her lips, then pulls back from whatever she was going to say. *That's not her*, or *that was taken ten years ago.*

'What's that?' she says instead, after a few moments.

'That's a photograph of your wife, with a child, on Dingwall High Street last Friday afternoon. Can you tell us who the child is?'

'How would I know?'

'She's your wife, Ms McIntosh. It's not too far-fetched to suppose you might.'

She lifts the photograph and studies it more closely.

'Seriously?' she says, and now there's a rueful, almost mocking tone in her voice. 'You expect me to buy this? Look at it. You probably had someone mock this up in the last fifteen minutes. Do I know who this kid is? Sure. He's yours. Or his,' she adds, indicating Sutherland without looking at him.

'Neither of us have kids,' I say, deadpan.

'Sure you don't. Whoever he is, it doesn't matter, does it? You faked the photo. I don't know what your endgame is, but—'

'Can you tell me the name of the boy in the photograph?'

'No,' she says, a little more harshly. 'No. I can't. I've never seen him before in my life.'

'Can you remember how long your wife was gone on Friday afternoon?'

A roll of the eyes and with it the spark seems to go, the shoulders slump a little further down, the eyes drop.

'I'm not sure. Three hours maybe, far as I remember.'

'You know where she was going?'

'No. Just out. Can't even remember if she said. Sometimes she told me, sometimes I'd look for her and she'd just be gone.'

'How often?'

'How often did she go out?'

'Yes.'

'Shall I consult my diary? My special Wife Stalking Diary that she got me for Christmas last year so I could keep track of her every movement?'

'How often did she go out?' I ask again.

'I don't know. A few times a week, maybe. Maybe more. Maybe less. Why don't you tell me? You people know far more about the lives of the citizens than they themselves. You've got us all tracked. You probably make sure there's a chip implanted at birth.'

'That's all you've got for us?'

'Yes, Inspector, that's all.'

'You *never* knew where she went, or you didn't know last Friday?'

'Sure, sometimes she went to the shops.'

'Did she have any friends? Did she have friends who have children this age?'

'She probably had friends. We didn't talk about them. I don't have friends. That's how it is, and so I'm not interested in anyone else's.'

'Even your wife's?'

'That's correct.'

She sits back, her lips purse, she stares harshly across at me, and she has given everything she intends to give.

Sutherland and I walk up to the well to see Constable Ross. The scene is unchanging, the crowd shifting in composition but not in number, people coming and going. Another death, a new twist to the tale of the boy in the well. Maybe, some will begin to suggest, this isn't about the boy, or the well, but about this farm and the curse that sits upon it.

'Alex,' I say, as we come up alongside.

Sutherland stops just short, drawn once again to look down over the hillside.

'Sir,' says Constable Ross.

'Do you ever go home?'

He smiles. 'Finished at ten last night, sir, back on at ten this morning.'

'That's good. I thought maybe you were just stationed here permanently to make sure I didn't go down the well without a hat.'

'Well, obviously,' he says, smiling, 'Bernie's primed to rugby-tackle you if you try it when I'm not here, sir.'

We laugh lightly together, and then I indicate the need to get back to business with a thumb pointed in the direction of the farmhouse.

'The farmer says you spoke to Catriona Napier last night?'

His brow furrows a little and he nods.

'Aye,' he says. 'I was going to talk to you about that. I mean, it was nothing major, and I wouldn't have said anything if she hadn't died. Even then—'

'Go on.'

'She was out walking. After dark, obviously, didn't have a torch. I suppose she knows the ground. She came by the tent, and she asked if she could go inside, take another look in the well. Not sure why, and I said no anyway. She didn't argue. Then she stood for a while looking down over the view, or, you know, into the darkness. There were the lights on the rigs, I suppose.'

He pauses, straightens out what else he wants to say about her, then continues, 'Funny. I was wondering if she was waiting for a moment to dive into the tent, like she thought I might get distracted or something. But I got this sense from her . . . I'm not sure what it was. Like . . . sadness. Does that sound mental? I could sense the sadness in her.'

His face is slightly twisted, uncomfortable with what he's saying.

'Don't worry about it, Alex,' I say, 'I sense that all the time.'

'Really?'

'Yes. She didn't say anything else?'

'Aye, well, she said she was tired, then she left. Watched her head back to the house.'

He holds my gaze, I can tell he's thinking about it, trying to remember the moment, then he shrugs.

'That was it. Well, she didn't actually say she was tired, but that was what she meant.'

'What did she say?'

'The Sandman's coming for me.'

He says it, then he smiles.

'Aye, I remember that. Sounded kind of childish.' A moment, then he repeats, 'The Sandman's coming for me. Ha.'

He smiles again. I don't return the look.

The Sandman.

That's not weird, is it? The Sandman. Why shouldn't she talk about the Sandman if she was tired? Except, that other man of sand comes instantly to mind. Elizabeth's Beige Man. I don't know who he was, and I couldn't tell if Elizabeth knew who he was. The story seemed so unreal. The story seemed to be about something other than what it was about. I wish I could remember it all. But there was the Beige Man who blended into the sand, and now the last words we know to have been spoken by Catriona Napier were about the Sandman.

Is this some new strangeness, or is it me, once again, casting the net far and wide in desperation?

'She was probably just tired,' I say, absent-mindedly.

'Yes,' says Ross, nodding curiously, 'I'm sure that's what she meant.'

I'm standing here, trying to put my thoughts together, trying to connect these two women and these two stories, and wondering how on earth there could be anything. Except that Elizabeth is married to a councillor, and a body was found at the bottom of a well in Napier's home, and there's another well beneath the home of another councillor, and the two women talk of there being a Sandman.

Is that any kind of a link? Is there anything there at all that's not plucking at particles in the air, desperate for something to make sense? Reaching, stretching, pulling; reckless in the end to make connections that don't exist.

'Sir?'

I turn and look at Sutherland, who's walked up alongside, and I catch the glance between him and Ross. The look that says, *uh-oh, the boss has gone full Walter Mitty again.*

'Yes, you're right, we should be heading. Thanks, Alex.'

'Sir.'

And so we turn away from the well, and start walking back to the car.

24

'What d'you think?' says Sutherland, his words jarring, coming from nowhere.

Heading back into Dingwall, still internally crunching the data on the Beige Man/Sandman crossover. Except, there's no data to crunch, and there may not be a crossover, so my thoughts are inevitably vague and remote. As much about whether I'm forcing the issue, as they are about trying to work out what the issue even is.

As seems to be happening more and more in the last couple of days, I have to take a moment to retrieve the sergeant's words from the past in order to hear them.

'McIntosh?' I say, giving myself time to become acquainted with the present.

'You think she killed her wife?'

'No. Yes, she could be lying about all sorts of things, and there may well be plenty more to come out, but on this . . . No. Even before Napier died, you could see there was nothing between them. So it feels wrong. In order to want to kill someone, at least in this kind of situation, there has to be something there. Some feeling. Some intensity. They were just two people who lived in the same house and shared a business. And now one of them's dead.'

'And the boy in the CCTV?'

'Don't know,' I say. 'Maybe McIntosh was lying about that. We need to get that picture out as quickly as possible.'

'Presumably someone'll know who this kid is,' he says. 'We're not going to have lightning strike twice.'

We drive on in silence for a while, off the bridge, along the A862, into the outskirts of town.

'I'm not so sure,' I say eventually.

'Sorry?' he says, his thoughts obviously having moved on.

'I'm not so sure that someone's going to come forward. Maybe this is the connection we've been looking for. Maybe that's why she killed herself, because she knew we were on to her.'

'That there's a secret stash of children somewhere?' he says, his voice disbelieving.

'That's one way of putting it, but yes. Really, d'you think the police, the authorities, know about every living person in the UK? D'you think all immigrants are recorded? Maybe there's some child labour camp somewhere that we're unaware of.'

'Really, sir?'

'Iain, come on. There's something weird with Boy 9 and, whatever it is, it's going to be an eye-opener. Maybe it'll be the same with this kid, and maybe that's why Catriona Napier felt she had no option but to take herself out the game. Or why someone made that decision for her.'

'Hmm,' he says.

'We'll find out soon enough. It was a picture of a child on Dingwall High Street five days ago. Someone's got to know him, and if they don't . . .'

Pull into the car park, glance at Sutherland, can see him staring sceptically straight ahead, and then we're parked, out the car, and heading into the station.

Sometimes walking past Mary on the front desk can feel like running the gauntlet. In quiet times, we're liable to end up in conversation, with Mary enquiring after my personal life, regularly doling out unneeded advice. Fond though I am of her, there are plenty of occasions when I don't want to talk.

In busy times, when there are too many things to do, one passes her with trepidation, as much as one returns to one's desk with trepidation, waiting for the thing that's going to be added to the list, that's going to throw your well-planned next two hours out the window.

This time, as we enter, I know it's coming, as sure as if there had been a notice attached to the inner glass swing door.

I pause just inside. Sutherland, who seems to hold none of my expectations of being grabbed by the front desk, walks quickly past and on up the stairs. Mary catches my eye, lifts her eyebrow in that way of hers, and I approach the desk, ready for the worst.

'I know that look,' I say.

She smiles. 'I'm sure you do.'

'Quinn?'

'Yes,' she says. 'There's someone in the office. Seems the local council are taking an interest in the investigation. Was bound to happen once it got on the news. They'll be wanting their own fifteen minutes in the picture.'

'The council?'

Wonderful. Here comes Councillor Rollins with his objections about Sutherland and Kinghorn pitching up at his house. Here comes Councillor Rollins with his official complaint, which he will demand is immediately staffed through the appropriate channels, and is, of course, much more important than any investigation currently taking place. Here comes Councillor Rollins, officious and pedantic, bureaucratic and dull, putting himself in the middle of the investigation, painting himself as the victim.

'Harry Rhodes,' she says.

Harry Rhodes. Well, that makes even more sense.

'Apparently he's returned early from a trip to *take charge* of the situation. That's how it was presented.'

'He doesn't have any authority,' I say, blandly, although I'm not thinking about his level of authority.

'He does front the police and town council liaison committee.'

'That doesn't mean he tells us what to do,' I say, although my heart and confidence are not in it.

'Maybe you could point that out to him.'

I turn and look up the stairs to the door of the open-plan. I would hope that Quinn is pointing out Rhodes's lack of authority, but I wouldn't put it past Quinn to be playing his usual cards, cautious and steady.

'Thanks, Mary,' I say, and she smiles.

The implications quickly run through my head as I walk up the stairs. Busted for sleeping with a councillor's wife, and more or less in the course of my duties. Me, the dull detective who never does anything interesting. Kicked off the investigation. Will it be handed over to Sutherland, or will they bring in someone from Inverness? Sheerin maybe, or Monk.

I walk through the office. Stop for a moment, look around, ponder going to my desk to check for messages, but decide against. The office is busy, no one immediately comes flying over, which means there's no particular news to be imparted. Boy 9 remains unidentified; there have been no further revelations in the death of Catriona Napier during the short time it took Sutherland and me to drive back here.

Cole, Fisher and Kinghorn are at their desks. Sutherland is at the coffee machine. He looks round, catches my eye, asks the question with a look and I shake my head.

Harry Rhodes awaits, and suddenly I'm aware of a feeling of almost total disinterest in him. So what if he is here to denounce me as an adulterer? Let him have his say, and let me get back to work or let Quinn do what he's going to do.

Quick pace in my step now, knock on the door and enter without waiting for the call from within.

Neither of the men is sitting. Quinn has his back to the window, his backside against the window frame, arms folded. Rhodes is standing to the side, hands in his pockets, broad shouldered, white shirt tight against his round belly, the sides of his navy blue suit jacket hanging back behind his forearms.

'Sir?' I say, then give Rhodes a nod.

The cuckold stands imperiously, barely thinking me worthy of a nod in return.

'What's the news from the farm?' asks Quinn.

I take a moment, glance at Rhodes, then turn back to Quinn.

'It's all right,' says Quinn, 'Councillor Rhodes is on the local police committee, as you know.'

That does not, in my opinion, make any difference, but since I'm not about to impart any information that counts as even remotely classified, it hardly seems the time to take a stance.

'Catriona Napier is dead,' I say. 'Apparent suicide, although we'll know more when we hear back from Dr Wade.'

'Hanging?'

'Yes. There's nothing to suggest outside involvement, but we should wait to get all the facts before rushing to judgement.'

'Is it possible that all this is over?' asks Quinn, a question that is so unexpected to me, I'm not really sure how to answer it. 'Ben?' he says, when a moment or two has passed in silence.

'No,' I say, 'it is not over. How could it be over?'

Harry Rhodes makes some sort of noise, as though he's about to speak but decides to leave it to the chief.

'Catriona Napier killed the boy,' says Quinn. 'She realised

we were closing in. We'd seen her with another child, we'd made some sort of link, and although we don't know exactly what that is yet, it's apparent she knew that the truth, whatever it is, was about to come out.'

He pauses to see if I'm going to say anything about all of that, then adds, 'And she killed herself.'

Still nothing from me. I wonder where he's going with this. It has the feel of him being about to close the investigation, or say that we need to redirect resources to policing the school run or traffic control at the roadworks on the A834. But it can't be. It's not just too early for that, it's like a twenty-year-old preparing a bucket list because his doctor says he won't live to see one hundred and six.

'Ben?' says Quinn.

'Inspector?' chips in Harry Rhodes.

'We don't yet know the identity of Boy 9,' I say, voice steady, trying not to betray my general incredulity. 'Someone has lost a child, and it's not Catriona Napier. We don't know how he came to be at the bottom of the well. We don't know the identity of the child seen with Napier last Friday. We don't know if there's a connection. We don't know if that child is in danger. We don't know if someone staged Napier's suicide, or, if she did kill herself, did someone coerce her into it? The list of things we don't know is currently far, far longer than the list of things we do. So is it possible that this is all over? No, sir, it is not. Even if there's no more death, it doesn't mean it's over. Usually when someone is murdered, there isn't immediately someone else murdered a couple of days later. Just because no one else is going to get killed, doesn't mean it's over. And, in any case, we can't say with any certainty, with anything even resembling certainty, that no one else will get killed.'

The tone was coming into my voice by the end. I have an investigation to be getting on with, and here I am, talking to a couple of suits who are about to come out with some bullshit or other about the town's reputation and the police's reputation. Another grunt from my right, and this time I turn and look at Rhodes.

Maybe if I get mad enough, he'll finally come to what must surely be the point of this meeting. That I slept with his wife. We can't really be here discussing wrapping this up because someone else died.

'Councillor?'

'This isn't . . . we're not living on the set of some American film, Inspector,' he says. 'This is a sad business, but don't go implying that there's some serial killer on the loose, and that the death of Ms Napier is the start of a series of random Ross-shire killings where people are forced to commit suicide.'

I look curiously at him, and then switch back to Quinn.

'Sir?' I say. 'I'm not entirely sure where this is going. We're investigating the death of a child. We are so far from a conclusion, we are so far from knowing who he was and what was behind his death, that the death of Catriona Napier can be said to neither complicate nor illuminate the investigation. At the moment it represents just another fact to be added to the list. At the moment—'

'We're a laughing stock.'

I turn slowly back to Rhodes. He holds my gaze, and we stand in angry silence for a few moments. That phrase, even if it hadn't just been directed at me, is one of the tropes of modern life, tossed out with ever-increasing volume and usage, alongside words like disgusting and disgraceful. It makes me angry every time I hear it, and not just when it's being applied to the work of the department.

'You look annoyed, Inspector,' says Rhodes. 'Good, and so you should. You should be annoyed, because this investigation has been a joke from the start. If you'd got anywhere with this preposterous Boy 9 story, if standing up in front of the world's media had produced results, your actions would still have been questionable, but at least you'd have something to show for it. But instead, what do we have? The entire world is looking at Dingwall, millions of people who never even knew we existed have now heard of us, and what's their first impression? A dead boy in a well, and a community that has to rely on policing by Twitter. We don't have bobbies on the beat, we have spotty youths sitting at computers, hoping the public are going to do their work for them. That's how it looks.'

For a moment the room seems lost in a suffocating drench of words that I would rather not have heard. But how can I switch them off? How can I not listen to someone with absolutely no authority tell me how badly I've been handling the investigation? How can I not hear the irrefutably bad logic that if something speculative works it's a good idea, but if it doesn't, then you shouldn't have tried it in the first place?

I turn back to Quinn, waiting to see if he's going to take a stand on behalf of the station. There's absolutely no reason for him to be beholden to Harry Rhodes. It's not like we've got the First Minister or the chief constable in here.

'I need to get on with the job,' I say in response to Quinn's silence. I've had enough of the conversation; I've had enough of the room. 'Is there anything specific you would like me to do in relation to Councillor Rhodes's comments?'

Quinn looks caught in the moment, in the way that sometimes happens with him. Part annoyed, part determined, part confused. Annoyed at me for not bowing down, or annoyed at Rhodes because he deserves Quinn's annoyance, and a lot more besides. I don't know. Nor do I care. We have an investigation to progress, and the trivial politics unfolding in the room are nothing but a hindrance.

'Be mindful, Inspector Westphall,' says Quinn, 'that this does not look good for Dingwall.'

Strangely it feels as though I'm speaking to Olivia. Olivia, my ex-girlfriend, of whom I so rarely think any more. Olivia, who coloured my view of relationships for so long. Olivia, whose thoughts so rarely seemed rational. Olivia, with whom one could never have a discussion, never mind an argument. Olivia who drew me in and who then chose to never spit me back out, until I came to the far north of Scotland and she would not follow.

'So, sir,' I say, a completely trivial thought coming into my head, one that befits how petty and small this conversation has been, 'if this is *Jaws*, and I'm Brody and the councillor is Mayor Vaughn, who does that make you?'

I let the analogy hang there for a moment. It feels lightweight and stupid, and yet utterly appropriate to the occasion. Quinn's face hardens now. His annoyance, split between us before, is now all directed at me. As usual, however, he's not quick to words, so before he can bark anything at me, or choose to side with the councillor in the denunciation of his own station and the decisions that he's been party to and has authorised, I turn, open the door and leave.

With the door closed behind me, I stand for a moment, staring straight ahead into the office. Quint. That was Robert Shaw's name in the movie.

I don't think Quinn is Quint. Not by a long shot.

I catch Sutherland's eye from a distance, shake my head at myself, that positive act of clearance, of removing the previous five minutes from my mind, and walk quickly back to the desk.

'We're ready to go live with the picture, sir,' says Sutherland.

'That was quick.'

'Yes,' he says. 'Nothing elaborate. News media, Internet sites, the usual sources. Ping it out now, follow up with a press conference at five if we haven't heard anything.'

'Yep, sounds good,' I say.

'Thunderbirds are go?'

I nod, he turns back to his computer and gets on with the job.

I take a second, then look back over the office. No one looking at me, no one waiting for my direction, everyone getting on with the tasks in hand. So many strands flying in from various directions, and I feel that I need to take the step back now, into the ops room, lay out everything that we have. I consider calling everyone in and having a round table, then decide instead to go into the room myself, put things in order, then get the team in one by one to make sure that I have all the latest.

All that, then more than likely back through to Inverness to see Wade about our latest victim, and to talk to a forensic anthropologist about the peculiar decay displayed by the body of Boy 9, if this really is the body of Boy 9. I need there to be a regular explanation, no matter how much of a stretch.

Witches, I can suddenly hear this woman I've never met before say. *Looks like the work of witches.*

Shake off the thought, nod to myself at the decision I've taken for the next half-hour of the investigation, then head first of all for the coffee machine.

25

The Sandman is coming for me.

The last words of Catriona Napier are back in my head, as soon as I walk into the grim room that PC Cole tries to lift through her relationship with the ficus. Those words could, at some other time, have been innocently meant. Surely not now, however. Not when someone actually was coming for her.

And, regardless of how much of a stretch it may be, I cannot escape the connection with Elizabeth's tale from last night. And that's the thing: I don't in fact find it a stretch at all. It seems so glaring, so obvious.

What would Quinn think? What would Harry Rhodes think of this story, told by his wife in the bed of another man?

There seems no possible connection between them, of course. I stumbled upon Elizabeth Rhodes through my decision to go to the land registry office, our meeting entirely accidental. She did not invite us; she did not manoeuvre or finagle in order for the meeting to happen. She did not force herself into my bed.

And so I drove back from the farm wondering about this peculiar coincidence, thinking that maybe it was me stretching the story to make something out of it, assuming that there was no other possible connection. And then, there he was, waiting for me in the boss's office. Harry Rhodes. There to talk about Boy 9 and the death of the woman who had talked of the Sandman.

Strange things happen, that's just how life works. There needn't always be a connection, there needn't always be something sinister waiting beneath the table to spring out at you.

So, why am I standing here with the Beige Man sitting in the middle of my head?

The Beige Man. The Sandman. Morpheus. Greek mythology and the mythology of DC comic books, Hans Christian Andersen and ancient folklore. Legend and lore and imagination combined through the ages.

But not here. Here we have a Beige Man becoming one with the land; now Harry Rhodes, cuckolded and interfering. Whether he's interfering because he's been cuckolded, I did not care to stand around long enough to find out. I can deal with that thought later. I can deal with the fallout later, should it come to it. At the moment, regardless of me stupidly putting myself in the story, I need to get the mystery of Boy 9 solved.

About to stick my nose out the door and call the first of them in, when there's a knock, and before I can begin to assume that this will be Quinn turned up in an attempt to assert some authority over the investigation, the door opens and Constable Cole sticks her head in.

'Got it, sir,' she says.

'Good,' I say, feeling slightly adrift, having been so lost in thoughts of the Beige Man. 'What have you got?'

'Just spoke to a woman, living in Golspie, who's the daughter of the youngest of the Balfours. I mean, the youngest one who moved to the house in Tain after the Great War.'

'She's the first Balfour you've been able to find?'

'Sounds like she might be the only one. I said someone would be round to see her. I asked if she'd be happy to give a DNA sample.'

'And?'

'She said, sure.'

'Really? We just call out of nowhere asking for DNA, and she doesn't mind?'

'Sense of duty, I think, sir.'

'Sense of duty? That seems wonderfully old-fashioned. Is she from the forties?'

I can see Cole ignoring the facetiousness of my comment, doing the arithmetic in her head.

'Nineteen forty-four. Her name's Marion Stone, been living in Golspie the last fifteen years. She sounds American, but I didn't get the story. She was pretty busy. Parents are both long since dead.'

'Any other family? Aunts, uncles, cousins.'

'Didn't have much to tell me, sir. And she couldn't, off the top of her head, think of a nine-year-old boy in the family.'

'Still, it's a start,' I say, and she nods. 'OK, thanks, Alice. I'll give her a call, probably head up there. I'll get the details from you on the way out.'

'Yes, sir.'

And with the closed door and the sudden silence, I return to my previous state. In thrall to the Sandman.

Focus. Press conference regarding Catriona Napier and the unknown child at five. Wade and the forensic anthropologist at six in Inverness. Then I need to head up the road to Golspie to see Marion Stone. Likely not get there this evening until seven thirty, maybe closer to eight. Go tonight, or in the morning. Or call the local office, get them to go in and see her. Or get Sutherland to go up there now.

The micromanager in me already knows the answer to that.

Check my watch. Things would be simplified if, in the next few minutes, someone were to come forward with the new child's identity. I feel like that's not going to happen, but perhaps there's a straightforward explanation.

It's the same as always, of course. Don't hope for anything. Don't think about what would be helpful to your cause.

Concentrate on what you can do yourself, right now, and get on with it.

Eyes back on the board, dismissing the voices, wherever they're coming from. Try to create a logical sequence of events, something that could explain how we got from where we were this time last week – i.e. there was no story – to where we are now, with two unidentified children, one of them dead, and either a murder, or a suicide that was induced by the event that started this all off.

And at the centre of both of these things is Belle McIntosh, disgruntled and alone, facing an uncertain future, or hiding enough of a past to try to keep us at bay.

The board remains incomplete. Facts to be added, ideas to be shifted around. I open the door, manage to catch Fisher's eye, and indicate for her to come and join me in the room.

'Suicide.'

We're standing over the corpse, Wade and I, in familiar pose. Heads bowed, as though in respect, although of course, just looking down, that's all. Looking down at another body, we the butchers, studying the dead meat of today's investigation.

'You going to give me any leeway on that?' I ask.

'There's nothing to give,' she says, her voice flat. 'Nothing to suggest there was a struggle, nothing in her body to suggest she wasn't fully *compos mentis* when she made the decision to kill herself. As to whether there was someone standing with a gun forcing her to do it, you'll have to work that out. Though, of course, why would you commit suicide to save yourself from getting shot?'

'Maybe the gun was at aimed at someone else,' I say, although I'm not really thinking about that. This story, whatever it is, is not about guns.

'Hmm,' she says. 'You can get people to do most anything with a threat directed at someone they love. Who did she love?'

'That's a good question,' I say. 'No one, far as we know.'

'What about the boy in the photograph you put out this afternoon?'

I finally lift my head away from the cadaver and nod.

'Yep,' I say, 'that's a good question. So far, just like our mysterious Boy 9, we don't have an answer to that.'

'You think that's the answer that'll help you unravel the whole thing?'

'It'll be a start.'

Hands in pockets, look around the mortuary. One other body lying out, our boy in the well, brought out for the anthropologist's inspection.

'Have you had a look at Boy 9 today?' I ask.

'Yes. Same as yesterday.'

'Hasn't deteriorated any further?'

'Nope. Whatever it was that induced it, it was a one-off event. Boom.'

'Boom,' I say, looking back at her, and she smiles humourlessly.

'I foresee a regular rate of decomposition from here on in,' she says. 'I can't explain it, but maybe our guest will be able to.'

'What about the SOCOs? Have they been down to check for a break-in?'

'Yeah, they were here a couple of hours ago. Miserable pair, didn't say much.'

Need to call and check, something else on the list.

'Where is she?' I ask, mind moving on, eyes drifting up to the clock. 'The anthropologist?'

Late arriving here, already nearly six thirty, time marching inexorably on, realising I'm going to be late getting to see Marion Stone. I don't mind, but she might. I haven't called her yet, in case it wasn't going to work out, and I should try to do that before seven.

Already long since night-time outside, the dark bringing the rain. It has turned into a lousy, cold, bleak November day, miserable for driving up the A9 to interview an old lady, but it can't wait until tomorrow. I might not be able to do anything this evening with whatever information the interview throws up, but at least I can get on with it first thing in the morning, without having to start the day with a two-hour round-trip up north.

'She's getting a coffee, she shouldn't be too long.'

'Coffee?'

Wade shrugs. 'She drove through from Aberdeen. She was tired. Wanted a coffee. Everyone wants coffee these days, right?'

'I guess so.'

I turn away again, looking once more at the sheet covering Boy 9. I contemplate going over there but I'll see him soon enough. The same withered, decomposed face, dried skin drawn tightly across his cheeks.

'You ever . . .' I begin, then I stop to reformulate the sentence, not looking at her, just staring idly around the room. 'Sanderson left in such a rush. You ever find anything personal of his around?'

'What are you thinking?' she asks.

'I'm not sure,' I say, because I'm not. The investigation feels so nebulous that it is possible some things may be lost. One of those is Sanderson, and the curious intrusion that he's been making into my head since the weekend. Since he died. 'I just wondered if there was anything of his left here. We stood in here often enough, the two of us, like you and me now,' and I turn back to her, 'and I never knew him. And then he was gone, and it was hardly a surprise that he never said goodbye, to me or anyone else. I just wondered. Did he leave anything of himself, that's all?'

'Apart from his CD collection?' she says. 'I don't think that's what you mean.'

I smile and shake my head.

The door opens, and we turn at the arrival of the woman who is, presumably, the anthropologist. Coffee in one hand, taking the last bite of a Danish with the other. Good thing Sutherland isn't here or he'd be feeling left out. Immediately some Pavlovian thing would have kicked in and he would've had to go and get something to eat in order to think straight.

'Hey,' she says.

Mid-thirties, blonde hair, an attractive smile.

'Sorry about that, I was dying there.'

She stands in the middle of the room, eyes moving from the covered cadaver, to the uncovered body of Catriona Napier.

'I heard about that,' she says. 'Suicide?'

'Yes.'

'Bummer.'

She turns to the body of Boy 9, stopping beside me as she walks towards it.

'Charlotte Muir,' she says. 'Aberdeen Uni.'

'Ben Westphall.'

'Cool. Saw you on the news the other day. You look younger in real life. Hey, Dr Wade, is it?'

Wade nods, does not look particularly comfortable with Charlotte Muir's easy-going manner.

'Hmm. There used to be a Wade through in Aberdeen. Not related, I suppose. No, sorry, that would be weird. Why would you—'

'The same Wade,' says Wade. 'I moved.'

Muir looks at Wade for a few moments, hard to read her face, then she smiles.

'Right. Cool. I'm sorry.'

'That's OK.'

'OK, great,' says Muir, almost forcing the conversation forward, and I wonder what that's about, then Muir is behind me, and over beside the body.

'Can I?' she asks. Wade and I simultaneously answer in the affirmative.

Wade covers over the head of Catriona Napier, and then comes to join me beside Boy 9, as Muir pulls back the sheet, the full length of the body, and leaves it loosely folded at the bottom end of the table.

'OK,' she says, still with her coffee in one hand. 'Tell me what you're looking for.'

Wade gives me a glance and I indicate that I'm happy for her to answer.

'The boy was pulled out of a well on Monday morning. At the time his body showed very little . . . no, the body displayed as having been dead for around forty hours. That's what I thought at the time. A couple of hours later, undertaking a more thorough examination here, I pushed that back to forty-eight, maybe even more. I didn't think much of it at the time. It didn't occur to me that the body had rapidly begun to speed up decomposition in that two-hour period. I just assumed my initial analysis on-site had been a little off. I made all the necessary checks, I had everything I thought we needed. The body was stored,' and she indicates the large, rectangular drawers around the room, 'then we took it out yesterday, forty-eight hours later, and this . . .'

'Shit,' says Muir, 'that really is the story, huh? I thought you were exaggerating.'

'No,' says Wade, not responding to the flippant tone.

'Wow. That's awesome. They're not saying *that* about Boy 9 on the news, are they?'

'And neither will they,' I say.

'Yep,' she says. 'And hey, don't worry, I'm all in. I mean, on keeping the secret. This is awesome.'

'Have you any idea how it might've happened?' I ask, ignoring the fact that what I would take for granted, she seemed to think worthy of mention.

She lets out a low whistle, shaking her head as she does so. 'Witches' curse?' she says, looking round at me.

She holds my gaze for a moment, then suddenly the wide, white smile comes to her face.

Beautiful teeth.

'I'm kidding,' she says. 'I mean, if we were to acknowledge the existence of witches' curses, that'd be the answer to like, almost everything.'

'That's good,' I say. 'We might have to fall back on it, though. Have you anything that doesn't involve witches? Anything, that has, I don't know, an anthropological angle, for example.'

She laughs, then looks round at Wade to include her. Wade does not look like she wants to be included.

'Awesome,' says Muir, to no one in particular. 'A policeman with a sense of humour.'

Then she lets out a heavy sigh, stares down at the corpse, and says, 'You have gloves?' to the room.

Wade walks away to her right, then returns shortly, placing the gloves in Muir's hands. She hands me her cup with a smile, then puts on the gloves, taking pleasure in the smack of the latex, and then she starts to slowly run her fingers over the corpse, feeling the tension of the skin, and the firmness of the bones.

Wade and I watch her at work, although she's not carrying out any forensic examination into the cause of death. Presumably giving herself time to think.

Soon enough the movement of her hands across the skin of the dead boy comes to an end. She stands for a few moments, one hand on the boy's face, the other resting lightly on his stomach, and then abruptly she straightens up, removes the gloves, looks at Wade who indicates the pedal bin behind her, deposits the gloves, and goes to the sink to wash her hands.

Wade and I glance at each other while the anthropologist has her back turned, but Wade is looking sceptical and nothing else.

Tap off, Muir dries her hands on a paper towel, towel in the bin, and then she turns back to us, smiling.

'And we're done,' she says, once more approaching the body of Boy 9, who lies between us.

'What d'you think?' I ask, as she takes her coffee back with another smile.

'You're sure it's the same person?'

'All initial indications suggest as such,' says Wade. 'Still waiting on the DNA.'

'Hmm,' says Muir.

'If it's not,' I say, as I feel there might be an edge creeping in between them, 'then we're wasting your time, but we needed to cover all the bases. Since you're here, work on the basis that this is absolutely the same boy, whose body has decomposed two hundred years more or less overnight.'

'Will do, Inspector, sir,' she says, looking back at the corpse, the mock salute in her tone.

She nods, smiles to herself, then looks up at me again.

'You're an interesting guy,' she says.

'I don't think this is about me.'

'Well, maybe you don't, but this is kind of intriguing. I reckon a lot of people wouldn't even consider this. I mean, I don't mind you asking me through here 'n' all, but it's kind of a stretch. Think about it. We're examining the possibility that this body somehow magically aged two hundred years in a . . .' and she snaps her fingers. 'Now, I guess there's some possibility he's been held in a total vacuum by some miracle of early nineteenth-century engineering, and that once he was brought to the surface, he turned into baby Benjamin Button here. But, really, a total vacuum? Created out of what?'

'So, you can't give us an answer?' I say, and Muir smiles.

'No,' she says, 'I'm afraid not. Not from looking at the poor little fellow,' then she looks around, as though there might be a window out of which she can look. Deep in the basement of the hospital, however, there's nothing. She checks her watch instead. 'Long since dark, of course . . . I need to have a look at the well. Gauge the conditions out there, check out the state of the ground around the well, inside the well. I've arranged to see my sister for dinner,' and she looks up, as though this might be of interest to either of us. Neither Wade nor I reply.

'Great,' says Muir, presumably in response to herself, 'so it's all right if I go out to the well later? There's someone out there?'

'Yes,' I say.

'And there are lights and shit down the well?'

'Lights and shit, yes.'

'Awesome. Can you let them know I'm coming?' Another check of the watch. 'Some time around nine. Might end up later.'

'Why don't you do it in the morning?' I ask.

'Not staying over. Don't mind driving back late. Got the new Turin Brakes to listen to; that'll keep me going.'

Ah, she's one of my people, I think, but I don't say anything. Hardly the time.

'I might see you there,' I say. 'I need to take another look at it myself.'

'Cool. You want to coordinate?'

'No. I have something I need to do first.'

'Cool,' she repeats. 'Well, I'll see you later if it happens, otherwise . . .' and she finishes the sentence with a hand tossed to the side. 'But I've got to say, my credulous detective, that I'm not sure I'm going to find anything. I'll look for you, but unless what we've got there is a hermetically sealed, steel-lined vault . . .'

Another sentence left unfinished, and then she takes us both in with a smile, turns and walks around the body, heading for the door.

Wade waits until she's gone, and then she lifts the sheet and once more covers up the body of Boy 9, from the feet to the wasted and stretched young face.

'Baby Benjamin Button,' she says, kind of smiling. 'That was funny.'

'She's right, of course,' I say. 'The answer is far more likely to come from the SOCOs investigating the possibility of a break-in than from anthropological science.'

'I think the SOCOs will have nothing. At our peril do we ignore the possibility of witches.'

She says it without a trace of humour. I wait for the smile or the laugh, but neither come, and then I turn and head towards the door.

'Maybe you should speak to the McIntosh woman,' she says to my back, and I turn round.

'How d'you mean?'

'Remember when she walked into the tent, right at the beginning? She just stood, staring at the body. What was that about? What was she doing?'

A moment, then I say, 'You think she was casting a decomposition spell that took a few hours to kick in?'

Wade doesn't answer. A few moments later she looks down at the body, then turns back at me.

This happened, she's saying. Whatever the explanation is, it's going to be incredible.

'I'll keep the witches in mind,' I say.

'Inspector.'

And with that, back out the door.

26

A long, wet drive up the A9 to Golspie, the rain increasing in intensity as I head north. Squally rain, flashing inconsistently in from the sea. Stuck behind a bread van for over twenty minutes. Contemplate putting on the blue light and accelerating dangerously into the right-hand lane, but decide against. Patience, Inspector.

What had I been expecting from the anthropologist? Seriously, there was never going to be a scientific explanation for the body ageing so much, so quickly. Never. There seems to be so much going on, so many angles to tackle, I was doing that thing, of parking a problem until we had a little more information. We don't have to worry about that yet, because it might be this. It might be this other, utterly incredible thing that we need to get specialist input on.

There comes the time, though, when I need to address this. No bizarre ageing, no witches. The body on the slab is not our boy. Switched. Yes, that might have been the first thought that we had, almost the first thing that any of us said as the explanation for the peculiar occurrence of the wasting of the body. Darnley, for one, was very sceptical from the off. But even then, even in that moment, I know what I was thinking: this isn't what it seems, it isn't straightforward. There's something strange going on here.

From the beginning the tale of the boy in the well could have been a story from Victorian times. The strange case of the unidentified child. An explanation beyond the mundane.

And I, on the one hand happy to park the issue, was also happy to consider anything that fitted the matrix of this narrative of dark, gothic mystery.

But the anthropologist arrives, with a beautiful smile, a coffee and a Danish, and she has nothing. Of course she has nothing, and her taking a look at the well is highly unlikely to give us anything either. Bodies do not waste into oblivion overnight. However remarkable any single event or occurrence appears, there is always an unremarkable explanation. Or, at least, an explanation firmly rooted in orthodoxy.

Add a little realism to any discussion, and suddenly the last twenty-four hours of tortured thought on where this was going seem absurd. And the bonus of this particular piece of realism is that it makes sense, and helps pieces fall into place.

If the body at the mortuary is not our Boy 9, then there is a chance that it is the original Boy 9. The son of the Balfours, who went missing two hundred years ago, whose heart was placed on the doorstep in a box. Which means that someone on this blasted Black Isle kept that body all this time. And, over two hundred years, that takes organisation. It takes handing down a legacy, from one generation to the next. And at the end of that, when the body was finally given up, perhaps it was to replace the latest in the line of Balfours, who'd been killed in the same way as the boy two hundred years previously.

Along Golspie Main Street, turning off into Duke Street at the far end, on the way out of town, nearly 8 p.m. The town is deserted, everyone forced indoors by the weather. Raining heavily, largely in horizontal sheets, driven in from the sea.

I need to get the answer from Inverness on whether they've found anything amiss at the morgue. It may suddenly seem obvious that someone broke in and switched the bodies, but

I shouldn't make the same mistake again. I shouldn't latch onto a theory that sounds right, just because it's more grounded in reality. Breaking in and switching the bodies, while making it look as though nothing happened, is not in itself a straightforward task. The truth could be stranger, the truth could be even more mundane, the truth could be anything. It could be that, after four days of investigation, we are absolutely nowhere nearer the facts.

I park the car at the far end of the street, beside the bridge that crosses the Golspie Burn, and sit for a moment. Marion Stone lives in an old, converted signalling station, a single-storey, flat-roofed house that overlooks fields, with the Dornoch Firth a couple of hundred yards in the distance. Her front door is no more than ten yards away, but I will still be soaked by the time I get there.

I'm not waiting for the rain to stop, however. I'm just sitting here with a sense of this. A sense that at last we have a connection, and that the next few minutes is going to reveal the direction in which we will be heading. I need to get this right. I don't know yet how cooperative this woman will be, although she appears to have been unusually accommodating up to this point, but I need to leave here with something positive, and not let her get away with obfuscation, should I suspect that that's what she's doing.

Out the car, door locked, a quick run up the garden path and then ring the bell, standing beneath the slender awning above the door. With the rain sweeping in from the sea, driving against the other side of the house, this is as dry a spot as I'm likely to find, though my hair is already soaked from the few seconds' exposure.

The door opens to a blast of warmth, the smell of cinnamon, and a woman in her early eighties, wearing an apron.

I don't know what I'd been expecting. I don't think I'd thought about it, although my subconscious must have made up its mind. I was to be greeted by a grey-haired spinster lady, poor teeth, timeworn, smoker's skin, slightly forgetful, wearing an old red cardigan and tartan slippers, and I'd have to remind her why I was there.

'You're here,' she says. 'Lousy night for it. Shoulda waited until morning, kid, gonna be a beaut. Come through, I'm in the kitchen.'

And she turns her back on me, walks quickly along the short corridor and through the third of three doors on the right.

Looking like something from an American TV show, and with the accent to go with it, Marion Stone is gone, yet she has such a presence I can almost still feel her standing in front of me.

'Will you come in and shut the goddamn door!' she shouts from off set, and I step quickly into the house, closing the door behind me.

The corridor is narrow, with a wooden floor and a long, slim, Persian rug running its full length. On either side there is a set of four paintings, identically framed. Rothko prints.

'What're you doing out there?' she shouts. 'Just 'cause you're a cop, don't think I trust you for one damn minute.'

Smile to myself, take my jacket off, hang it on the only spare peg of four by the door, then walk through to the kitchen.

It's a small space that's been expensively redesigned, with the clean, sleek lines of a Scandinavian model kitchen, neatly and immaculately kept. There's a large window, with the blind undrawn so that you can see the rain silently streak across it, and beside it a back door. In the air, the smell of baking pie, autumnal and delicious.

On the kitchen top nearest the door are three pies, two with crust over the top, a pumpkin pie in between them. At the central island, Marion Stone is preparing more pastry, rolling it out, her movements quick and business-like, tempered by an obvious feel for her work.

A glance down at the oven reveals another pie currently cooking, and on the hob there is a pan with a lid on, steam escaping in a slender trail.

'I make pies, Inspector,' she says. 'It's my job. You can stop staring if you like.'

'Who buys the pies?' I ask.

She stops for a moment, turns to look at me with a smile, then turns back and continues rolling the pastry, before stopping, folding it in half, and rolling it out again.

'I sell direct to the consumer,' she says. 'Top of the range. You want one?'

I don't answer, looking back at the three pies sitting on the kitchen top.

'It'll set you back anywhere between thirty and fifty pounds, and there's a six-week waiting list.'

'Those must be some pies,' I say, with an accompanying low whistle.

'People pay for quality. That's how it works.'

'How many d'you make a day?'

'Seven.'

She lifts the pastry, lets it hang for a moment in its flattened state, and then lays it out on a board that's almost precisely the same size. Then she covers the pastry in greaseproof paper and places it into the large fridge to my left.

When she closes the door she looks at me for a moment, waits to see if I'm going to say anything, then turns to the cooker, lifts the lid and gives the contents a stir.

'How much d'you clear per pie?' I ask.

'An economist, eh?' she says. 'Well, why not? Ingredients average out at around seven-fifty each, so I'm clearing roughly thirty pounds across the board on any given day.'

'Thirty pounds each pie?'

'Sure. Seven pies a day, five days a week,' she says, giving me another quick glance, 'you do the math.'

'Around a thousand a week.'

'Yeah.'

'Not bad.'

'Yeah.'

'Tell me about your relatives.'

She barks out a laugh, and then puts the lid back on the pot, lays down the spoon and turns to face me.

'Perfect timing, Inspector,' she says, 'I can leave them to improve for a few moments. So you're not here to talk about pie crust?'

'You don't mind me taking a DNA sample?'

'Whatever. You're trying to find out if I'm related to this kid you found. The one no one wants?'

'That's right.'

'The young lady on the phone said there was some connection between this case and the Balfours?'

'Also correct.'

'So if you find we have common DNA, then you start investigating me in case I've got something to do with the kid dying?'

I don't immediately answer, and she smiles.

'Well, I've got nothing to hide, detective, do your worst. What d'you want? Swab from inside of the cheek?'

'That should do it.'

'But, you know, right, that I don't know who he is. I already said that to your people.'

'That's all right,' I say. 'Families are big. They split apart and go off in all sorts of directions. Maybe if you could give me as many details as you can remember about your family, and I'll take it from there.'

'Where'd you like me to start?'

She asks the question, and then looks at the oven. Opens the door, glances in at the pie, takes a small knife, gently lets it bounce off the pie crust, then closes the oven door again.

'Another five minutes,' she says, to no one in particular.

'How about you start with the accent.'

She opens the fridge and takes out yet another pie, this one complete but uncooked, and lays it on the worktop beside the cooker.

'I just put it in there for a few minutes while it was waiting,' she says, again not really directing the words at me.

'The accent?'

She mutters an affirmative, and starts to clear up various items around the kitchen, stacking the dishwasher as we talk. It could be that she wants to talk under cover of a distraction, or it could be her business-like way of making best use of her time.

'Mom and Dad moved to the States a couple of years into the war. He was in intelligence, did some sort of thing at the Pentagon. I was born in DC. When the war ended, I was one, and my folks got divorced. Dad went home, Mom stayed in DC with the reason for the divorce. His name was Brad. My stepdad. I was an only child, they never had kids.'

'What about your father? Did he remarry?'

'He did not.'

'Did he have any children?'

'Not so's I'm aware.'

'You have any cousins?'

'First cousins?'

'Any kind of cousins.'

'No cousins,' she says, clanking a glass bowl into the dishwasher. 'Small family on all sides. I'll have one of those funerals attended by a gravedigger and a dog.'

'And what about you? Is your husband still alive?'

'Ain't seen Mr Stone in fifty years.'

'But is he still alive?'

'Wouldn't know. He was an asshole back then. If he's still alive, he'll still be an asshole, and if he's dead, then he's a dead asshole. Doesn't pertain to your DNA investigation anyway, does it, Inspector? The kids you're looking for, the bloodline, would have to be mine, so it barely matters if he's still alive, has remarried, and has spent fifty years producing children on a conveyor belt.'

'And you had no children?'

'Had my moments of wanting them, but thank God those passed.'

'So, what brings you to Golspie?'

'Why d'you ask?' she says, having moved to the sink to gather up a small amount of cutlery. 'D'you think I might've spread my DNA through infection?'

'How long have you lived in Scotland, Mrs Stone?' I say, humourlessly.

'Sixteen years, give or take. Was living in Manhattan at the time of nine-eleven, then I upped and ran, you might say. Don't judge me.'

'I'm not.'

'Sure you are. Everyone judges me. Let's say I was afraid. It doesn't matter. I'm here now. I'd visited, of course. You know what us Yanks are like, can't get enough of our Scottish heritage.'

'And you're making pies.'

'That's right. Making pies.'

'So you have no idea who the nine-year-old boy at the bottom of the well in the Black Isle might be?'

'You're persistent, I'll say.'

'I didn't come all this way to talk about home baking.'

'Cute. No, Inspector, I do not know who the boy might be.'

'I'm curious why you're so happy to submit to a DNA test. Usually people are pretty reluctant.'

She looks around the kitchen, can't see anything else that needs washing, and closes the door of the dishwasher with a backwards slide of her foot.

'Nothing to hide, Inspector. You guys created a bit of a shitstorm, and I'm just trying to help you out. Truth be told, Mr Detective, I doubt I'll share DNA with the kid, and you'll be wasting your time.'

'We'll see.'

'Yes, we will.'

'Any idea how you and the boy could be related, if you are?'

'Now you're clutching.'

'I won't deny it. I've been clutching for four days now.'

'Least you're honest. Look, I lost touch with Dad for the longest time. It was inevitable given the distance in those days. Maybe he had another kid. Maybe I've got a half-sister or -brother out there, and maybe they had kids, and maybe one of those kids had another kid, and now maybe that kid is dead on a slab in your mortuary.'

'That's a lot of maybes,' I say, my voice a little forlorn.

'You asked for a wild stab in the dark,' she says, with a shrug.

'Yes,' I say, nodding, and finally I take a step away, stepping back from the interrogation.

She's right, of course. Here I am, clutching at straws, but if there is a connection between Boy 9 and Ewan Balfour – and if we accept the swapping of the bodies in the morgue, then we already have a possible connection – then there must be a connection with Balfour's descendants. Except, of course, her father wasn't one of Balfour's descendants. The line comes through her mother.

'What was your father's name?' I ask, nevertheless.

'Richard Lester,' she says.

'Like the film director?'

'That's right.'

'But not the film director?'

'No. Like I said, he was in defence intelligence.'

'Where did he live after he came back to the UK?'

'Worked in London for a time, moved to Edinburgh, then eventually ended back north. Inverness.'

'You said you lost touch for a while?'

'Sure. Saw him a few times later on. Last time, we played golf at Royal Dornoch. The Yank and her old man. Classic. It was 1976. Long hot summer, you remember it?'

'Too young.'

'We played golf, we ate dinner, and the following afternoon when I was on the flight back to New York, he had a heart attack and died. That was it for Dad.'

'Did he have a partner, a girlfriend, a—'

'A mistress with his illegitimate child? He never said, and no one came out of the woodwork after he died either.'

'You never asked if he'd had another family, another wife?'

'Nope.'

'Our best logical deduction here, though, is that there was someone,' I say.

'You said it, Sherlock, not me.'

I give her the appropriate look and she laughs.

'Right, got you, cowboy. Total cliché. Look, I got things to do, son, so if you've got any more questions, can we just get to it? These people ain't paying fifty pounds a pop for me to talk to you.'

'You said you had no cousins. That seems unlikely. Everyone has cousins.'

'Look, if you guys want to do the genealogy, go right ahead. I don't mind. I mean, you found me, so you know where to look. You dig anything up, give me a call. But honestly, for now, I've got nothing else, so let's get the swab done, and you be on your way. Shall we do it in here, or d'you want to go into the antiseptic swab room I keep in the basement?'

★   ★   ★

Five minutes later, I'm in the car, driving along Main Street on the way back south, the rain still swirling all around, wipers on full.

'Boss?' says Sutherland, picking up the phone after one ring.

'You still at work?'

'Yep, but about to head back out to the well.'

'Can you get someone to check out a guy called Richard Lester. He was Marion Stone's father. Died in '76. Worked in Washington DC during the war, came back to the UK, London, Edinburgh, ended up in Inverness. Did he have any other family, that's what we need to know?'

'A second family?'

'Yep.'

'You're thinking, that maybe Boy 9 came from that side, and there's the connection to Marion Stone?'

'Yep.'

'Does that make sense?' asks Sutherland. 'The last of the Balfours were women.'

'You're right. It was Marion Stone's mother who moved to the house in Tain from the Black Isle, married Richard Lester, and moved to the States. So, although there would be a genetic connection between Marion Stone and any potential sibling from her father, there wouldn't be the direct bloodline that we need.'

'So . . .?'

'Let's keep running with it for the moment. I got the swab from Marion Stone. I'll get it over to Inverness later. I'd like you to check out Richard Lester anyway. We need to get ahead of the game, in case we do get a positive match.'

'Right, boss, will do. Got a call from Raigmore, by the way. They said there was an anomaly in their CCTV footage from Tuesday morning. What were you looking for?'

'An anomaly? Really? Did they say what kind?'

'They're still running with it, but it looks as though there might have been finagling with the footage; you know, the classic, insert the same still footage into a five-minute time period, so that someone can do something without being watched.'

'Seriously? They're telling us this *now*? The hell have they been doing?'

There's a pause, as he obviously doesn't have an answer, and I fill the silence with an exasperated exclamation of 'Jesus!'

'It's like we're always having to say, boss,' says Sutherland, the diplomat. 'We're not a TV show . . .'

'I know.'

'You ask someone to do something, and they say sure, I'll do it. Oh, but by the way, our department was cut in half while our workload was doubled, so that thing that's really important to you, is just number three hundred and seventy-six on my to-do list.'

I make the curse silently in my head, but I know he's right. This time he allows the silence, the time for my anger to dissipate in the face of reality.

Heavy sigh, head shaking in the darkness.

'That's going to take some know-how,' I say, trying to get back on track.

'And it would've given someone time to switch the bodies. They're checking it out, but it's likely the hospital's security could've been hacked from anywhere in the world, so we needn't assume that it was an inside job or anything.'

Well, that explains that then. Twenty-four hours of running after the bizarre, down the drain. And yet, it leads us more pointedly towards a believable and manageable hypothesis. The bodies were switched, this case is linked to a 200-year-old murder, and someone somewhere has held a grudge an awful long time.

'Anything else?' he asks.

'Not yet, but I expect there will be in the next fifteen minutes.'

He laughs, we hang up, and I'm out the other side of Golspie, and driving into a torrential downpour.

27

The night flashes by, the drive long and slow. Normally it would take under an hour, but the rain still falls, the water lies on the road, pooling in places, and the cars that usually travel along here at anywhere between sixty and eighty, limp in slow procession, barely doing forty miles an hour.

Just south of Tain, close to the exit for Cafferty House, a car lies in a ditch, an ambulance and two police cars behind. The traffic slows to a single lane as we pass by, two officers out on the road, rain lashing against their fluorescent yellow jackets.

As I pass, a stretcher is being loaded into an ambulance. The head is covered, the rain drenching the shroud. Behind the body stands a young woman, her hands at her mouth, a waterproof draped ineffectually over her shoulder.

No more than fifty yards along the road is the exit to the house, and there are five people standing, watching the scene. Commune members, by the gate, looking along the road at the flashing lights, the stretcher being wheeled towards the ambulance. They could have got closer if they'd wanted to, but it's almost as though they can't leave the protection of their property, like there's a force field restricting them to within a couple of yards of the boundary of the commune.

I slow even more as I pass, and I can feel them looking into my car. And there, just for a moment, I catch her eye. Franklin. In amongst her throng, wearing a large, dark raincoat, the hood pulled up. And when we make eye contact, it's as though the traffic stops, and my car stops, and time stops, and Franklin is looking right inside me.

'*On you go, detective,*' her voice inside my head. '*On you go. Find your witches, and burn them where they lie. Where will that get you? What answers d'you think you'll find when you rake through the embers?*'

And I've passed them by, a shiver running through me, head twitching at its conclusion. Then she's behind me, and when I look in the rear-view mirror all I can see is the aftermath of the accident, the heavy rain picked out in the flashing lights of the ambulance; the slow queue of traffic, the fluorescent jackets of the officers on duty. Once again the traffic begins to pick up speed, but now, however, with everyone having been a spectator to the death on the highway, the speed is even lower.

It's not about Franklin. Franklin is mocking me. Franklin wants me to turn up on her doorstep, with a full crew. She wants her house ripped apart and her people taken into custody, she wants her stone monument dismantled, the ground beneath it burrowed into, because, ultimately, her house and her people have nothing to do with this; there will be nothing to find beneath the stones.

Grip the steering wheel, glance out to my right past the queue of cars in front, wonder about making the dash up the outside lane. Yes, I'm in a hurry, because I want to get back down that well tonight, but the well is not going anywhere. The road is dangerous this evening, and more than one car, and more than one person will end up broken in a ditch.

There's no reason why the well can't wait until tomorrow, of course, except I had determined that it would be done tonight, and if it's not, then I will go to bed, restless and uncertain, aware that I didn't do everything I'd set myself. It will feel indolent, the day unfulfilled.

Lights flash by in the opposite direction, blurring in the rain. The road becomes monotonous, the wipers on full, water splashed up from the car in front, rain, impelled by the wind, swirling in off the coast.

My thoughts seem to blur with the lights. I could be using the drive to think this through, assemble the pieces into some sort of order. Maybe that part of my brain has already decided that there's enough order been established for now. The bodies must have been switched, we have our connection to the historical death, the coldest of cold cases, and we are one step closer to knowing how this investigation plays itself out.

'They say you can talk to the dead.'

I look in the rear-view mirror. Nothing to see here. Just Boy 9 staring back at me, his face colourless, lips thin and pale, his eyes dark and full of sorrow. There is a collar around his neck, the dark blue of a polo shirt maybe, but I can't see what he's wearing.

I look back at the road.

'Is that right?' he asks after a few moments. 'Can you talk to the dead, Inspector?'

Does engaging him make him real? Does it make this situation real? Lights flash by, rain falls, the steady drone of a car travelling at thirty-six miles per hour in fourth gear.

After a while I glance in the mirror to see if he's still there. Eyes back to the road. The car in front. The rear lights and the plume of rainwater.

'Yes,' I say eventually.

'Well, why can't you talk to me?' he asks.

I don't look in the mirror this time. There's something about the eyes. I should be looking at blue eyes. The boy in the well, Boy 9, had blue eyes. This kid sitting in the back seat, his eyes are much darker. Drained of the soul, they are also drained of colour, drawing in all the life around them, banishing it into darkness.

'I'm talking to you now,' I say.

'No you're not.'

I keep my eyes forward.

'You could have asked me what was going on,' he says. 'You could have asked me how I came to be at the bottom of the well. You could have asked me how it is that no one knows who I am.'

And he's right, I can't ask him now. The words, the questions, form in my head and in my mouth, but they have no outlet. Because I can't speak to him, even though I have so often imagined myself speaking to the dead, even though some of those words escape from my lips.

'Who is the Beige Man?' I say, and I risk another quick glance back. The face does not change.

This time it is Boy 9 who does not answer, and we drive on in silence for a while. The detective, staring fixedly on the blurred lights of a red Toyota Corolla, and the dead child, who can't possibly be sitting in the back of the car.

'They say you can talk to the dead,' says the boy.

Didn't he say that before? Yes, he did. At the beginning. That was the first thing he said. Maybe he's come full circle, and will now be gone.

Another look in the mirror says otherwise.

'I tried speaking to you before,' he says.

'Tell me now.'

'I told you it was the wall. That's all.'

'When?'

'I told you. Bodies don't just appear magically at the bottom of a well. Not now. Not in these times.'

Like there was a time when this did happen?

'You have everything anyway,' he says. 'You just have to put it together.'

I glance back in the mirror. The dark eyes are still there, still staring at my reflection. For the first time I begin to feel the hairs standing on the back of my neck. The look lasts a little longer, and when I finally turn back to the road I have to hit the brakes for the first time in a while.

The car in front moves away to a safe twenty yards, and I speed up again.

'You know it's the Beige Man,' he says.

Yes. I do know it's the Beige Man. I don't know how it's the Beige Man, and I don't know how I'm supposed to know.

'Look at the wall. Find the Beige Man.'

I look back in the mirror.

Now he's gone.

Another shiver courses through me, I check the gap to the car in front, and now I turn round properly and look in the back seat.

A half-drunk bottle of water, a damp waterproof coat, a foot pump lying on the floor.

I turn back to the road. The car in front. The rear lights, and the plume of rainwater.

The boy in the well. That's where it started, that's where the answers will be. The boy himself, of course, if the body has been switched, is missing. Haven't even begun to get into that, and it's another great complication that I'm still some way away from sorting through. But if not him, if not that body, then perhaps the answer lies up here, on the side of the hill, at the edge of a field by an old farmhouse building.

I drive up the lane of the farmhouse and park the car to the left, facing the house. The lights are out, the place is dark. It does not look as though Belle McIntosh is home.

There are two cars, one of which is Sutherland's. The other I don't recognise, and assume that it must belong to Muir, the anthropologist. I glance over at the tent, grey in the darkness, but there is little sign of life. The officer who should be on watch is not present, although there is a light shining inside.

Get out the car, grabbing the waterproof as I go, and put it on even as the rain soaks into my coat. The night is cold, and perhaps it's not so far from this rain being sleet, the wet ground turning white.

I get a torch from the boot, aim it at the ground in front of me, and start walking quickly around the side of the house, towards the gate that leads into the field.

I stop for a moment, as I close the gate behind me. Turn and look down over the land, towards the firth. There's little to see through the dark and the rain. Having put the hood up on the jacket when I'd put it on half a minute ago, I now push it back and let the rain soak my hair. Rub my eyes, look round at the house, then turn back towards the tent.

The beam of a torch flashes across the fabric of the top of the tent from inside, then turns away and is gone and I quickly start walking across the field, my own torch illuminating the sodden grass before me.

The sound of the tent in the wind is loud now, the closer I get. Hesitate outside for a moment, and then pull back the flap.

Muir, the anthropologist, is sitting with her legs dangling over the side of the well. Sutherland is kneeling down, examining a stone in the side wall. Constable Ross is standing back, his arms folded.

'Hey,' says Muir.

There's something peculiar about her, then I realise it's because she's completely dry. A quick glance around the tent, and what are obviously her waterproofs are dumped casually in a pile in the corner.

'Sir,' says Sutherland, looking up, and then he stands as I more fully enter the tent, closing and securing the flap behind me.

'You been down?' I ask Muir.

The well is illuminated, and as I ask, I stand over it, staring down to the bottom of the shaft.

'Nah,' says Muir. 'The constable here wouldn't let me go down without wearing enough safety equipment for a space station worth of astronauts. Anyway, I think we're good here. It's just a well. Nothing to get excited about, nothing to change my original diagnosis.'

'Thank you,' I say. 'Sorry if your trip through was a waste of time.'

'Hey, it's cool,' she says.

'It was a stretch.'

'A change is as good as a rest, right?' she says, smiling, then adds, 'No cliché left unturned.'

'If you don't mind me asking,' I say, 'what was that back at the morgue? You apologised to Dr Wade.'

'Did I?' she asks curiously.

'You said sorry when you mentioned the Dr Wade through in Aberdeen.'

'Oh, that. No, I wasn't apologising, I was saying sorry. You know, for what happened.'

I ask the question with a raised eyebrow.

'Sure, of course,' she says. 'Wasn't like it was on the news. There was a thing. She was in a relationship with someone at the hospital. Another doctor. Her partner killed herself. The story was a little vague, there was talk of another woman. It was . . . you know, it was kind of sad, that's all.'

'Right,' is all I manage, feeling as though I've intruded into Wade's life, learning too much along the way.

Everyone's got a story, after all, and that was one I didn't need to know.

'Anyway,' I say. 'Sorry for dragging you through, nevertheless.'

'Really, it's cool. And I had *the* best steak-frites for dinner you ever had in your life.'

'Yeah?' says Sutherland, looking up. 'Where was that?'

'Sergeant,' I say, though without my common sharpness.

'Sir,' he says, and he glances at her apologetically.

'D'Olivera's,' she says, anyway. 'It was awesome.'

Sutherland swallows, tries not to look too interested.

'You found something?' I say to him, rubbing the water from my face again.

'Not really,' he says. 'I was wondering . . . there are a couple of loose stones here, and they seemed pretty small, but I was wondering if they could've squeezed his body through them. But as soon as you start thinking about that, and it seems obvious, then you have to ask yourself why there were no marks on the body, no trace at least of the corpse having been dragged through stone.'

'I was thinking about that,' I say, and I bend down to take a look at the stone that Sutherland was studying when I entered, running my fingers around its edge.

'We're still waiting to hear from Lyle?' I ask.

'Yeah,' says Sutherland.

We exchange a glance, in which we silently repeat the discussion we had over the phone about how busy every single publicly funded department is.

'Do you still call them SOCOs or does everyone call them CSI now 'cause of the TV shows?' asks Muir from the wall.

Sutherland waits to see if I'm going to answer, then says, 'Either. Doesn't matter.'

'So, how does this sound?' I say, ignoring their conversation. 'The stone was carefully eased out. The body was then put inside a tube of some description. A strong plastic, something that wouldn't tear. He was placed in the hole and squeezed through, pushed out the other end of the tube. He plummets down to the bottom of the well, the tubing is removed and disposed of, the stone is placed back into the gap, but not re-fixed with any new adhesive. We noticed it, this loose stone, but we weren't completely focused on it because it's such a small space.'

Sutherland bends down beside me now. We know the stone was removed and placed back in position by Lyle's people, but there's no need for us to force it out again now. The size of the space is evident.

'It's not terribly exciting,' I say, 'but it makes sense. Sure, there might've been residue from the wall dislodged, which would've fallen down into the pit, but then the same would've happened when the cover was removed.'

'How would they have known we wouldn't notice it straight away, though?' says Sutherland. 'Any attempt to cover their tracks would have made it obvious that they'd covered their tracks, so they just had to hope we didn't see it.'

'Maybe it didn't matter. They knew McIntosh and Lachlan were going to be opening up the well, so they were happy for the body to be found.'

'Why not just rip the cover off?' he asks.

'They had this plan all along. To create the mystery of how the body got down there. Maybe we work it out, but it's not a great explanation. It's not definite. And then they switch the corpses at the hospital, and it creates the link between the two, and sets us off in a particular direction.'

Hands in pockets, I look down into the well again, as though the answer is suddenly going to be lying there.

'Which means we're kind of ruling out McIntosh and Lachlan,' says Sutherland.

'Unwitting stooges perhaps,' I say. 'But we're not ruling out Catriona Napier.'

'Yep,' says Sutherland. 'Then someone found out it was her, and ...' and he finishes the sentence with a pointed thumb dragged across his neck.

'If Catriona Napier was trying to tell us something, why not just tell us? If she wanted us to know, but didn't want someone else to find out that she'd told us, why plant the clue on her own property? That . . .' and I look up, shaking my head.

Ross, Sutherland and I share the look, the one that says there's thinking being done, that someone has to have an idea. Dredge it up, toss it out, it doesn't matter what it is. If it's easily dismissed, then fine, and we move on to the next hypothesis.

'Constable?' I say to Ross, recognising that he's swithering over throwing something into the mix. 'Spit it out.'

He makes the measured face of someone stating some-thing in which they don't have a lot of confidence, then says, 'Maybe the well's the clue.'

'Keep talking,' I say, when he leaves it at that.

'We examined the closed-off wells. She didn't even have to suggest to us that we look to see if there are any others, we did it anyway. Maybe this was a way of saying, you know, look at the other wells. Look at them! Napier knew this well would be opened, so she prepared the ground.'

'Why?'

A beat.

He naturally doesn't have an answer to that.

'We'll need to look at the other wells to find out,' says Sutherland.

'You did that already.'

'Yes, but what were we looking for? We didn't know. We basically made sure there wasn't a dead body lying at the bottom.' He pauses, and then shrugs. 'Maybe we missed something.'

Check my watch. Already well after nine thirty.

'Seems a hell of a convoluted way to send us off in any direction,' I say.

'We can't say that yet,' says Sutherland, 'as we don't know which direction we're actually going in.'

Smile grimly. 'Yes,' I say, 'can't argue with that.'

'You want to go and look at them now, or leave it until the morning?'

I give him a single, raised eyebrow in reply, and he nods.

'Torrential rain, late evening stretching into the middle of the night, bitter cold . . .' he says. 'Why wait until the sun's shining?'

'Lives could be at stake, Sergeant.'

'How many of us d'you want?'

Phone starts ringing, and I take it out my pocket and check the call. Fisher.

'I don't want to turn up anywhere heavy-handed. You know where you're going, right?' He nods. 'You and me'll do.'

'Yes, boss.'

'Fish?' I say, answering the phone.

I catch Muir's eye as I do so, and she smiles and swings her legs back over the side of the wall.

'My work here is done,' I hear her say to Sutherland.

'Sir,' says Fisher. 'I've tracked down Richard Lester for you. Didn't take long. He was convicted of fraud in 1973, so he was on file.'

'Fraud?'

'Very minor case involving the Post Office. Anyway, it just served to make him easier to find.'

'OK, good. How about the family?'

'Yes, there's something positive there too. He had a daughter, although there is no record of who the mother was. Or indeed when the daughter was born. I'll keep looking.'

'And did the daughter have any family?'

'She married, and she had one child named Elizabeth,'

says Fisher. 'Elizabeth is also married, now called Rhodes, doesn't look like there are any children. In fact, pretty sure it's Councillor Rhodes's wife. He was in the office today, I think. Small world, or do you think there's a connection?'

A few moments, then she says, 'Sir?'

28

'But I thought we decided that the bloodline had to come down through the mother? This wouldn't make sense.'

'No, it doesn't.'

'So what are you thinking?'

'There's too much we don't know. But this can't possibly be a coincidence.'

'It could be,' says Sutherland. 'She's just some woman whose office we chose to go to. That was entirely coincidental.'

'But then, there's the Beige Man business. Back-to-back coincidences don't happen. That's not chance, that's a pattern.'

A moment, then Sutherland says, 'The Beige Man, sir?'

I can feel him looking at me. I didn't blurt it out, it was a controlled release of the information, but he obviously isn't going to know what I'm talking about.

The tenuous link. The unnatural thread running through the strange case of the boy in the well.

We are closing in on the Rhodes's house, just outside Culbokie, travelling together, Sutherland having left his car back at the farmhouse. One car slithering through the night is quite enough. The decision to come here before visiting any of the well sites was related to immediacy of location rather than time.

'It was a story Elizabeth told me.'

'Yes?'

We approach the house. The road is in the lee of a hill, and the rain, swirling less in the wind, a more consistent downpour. As I pull up across the road, I can see there are no lights on.

'About a man on Nairn beach. She used to see him every day. The same man, dressed in beige, seeming to slowly disappear into the sand. Her dog disappeared, and this man, the Beige Man, brought it back.'

I say that without looking at him, then turn to gauge his reaction. Unsurprisingly, he looks puzzled.

'I'm not sure where this is going, sir,' he says.

'I know, as a story it was strange. It didn't make any kind of sense. But I'm sure she was trying to tell me something. This man, this mysterious figure, is an actual person. There is a someone, a real someone, that this character represents.'

'What?'

'And the story of the dog. There's something going on with the dog.'

'Sir?'

He's half-smiling as he looks at me, but he's no less puzzled. Rightly so, as I'm not making it easy for him.

'It was just a story that Elizabeth told, and one that I've been struggling to see the point of. But then Alex told us Catriona Napier's last words, and since then the story of the Beige Man has been in my head: *the Sandman's coming for me.*'

A moment while Sutherland processes this, putting these two things together. Finally, he shakes his head.

'She just meant she was tired,' he says. 'I don't even know that it counts as a coincidence.'

'Someone obviously *was* coming for her, though. She was dead the next day.'

I say it with more conviction than I feel. I've squeezed the narrative into the appropriate box, now I need to know what Sutherland thinks of it.

'Elizabeth Rhodes told me a story about a Beige Man,' I say, when Sutherland still doesn't say anything. 'A Beige Man *on the sand*. A Sandman, though she didn't use that term. OK, just a story, nothing more. But then today we hear that Napier spoke of the Sandman. It seemed a peculiar coincidence, yet it felt like I was forcing the two things together. It felt like it needed something more. And now we find that Elizabeth might be related to Boy 9, and I wonder, just how much more is it that we want?'

He doesn't immediately reply, and I give him a few seconds.

'Shoot me down, Sergeant,' I say eventually.

He doesn't look at me, brow furrowed, thinking it through.

'We'll need to wait and see,' he says.

'That's all you've got?'

He turns to look at me, face expressionless.

'When did she tell you this? You interviewed her on Tuesday evening?'

A moment, then I open the car door.

'Doesn't look like there's anyone in,' I say, pivoting away from Elizabeth Rhodes, 'but we can ring the bell. Just stay here, there's no need for us both to get soaked.'

Out the car, door closed, running up the garden path, Sutherland ignoring my instruction, slamming his door and running just behind me.

Ring the bell, huddled by the door, no cover, the rain coming down straight upon us. I give it little more than a second or two and then bang the door, an act of impatience rather than anything else. If they're here, they'll hear the bell.

'It's not just the lights,' says Sutherland. 'You can feel there's no one in.'

'Yep. Come on.'

Back down the path, throw my waterproof, for what it is now worth, into the back seat, and we're back off along the road.

'Which well are we going to stand in the rain getting soaked next to first?' asks Sutherland, after he's struggled to get his coat off, slung it in the back and buckled up.

Steady through the rain, we'll head towards the A9, up to the roundabout at Tore, then a left towards Fortrose.

'You looked into two of them already. We need to check out the house first, then we'll double-check the others.'

'I was thinking that was the one we'd leave until morning. They might not appreciate us turning up at their door at ten at night. Not that the council'll appreci—'

'They might not, but that's what they're getting.'

'What's the plan? I mean, the well is beneath the foundations. They said it'd been filled in, concreted over.'

'But you didn't get a visual on that?'

'Did I get a visual on the foundations?'

'Yes.'

'No.'

'You looked in the basement, though?' I ask, aware of his annoyance.

'I checked the basement. Like I said, there was a floor covering. But it did look like a permanent floor covering. Nothing to get us suspicious, particularly since the reason we were there was entirely speculative. But, you're right, sir, I didn't get down on my hands and knees and inspect the floor.'

'Of course,' I say, trying to take the edge out the conversation. 'You had no reason to. And maybe we have no further reason to now, but we're going to go and do it and they can lump it.'

He doesn't say anything, retreating into silent agitation. There's no need for me to say anything else, no need to reassure him or to chastise him. The business will be resolved soon enough, either way, though it's impossible to know what we'll find, even if we're right about Catriona Napier attempting to steer us in a particular direction.

No other cars in sight as we turn left onto the A9, rivers of rain running either side of the road down the slope towards us.

In silence until we're almost at the roundabout, though Sutherland's restlessness is obvious. Fingers tapping on his knees, constant looks out the side window at the dark wet of evening flitting past.

'So, we're going with the idea that the body was pushed through that small gap?' he says, finally, after we're through the other side and heading along the A832 to Fortrose.

'I think it's possible. We need those test results from Lyle.'

'Yeah, poor bastard. I'll give him a call first thing. It could be that we were focused on the cover; they picked up on that focus, and hadn't paid so much attention to the stones in the side.'

As he says it, he shakes his head, as though he's constructing a reason to cover for Lyle and his team.

'What d'you mean, poor bastard?'

'You haven't heard?'

I don't immediately reply, as the answer is obvious, though he seems to wait for me to say something.

'Maybe I'm not supposed to have heard,' I say finally.

'Don't think it's a secret. Anyway, his boyfriend's HIV. He's waiting to hear about himself. I mean, there's so much they can do, it's not the death sentence it used to be . . . God, that's such a twat-brained cliché, isn't it? It's not a death sentence! Great! Let's all get HIV! Anyway, still . . . you can imagine.'

'Crap,' I say, voice low.

I'd forgotten about Lyle, his demeanour when I was in his office a couple of days ago. Too many other things going on. I left his office meaning to get in touch with him again, to see if he wanted to go for coffee, or at least to have a chat that wasn't about work. Instead, the case took over, as cases always do, and I'd not thought about him again.

Not that that will make any difference to Lyle, of course. That's all about me, and I need to not think about it. There are enough things to beat oneself up about in life.

'That doesn't sound like something he'd want everyone to know. I mean, really.'

'Elvis told me, he'd heard from Andy in Lyle's office. And he's been talking about it on Facebook.'

'Lyle?'

'Yep. You know what he's like. Forty going on fifteen. Everything goes on Facebook. A life lived in public.'

'I spoke to him three days ago and he wasn't saying anything.'

'Hmm,' says Sutherland. 'He probably presumed you knew and was bummed you didn't commiserate with him.'

'Jesus,' I say.

Shake my head at the thought, although I don't think that was it.

Lurch back into silence. A car approaches us in the other direction, the water sprayed from our wheels clashing as we pass.

'How long have they been together?' I ask.

Agitated. Need the conversation, though don't need to be talking so much. Just listening. Just the sound of something else to help concentrate the mind, driving through this dreadful weather, no real idea of what we're heading towards.

Logical thinking suggests nothing, because I'm not sure it was logical thinking that helped us get to this point. Standing back in that tent, the three of us aided by the young anthropologist, who walked in out of nowhere to point us in the right direction, and will likely not be seen again, everything seemed to fall into place. Now, however, twenty minutes detached, warm and damp in the car, trying not to skid, trying not to have to drive too slowly, it seems like we're stretching. We, like all detectives in this situation, want something to happen, and so we twist and contort and bend, hoping that what we're twisting, contorting and bending doesn't break.

'Don't know,' says Sutherland.

The conversation doesn't happen. Past Munlochy, on towards Avoch, a drive that should be little more than ten minutes, taking double that. Wheels twitching, the car constantly aquaplaning. I think of the car at the side of the road just south of Tain.

Muir's smiling, casual face enters my head. So down to earth, so instantly part of the team. Seemingly of little use given that she had no explanation for the decomposition, yet a nil return that somehow helped steer us in the right direction. Or, at least, in a direction that feels right.

Maybe when we finally get back to the station this evening there'll be a report waiting for me. She died in a car crash on the A96 earlier this afternoon. Car crumpled from the side, body crushed, the seatbelt and airbag of no use. She's another Sanderson, delivered to the investigation from death.

Maybe she's just an intelligent young woman, with more common sense than I frequently bring to an investigation. That's probably more likely. Not everyone's dead.

There's a thought.

'When did you interview Mrs Rhodes?' asks Sutherland. 'I mean, was it an interview, or were you just chat—'

Sharp intact of breath, from us both, as I nearly lose it coming through Avoch, past the Post Office onto the shore road. Foot off the accelerator, slow without braking, regain control, straighten up, and back onto the left side of the road, glad there had been nothing coming in the opposite direction.

'Shit, sorry, Iain.'

'That's all right. Maybe if you could stop somewhere for me to change my underwear . . .'

We both laugh, forced, nervous.

'I'll slow down,' I say, stating the obvious, as I haven't picked up to the same speed as before.

We drive on, just the short stretch of the shore to go between the two towns, water lying in great puddles now on either side of the road. As we've driven from the farm, via the Rhodes's house, the tension seems to have increased with each passing, slowly driven minute. Is it just the weather, or is it the knowledge, or the sense at least, of what awaits us at the other end?

'You're avoiding the question, sir,' he says.

I have to think back, to that time which seems much earlier, before I nearly skidded off the road, to try to remember what the question was.

Elizabeth.

'We talked yesterday,' I say.

I can feel him looking at me. Some espionage officer I used to be. Shorn of the skills through lack of use.

'Just talked?' he says.

'We talked, yes.'

'I don't understand about the Beige Man,' he says. 'A metaphor of a guy disappearing into the sand? What kind of conversation were you having?'

Pinned down. Trapped behind the wheel. A conversation that can't really be avoided. A conversation that I introduced, after all. Alec, my old boss back at Vauxhall, would be shaking his head. *Walked right into it, Ben*, he'd be thinking. *Rookie error.*

'It was a half-asleep conversation at the end of the evening,' I say.

'Oh.'

'I wouldn't have been having the half-asleep conversation if I'd thought that this was somehow going to lead us back to her door, and I certainly wouldn't have been there if I'd thought that Councillor Rhodes was going to be turning up in Quinn's office telling us how to run the investigation . . .'

'The two aren't related?'

'I don't know,' I say, shaking my head.

Shaking my head at myself, my own stupidity. Not that, on the face of it, it was stupid at the time, but it looks nothing but stupid in retrospect.

'But then, if she hadn't told me the story of the Beige Man, I would have thought nothing of Catriona Napier's *Sandman* remark.'

He doesn't say anything, but I know he's thinking that maybe there's nothing to think of that Sandman remark anyway.

The lights of Fortrose begin to glow more brightly through the murk, although perhaps glow is not the word. Blurred images of light, indistinct in the darkness. We're done now for conversation, nothing to be said until we arrive at the house.

Into town, take the left as indicated by Sutherland, right and then another left into a small street, the large house at the far end of a cul-de-sac. A few cars are parked on either side of the road outside the house, three more in the driveway.

'They're really going to love us,' says Sutherland.

'All the best parties get police call-outs.'

'Yeah.'

Park the car untidily out on the street, glance at Sutherland as I turn off the engine and pull the handbrake on, take a moment before subjecting ourselves once more to the rain, and then, with the peculiar feeling of nervousness growing stronger by the second, out the car, doors shut, a quick run up the front garden path, and we huddle together beneath the small awning.

'Are we fit, Sergeant?'

'Fit,' he says, and he smiles and pushes the button.

The doorbell rings with a dull tone.

29

'Nothing better to do on a dark, wet Thursday night on the Black Isle, Inspector?'

The house is quiet, neither sight nor sound of revellers, or committee members or party members or church elders, or whatever it is that this is a gathering of.

'We'd like to look at the basement, please.'

Jack Rollins, yet to allow us over the front door, takes a step back, folding his arms at the same time.

'Really?' he says. 'Your sergeant was here this morning.'

He glances at Sutherland as he says it.

'We want to see the exact area where the well was covered,' I say.

Play it straight, don't give them anything to rise to. Standard procedure when looking to effect entry. Not that rising doesn't usually take place anyway.

'The well was filled in, the top of the well cemented over. There's nothing to see in the basement.'

'We'd like to see the basement,' I repeat, deadpan. There's not a discussion to be had. I don't care what his position is in this one-horse town.

He's sizing me up, wondering how far to take it. Impossible to tell at this point whether or not it's because he's hiding something, or if he just objects to the police turning up at his door at ten o'clock on a Thursday evening. The latter, I have to admit, is not unjustified.

'Do you have a warrant?'

'No.'

Give it a moment to see what he's going to do with that information. It would be easy enough for him to tell us to leave, but then, of course, we'll be back, there will be more of us and our presence will be much more evident. It doesn't always need explaining.

'And you think it's all right just to turn up on the evening of a private dinner party? You do know who I am, Inspector? You do know the name Jack Rollins? You do know that, inside this house, through that door there, is Councillor Rhodes, with whom I'm sure you're familiar? There may be others here who would also be of interest to you.'

Jesus, the bullshit you get from people. I've met Jack Rollins on at least four separate occasions before, but he still has to do the *You do know the name Jack Rollins?* line, implying that we've never met, and that, even if we had, he wouldn't remember me. Which I also know is bullshit.

'The evening, just like the private dinner party, is irrelevant,' I say, voice level. 'We're in the middle of a murder investigation, and while there's nothing here to implicate you or anything about this property in the investigation, as I'm sure you'll be aware, investigations are as much about eliminating strands and people and places, and—'

'And there's a reason this house was not eliminated after your sergeant's visit?'

'Sergeant Sutherland carried out a cursory inspection to establish the whereabouts of the well. Further evidence has come to light in our current enquiry, and now we wish to carry out a more thorough investigation.'

'Even though you have been repeatedly told that there's nothing to investigate?'

I have a banal line on the tip of my tongue – *there's always something to investigate*, or some such – but decide to rely on the even greater police cliché of silence. He holds my gaze for a few moments, his lips tightening as we stand there, playing the testosterone game. The *who will crack and who will hold fast* of it.

I really don't want to have to go and get a warrant, not at this time of night, not for this property with this guy. And it wouldn't happen tonight anyway, of course. The warrant would be requested tomorrow, and questions would be asked, explanations demanded, and his party affiliation would be brought up and added to the muddle of bullshit that this kind of thing inevitably leads to. And it might just be that the warrant wouldn't be granted, and the likelihood is that he's standing here working out the odds.

A door opens behind him, and a woman enters the hall and approaches. Without turning, Rollins moves to the side and allows her the space to stand beside him. Like Elizabeth Rhodes before her, I also recognise Jill Rollins from the *Journal*.

'Mrs Rollins,' I say, nodding.

She stares at us for a while, seeming to immediately fit into the silence that has descended over the doorway, while her husband decides how this thing is going to go.

'The police would like to search the basement, again,' says Rollins. 'Apparently they didn't get a good enough look this morning. Hard to imagine what they were doing down there . . . They're just leaving.'

'That's all right,' says his wife.

There's a tenseness about her, which is hard to pin down, but then, there are plenty of people who'd be tense under these circumstances. We have to aim off for the fact that our presence can do that.

'What is?' asks Rollins.

'Let them in, they can look all they want. If we turn them away now, they'll only be back, making things awkward at some other time.'

She takes a step back from the door, without taking her eyes from me. Rollins finally turns and looks at her.

'We have guests,' he says.

'I'm sure the officers will be quiet. Let them in.'

Another step backwards, something unreadable about her face, and then Rollins turns back, his demeanour instantly changing.

'Great,' he says, as though a switch has been flicked. 'Your sergeant knows where to go. I'll ask that you make as little noise as possible.'

And with the sudden acquiescence he turns, ushers his wife ahead of him, and walks down the corridor and through a door at the side.

Walking along the corridor we glance into the side room. They did not close the door behind them. There are people standing around. After-dinner drinks. A large glass with a small amount of cognac, whisky on the rocks, a Baileys. A waiter in a black waistcoat, guests in small groups.

I catch her eye, just for a moment. Elizabeth. The moment seems to extend, almost as though I was walking in slow motion. Like the moment I caught the eye of Franklin, the witch; the same yet so different. A scene from a film, a passing glance, not enough time for the look to develop into anything, or for me to see to whom she's talking. A look, so fleeting, time slowed down, and then a rush of reality, and I'm beyond the doorway, the glance is broken, and we're walking quickly along the corridor to the door that leads down to the basement.

I can't turn back, I can't walk in there to talk to her. What would I say anyway, in front of all those people? *We need to talk about the Beige Man.*

We enter a study at the back of the house, a dark room, lit by a single lamp on a table beside a wooden Chesterfield sofa. There is a desk by the window, but I know that the window looks out onto the wood behind, and so will not get much light, at any time of day. There is another two-seat sofa, a single, winged armchair, an ottoman, the walls lined with books.

The room looks flawless, like the picture-perfect study in a photograph on the back page of a Sunday supplement. An advert for wooden flooring, or a twenty-five-part encyclopaedia available in monthly instalments of £9.99, or bespoke globes, or hand-crafted scale models of tall ships.

At the back of the room there is a railing, with a set of wooden steps leading downstairs, and I follow Sutherland as he flicks a light switch on the way down. The stairs double back on themselves, at the bottom of which there is another door.

'This is us,' says Sutherland, then he opens the door, hits the light switch inside, and we walk into the basement room together.

Unsurprisingly, given the room upstairs, this is not the dusty, undecorated dingy basement of popular perception. Walls painted off-white, a couple of film posters on each – *Casablanca* and *Apocalypse Now*, *Fight Club* and *The Godfather* among them – the floor carpeted, an old music system against the wall, and a bar billiards table against the other. A drinks cabinet, a dartboard and, tucked unused in a corner, an exercise bike.

'What's through there?' I ask, indicating the wooden door, in between the posters for *You Only Live Twice* and *Goldfinger*.

'Storage,' says Sutherland. 'I looked in there too.'

And he opens the door, standing back for me to see in.

A large pantry, three rows of shelves stacked with drinks, water, canned food, with shelves against the walls at the back, laden with a more eclectic range of items, dumped down here out of the way. I walk inside, taking a closer look at the tiled floor.

'The well's exact position? It was under here, or in there?' I ask.

'Here,' says Sutherland, indicating the sitting-room part of the basement, in which he still stands.

I walk back through, closing the pantry door behind me. Pause for a moment, getting a peculiar feeling of unease. Look around the room, at the faces on the posters, at the records lying on top of the music cabinet.

'The exact spot?' I ask, and Sutherland shakes his head.

'D'you suppose it's under there?' I say, indicating the wooden music centre, large cabinets either side of the turntable, with an old-fashioned radio panel on the front of the unit.

'I didn't think,' says Sutherland, trying to see what he missed.

'It's on wheels,' I say.

'Crap.'

'It's not unusual for furniture to have wheels, of course, but it's worth a look.'

We take an end each of the unit and start to move it away from the wall. It comes easily, on well-used wheels. I reach behind and unplug it as it goes. A few feet away from the wall, and then we both move behind the unit to look at the floor.

There is a rectangle cut into the carpet. Sutherland curses. He bends quickly, lifts it, and there's the trapdoor, a metal ring flush within the hatch.

'Crap,' says Sutherland again.

'We've got it now.'

He bends to start lifting the door, gives me a look, and I nod for him to go ahead. He raises the door, and already, even without the light on, it's possible to see how this shaft differs from the well at the McIntosh Farm. A moment, and then Sutherland reaches in, finds the light switch at the top of the shaft and flicks it on.

'Jesus,' he says.

I look down into it, staring all the way to the well-lit bottom.

'Shit,' I say. 'That lying bastard. Come on.'

First foot, second foot down into the hole, about to descend into the pit. And then the voice comes from behind.

'Ben, what in the name of God d'you think you're doing?'

Turn quickly, and there he is. The boss. Quinn, a guest at the party.

I'm standing on the third rung inside the hole; he is standing alone on the bottom step of the stairs. Sutherland takes a step back, retreating from the fray. This isn't going to be his fight.

We stare angrily at each other for a moment, Quinn and I, and then I lift myself back up out of the pit.

'Look at it,' I say. 'Come here and look at it.'

Upstairs there is the sound of movement. The shuffling of feet, low conversation.

'Dammit, people are leaving,' I say.

'You think?' snaps Quinn.

'Sergeant, get upstairs and stop them. I want to know who's here, and I don't want anyone leaving. And put a call through, get some back-up out here.'

'Stay where you are, Sergeant,' says Quinn slowly.

Sharp breath, teeth clamped hard together, Quinn and I staring harshly at each other, both of us bristling with anger, and poor, bloody Sutherland, stuck in the middle.

'Iain,' I say, needing to get him out of his hole, but not wanting to back down myself, 'go upstairs. Don't stop them leaving, but I at least want to know who's here. And search the house, I want to know if there's anyone hiding anywhere.'

Quinn's knuckles are white, but he doesn't look at Sutherland, and when, finally, Sutherland turns away, he doesn't stop him.

Sutherland's footfalls on the stairs, then he disappears from view, and Quinn and I are alone in the basement.

A long silence, we can hear Sutherland's low voice coming from the ground floor, and then Quinn says, 'You don't think I would have told you who was upstairs, Inspector?'

Right at this moment, beyond my immediate team, I don't think I trust anyone.

'Come here,' I say coldly, 'and look at this.'

Jaws clenched, the anger still hot in his eyes, he steps forward.

30

We stand, the two of us, looking down into the well. Or what, at one point, would have been a well. Now it is a well-lit, steel-lined shaft, a dark grey ladder running the full length, with a full-sized metal door at the bottom. This shaft, which has had a lot of money spent on it, was designed to go somewhere. Somewhere strange, somewhere out of reach, and somewhere that they didn't want anyone to know about.

'Look at it,' I say to Quinn again, voice harsh, staring down into the shaft, about to resume climbing down the ladder. Pointless, heated words, as he is already looking.

He's standing a couple of inches from me, and I can feel his anger, and my own anger continues to rise at his attitude, his bearing. All in it together, I think, even if I can hardly be considered to be so detached from the establishment. But here they are, Rhodes and Rollins and our own chief inspector and God knows who else, all comfortably spending the evening together, you scratch my back and I'll scratch yours, like a Davos of the Dingwall elite – ha! – dividing up the town between them; the kind of evening that would have Belle McIntosh pointing and saying, *I told you so*.

'Did you ask him why it's there?' he says, voice seething.

'How could I?' I snap. 'He denied it even existed. Jesus.'

Shake my head, although it's more of an angry twitch, and don't even look at him. What would be the point in going back upstairs to speak to Rollins now? Just to give him another chance at obfuscation and deceit?

Legs into the shaft, turn, and then start descending the ladder.

'Inspector,' says Quinn, more slowly, 'did you ask Councillor Rollins what's down there?'

I stop for a second, staring straight at the steel wall of the shaft, a few inches before me. There was a slight change in his tone that time, and now, finally, I get the sense of it.

I don't know what I'm going to find down here, but I'd presumed it would be another dead child, or a clue to our first dead child. It would be something that validated how I've been leading this investigation, an endorsement of the way I've taken the disparate pieces and slotted them into place; it would be something that had made Rollins need to lie about what was beneath his house, something tied to our case.

Quinn knows, however. He's standing over me, letting me know that I've screwed up. I look up and catch his eye, and for once I feel like Quinn has the better of me. That he is crushing me. It's not that I usually feel in competition with him; but I'm the detective, I know what I'm doing, and he lets me get on with it.

Not at the moment. The look says it all.

I break the stare after a few seconds, then head further down into the shaft. I get to the bottom, and turn to the left to the door. A plain, steel-grey metal door with a steel-grey metal handle. There is no external lock. You cannot lock anyone in.

'Dammit,' I mutter. I just need to get on with it, stop creating so much internal drama.

Open the door, light floods into the room from the shaft, then I reach round to the wall, find the switch and turn on the lights.

And there it is, the room stretching out before me. Set up for one specific purpose, just as Quinn knew I would find.

'Fuck,' I say this time, voice low, the word barely audible.

⋆   ⋆   ⋆

1:12 a.m.

Standing at the sitting room window, in the dark, watching the rain. The drops against the glass collecting and running; on the street below, the rain sweeping past the orange lights at a forty-five-degree angle. A cup of tea going cold in my hand as I stare out into the night.

There was one time. Early 2004. Classic screw-up in Eastern Europe. *Haven't seen anything like it since we were making an arse of the Cold War*, my boss back at SIS said. I was in Moscow trying to set up an inside track on the Putin presidency, back when he was being welcomed with open arms by Western democracies, who'd happily ignored the slaughter of Grozny, and who were happily ignoring the warnings of the Baltic States.

Unfortunately, I was the one being set up. That time, I spotted it before anyone else on my side, and managed to extract us from the situation before too much damage had been done. Still, it was a colossal debacle. Belevich ended up with a bullet in his head, and I had to leave Moscow at two hours' notice. Straight to Afghanistan, for my trouble, where I went about repairing my reputation. That, ultimately, wasn't so hard, given that in Moscow I'd played it pretty straight and hadn't done anything wrong.

Tonight, however, I blundered into the house of a prominent local councillor while he was hosting a dinner party, because I suspected there might be dead children, or a clue to the case of a dead child, at the foot of a well beneath his house. It turned out that what was at the foot of the well was a very expensively kitted-out nuclear fallout shelter. Enough food and water to last four people a year, medicine, fuel, clothes, blankets, and with its own independent power source.

Rollins had the receipt for the building work, dated five years previously, and an absolutely legitimate, if selfish, reason for lying about the shaft's existence, in that he didn't want it generally known that his house was the go-to place on the Black Isle at the onset of the coming apocalypse.

'It could be that Rollins worked out that we might come,' Sutherland said to me, as we drove back to the station, before we were hauled into Quinn's office. 'So he cleared the place out, and filled it up with all the nuclear fallout shelter schtick.'

'He could, Iain, you're right,' I said. 'And that's all we've got. But it's weak. It's clutching. I got a quick look at the shelter. I *wanted* to find something in there, some proof that he had set it up in the past two or three days on the off-chance that we'd pitch up. But I'd stretched storylines and suspicions and clues that were barely more than hints just to get us there, inside that room. How much further can we take it? Maybe a close forensic examination of the room would reveal the kind of set-up we're looking for, but asking for it is going to look desperate, and we haven't a chance of getting it authorised in any case. After this, I'll be lucky if I'm so much as allowed to buy the coffee again.'

'You've never bought the coffee,' said Sutherland, and he laughed, and I told him to fuck off, and not long afterwards we were at the station and Quinn was giving me the *what were you thinking/do you realise the damage you've caused/starting right now, you will run every aspect of this investigation by me* speech.

I also got the full list of people who were in attendance at Rollins's dinner party. Not names necessarily, but job titles and positions and level of importance within the community.

I was hearing him out, hands behind my back, head slightly bowed, until he said, 'I'll do my best to not suspend you tomorrow, Ben, but if it comes to it ... if that's what's required, if that's what I have to do to save this station, well that's what's going to have to be done.'

I stopped myself making a comment about him throwing me under the bus. It would have been petulant and undeserved. He was right after all. I'd blundered in, leaving behind problems and hurdles that it wouldn't be my job to overcome.

'I need to speak to Elizabeth Rhodes,' I said.

Quinn looked unimpressed, perhaps even shocked.

'Harry's wife? Why?'

'There's a possibility she's related to Boy 9.'

That gave him pause, and he stared at me, his mouth slightly open, for a few moments.

'What?' was all he could say, when he finally managed to find some words.

'We suspect that Boy 9 was related to the Balfour line, the old lairds of the land on that side of the Black Isle. We're waiting on the DNA, though it'll likely be a day or two before we get that back. The trouble is, we can't find record of any existing descendants of the Balfours of that age.'

'What?' he said, the agitation in his voice increasing.

'Listen,' I snapped, my tone matching his. From the corner of my eye, I noticed Sutherland make a slight move towards me, as though of a mind to reel me back in, but he didn't go beyond that. 'We've potentially got a line from the Balfours, whose son was kidnapped, his heart left on a doorstep, to Elizabeth Rhodes. It doesn't make sense, but it's a start. I need to speak to her.'

He was staring at me by the end of that, his head moving from side to side. A moment, then he said, 'No. Just no.'

'We need to!'

'Inspector!'

I backed off a little, but only in a straightening of the shoulders.

'I have to speak to—'

'Write it up for me,' he said, his voice straining. 'I'll look at it in the morning, and I'll make the decision. But don't be surprised if this investigation is turned over to Inverness.'

I switched off after that, although we weren't in there much longer in any case. The upshot is that I have no backing from the boss, and it's not entirely impossible that tomorrow I get tossed off the case. I have eight, maybe nine hours to solve this thing, and then I'm done.

The boy in the well, just like the boy seen in CCTV footage with Catriona Napier, remains unidentified. We believe that Boy 9 is connected to the Balfour line, a line that potentially leads through Elizabeth Rhodes, although there's a peculiar kink in it that does not make sense. However, she's the only link we have. And if there is any significance in the last words of Napier in her reference to the Sandman, that significance also comes from Elizabeth Rhodes.

Perhaps she did not find her way into my bed for nothing. Perhaps she did not just find herself irresistibly drawn to me. All those years of intelligence training, guarding against the old-fashioned honey-trap, have been forgotten, and there I was, falling into bed with someone I'd met through an investigation.

What was in it for her, though? Sure, she planted the idea of the Beige Man, but she could have done that anyway. Yes, the manner of the telling and the dreamlike nature of the narrative lent itself to late at night, lying in bed on the cusp of sleep. But surely there could have been another way to get that story across. She didn't need to sleep with me, twice, just to tell me a tall tale, a parable that took me off in a direction of her choosing.

I put the tea to my lips, immediately put it down again when I realise how cold it's become. Rest the cup on the window ledge, take another look at the time.

1:17 a.m.

I need to speak to her again, and I can't leave it until the morning. I contemplate texting, wondering if I could lure her out secretly into the night. But subterfuge is no longer my game and, despite the last disaster, stemming from me striding purposefully up to a door and blundering in full bore, I decide that this is once again the only thing for it.

Nothing gets done standing staring at rain on a window. Nothing gets done while you sleep.

I turn away, head to the front door, clothes still damp from earlier, having not taken the time to change. Shoes, jacket, car keys, and I'm off.

31

As I stand at the front door of Councillor Rhodes's house, the rain pouring, soaked through, having made the decision to leave my ineffectual rain jacket in the car, for some reason I think of that stupid Andie MacDowell line at the end of *Four Weddings*. *Is it still raining? I hadn't noticed.*

Usually the awfulness of it makes me smile. I can remember the argument with Olivia. She thought it was fine. Romantic. I've never known anyone else who liked that line.

I knock. Somehow that seems more appropriate for just gone one thirty in the morning. As though the bell will wake up the whole neighbourhood. Even if there was such a bell, there isn't really a neighbourhood; the nearest house no closer than a couple of hundred yards. And, of course, the sound of the knocking carries louder out here than the bell, though not much sound is carrying at all in the rain.

I leave it about half a minute and knock again. First knock to stir them, the second to confirm that there is someone at the door. I stand back, waiting to see if a light goes on, or if a figure emerges.

I'm not at all focused, here with little aforethought or planning. I don't know what I'll say if Harry Rhodes comes to the door, other than to ask to see Elizabeth. And with what authority will I make the demand, should he refuse? Certainly not any that would be backed up by my senior management.

For Elizabeth I have the mundane questions – can she remember her grandparents, does she know she has a blood relative living just up the road in Golspie? – and I have what is likely to be ill-disguised anger. The feeling of having been used, remorse at my own foolishness. Perhaps most of it will be anger at myself, but I need to know how much I've been played.

The second of those questions, of course, I'm asking from a position of total ignorance. Perhaps they have Sunday lunch together every week. *Of course I know about Aunt Marion, she's the only family I've got!*

And there's the gnawing, nagging question that's just been sitting there waiting to be addressed. Perhaps her Aunt Marion was not her only blood family. Perhaps there was a nine-year-old boy, now dead.

But why would Elizabeth have left him there? Why didn't she come forward?

I've been thinking about her, that first time Sutherland and I walked into her office. She seemed, in some way, to be defined by her sadness, that's what I thought then. Given what ensued, my thoughts moved in other directions, and there was no reason to think that her sorrow was related to the boy in the well.

Yet, she was trying to tell me something with her tale of the Beige Man, and I was too tired to work out what it was. Now, I feel as if I missed my chance. I should have been listening more closely at the time. I should have chosen my moment to ask the apposite question. And I fell asleep.

The door opens, and there she is. Elizabeth Rhodes, dressed in white, patterned cotton pyjamas, the look of top-of-the range M&S about them. She hasn't been sleeping.

She doesn't speak. Doesn't remark on the time, doesn't remark on me standing there, soaked through. We stare at each other for a few moments, and then she takes a small step to the side, and opens the door a little further. She knew I was coming. Lying awake, waiting for the bell to ring, the phone to vibrate, the knock at the door. Expecting me.

I walk past her into the dark house. She closes the door behind me, then walks along the corridor, squeezing my hand as she passes but quickly letting go, and I follow her into the kitchen.

She turns on the lights beneath the wall-mounted cabinets, and the room is illuminated in low, night-time yellow. Then she pours herself a glass of water from the tap and turns to face me. I'm standing in the middle of the kitchen, dripping rainwater onto the floor, the other side of the island. A square of kitchen worktop, with a block of knives at its centre, beside a small wooden container of kitchen oils and vinegars. Above it hang neatly arranged pans and cooking implements.

And there we stand. The questions are standing there with us, waiting to be asked.

Who was the boy in the well? Who is the Beige Man? Where is Harry? Was there a subplot to the dinner party at Rollins's house this evening?

She takes a sip of water then lays the glass down on the worktop beside her.

'You didn't go to look at Nairn beach, did you?' she says finally. 'I didn't mean you to go to Nairn beach.'

'I didn't.'

'Good.'

Conversation forced out from the smallest cracks in the still of the night. In here there is no suggestion of the squall outside.

'You know where we'll find the boy in the well?' I ask.

Anyone unfamiliar with the case might assume the answer to that is the mortuary at Raigmore. It's not public knowledge that that corpse has been replaced.

'How much do you know?' she asks, the classic cagey question from the accused to the police. I almost feel disappointed that she asked it. As though I expect more of her.

'Were you his mother?'

I hadn't been intending going straight there, but her demeanour is unexpected. She looks defeated. She looks as if she's about to give up her power over the story. Whether she gives up everything I need, however, depends on how I play this. That's what I have to believe, anyway, to assume that I have any control in this situation.

Nevertheless, if she is giving up, she's not doing so yet. She's not doing so in words. She's not saying anything.

'We have the body of Ewan Balfour, who disappeared two hundred years ago, and we *had* the body of Boy 9. We think the two were related, down through the centuries. We traced the Balfour line to Marion Stone, who lives in Golspie. Her father was your grandfather. You are part of that family line, although I know it doesn't make sense for you to be Boy 9's mother. But you fit in there, somewhere, and you have to—'

'My grandparents, who went to Washington during the war, had two children. Two daughters. When they separated, they took a child each. They split them up. Who does that, Inspector? But it was 1946, and that was what happened.'

'She never said. Mrs Stone. She said she'd been an only child.'

'She wasn't going to lead you directly to me, was she? She wasn't going to—'

'So you are directly descended from the Balfours who were lairds on the Black Isle two hundred years ago?'

A long silence. In the heart of it, the heart of the quiet, the fridge clicks into life, the hum and the vibration a little louder. For the first time since we got in here, there is the sound of rain against the window, on the back of a strong gust of wind.

'But it doesn't mean what you think it means,' she says, her voice even lower.

'What was his name?' I ask. 'Boy 9. What was his name?'

'Adam.'

For the first time there is a break in her voice. I try to take my time, not to rush into the hundred questions that need to be asked. She's talking at least, and I can't lose her, regardless of how opaque some of those answers might be.

'Who killed him?'

I have barely even approached that question up until now in this investigation. All our efforts concentrated on establishing the boy's identity, and we've barely come close to even talking about why anyone wanted him dead, or who that might have been.

'They killed him,' she says, with a peculiar emphasis. The stress not on the word *they*, as though who *they* are is obvious.

'We know they killed him. They cut out his heart.'

I can hear her swallow. She closes her eyes for a moment, her lips squeeze together.

'They cut out his heart,' I repeat.

'Don't say that,' she says. 'I know what they did.'

'Who are they?'

Her eyes drop; the words that had started to come stall in her throat. Her head dips a little.

'Is that what this was? Someone still taking revenge for the Clearances? A blood feud, dating back two hundred years?'

A moment, and then she looks up. There are tears in her eyes now, just beginning to rise, though her face remains expressionless. She's leaving me hanging.

'Was it about the Clearances?'

Now, the merest shake of the head, her eyes dropping again. Can't look at me while giving me information, although it doesn't feel as if it's because she's lying. Too afraid to tell the truth, and so she hides behind vague words and small gestures, and she doesn't really look at me, as though that might absolve her in someone's eyes.

'But you wanted me to find that old story. You wanted me to know about Ewan Balfour.'

She swallows, another shake of the head, but does not lift her eyes.

'Why? Why did someone keep that boy's body all this time?'

The hum of the fridge settles back down to its lower level, and seems to disappear. The wind does not drive the rain against the windowpane. Silence creeps back into the room. Finally she lifts her eyes and we stare at each other across the island in the middle of the kitchen.

I realise that I feel nothing for her. I'm not sure why we ended up in bed together, but there was no emotion. I've been completely wrapped up in the case this week, and perhaps I needed the release, but it left me with nothing for her. I'm not looking at her as someone I care for, I'm not even looking at her as a member of the emergency services would look upon a mother who has lost a child. She is information, that's all. She's standing there, knowing things I don't, knowing things I need to know.

The silence grows so strong. It crawls over us, it wraps us up, almost as though it's a physical entity. Clamps our mouths closed, creeps down inside us, encircles our heads and seeps insidiously inside, cutting off communication between brain and speech.

The silence owns us. The room has become this silence. I don't know how long we've been standing here, but it begins to feel as though I won't be able to speak, even if I try.

There are four lights beneath the wall-mounted cupboards, and one of them begins to blink. I hadn't noticed it when I came in. Perhaps it's just started, the stutter of the bulb. Or perhaps the silence is enveloping it too. The silence, encircling the room, taking control of everything.

I need to speak. I need to force the words from somewhere. Dredge them up, spit them out, scream them if I have to.

And then, when finally words cross my lips, they just sound like regular words. Plain spoken, little drama.

'We should go down to the station. Can you get dressed?'

'I just wanted someone to hold,' she says, her voice thin and broken. 'Someone to love. Is there anything wrong with that?'

'I don't understand.'

'How could you?'

'Tell me.'

'I can't tell . . .' she starts, then her voice breaks.

Jesus. I need to get her down to the station. Yes, there's some part of me wants to walk round there, take her in my arms, hold her, comfort her. Even from a practical point of view, it might be the way to get her to talk.

But I've had enough of this. We need to get on, we need answers, and I'm in no mood for comfort. No mood for the hand run through the hair, the face pressed against the chest, the soft words.

I wonder if I'm going to have to physically force her out the house, and decide at this point, regardless, that I really ought to have someone else here. Take the phone from my pocket, let out the low curse at the fact that there's no signal. Turn my back, walk out the kitchen into the hall, holding the phone aloft, as though that might help it connect with a mast or a satellite or whatever it is that I need.

A movement behind me, and I turn quickly. Elizabeth is still on the other side of the island, but now she has a knife in her hand. Long, large. A carving knife. She's not brandishing it in any threatening way, and I know immediately. It's not meant for me.

Step back into the kitchen.

'Don't,' I say.

In the silence I can hear her swallow, I can see the tears on her cheeks. She grips the knife in her right hand, no tremble in her fingers.

'Put it down. We'll go down to the station, we can talk it through.'

Her head moves to the side, her damp eyes stare helplessly back across the kitchen.

'You should go and get them,' she says. 'They'll move them tonight. Maybe they've moved them already.'

'Where from?'

The words automatically out of my mouth, although I don't even know who it is that she's talking about.

And yet, I do. Of course I know. An unknown boy dead. An unknown boy seen on camera walking along Dingwall High Street. There are, quite conceivably, going to be more than two of them. I think of the notion I posited to Sutherland, and his dismissive line in response: *a secret stash of children* . . . That this is what we have come to has a cold, grim hand gripping and twisting my stomach.

She smiles weakly, her lips faint, her eyes empty. I need to keep her talking. I can't rush towards her or she'll make her move. Engage and distract. Get her interested in something or, at least, interested in telling me something.

'Talk to me,' I say. 'It's the only way you can help them.'

And that's all. The knife is up and thrust into her stomach. Blood spurts forth, she bends double, her eyes are big, and her mouth opens in silent shock.

I rush forward, but it's far too slow, far too late. Round the side of the island, our eyes on each other the whole time, and then, as I get there, her head slumps forward and bangs off the worktop, and then she's falling back and I'm catching her, and I stagger back, propping up her dead weight, reaching for the knife which is still embedded in her stomach, blood everywhere.

And when it's over, the movement and the noise and the pulsing of the blood and the staggering backwards, I'm sitting back, slumped against the unit beneath the sink, with Elizabeth Rhodes, dead and bloody, in my arms.

32

To the left of the kitchen there is a small breakfast bar with two stools. I sit there now, blood on my already damp clothes, staring straight ahead. My eyes are on the knives in the block on the island, but I'm looking through them.

I can think about the knives later. I can think about the sad, bloody cliché of them. The obviousness of it. A rack of knives between me and her. The knives, right in front of my face, waiting to be used. And I turned my back.

Elizabeth lies where I laid her on the floor, her head resting in a dark pool, the blood soaked into her hair. I made a quick search of the house, presuming that Harry Rhodes would not be here, and sure enough there is no sign of him.

She was alone. Alone and waiting for me to come. I could have been here earlier, but then, how would the outcome have been any different?

She has only been dead ten minutes. I haven't made any calls, I haven't made any decisions, but whatever it is I'm going to do, I need to do it quickly.

They'll move them tonight.

I don't know who and I don't know from where, but I can work it out. That's what I'm supposed to do, isn't it?

Lost boys, invisible boys, boys concealed from society. Maybe girls too, I don't know. And it makes sense that they're being moved from Rollins's house. The house built over the well.

Whoever put Boy 9's body in that well was pointing us in this direction from the start, just as Elizabeth was pointing me in the direction of the story. From the tale of the dog that wasn't a dog, to what she just said to me, the words I so dumbly and helplessly batted back. *I just wanted someone to hold.*

She lost something in her life, and it wasn't a dog. The same thing that Belle McIntosh lost, and the same thing Catriona Napier was never able to have.

And this story is about someone, the Beige Man of Elizabeth's peculiar late-night narrative, helping these women deal with that loss.

I'm not sure why Quinn allowed me to instruct Sutherland to search the house. Perhaps he just wanted me landing myself in even more trouble, digging myself an even bigger hole. But, despite Rollins's objections, Sutherland did what he'd been told, and went into every room.

He found nothing. No one sneaking out of windows, no one hiding in rooms. And, although Quinn might have been angry about it, he did then use the fruitless search as *proof of the legitimacy of the nuclear fallout shelter by elimination.*

But sitting here, now, staring at those bloody knives, I'm even more convinced of the fact that there was something wrong with the story. That the basement is not what Rollins claims, and that there are answers to be found there. I need to go back to the house, and I need to find whoever was being hidden down at the bottom of the old well.

I can't call Sutherland. Nor, in fact, any of the officers from the station. However I'm going to do this, it can't involve the others. They'd all do it, but they'd be in as much trouble as I would, and I can't ask them to take the risk.

Even if this works out, even if this goes as well as it possibly could go, the fallout will be bad, the ramifications of turning up there again after this evening will be ugly. It feels like the kind of rogue action that I would've taken in the old days, in the old job.

Leaving Elizabeth's body lying here feels like a similar kind of thing. Something from the old days. But I can't risk calling it in just yet. I don't want word getting out that I'm on the move. I can worry about the consequences later.

Another five minutes and I should go. Another five minutes, and I need to have come up with a plan, even if it's just sitting outside Rollins's house, waiting for dark, shadowy figures to emerge in the middle of the night.

With Quinn at my back, with Quinn breathing down my neck, I didn't get a proper look at the shelter. Could there have been another room? There was one door leading to a toilet and a rudimentary shower, that was all.

My search for another door was curtailed as Quinn followed me down the ladder.

'Where's the other route out?' I said to Quinn, as he looked at me in the small, airless room.

'What d'you mean?'

'If you pay this much for an underground shelter, aren't you going to guard against someone being able to shut you in? You're down here, no idea who's up there. Wouldn't you want another way out?'

He looked at me with a contempt I'd never seen in him before. A moment, he let his disapproval and his authority permeate the room, and then he said, 'Inspector, you are finished here. You've seen what you came to see. Now get out. Get out!'

But that thought is still with me. The other way out. Maybe there are plenty of fallout shelters beneath homes, designed to be evacuated after six months using nothing other than a trap-door and hope. But Rollins is wealthy, and while that fallout shelter might not be like the one they have beneath the White House or the Kremlin, it was built with money, and anything constructed with that level of aforethought, and that amount of financing, is surely going to have had another means of escape.

I can't go to the front door again. I can't enter the house without breaking in.

When I do think of what I can do, and who I can call – as the red digital clock in the dim light of the kitchen moves silently and remorselessly through the digits, with the body of Elizabeth Rhodes lying dead and bloody on the floor – my head snaps back, and I stand quickly, phone in my hand, already checking I have the number I need.

The rain, not as heavy as it was previously, is still falling, the depths of night bleak and cold. Sitting in Lyle's car, around the corner and about two hundred yards from Rollins's house.

The drone that Lyle used to check the ground around the McIntosh well has just set off from the pavement beside the car. Lyle is following its movement on a laptop, controlling it as it goes. I'm sitting with another laptop – resting on Lyle's dry jacket on my lap, as my trousers are still soaked – following the feed from the drone, as it scans the ground beneath it.

Were this a movie, in fact, were this an operation from my old work, we'd be sitting in the back of a high-tech van, rather than in the front seat of a lousy old Peugeot 307. But we're parked behind some trees at just after two o'clock on a grim and wet November morning, and we can monitor our target from afar, so subterfuge and concealment are not so important.

'So, like, whose house is this?' asks Lyle, taking a drink of coffee. He had the thought to bring me one too.

He was wide awake when I called, playing the new Call of Duty, one eye on Thursday-night American football. Answered the call to arms with an attitude of act now, ask questions later. Like he was bored at two in the morning, and looking for something to do.

Having met me here, and established the parameters of what I'm looking for, set up the equipment and got the operation under way, now is the time to find out what exactly it is he's got himself in to.

'Jack Rollins.'

He looks at me, smiles, then lets out a low whistle as he turns back to the drone.

'The travel guy?'

'The travel guy.'

'The travel guy who's the councillor and who's going to be an MSP, and like, President of an independent Scotland at some point?'

'I think you might be exaggerating his place in the world, but yes.'

'Jesus. What's the story?'

Take a drink, accept that there's a little too much milk in it for me, take another sip, then nod as I watch the flight of the drone through the images of the ground it's sending back.

'The sergeant and I decided that whoever planted the body of Boy 9 in the well was sending us a message. There are other wells, and there's something to find there.'

'Cool,' says Lyle.

'Rollins's house was built over a well.'

'Built *over* a well? Seems weird.'

'He said it was filled in and concreted over.'

'And we're checking, in the middle of the night, to see if that's the case? Epic.'

'I know it's not the case. We were there this evening. The well has been turned into a well-lit, steel shaft, leading to a nuclear fallout shelter.'

'Shit. That guy really does have money.'

'No dispute about that.'

'So, what're we looking for, then?'

'I was wondering if there was another exit from the fallout shelter.'

He looks at me for a moment, then turns back to his monitor, holding steady on the small control panel in his hands.

'OK. You think . . . wait, what? You think someone's hiding down there?'

'Being kept prisoner.'

'OK, cool. So, I know you used to be a spy 'n' all, but is there a particular reason we're being covert? Can't you just get a warrant?'

'I can answer that if you like, but at this point you might like to have *some* deniability.'

He laughs.

'Oh, I'm all about deniability, man.'

'So, I'm tasking you to do something, you've made sure the budgetary requirements have been met, and that's all we need to know.'

'I'm cool with that,' he says, with another laugh. 'Going rogue. Epic.'

He concentrates on the drone's movement for a few moments, and I look down at the dark images; nothing much yet to see.

'Oh, yeah, we got some more results back, by the way. Sorry, total logjam at the factory. Been chasing them for two days. We found traces of a fluoropolymer around a couple of the stones. Seemed unusual. We were thinking, maybe some sort of pliable tube was used, and the kid pushed through it . . .'

I say the words *the kid pushed through it* along with him, and he nods and smiles, still concentrating on the screen.

'You'd already got there,' he says.

'Just needed confirmation of the tube's material.'

'Well, we got it, man,' he says, then he nods and adds, 'I'll switch to the Burton scanner in a few moments. All you've got for now is the surface look. So, we're approaching the house.'

'Pretty shaky in the wind.'

'Yeah, but it's cool. We'll still get the reading you need.'

I keep watching the screen, take another sip of coffee. Beginning to feel a little nervous, even though I haven't outright stepped over Quinn's mark as yet. Not so that anyone in there will have noticed, at any rate.

'You all right, by the way?' says Lyle.

'What d'you mean?' I ask, without turning.

'You're fucking soaking, man. How long you been like that?'

'A few hours.'

'Jesus. Shoulda changed before you came here. And is that, like, blood?'

'It's not mine.'

'Oh, well, that's great,' he says with a smile. 'You still look terrible.'

'Thanks. You all right?'

'Yeah, really,' says Lyle, shrugging. 'I'm happy to do this, man, don't sweat it.'

'I didn't mean that.'

He lowers his eyes for a moment, turns and gives me a glance, then looks back at his monitor with a small nod.

'Yeah, right,' he says, acknowledging the real meaning of the question. He lifts his coffee, puts it back down without taking a drink, concentrates on the drone for a moment, and then returns to the question with a nod. 'What can you do, man, right? It's a shit world. Shit happens. You can let it beat you, or you can just say, fuck this, man, I'm all in. I'm going to ride the fucker long as it lasts, and when it's over, it's over. No point sitting around feeling miserable.'

'How's Ray?'

Another lift of the cup, a sip of coffee, cup back in place.

'You know, he's cool. He's coming round. Look, man,

there's worse, right? There really is. We've just got to get through this, adjust to the new reality. Once we do that, man, what's not to like about life, right? We're still going to be playing Call of Duty, we're still drinking cups of Joe, I'll still be doing this kind of weird shit in the middle of the night, and I'll still be telling him about it when I get home.'

I nod along with him, smile for a moment, but that's it for the distraction.

'Hey,' he says, 'we're here. Right overhead. I'll switch to the Burton. You focused? I'm not going to have it on my screen.'

'Yep.'

'Cool.'

The image on the screen changes, and now it becomes largely black, with various coloured areas superimposed on the dark in degrees of yellow. I scan the image quickly, try to adjust to it, to the colouring and the way it is presented, to work out what it is I'm looking at.

Nevertheless, despite looking at a geological survey tool that I've never used before, what we're looking for is immediately apparent. There is a mass of yellow, representing the basement and the other underground areas of the house about which we know. And then, leading away from that, a straight area of darker yellow leads away to the right, to the edge of the screen, interrupted by a slightly wider bulge in the middle.

I turn the monitor round towards Lyle so that he can get a better look.

'What d'you think?'

'Underground tunnel, man,' says Lyle, something of a laugh in his voice. 'That's what we're looking for. You can tell from the darker shade of yellow that it's a little deeper than the broader area beneath the house. And there in the middle, there's like a little chamber or something. Coolio. I'll swing the drone over, see where it takes us.'

He manoeuvres the drone, and the image on the screen begins to shift a few seconds after he operates the controls.

'There's a delay?'

'Of 2.47 seconds,' he says. 'We're there.'

He glances over at my screen, which is still turned towards him, and we watch as the drone tracks the path of yellow, as it stretches away from the house, the intensity of the yellow gradually getting less along the way.

'Coming up to the surface,' he says. 'Decent.'

And then, suddenly, it stops, with a more intense patch of yellow, indicating another short shaft, rising to the surface.

'Fucking bingo, man,' says Lyle. 'We have lift-off.'

He stops the movement of the drone, so that it's now hovering over the site of the end of the tunnel, and I look over at his monitor.

'Nothing there,' he says. 'Trees and shit.'

'The shaft comes up in the middle of a wood.'

'Yep.'

'You got an app where we can record the exact coordinates and go over there to check it out?'

'Already on it,' he says, and he is, phone in hand, quickly typing away.

'I can close this?'

He nods. 'Sure. We've got all we need. You want me to come with you?'

'There's something you could do for me, but it's your call,' I say. 'The more involved you get, the worse it could be for you.'

He glances at me and smiles.

'Deniability, man. I don't know what we're doing, I'm just following you over there.'

'OK, thank you. I need you to take your car, and sit in clear sight of the front of the house.'

He nods approvingly.

'Coolio,' he says.

33

Standing not far from the exit to the tunnel. I'm not sure who's going to emerge, or when it'll happen, but they're coming.

No check of the watch, no look over my shoulder, no fear. At last it feels like we're about to get some answers. Maybe not all of them today, and maybe not tomorrow, but we're getting closer.

I can't be one hundred per cent confident that someone will emerge from this tunnel, but if I'm wrong, it's only because I've missed them already. However, the tumult at the house lasted well over an hour, and I know that after Quinn had ripped into Sutherland and me at the station, he was heading back out there to apologise once more. A midnight run of supine submissiveness, reporting on the steps he had taken, while making the police beholden to the local council.

If these people have a move to make, and I'm sure they do, they were not going to risk making it while there was still a chance of discovery. It will be done in the dead of night, and I can only hope it didn't happen while I was watching Elizabeth die, and while I was constructing this next part of the game-plan.

I'm sure that Rollins, at least, will be amongst them, and I'm also presuming Harry Rhodes. Perhaps Rollins's wife. And that there will be several children, including the boy we saw in the CCTV footage with Catriona Napier on Dingwall High Street.

It would be so much easier if I hadn't made a mess of everything up until this point, and we could have officers knocking on doors, checking on whereabouts, asking questions. Now something prevents me lifting the phone, calling Sutherland, and bringing in reinforcements.

There may be one or two adults about to emerge here, or there may be fifteen, and they are unlikely to happily lie down in a gentleman's agreement. *Uh-oh, police are here, we'll go quietly, we don't want any fuss* . . . But I can't risk it. I can't risk landing the others in trouble, and I can't risk the information somehow getting out. If it got as far as Quinn, the call would be put through, and I'd be standing out here for nothing.

A cold shiver runs through my body. Having moved around a little, I know there's nowhere to stand to avoid the rain, or the water cascading from the bare branches of trees.

Hands by my sides, I stand and wait, the woods impenetrably bleak, the lights of the town through the trees down the hill, but distant enough in this forbidding, wet night to make no difference to where I now stand, entombed by darkness.

Another shiver, and then a skip of the heart, a quick intake of breath, and I crouch and turn. A noise behind me. The snap of a damp twig, footsteps in the undergrowth. I'd been concentrating on the area of ground from which I expected people to emerge. My mind set on that, not on an approach from behind.

I can see the figure moving, advancing slowly, but as soon as I can make out the shape in the darkness, I know there's nothing threatening about it. I can't tell who it is, but they're not sneaking up on me from behind. I wonder if there's a dog somewhere – I really don't want there to be a dog – but there's no sign.

And then he's emerging from the trees, and coming straight for me. I feel confused for a few seconds, disconcerted enough that I take a couple of steps backwards, backing against a tree, and then he's in front of me, that curious smile on his face.

'Ben,' he says. 'This is unexpected. Although, I guess you were going to work it out in the end. Makes a change from a sunny mountaintop.'

'What are you doing here?'

Sanderson looks uncertain, then he shakes his head.

'Hmm. Not sure. Keeps happening. What've you been up to?'

'The boy in the well case,' I say, falling into conversation, as though meeting Sanderson in the middle of this dark wood is perfectly natural. 'Though it seems to have gone a little further than that.'

'Huh,' he says, nodding. 'Interesting. What's the prognosis?'

'I'd been working on the assumption of it being a centuries-old blood feud, or maybe a secret cabal of powerful people—'

'Such as that is, in these parts.'

'I'm not sure, but I think it might just be much sadder than that.'

'Simple,' says Sanderson.

'Yes. If a cellar full of children can be simple.'

'Hmm.'

Another shiver, and this time I begin to feel the discomfort of it. This isn't the shiver of nervousness.

'As a doctor, I recommend you go home, get dry, take paracetamol and a shot of whisky, and get into bed.'

'You know I can't.'

I turn away from him and look back at the spot between the trees where the underground shaft ends.

'Why would you keep children locked away like that? Why would you give up your children?'

Sanderson walks up beside me, and looks down at the same spot on the damp forest floor. From here it looks like nothing, although I do not worry that I have the wrong place. I seem to trust Lyle's technology far more than I trust my own intuition.

'Witches' cult,' says Sanderson.

'No,' I say, shaking my head. 'I'm not accepting that.'

'Members of the same family, hidden away for purposes of abuse and sexual exploitation, like the Fritzl case. The cops involved in that one must've been shocked. I mean, that was all kinds of a maelstrom out of the blue. This could be anything, and you're about to welcome it above ground. I don't envy you.'

'You're here too,' I say.

'Not really,' he replies, patting me on the shoulder. 'The awfulness of human beings knows no boundary. That's a really trite line. Clichéd, cloying, banal, the line of a dullard. But you know what? It's true. What goes on behind closed doors, what goes on in the minds of men and women, what depravity slithers out into the world . . .? There are all sorts of reasons why invisible children could be kept beneath ground, and none of them, *none of them*, are good. Steel yourself, Inspector, for the worst will soon be upon you.'

And there it is, the first movement in the turf. I feel his hand on my shoulder again as I crouch down, tucked in behind the trunk of an old oak tree, eyes peering ahead into the darkness.

A disturbance in the foliage, a door is raised, pushed back, and then lowered back onto the forest floor. I take a quick glance round at Sanderson, but he's gone. Somehow there still seems to be the remembrance of him, in the space where he'd been, and then even that goes, and there's nothing, just the wet darkness of night.

A head emerges from the dark space on the forest floor, hidden beneath a hood. A moment, and then the figure rises and comes fully into the woods. A slight build, and I think of the men who've been involved thus far, and wonder if any of them are small enough of stature, and decide that it must be one of the women.

She steps away from the entrance to the shaft, looks around the dark of the woods, and then turns back round.

Silent in the night, another figure emerges. Smaller this time, the pale face of a child beneath a dark hat. He is pulled up to the surface, and then he steps to the side, where he stands still, head down, arms hanging limply by his side. He is then pushed gently back, away from the entrance, presumably to make more room.

I wonder if the boy is going to take the chance to turn and run, but he stands there, unmoving. Not even looking around, not even considering giving it a go. Is he cowed and beaten into submission, or does he not want to go? He wants to be with these people, perhaps because he does not know anything else.

A few moments, and then another child is hauled up, and ushered over to the side. Slightly taller, he carries the same beaten deportment, and they stand together in defeat. Do they know no rebellion? Have they no curiosity, no annoyance, no affront, at being brought out into a cold, wet forest in the middle of the night?

I study the adult, as she bends to pull up the next child, but I don't recognise anything about her. Not in this light, not when I can't see the face.

Another child is brought up; he is moved over to the side to stand with his subdued comrades in arms, and then another adult emerges, up onto the forest floor, unaided. Larger, and more difficult to tell this time if it is a man or woman.

I wonder if this is it, and that the door will now be closed. I begin to ready myself for the advance, but then this second adult also stands to the side, and the first to emerge once more reaches down to help another child up out of the trap-door in the forest floor.

Presumably then, as well as an indeterminate number of children, there will be at least one more adult bringing up the rear. Time to start thinking about how I should play this. Making the call to the station is the obvious first option, but to do that I would have to back off out of earshot. I could take my phone from my pocket and send a text, but there's no guarantee that it would be answered quickly at this time of night, and I'd need to worry about the light of the phone, which will shine brightly in the darkness, if just for a moment before I can dim it. And either way, here we are in Fortrose at two in the morning, and when exactly is it that I could expect the cavalry to arrive?

I need to step forward and make the intervention. No nerves, no doubts, just get on with it. Make the call when we've established where we are, who we've got, and I'm already standing before them, my presence revealed. Yes, I'll be outnumbered, and if they're willing to kill a child then there's no reason why they wouldn't be willing to kill a police officer, but there's only one of us here going to have any authority, and I will act upon it.

A minute, and it seems that this part of their work is done. A third adult surfaces, and this time the trapdoor is closed over. Two of the adults kick leaves across the area, and then the other bends down to the task, ensuring that the door is properly covered over once more.

Low voices, indistinguishable in the noise of the rainy forest, and then one slightly louder, a woman, turns to the children.

I strain to hear it, although the words are still unclear. But there's something about that voice. Something familiar, yet it's out of place. The voice belongs to a person who shouldn't be here, who shouldn't be in this damned wood in the pouring rain in the middle of the night, so that my brain can't quite compute. Like seeing someone so out of context, that you can't recognise the most familiar face.

And then, suddenly, the shock of recognition. The image falls into place, and I know who it is. This person who can't possibly be here, but is. Not just can't, but shouldn't. They shouldn't be here.

Another shiver, and a shake of the head to clear it. *Right, you're shocked, Inspector. We know. Big damned deal, now do your job.*

They start to move, this collective of nine. Six children, making no attempt to get away, and three adults, and it's time. I can't wait around any longer.

With no need to cover my tracks or mask my approach, I walk quickly out of the woods, footfalls loud on the forest floor.

They stop and turn, all nine of them as one, at my approach. The children recoil, grouping together behind the adults, who close in before them, as if to protect them. These adults who would murder one of these children, who would cut out his heart and toss him into a well.

'Show yourselves,' I say, and I've got my phone out, torch on and shining it into their faces.

They stare back at me, and then all three of them, as if one tightly bound unit, pull back their hoods so that I can get a good look at their faces.

No Beige Man to be found here. The adults are all women. I know them, and I've spoken to each of them in the course of this investigation.

'You're all under arrest,' I say boldly, as that had been my line on approach, and will not change on the shock of revelation.

There's nothing for a moment. The only sound from any of us, a slightly nervous shuffling, coming from the children, who all stand with heads bowed. And then one of the women steps forward. The one I did not expect to see at all. The one who amazes me by her presence. The one who cannot possibly be part of this.

'Interesting play, Ben,' she says. 'Do you have a gun app on that phone, or some other plan to overcome nine people in a forest, one of whom is armed?'

'You're not armed,' I say boldly, heart sinking at the thought of it.

Guns. Jesus. The blight of the bloody world.

And then slowly, with a minimum of show and fuss, she disproves me, and I'm looking down the barrel of a Glock G30, something I haven't done since I left the SIS.

34

'All right,' she says, 'I'm probably not going to shoot you. These things are so vulgar.'

'You're not Elizabeth's Beige Man?' I say.

'Well, I might be,' she answers diffidently. 'Do I look like a man?'

'What was Elizabeth's story, then? What exactly was she trying to tell me?'

'I don't know, Inspector. Seriously? Why don't you ask her?'

I don't answer. It's a small thing that I know Elizabeth is dead, and she doesn't, but knowledge is power, right?

So many questions, back and forth, like a game of Scottish football, where the ball never touches the ground.

'Kind of gave your hand away with the line about the gun, didn't you?' I say. 'I mean, if you're not going to shoot me, you might as well be holding a water pistol.'

'I said I probably wasn't going to shoot you,' she says, 'but it doesn't mean I won't. That's Lyle sitting out front, is it?'

I'm not going to answer that.

'He knows you're here, I take it?'

Again, I don't answer.

'A little too much of a coincidence for him just to be hanging around in Fortrose in the middle of the night. Maybe he has to die too. It'll take his boyfriend's mind off things for a while.'

The line delivered deadpan, then for a moment nothing but the rain on the leaves. She's talking though. The villain in control, the villain with the floor.

'Interesting that it's just the two of you,' she says. 'Scared off from calling for back-up after this evening's fiasco?'

She smiles; her eyes are bright in the dark. Her partners, Jill Rollins and Belle McIntosh, look impatient, ready to move on, wanting the irritation I'm causing to be dealt with.

'You got played, Inspector, you got played.'

'As I did with the body exchange of Boy 9.'

'Yeah,' she says. 'Classic piece of misdirection but, I admit, it was a bit of a cheat. Really, how were you to know that the new female pathologist would turn out to be . . .' and she pauses for a moment, a strange melancholy about her suddenly, then says almost ruefully, 'a cunt.'

'I had my suspicions,' I say, shaking my head, although it's a lie. I walked through this entire thing without the hint of a suspicion. Why on earth would I be suspicious?

'Liar. But, hey, say what you like.'

'What happened in Aberdeen? I take it your girlfriend didn't really kill herself?'

'No, not so much,' says Wade. 'She was getting upset. Sounded like she might be about—'

'Really?' says Belle McIntosh, taking a step forward. 'We're doing this? Come on, the kids are freezing, I'm freezing. We need to get the fuck out of Dodge. If you want to stand around talking with your police buddy, you're welcome. We're going. Come on, boys, this way.'

She moves to her side, indicating for the boys to follow, while Rollins looks unhappily over at me and starts to fall in behind.

'Looks like it's time for us to go,' says Wade. 'Been lovely chatting.'

'Stop!' I shout, and the raising of the voice has the right effect. They all look at me, the boys with fright, Wade almost regretful, Rollins and McIntosh annoyed.

'You're not going anywhere. You three are under arrest. Boys, you don't have to go with them.'

No response from them, and now the women look at me with disdain. As if I'd be able to make any difference with these boys. As if they would listen to a complete stranger when they have their protectors amongst them.

I see him now, the boy from the CCTV footage. The boy that Catriona Napier took for a walk. I look at him directly.

'You know why Catriona isn't here? Do you know why you haven't seen her?'

His eyes widen slightly, and I can tell that got through to him.

'Shut up!'

'They killed her,' I say, harshly. 'Just like they killed the boy they took away last week.'

'Stop it!'

It's McIntosh who's shouting, but Wade looks almost amused. Like she's curious how this is going to play out. She has a confidence in her control over these boys that McIntosh does not.

'What was his name?' I ask, my voice losing its edge. Calming down, contrasting with the anger that stands next to him.

I know his name already, of course, but I want to engage them. I want them to start talking to me.

'Jesus,' mutters McIntosh, shaking her head. 'Boys, come on, we're leaving.'

'What was his name?' I say again, but I can tell that there are no words going to pass the boy's lips. Too scared to speak.

'Adam,' says a voice next to him, the tallest child.

'Oh, for crying out loud!'

'That's enough, Paul, come on,' says Wade. She sounds like a schoolteacher chastising, with infinite patience, a slightly difficult child. 'Aunt Belle is right, we should be going.'

'They killed him, Paul,' I say. 'Adam is dead.'

'Jesus, they know Adam's dead, that was the point.'

'Just like Aunt Catriona,' I say, ignoring McIntosh. 'And do you know Elizabeth? You have an Aunt Elizabeth?'

He doesn't speak, but the answer is in his eyes.

'Elizabeth is dead too,' I say. 'So many people are dead, and it's all because of your—'

'She's dead? Jesus!'

McIntosh again, louder this time, an explosion of sound, and then there's a flurry of movement as she runs at me from a few feet away, and then she throws herself at my legs in a rugby tackle, and, completely unprepared, I fall back onto the wet ground. I try to push her off, but she's up and detaching herself anyway, and then her fist slams into my face, crunching my nose, then she's up on her feet, right foot stepping on my balls, and as I curl in pain, she steadies herself with her right, and stands on my throat with her left.

Blindsided and overcome in seconds. Fortunately, memories of some of the old training still linger. Take the force of her foot on my throat for a brief, non-breathing second, and oblivious to the pain in my nose and my groin, I slam the edge of my hand into the back of her knee, and then jump up, throwing her over, as she loses balance. As she staggers, I clip her leg, and suddenly she's on the ground and I'm the one standing over her.

I've lost the killer instinct. Ten years ago I would have finished an assailant off from this position. Man, woman or child, I wouldn't have stopped to judge. Now, however, I'm back in Kansas. This isn't how we do things up here, and I take a step back, looking down warily at her, waiting for her next move, while also being aware of Wade, the gun in her hand, and Rollins, still standing behind.

Put my hand to my lips, as blood from my nose mixes with the rainwater dripping down my face.

'What happened to Elizabeth?'

I glance at Wade, keeping my eye on McIntosh as she gets to her feet, but for the moment she stands back, at least until the next time her temper boils over.

'Killed herself.'

There's a gasp from Rollins, behind.

'Shit,' mutters Wade. 'That's on you, Inspector. She was fine until you got involved. Jesus.'

'She *was* fine, perhaps, until you murdered her child.'

'What? I didn't murder her child. Her boy died on an operating table, eleven years ago. One month old.'

'Adam wasn't her child?'

'What? Why would you think that?'

I look at her quizzically, but of course I already knew that. Elizabeth told me. It may have been in a roundabout way – *it doesn't mean what you think it means*, she said – but she said it all the same.

Yes, I'm here, and these people are standing right in front of me, and, as far as I know, no other children have died, but I've made so many mistakes in getting here.

'Haven't you been paying attention?' says Wade. 'I did it all. Sure, Adam's DNA was accurate. When I switched the bodies, I just submitted the same DNA strand for testing. When it comes back, no one's going to know any different. Might be tricky for a while, but we'll be cool.'

'But why?'

'Because Catriona and I had a disagreement. Because Catriona had to make a stand, and she couldn't just do what she was told. She took Adam's body, and she dumped it down the well, and she knew Lachlan would be there when it was found. And Lachlan, however much of a buffoon he may be, was not going to cover up murder. And then you got your hands on it, and here you are, talking to me, and about to die.'

'Can we just get on with it, then?' says McIntosh. 'Jesus. He killed Elizabeth.'

She can think what she likes, I'm not getting into a discussion about that. I'm not going to be offended, I'm not going to defend myself. Elizabeth had a part to play in this, she died, and now we're on to the next thing.

'Fine,' says Wade, 'move them away, there's no need for the children to see it.'

'About bloody time,' says McIntosh, and she starts to walk around me, looking at me angrily.

'You stay here,' says Wade to her. 'Jill, take the boys off to the van, we'll be there in a couple of minutes.'

We stand for a moment, as the children begin to dutifully walk off into the forest, away from me, trailing behind Rollins. This is them, the ones I came to save, leaving. Heading out of sight, and possibly never to be seen again. But not for a moment am I assuming that I'm going to die here. I need to make sure the children are safe, and that's all.

The sound of the small troop marching into the woods mixes with the backdrop of rain and water dripping from branches, then slowly the sounds of this grim early morning begin to mix, and then the sound of the children is indistinguishable from the ambient hum of the wet forest as they are lost in the dark.

'Right,' says Wade, indicating with her gun, 'follow them, but don't get too close.'

'The fuck?' says McIntosh. 'We're not taking this idiot with us?'

'Really, Belle?' says Wade, as I start walking. They're pointing me in the direction in which I want to go, there's no reason not to just get on with it. 'We have to dispose of his body, we can't leave him lying here. We're taking it in the back of the van, so we might as well get him to walk in that direction. Do you want to drag it two hundred metres?'

'Jesus,' mutters McIntosh with a grunt.

It's dark, we're in among trees, Wade is obviously reluctant to fire the gun. Aside from wondering how it is she intends to kill me without using it, as I walk, I calculate the odds of me just rushing away and losing myself in the woods as quickly as possible.

First sign of a move, she pulls the trigger. Let's say I have half a second. A sudden move to the side, I can be behind a tree in that time, and thereafter I'm taking my chances with however good she's going to be with that thing.

Guns, dammit. I thought I was done with that crap.

I stop and turn, and she stops quickly, making sure she doesn't get too close.

'Fuck's sake,' says McIntosh, and she walks around Wade and pushes me back. 'Get a fucking move on.'

It's time.

Foot hooked quickly around her leg, she starts to fall back, and then I'm forward and bringing a heavy fist down into her face. As she hits the ground, I do to her what she did to me, though much more brutally, stamping my foot down into her throat. So much for losing the killer instinct.

A jab in the stomach. Pivot. Noise. Pain.

The Glock, thrust into my midriff, is fired, and I fall back as the pain of the bullet ripping right through me surges around my body. And then I'm lying back on the ground, Wade suddenly standing a few feet back, leaving herself plenty of reaction time should I make a grab for her.

'Nice move,' she says. 'Does that hurt? Speaking as your doctor, I suggest some antiseptic, a dry bandage and plenty of bed rest. Now get the fuck up, start walking, and don't do anything like that again or the next bullet will be in your face.'

I lie there, wet and cold, the shock of the bullet still career-ing through my body and my head, wondering if I *can* get up.

'Jesus!' croaks the voice next to her, as McIntosh drags herself to her feet. 'Just finish him the fuck off now. Give me the fucking knife, I'll drag him the rest of the way myself if I have to.'

Wade, dismissive in her movements, reaches inside her jacket and hands a sheathed knife to McIntosh. Interesting that Wade gets to hold the weapons. Not a lot of trust amongst this group of thieves.

'About time,' she mutters, and then she's coming towards me, and I'm suddenly pushing myself back, insomuch as I can, still reeling from the pain of the shot, left side completely useless, lopsidedly trying to force myself to my feet.

And then it comes.

The flashlight scoring the dark of the woods. The shout. The whistle. And now I'm not fighting for my life against the gun and the knife, I'm fighting for the next ten seconds, and after that the back-up that Lyle must have called will be here.

A curse from them both. Wade does not hesitate, and immediately runs by me. McIntosh is determined, however. She wants me dead before she goes. And she's on me, swing-ing, slashing either way with the knife. I push up and back, crash against a tree, duck to my left, as her arm slashes the bark by my head. Adrenaline roaring in, ignoring the pain and blood loss, and I'm looking for an in, the break in her form that allows me the counterattack.

I see it as she stumbles. I step into her path, fist up into her face; as she falls she slashes at my leg with the knife. The pain shoots through my shin. Then suddenly there's a rush of noise, a cascade of activity through the trees and a burly figure has leapt upon her. She's pinned down, the knife glint-ing in the glare of a flashlight as it's knocked from her hand. We're surrounded, McIntosh quickly subdued.

'You all right, boss?' shouts Sutherland, voice gasping and rushed.

'Keep going! After them! But watch, she's got a gun. Wade. Wade's got a gun! They'll be parked out on the back road. Come on!'

I force myself to my feet, and as soon as I do, the pain shoots through my abdomen, my right leg caves in beneath me, and I pitch forward.

'Wade?' shouts Sutherland, confused, but already running.

'Go!'

And I want to shout more, I want to shout to be careful, but Sutherland and three others are already on their way, crashing through the trees, out of earshot, and I start crawling after them, all I can do, hoping that for God's sake I don't hear the sound of a bullet.

35

'All the best detective stories end up with the hero in hospital.'

A long night. At some point – when was that? – someone told me I had a temperature of one hundred and five. Point nine, they added, with significance.

I slept on and off, patterns dictated by a peculiar dream. Lying in bed, my limbs displaced, wrongly attached to various parts of my body, and only by putting them in the right place would I be able to settle down and get to sleep. Yet every time I had my legs finally on the right way, some other body part would be in the wrong place, and so the endless quest to finally settle down continued. On and on, through the night.

One hundred and five point nine. Because I didn't change out of my wet clothes, apparently. That's what they said. I think that's what they said. But what with the gunshot wound and the knife wound, who knows?

Wait, someone said something.

'What?'

'All the best detective stories end up with the hero in hospital.'

I'm staring at the white wall directly in front of me. I'm going to have to turn my head. That should be all right, as long as I don't move my body. My body hurts. Ribs, stomach, side. All sore. The sharp pains in my leg, however, seem worse. Just from a pain perspective.

Look to my left. My line of vision sweeps past a formless painting of light greens, a television, a small vase of flowers, to the window. Outside, the bare branches of trees, buildings set back, hills rising behind. I don't know where I am. Hospital obviously. Must be Raigmore. If I'm in a hospital, it'll be Raigmore.

This is where the boy in the well is being kept. That'll be why I can hear his voice. Although didn't Wade swap out the body?

There he is, sitting beside the bed. Boy 9.

'All the best detective stories end up with the hero in hospital?'

'Yes,' he says.

'That makes me the hero.'

'You worked it out,' says Boy 9.

'I don't feel much like a hero.'

He nods. He looks sad, but I guess it'd be hard for someone in his position to look anything else.

'Why are you here?' I ask.

'Not sure. I think just because of you.' He smiles weakly. 'That's funny, isn't it?'

'You were kept underground all that time? In that little room?'

'Oh, no, nothing like that. They were all really nice. Except, Mum sometimes. Mum could be mean, but I suppose she meant well. She looked after us.'

'Mum?'

'Yes.'

'Was Dr Wade your mum?'

'I guess. Aunt Catriona's dead now, isn't she? Do you talk to her too?'

'I don't think so. I don't remember.'

'Oh. That's a shame.'

'Why didn't your Aunt Catriona come to the police? Why did she plant your body in the well?'

'She must have been scared. That was her way. It's always hard to know what other people are thinking.'

'Yes. Even when they tell you what they're thinking.'

'Really?' he says. 'Do people lie?'

'All the time.'

'Oh.'

This seems to make him even sadder, and I wonder if there's anything I can say to cheer him up.

There's a notion of the absurdity of that idea somewhere in my head, but nothing's really sticking at the moment.

'They didn't keep you locked up?'

'No, not much. We stayed in a house. We went out sometimes, but mostly not around other people, and when we were around other people, we weren't allowed to say anything. Ever.'

'You never went to school?'

'No.'

'The doctor or the dentist?'

'Mum was a doctor.'

I'm not looking at him any more. It feels too painful. Real pain, real emotional hurt, far greater than that stupid pain jabbing through my leg.

'Did they . . .?' I begin, but I can't get the question out at the first attempt. I don't want to know. I don't want this to be any more disheartening.

'Did they what?'

Come on, detective, where's the steel that saw you happily back Elizabeth Rhodes into a corner until she took her own life?

'Did they force you to have sex?'

'What does that mean?'

My brain isn't working properly enough for this.

'Did they touch you? Do things to your bodies?'

'When I was a kid, they gave me a bath. Is that the kind of thing you mean?'

I don't answer. It's not about sex. It was never about sex. Wade said it herself, didn't she? I remember that. Elizabeth's baby died eleven years ago. Belle McIntosh's baby died. Catriona Napier could never have children. I know nothing of Wade or Rollins, but I do know Councillor Rollins has no children. There's a clear pattern of what was going on.

'Why did they kill you?' I ask. That seems important.

'I didn't know at first I was dead. Then I worked it out. Funny how that happens.'

'But why?'

'Mum was getting mad, that's all. Oh yes . . .' he says, and his voice drifts off.

'Oh yes, what?' I ask.

'Sorry?'

'You said, oh yes, as though you'd just thought of something.'

'Yes, I had. There was this . . . there was a girl I started talking to. She was my friend. Mum said I wasn't allowed friends.'

'Who was the girl?'

'I met her at the park. She said I could come over to her house, and I really wanted to, but when Mum found out about it, she was cross. We had a big fight. That was bad. I shouldn't have had a fight with Mum like that. I shouldn't have tried to run away.'

I finally turn back to look at him. There you have it, I think. Breaking ranks from authority will get you killed every time.

'How did you get to the park?' I ask.

'Aunt Catriona used to take me. I think Mum was angry at her too. Wait, d'you think Mum killed Aunt Catriona?'

I hold his gaze for a moment, his doleful, forever-young eyes.

'Yes,' I say.

'Oh,' he says. 'That's sad.'

'Yes.'

He looks away this time, staring blankly at the wall at the end of the bed, then a slight, melancholic smile comes to his face.

'What?' I ask.

'Sometimes we called Mum the Sandman,' he says. 'That's funny, isn't it? She used to come to put us to sleep at night. Mum didn't like it, though.'

He pauses, his eyes drop; he looks, inevitably, like the lost child that he is.

'I miss Mum,' he says.

I let out a long sigh at that. He would miss her, of course, regardless of what went on between them, regardless of what the situation was. And I'm pretty sure Dr Wade wasn't his mum.

'How many adults were there?'

'Oh,' he says.

'Don't you know?' I ask.

'Well, there was Aunt Jill, who looked after us mostly. Aunt Belle and Aunt Elizabeth. And Aunt Catriona, of course, though she's dead now. Aunt Elizabeth's dead too, did you know that? It won't be the same for them now. My brothers, I mean. No Aunt Catriona, no Aunt Elizabeth. Without them . . . Maybe they'll get to see more of Mum.'

'The boys have been taken into care. They won't see your mum any more.'

'Oh,' he says again, and his brow furrows. 'Who's going to look after them now?'

'We'll take care of them and find places for them to go.'

'Oh.'

He looks thoughtful, and although I'm looking at him, he's not returning the stare. His face, as though it were possible, has become more and more downcast.

'They won't like that,' he says after a while.

I can feel the tiredness crawling back in, an almost physical sensation of it creeping into my head, spreading through my brain, through my thoughts, infecting all, slowing everything down.

'Why?'

'People don't like change,' he says.

I look down at the bed sheets, feeling ever more tired, thinking that I agree with him, and that I understand everything he's saying, and that perhaps it's just because everything he's saying is actually coming from me. All those thoughts are in my head, not his.

Isn't that what's happening?

I close my eyes for a moment, or what feels like a moment, but when I open them again, the quality of the light in the room is quite different, as though the day has progressed significantly.

'They'll come to understand,' I say.

'Who will?'

I turn my head to the left again. Detective Sergeant Sutherland is looking up from a copy of the *Press & Journal*. On the table beside him is a takeaway cup of coffee and a doughnut with a large bite taken from it.

36

'Sir.'

I nod at Fisher as she comes to the table. She smiles, then looks worried and says, 'You still look like shit, sir, by the way,' a little sheepish as she says it, in case that level of familiarity might be too much.

'Thanks,' I say, taking the joke, but I notice the look that Sutherland slings her, and she nods apologetically.

Sitting in the hospital canteen. Beside me, the crutch on which I hobbled here.

Quinn has told me that I can't come into the station for another week. I, of course, do not want to sit on the sidelines. However, that damned, antiseptic room is the last place I want to be talking about work, and so we have come here, to the view down over the town, to the Kessock Bridge.

'Who have we got?' I ask, looking between the two of them once we're settled in, beverages of choice to hand.

'So,' says Sutherland, 'sorry, sir, I gave you some of the details a couple of days ago, but I wasn't sure whether or not the information went in.'

I stare across the table and try to remember. I recall him being by my bedside, I recall him talking, and me trying to listen. Wasn't there also something with the boy?

'We got the three of them on Thursday night,' says Sutherland, deciding to press ahead, correctly taking my silence as lack of awareness. 'At first none of them were talking. It was pretty clear, even after we split them up, that Dr

Wade was the boss. I mean . . .' and he lets out a whistle, shaking his head. 'I mean, just no one saw that coming.'

'Who opened up?' I ask.

'McIntosh and Rollins were both cold, but you know, we got that chink with Rollins. We looked into her background, found out that she'd had seven miscarriages.'

'Jesus,' escapes my lips.

'I know. You have to wonder. You'd think at some point . . .' and he glances at Fisher, then shakes his head. 'Anyway . . .'

'She was protecting her husband, not Wade,' says Fisher.

'Yep,' says Sutherland, nodding. 'We got her lawyer in, did the deal. Not that she's any less liable than the rest of them, so it'll be interesting how it pans out.'

'So this was . . .' I begin, but can't quite think straight. 'This was a group of childless, heartbroken women? Doing what, exactly?'

Another glance between the two of them, then Sutherland leans forward a little, takes another drink.

'It starts with Wade. I keep wanting to call her General Wade,' he says, smiling apologetically, and Fisher makes a *tell me about it* roll of the eyes. 'Rollins told us her story, but we can't know for sure, as Wade ain't saying anything. She got pregnant in school, didn't want to tell her parents, gave herself an abortion. And . . .' and again he looks at Fisher, as though he has to apologise for talking about women's reproductive matters, 'screwed up any chance of future childbearing. Seems almost like she might have gone to medical school in a *Magnificent Obsession, I can learn to fix this* kind of a way. You know that movie?'

'Surprised that you do,' I say.

'I know movies,' he says, defensively.

'Sergeant,' says Fisher, in the way of someone telling off their line manager.

'On point, right,' he says, nodding. 'Whatever her reasons, she ended up in pathology rather than gynaecology, and meanwhile she became consumed by her need to have a child. Then, at some stage, she took someone's baby.'

'Stole someone's life,' says Fisher, and this time it's Sutherland who gives her a slight rebuke for the interjection, part of the back and forth.

'Rather than adopt, or learn to live with her sorrow, or not learn to live with it and suffer,' says Sutherland, 'she chose to steal a baby, from somewhere. We don't know where. Obviously not from her own hospital, as that would've been too obvious; and, anyway, there are no records of newborns or children of any age going missing. We think perhaps she went onto the Continent. Impossible to tell. It's going to be a long journey trying to track down who these boys really are.'

'She stole seven children?'

'Far as we can tell. She's not talking, but we've checked. None of them are hers, none of them are from any of the other women. She obviously did it once, it worked, she kept on doing it.'

'And the other women? Elizabeth, Napier . . .' and I finish the list with a gesture.

'So Wade had these children, and she lived a couple of hours away from where she worked, and kind of had these two separate lives. But she never accommodated for how these children would come into society. She wanted babies, she wanted young boys . . .'

'We presume she aborted a boy,' says Fisher, and this time Sutherland just nods at the interjection.

'What she didn't necessarily want, or at least know what to do with, was an older child who would question his place. I mean, that's a thing, isn't it? Most people who have kids, they talk about wanting a baby. How many seriously think ahead? No one talks about wanting a seventeen-year-old who'll sit around on his arse all day and tell you to fuck off when you ask him to study for his Highers.'

Neither Fisher nor I have anything to add.

'So they lived their lives in secret,' continues Sutherland, 'and if they ever went out, they were barred from talking. But children grow up, and Boy 9 was getting older and was beginning to ask questions. Anyway, she needed help with these children, and she sought it from women who were, mentally, coming from the same place she was. We don't know . . . we're going to have to ask a lot of questions to get to the bottom of it, but at the moment, we don't know their level of complicity at the beginning. Did they really not know when they began, as Jill Rollins is saying, that the babies were stolen? They obviously weren't all Dr Wade's children. Maybe that was the case at the start, but two or three children in, they'd all become complicit.'

He called him Boy 9. It seems wrong to still be calling him Boy 9. I don't say anything.

'Hard for us to say at this stage how torn they were by it,' says Fisher, 'by the right and wrong of it. But once they'd held the baby in their arms . . .'

'Once they'd held that kid, and started to play a part in the life of the child, if they'd reported it, then . . .' and Sutherland finishes that thought with a couple of raised eyebrows and a shrug. 'One of them had to make the call the instant they learned where the child had come from. Right then, or else they were complicit. And either they just couldn't do it, or Wade held something over them.'

I stare at the table. Feel tired already. That didn't take long. Maybe they were right. Shouldn't be working yet. Apparently I lost a lot of blood, and have been told repeatedly about my high temperature. The wound in my leg still aches, all the more when I put the slightest weight on it.

'They weren't kept in Rollins's basement the whole time,' I say, more of a statement than a question. How is it that I know that already? Sutherland must have said previously.

'No, they lived in Wade's house. She's near Tore, but kind of detached. When she killed Boy 9, she told Napier to dispose of the body, and moved the kids to the Rollins's basement. Partly to subjugate them further, on top of having killed the eldest of them, and partly to put them out of the way for a week or two, just in case anything went wrong. Napier used that against her, obviously. If it was meant to be a way of surreptitiously showing their hand, Wade worked it out pretty quickly. Napier was never going to last long.'

'Why didn't she just talk to us?'

They look at each other again, then both turn back with a shrug.

'Fear,' says Fisher.

So many questions, and I'm not sure that I'm yet in a fit state to think properly.

'How do you fight this kind of thing,' I say, both hands wrapped around the warm cup, 'when you don't even know it's there?'

'The things you'd find if you could just walk into anyone's home,' says Fisher, a woman who knows, and I nod. 'Yet society would be the worse for it, if we could.'

'You look like you're struggling, boss,' says Sutherland. 'We've got this, and it'll still be here when you get back.'

'I'll be all right for another few minutes. Let's just ... Where are the boys now?'

'The Social has them, and we haven't got near them yet. We've got their DNA, but as for questioning, it'll be another day or two. We're negotiating that one.'

'Quinn or Darnley?'

'Bit of both. Quinn's talking, Darnley's pulling his strings.'

'And we've no idea where they came from?'

'Not so far, but I think the net is going to have to be flung far and wide.'

'You've asked around about Wade in Aberdeen?'

'We're on it,' says Fisher. 'But there's a long way to go. It'll be about trying to track her movements over a long time span. Credit card bookings, border crossings. So many things. But it looks like the woman who died in Aberdeen was in on it, and Wade killed her.'

'The application's in for the body to be exhumed. Should come through in a couple of days.'

'The people that were there on Thursday evening? The dinner party. They were . . . what were they? They were part of the ring?'

'No, that seems kosher,' says Sutherland. 'Just dinner, which is just as well, given that the boss was there. We've brought Jack Rollins in, but he's claiming total ignorance, and so far his wife has his back. Still, there goes his political career, you'd think.'

Another drink of coffee, eyes dropping to the table. Getting there, slowly. Things falling in to place. Still questions to be asked, answers to be given, or long searched for and perhaps not found. And here I sit, facing the question that has bothered me, personally, more than any other, the last couple of days. When my brain has allowed me to focus on it, at least.

And I don't want to ask.

I notice the glance between Sutherland and Fisher. The one that says, we should probably leave him alone, let him get back to bed.

'Sir?'

'What about Elizabeth?' I ask.

Sutherland nods sympathetically, knowing more than Fisher what lies behind the question. I assume, anyway, that he still knows more than Fisher, although word may have got around.

'Harry Rhodes says they lost a son, and she never got over it. The same sad story as the rest of them, fuelling their journey into the same sad demise. You were there when she killed herself?'

'How d'you know that?'

'You said two days ago. I'm checking. You were a little . . .' and he makes the appropriate hand gesture beside his head.

I nod.

'Hmm . . .' he begins, something else to say, then he stops himself.

'What?'

'It's all right, it can wait,' he says, glancing at Fisher.

'Really, Iain, I'm convalescing, I'm not five. Spit it out.'

He lets out a long breath, gives himself another second or two, then says, 'You're going to have to fight your corner on that one. You were there when Elizabeth died, and you didn't call it in. They're going to want to know the whole story, which we didn't really get from you yet.'

I'm nodding, long before he's finished talking. Of course they're going to need to know why it happened, and why I chose not to make the call. The second part of that will be tricky.

I couldn't risk my chief finding out about it, in case he passed it on to the owners of the house I was about to stake out.

It's not like I want to make Quinn sound as though he might've been part of it. It needs to start with a conversation with Quinn, then we can move on from there, and I'll take whatever's coming to me.

'All right, sir,' says Sutherland, 'I think we're probably good for the moment.'

I stare at the table, still thinking of the moment Elizabeth killed herself, thinking of my stupidity in turning my back.

I'd like to say we should just talk about it now, but I can't. It's not the raw emotion of it, because I don't feel any. There could have been something there with Elizabeth Rhodes, another man's wife or not, but ultimately she turned out to be part of the problem. There was a job to be done, and the personal side of it was just getting in the way. Now that it's over, there's nothing to be gained from looking back. This cold-heartedness, at least, I recognise in myself from the old days.

For now, however, I know I'm not thinking clearly enough to have the discussion with Sutherland, and I need to wait until I am.

Another drink of coffee. Struggling to stay with it now. But the rest, it's all detail, isn't it? A little bit here and there, pieces to slot into the puzzle. At least now we know what the puzzle is, and how it's supposed to look. We know why no one identified Boy 9. We don't know who he was, or who his parents were, and maybe we never will. How many babies go missing from hospitals every year? How long will it take to find out, once we've trawled through the past life of Dr Helen Wade?

'Wait,' I say, as another thought comes into my head, as though wandering casually into a bar off the street. 'Where did they get the body? The 200-year-old body?'

'Wade dug it up. She knew where it was buried. It really is the body of Ewan Balfour. Wade grew up near Avoch; she knows the area, the history, she seems to know things that are not generally known. We're just at the beginning of understanding how that is.'

'But how does . . .' I begin, trying to formulate the peculiarity of the story into a clear-cut question. 'How did she know to cut the heart out when she killed Adam? She didn't know he'd be dumped in the well, that we'd go off on this tangent.'

'Here we come to the brutality of Dr Wade,' says Sutherland. 'And remember, she'd already killed her partner in Aberdeen, then taken the chance to move closer to home when Sanderson left so abruptly.'

'She was outraged at Napier when she discovered how much freedom she'd been giving Boy 9 . . .'

'His name was Adam,' I say.

'*They* called him Adam, sir,' says Fisher. 'We don't yet know what name his parents gave him.'

And I nod. She's right. Fisher, the station's voice of level-headed practicality.

'She felt he was getting out of control. Impossible to know at this stage why she thought that the way to deal with it was to kill him, but that's what she chose to do. She also knew the story of Ewan Balfour, and she copied it. Cut out the boy's heart, presented the heart to Napier, ordered her to dispose of the body. No aforethought with regard to the body substitution. She appears to have called that play at the line of scrimmage.'

I look blankly at him, and he waves away the comment.

'She made that call on the spot. Anyway, what she did to Boy 9 was brutal, and Napier finally rebelled. In her way.'

'We spent all that time on the bloodline . . .?' I say. 'It can't all have been a red herring.'

'She played us.'

'But Elizabeth? Wasn't she . . . she was in the line?'

'Wade is brutal, and she's brilliant,' says Sutherland, shaking his head. 'I mean, God knows what we're going to find out as this thing unravels. But it looks like she must have known. She was tying it all together, tying Elizabeth to the story. She's not talking, and Mrs Rollins is claiming ignorance, so it's hard to know for sure.'

'But why did she tie Elizabeth to the story?' I ask. 'I mean . . .' and the thought gets muddled, the words dry up.

'She was building a web around her,' says Sutherland, 'and attaching that web to as many others as possible. She was lining up her suspects, and if it ever got too close, she'd have been out of here, and we'd have been chasing all over the place. We had been already, after all. If you hadn't got ahead of the game, and caught her in the act ... And you know, we've got her, but she's not done here, she's really not. Much too clever. She's damned good, I'll give her that.'

'Well, we have to be better,' I say, and then shake my head and wave an apologetic hand at the facileness of the line.

'Now I think it's time you were going back to bed, sir,' says Sutherland.

I'm staring off to the side now, trying to focus, and don't immediately answer.

'We'll take you back to your room,' he says.

'Did we find his body at least? Boy 9. Adam. What did she do with him?'

Another glance between Sutherland and Fisher, and then a shake of the head from them both.

'Poor kid. We didn't know who he was, and now that we at least have some idea of his story, we don't know where he is.'

I think of him. Boy 9. Somehow it feels as though he came to see me. That he was in my hospital room. And he was in the car. Definitely in the car. Neither of those things makes sense, though. He's dead. Boy 9 is dead.

I wish I didn't see dead people.

'Come on, sir, back to your room,' says Fisher.

Realise that my forehead is resting in the palm of my hand, and straighten up.

'Of course,' I say.

Tiredness sweeping in, accompanied by a jab of pain shooting up from my shin as I move my leg.

'I'm sure there'll still be plenty to sort out when you get back,' says Sutherland, getting to his feet.

37

Mid-December. One month on. The papers have all had their scoops, and when Boy 9's true story, or what is known of it, came out, the Internet broke. Again. It appears to have quickly repaired itself. And now, as usual, everything has settled down, while we, in league with the Crown Office and Procurator Fiscal Service, go about the business of putting together a case, and our former employee, Dr Helen Wade, sits in prison, awaiting trial. Slowly, very, very slowly, her story begins to be told, but like Sutherland said, she is cunning, and her defence will be littered with snares, deceptions and diversions.

So far it seems that there are no others involved beyond the ones we took that evening, three women sneaking off into the woods with six boys. Elizabeth was dead, Catriona Napier was dead, and those three were the only others we can connect to this. Rollins and Rhodes, the men we could reasonably expect to have had some idea of what was going on, are both claiming ignorance, and so far we have nothing to prove otherwise.

And so we do the job we usually do. We take what we can get, we unearth what we can, we prosecute and seek conviction where appropriate, and where a case can be made.

Of the children, two have been helpful, however reluctantly. They have each gone into temporary foster care, they are being monitored daily, and none of the six is happy. It will be a long, long road back for them all; fifteen years from now,

I would expect more than one of them to be troubling my contemporaries of the day.

A beautiful day. Given that an hour is a long time in Scottish weather, a month is an eternity. We've had the usual full panoply of seasons since mid-November, but somewhere along the way, winter arrived, and now, sitting on the top of Wyvis, the sky above a perfect, unbroken, pale blue, there's little else to see except snow-covered hills and mountains all around, bar the occasional line of a dark grey road.

I'm waiting for him, not knowing if he's going to come. Sanderson himself obviously did not feel the need to wait until I was at the top of a mountain, as I'm pretty sure he spoke to me in the forest, the night the story unravelled. Nevertheless, it has to be said that my memories of that night are shaky. Indeed, my memories of talking to Sanderson are shaky as a whole.

I didn't really meet him at the top of Wyvis, did I? Well, I'm not sure, and if I'm not, no one else can be. This is the first day, since I felt my leg was suitably recovered, that I had the chance to get out on the hills, and so here I am, the weight of melancholy upon me, thinking that this will be me talking to Sanderson for the final time when, of course, the final time might have been and gone several weeks ago.

Sitting in the same spot where I first encountered him last month. None of this had happened then. Those children, those six children rescued from their strange cosseted life, the surrogate children of five sad, lost women, effectively did not exist then. Not so that the world knew about them.

Such is the nature of the work we do, and the work of all the public services. Constantly pushed to the limit, enough work on a day-to-day basis to keep everyone busy, and into its midst comes a case such as this, thousands of man-hours added to the slate, with no extra resources to handle it. Just the way it goes.

I've been staring out over the hills, lost in thought, watching the movement of a herd of deer, dark against the white background, when I realise that Sanderson is already sitting next to me on the rock. A few other people have gone by since I've been sitting here, but for the moment, there's no one else in sight. Looking around, I don't see any footprints in the snow approaching the rock, aside from my own. Perhaps he followed my footfall.

'Inspector,' he says.

'Doctor. Didn't see you coming.'

'I'm a ninja these days,' he says, and laughs.

He follows my look out over the hills, and for a while we enjoy the silence, and the chill of a perfect day in early winter.

'You get it sorted, then?' he asks after a time.

'Well,' I say, with an appropriate shrug of the shoulders, 'sorted might be something of a stretch. I don't think we've got any more suspects to chase, but we do have six small boys who have no idea who their real parents are, and whose lives are going to be pretty screwed up for a long time.'

'Hmm,' he says. 'Seems I got out just in time, though I don't suppose I'd be much involved. I presume people have stopped dying at least?'

'Yes.'

'We can be thankful for that. Sorry I wasn't around anyway. I guess it would still all have unfolded, even if I hadn't been there. Dr Wade would just have handled it differently.'

'I guess so. I haven't really thought about your place in it. Her part, and how she dealt with it, certainly, was altered by her being at Raigmore, but I don't think materially it was so different. The unravelling of Wade's story began with Catriona Napier dumping the body, and that was happening either way. So, no, you don't have to feel bad about dying of cancer.'

He laughs and pats me on the knee.

'You're a funny man, Inspector.'

'I never thought so.'

'Oh, yes. I'm going to miss you, that's for sure.'

I glance at him, although the turn of my head doesn't quite make it all the way round. I don't meet his eye. And then I turn away again, and follow the trail back out over the white hills to the herd of deer, far in the distance to the west.

'I should have left so much earlier,' he says, after a while. For a moment he looks as though he's going to continue on the theme, then possibly remembers that he's already talked about it. He's already expressed that particular regret.

'You were playing your part, doctor,' I say. 'We all are. We can't all just duck out, take to the hills and leave the awful stuff to everyone else.'

'Someone has to do it,' he says with resignation.

'Yep. And that was you and it's me, and it's all of us. You know Constable Fisher? You know her story? She's a brave woman.'

He shakes his head.

'Maybe you can tell it to me some day,' he says, even though we both know, as he says it, that the day will not come.

'Sure,' I say.

'Oh, nearly forgot,' he says. 'I brought hot chocolate. You want some?'

'Hot chocolate? Really?'

'This is quality hot chocolate, my friend,' he says, laughing, and he pats me on the knee again, then starts to open up his backpack. 'You will enjoy.'

'Well, you've sold it to me,' I say.

'Good man.'

He takes the flask from the pack, then a couple of porcelain mugs, setting them on the rock next to him. He unscrews the top of the flask, pauses for a second to take in the smell of the hot liquid as the steam rises, and then fills up the two mugs. Lid back on, flask set down on the grass, he lifts the mugs and hands one of them to me.

'Cheers,' he says. 'Drink it quickly. The heat'll go.'

We clink mugs and then, together, take our first sip.

'Did you ever find the body, by the way?' asks Sanderson. 'The poor, lost boy in the well?'

I shake my head.

'She's not saying. It's . . . I think she's holding it, waiting to use the information to her advantage at some point. She knows we want him, and she's toying with us. We still don't know who his parents were, so you know, we don't have a grieving family, the distraught parents in the news, but we need the completion. Boy 9 needs the completion. We need to know where he is, so we can bury him properly. Remember him properly.'

'There will be grieving parents,' he says, 'out there, somewhere.'

'I know, and they'll have been grieving for nine years. And not just them; six other sets of parents. Maybe she took them from orphanages, but there are plenty of orphanage children whose parents are still alive.'

'You haven't been able to find any of the parents?'

'Not so far. We've gone to hospitals and orphanages all over world. Starting to get enquiries and hints, possibilities just. We'll see. It'll be a long process. There will be DNA tests, there will be . . .' and I let the sentence, and the awfulness of what still is to come with those young lives, drift away into the day.

He nods, his head drops a little, as he lifts the mug to his mouth again.

'We can just hope that we don't need to wait upon Dr Wade's calculation,' I say. 'Because it will be a long wait, and when it comes to it, we won't want to give her what she wants.'

'Once they're behind bars,' he says ruefully, 'where the bodies are buried is their only power.'

'I'm not sure it's their only one, but she's certainly going to make the most of it.'

'Poor kid,' says Sanderson.

In the far distance, the white contrail of a plane eases slowly across the sky, the silver of the fuselage glinting in the sun. I lower the mug and indicate its quality with a nod and a small gesture, and he nods in return.

The steam rises from the mugs into the cold of late morning. Despite the chill there's absolutely no wind, and the sun is warm on our faces. The Highlands, white and beautiful and, from up here, stretching for mile upon mile, look majestic. If I was prepared, it feels as if I could walk down Wyvis in the other direction, and keep on walking. Snow upon snow, hill upon hill, the herd of deer still moving slowly in the distance.

The world is not all dark, for all the darkness that people try to inflict upon it.

And then, even before I turn, I sense that he's gone, and I'm once again alone. I glance round, and the rock beside me is covered in perfect, untouched snow.

No Sanderson, no backpack, no imprint in the snow from his approach or departure. And yet, in my hand there remains a perfect mug of hot chocolate. A final gift from the doctor to mark his passing.

Now, at last, I get the crushing sense of loss, I feel myself begin to choke up, and so I lift the mug and take a quick drink.

'Damn fine hot chocolate, doctor,' I say, and I raise the mug slightly in front of me.

I look across the mountains and wonder if he's out there somewhere in that great swathe of white, and I tip my cup to him one last time.

ACKNOWLEDGEMENTS

In its original state *Boy in The Well* was something of a shambles, and I'm indebted to Russel McLean, who helped sort through the morass, bringing order and focus to the narrative.

The first publisher of the Westphall series folded – we shall not dwell on such matters – and for a while the series was lost. History became legend, legend became myth, and for two and a half thousand years, the series passed out of all knowledge. Fortunately it was rescued by Mulholland, and for that I thank everyone there, and in particular Ruth for giving me the time when I first approached, and Cicely, for her advice and for being such an enthusiastic advocate.

And, more than anyone, I'd like to thank Kathryn, without whom neither this, nor any of my other books, would ever have been written, never mind published.

DI Westphall returns in

The Art of Dying

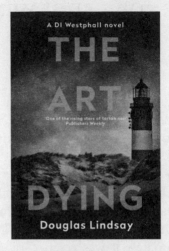

When businessman Thomas Peterson is killed outside a
football ground in the Highlands, there are several
witnesses. Yet the hunt for the killer is proving as futile
as the search for a motive.

Possible connections to Russian money and an eerie
retirement home are soon thrown into the mix. To further
complicate things, DI Westphall's MI6 past is coming back
to haunt him. Guilt stalks his dreams, but could there be a
message in these nightmares?

Westphall is in danger of losing his head just when he
needs it the most. He must find answers, and fast, before
the murderer strikes again.

MULHOLLAND
BOOKS
HODDER

You've turned the last page.

But it doesn't have to end there . . .

If you're looking for more first-class, action-packed, nail-biting suspense, follow us on Twitter **@MulhollandUK** for:

- News
- Competitions
- Regular updates about our books and authors
- Insider info into the world of crime and thrillers
- Behind-the-scenes access to Mulholland Books

And much more!

There are many more twists to come.

MULHOLLAND:
You never know what's coming around the curve.